Sharon Kendrick once won a national writing competition by describing her ideal date: being flown to an exotic island by a gorgeous and powerful man. Little did she realise that she'd just wandered into her dream job! Today she writes for Mills & Boon, and her books feature often stubborn but always *to-die-for* heroes and the women who bring them to their knees. She believes that the best books are those you never want to end. Just like life…

Irish author **Abby Green** ended a very glamorous career in film and TV—which really consisted of a lot of standing in the rain outside actors' trailers—to pursue her love of romance. After she'd bombarded Mills & Boon with manuscripts they kindly accepted one, and an author was born. She lives in Dublin, Ireland, and loves any excuse for distraction. Visit abby-green.com or email abbygreenauthor@gmail.com.

D0226483

Also by Sharon Kendrick

Crowned for the Sheikh's Baby
The Greek's Bought Bride
The Italian's Christmas Housekeeper
The Sheikh's Secret Baby

The Legendary Argentinian Billionaires miniseries

Bought Bride for the Argentinian
The Argentinian's Baby of Scandal

Also by Abby Green

Claiming His Wedding Night Consequence
An Innocent, A Seduction, A Secret
Awakened by the Scarred Italian

Brides for Billionaires collection

Married for the Tycoon's Empire

Rulers of the Desert miniseries

A Diamond for the Sheikh's Mistress
A Christmas Bride for the King

Discover more at millsandboon.co.uk.

HIS CONTRACT CHRISTMAS BRIDE

SHARON KENDRICK

CONFESSIONS OF A PREGNANT CINDERELLA

ABBY GREEN

MILLS & BOON

All rights reserved including the right of reproduction
in whole or in part in any form. This edition is published
by arrangement with Harlequin Books S.A.

This is a work of fiction. Names, characters, places, locations
and incidents are purely fictional and bear no relationship to
any real life individuals, living or dead, or to any actual places,
business establishments, locations, events or incidents.
Any resemblance is entirely coincidental.

This book is sold subject to the condition that it shall not,
by way of trade or otherwise, be lent, resold, hired out
or otherwise circulated without the prior consent of the publisher
in any form of binding or cover other than that in which it is published
and without a similar condition including this condition
being imposed on the subsequent purchaser.

® and TM are trademarks owned and used by the trademark owner
and/or its licensee. Trademarks marked with ® are registered with the
United Kingdom Patent Office and/or the Office for Harmonisation
in the Internal Market and in other countries.

First Published in Great Britain 2019
by Mills & Boon, an imprint of HarperCollins*Publishers*
1 London Bridge Street, London, SE1 9GF

His Contract Christmas Bride © 2019 by Sharon Kendrick

Confessions of a Pregnant Cinderella © 2019 by Abby Green

ISBN: 978-0-263-27363-2

MIX
Paper from
responsible sources
FSC™ C007454

This book is produced from independently certified FSC™ paper
to ensure responsible forest management.
For more information visit www.harpercollins.co.uk/green.

Printed and bound in Spain
by CPI, Barcelona

HIS CONTRACT CHRISTMAS BRIDE

SHARON KENDRICK

This is for the magnificent Joan Bolland,
whose wisdom and wry sense of humour
are greatly appreciated. Xxx

PROLOGUE

DRAKON KONSTANTINOU LOOKED around him, unable to hide the disgust which swamped his body like a dank, dark tide. But hot on the heels of disgust came regret, and then guilt. Regret that he couldn't have done something sooner and guilt that he couldn't have prevented this terrible outcome.

But the trigger to these grisly events had been pulled a long time ago and he couldn't control everything, no matter how much he had spent his whole life trying to do just that. Sometimes control just slipped beyond your grasp and there was nothing you could do about it. His brother had gone now and so had the woman he'd married—the sordid paraphernalia strewn around the room the last testimony to their degenerate lifestyle.

But life went on.

Life *had* to go on.

As if to confirm that indisputable fact, he heard an unfamiliar cry coming from an adjoining room, quickly followed by a voice and the sound of footsteps.

'Drakon?'

He glanced up at his business partner's face as she walked in from the adjoining room. Gingerly, she walked towards him, clearly uncomfortable as she carried her precious cargo—as if unsure just what to do next. *Join the club,* thought Drakon grimly.

'Are you ready, Drakon?' she asked.

He wanted to shake his head. To tell her he wasn't prepared for this latest responsibility which had come slamming at him like a weighted curve ball. To protest that he'd done enough of shouldering other people's burdens and their problems and he needed a break. But that was impossible. He could do this. He *would* do this. He just hadn't quite worked out how.

He needed a woman, that was for sure, but a quick flick through his memory bank of females who would be willing to do pretty much anything he asked of them failed to come up with anyone remotely suitable.

And then, as if in answer to the turmoil of his thoughts, a face unexpectedly swam into his mind. A face with soft blue eyes the colour of the bluebells which had grown beneath the trees in those long-ago English springs, in the heady days before he'd discovered how much his father liked hookers.

Forcing his mind back to the present, he thought about the face again. Not a beautiful face but a kindly one. He felt a faint beat of remembered desire, but far stronger still was his sudden sense of purpose as he allowed his mind to linger on Lucy Phillips for the first time in many months and his eyes narrowed speculatively. Maybe fate was cleverer than he'd imagined. Maybe the answer had been staring him in the face all this time.

'Neh,' he said, his harsh Greek accent echoing around the marble-floored villa. 'I'm ready.'

CHAPTER ONE

AT FIRST SHE didn't recognise him, which was pretty amazing when she stopped to think about it. Except that Lucy had done her best *not* to think about it. Or him. She'd tried to blot Drakon Konstantinou from her mind, the way you did when you were on a diet and didn't want to focus on cream cake, or chocolate, or toasted teacakes swimming with melted butter.

Because only an idiot would want to remember the man who had introduced them to pleasure then walked away so fast his feet had barely touched the ground. Or to recall her own participation in what could only ever have been an impossible fantasy.

But it *was* him. Lucy's heart slammed against her ribcage as she opened the front door of her tiny cottage and peered out through the protective chain at the figure standing on the step, silhouetted darkly against the fiery orange of the winter sunset. It was definitely him. And the first thing she thought was how different he seemed from the man who had seduced her on the beautiful Greek island of Prasinisos, an island which he actually *owned*.

It wasn't just that his features were ravaged and his

shoulders hunched, as if a heavy weight were pressing down on their muscular breadth, but his black hair was longer, too. Instead of being neatly clipped to follow the shape of his head, ebony waves were kissing the collar of his dark overcoat and there was a dark layer of stubble at his angled jaw. His appearance hinted more at recent neglect rather than his usual pristine perfection and it was an astonishing transformation. Suddenly Drakon Konstantinou bore more resemblance to a rock singer who'd spent the night on the tiles, rather than a powerful oil baron and shipping magnate, with the world at his fingertips.

Unwanted feelings flooded through her body and started making her skin feel as raw as if someone had been attacking it with a cheese grater. She told herself she shouldn't be so sensitive. Wasn't that what her former colleagues at the hospital used to tease her about? But sensitivity wasn't something you could just turn on and off, like a tap. Her memories of Drakon were mixed and…*complex*…and the overriding feeling she'd been left with when he'd walked away was that it would be better if she never saw him again. Better for her, certainly. Better to forget those three blissful days and nights which she suspected had ruined her for all other men. To try to get back into the groove of a life which had seemed very dull after her brief glimpse into *his* world.

But he was here now. Standing in front of her with all that dark, brooding power and she could hardly ignore him. She couldn't really shut the door in his face and tell him she was busy—something which her scruffy jeans and swimming club sweatshirt suggested was untrue. Because that would run the risk of making her look vulnerable and that was something she wasn't prepared to do. Okay, so he had taken her virginity. No, Lucy corrected herself sternly. She had *given* him her virginity—with an eagerness which had taken her completely by surprise. And him, if the look on his face had been anything to go by when he'd thrust deep into her body, while, outside, the inky waters of the Mediterranean had gleamed silver in the moonlight.

Just because they'd shared a passionate few days together and it had fizzled out like a spent firework didn't mean they should now be enemies. Or was she deluded enough to have expected that the amazing sex they'd shared would end in some sort of *relationship*, when they came from completely different worlds?

And yet...

She cleared her throat, trying to quell the foolish hope which was spiralling up inside her, knowing how foolishly persistent hope could be. False hope could raise you up and then dash you down again, making the pain even more intense than it had been before. And she was done with pain for the time being. Hadn't she been given more than her fair share of it during her twenty-eight years?

So she forced as wide a smile as she could manage and when she spoke, her breath rushed from her mouth like billowing smoke as it hit the cold winter air. 'Drakon,' she said. 'This is...unexpected.'

He shrugged his powerful shoulders. 'Maybe I should have rung first.'

He said it as if he didn't really mean it. As if any woman should be falling over herself with gratitude that the famous Greek billionaire had deigned to pay her an unexpected call. She wasn't really feeling it but Lucy attempted indignation. 'Yes, you should. You were lucky I was in.'

Dark eyebrows were raised. 'Oh?'

And despite everything, she found herself offering an explanation. As if she needed to prove herself to a man who hadn't even cared enough about her to lift up the phone and check she was okay after their long weekend together. She began to talk. 'Because this is a busy time of year in the catering industry. There are a lot of pre-holiday functions coming up and normally I would be working. In case you don't remember I work for Caro's Canapés and people eat more canapés at Christmas than at any other time of the year.'

'Of course. Christmas.' Drakon tensed as he said it, knowing he needed to choose his words with care—not a normal occurrence for him, since people always hung onto whatever he had to say with an eagerness which sometimes repulsed him. Like many powerful men he demanded servility while secretly despising it, but Lucy was different. She had always been different. Wasn't that one of the reasons he was here today? There were countless women who would have bitten his hand off to accept what he was about to offer—but only Lucy would understand the truth.

Only Lucy would accept the limitations of what he was about to ask her.

But first he needed to gain entry into her mini-fortress of a cottage. He fixed his gaze on the chain which was still stretched tautly across the door and wondered why she hadn't released it.

'Can I come in?' he questioned.

There was a pause. Not long enough to be insulting, but a pause nonetheless and he noted it with surprise and a faint flicker of irritation he knew to be unreasonable.

'I suppose so,' she said at last.

He watched her fiddle with the chain before pulling the door open and stepping back to let him in. He noted that she was keeping her distance but maybe he couldn't blame her for that. He hadn't behaved particularly well after that surprisingly erotic encounter which had taken place back in the summer and afterwards he'd cursed himself for allowing it to happen in the first place. He couldn't understand why he'd behaved in a way which had been so uncharacteristic, because usually he chose his lovers as carefully as he chose his cars—and normally someone like Lucy Phillips wouldn't have even made the cut.

He hadn't rung her or asked to see her again, because what was the point of meaningless phone calls which might have left her fabricating unfulfillable dreams about the future? She was way too unworldly to spend any time with a hard-hearted bastard like him. Not for the first time he found himself wondering what had possessed him to invite someone he'd known from his schooldays to his Greek island home, though deep down he knew why. It hadn't been because of the way she had looked at him with those soft blue eyes, nor the way she had blushed when she'd seen him again after so many years. It hadn't even been about her somewhat old-fashioned attitude, which had been obvious in pretty much everything about her—from the way

she wore her hair to the polite way she'd tried to refuse his offer of a lift home after the reunion, saying
it would take him miles out of his way—an attitude
which had undoubtedly charmed him.

He'd done it because he'd felt sorry for her because
she was hard-working and poor and had been through
a tough time. And yet, against all the odds, he had
seduced her, even though she was nothing like his
usual choice of bed partner. He was not and never had
been a player, for reasons which were rooted deeply
in his past. In fact, if anything, he'd been described
as not just formidable but indifferent to the charms of
women. He was not indifferent, of course. Far from it.
He loved sex as much as any red-blooded man but it
took more than physical attraction to engage his interest. Throughout his life he'd been able to have his pick
of any woman he wanted, but he was much too fastidi-
ous for that. When he did engage in a relationship, he
liked women who were experienced. Sexual equals
who were willing to experiment. Intelligent women
more focussed on their career than on the idea of marriage, who treated sex like an enjoyable form of exercise. Not someone soft and gentle and full of wonder,
like Lucy Phillips.

As she closed the door on the freezing winter afternoon, he was able to study her. Nobody in the world
could ever have described her as pretty, although her
soft brown hair was shiny and her skin was clear, and
she had a way of looking at you with that misty blue
gaze which was more than a little unsettling...

He narrowed his eyes. And, yes, she had a body
made firm by youth and exercise but the grey jeans

she was wearing did her curvy derrière no favours. Neither did her sweatshirt, which was scarlet and had the insignia of a dolphin embroidered just below one shoulder and disguised the luscious curve of breasts he knew lay beneath. Suddenly he couldn't hold back the flashback memory of her nipples—rose-tipped and tasting of coconut sunscreen—which had been positioned so tantalisingly beneath his questing lips as he had licked them into cresting peaks. He felt the hard rush of blood to his groin and thought just how much he would like to lose himself in her again.

Until a rush of shame made him wonder why the hell he was thinking about sex at a time like this.

Ever-present guilt washed over him and Drakon shook his head to clear it. Focus, he told himself fiercely. Focus. Think about the reason you're here. The only reason you're here. He looked around, realising that the cramped dimensions and obvious lack of investment in the property she had inherited from her mother was playing right into his hands. But before he put his proposition to her, he had to get her to relax and to lose that tight look from her face. Which wasn't going to be easy, judging from the way she was staring at him as warily as if a snake had just wriggled its way from the nearby riverbank into her tiny sitting room.

Stepping over the row of shoes lined up neatly beside the front door, he glanced around, at a jug of holly on a table and the way the scarlet berries echoed the colourful flash of cushions which were scattered along the sofa. A flickering fire was burning in the grate—scenting the small room with applewood. Everything was polished and shining and all the contents of the room seemed old and lovingly preserved. In pride of place on the wall were two photographs of different men, both in uniform, and Drakon felt a clench of pain and an unwanted sense of identification. But he forced himself to concentrate on the positive. On the future, not the past. Because that was what was important, he reminded himself fiercely. The only thing which was important.

'Nice place,' he commented, making the kind of benign social observation which wasn't usually part of his vocabulary.

Her blue eyes narrowed suspiciously, as if she didn't believe him. As if he was secretly making fun of her by comparing this matchbox of a dwelling to the sprawling square footage of his many homes. But he *did* mean it. He'd never been inside this riverside cottage before but he'd passed it often enough when he was rowing for the prestigious English boarding school he'd attended, where Lucy's mother had been matron. The little house used to symbolise home for all the boys who were so far away from their own. He remembered seeing fairy lights in the window and a wreath on the door every Christmas. He remembered hearing laughter coming through an open door in the lush months of summer when the green reeds grew tall and the riverbank was bosky. But there was no Christmas wreath today, he noted.

'It suits my needs perfectly,' she said, rather primly.

Her words sounded defensive and Drakon found himself staring at her left hand, registering each ringless finger before lifting his gaze to her eyes. It was unlikely that her situation had changed since the summer but you never knew… 'You live here alone?'

A faint frown appeared on her brow. 'I do.'

'So…there's no man in your life?'

Hot colour rushed into her cheeks. 'I believe that's what's known as a rather impertinent question.'

'Is there?' he persisted.

Her blush deepened. 'No. Actually, there isn't. Not that it's any of your business,' she said crossly, before fixing him with an enquiring look. 'Look, what can I do for you, Drakon? You turn up without any kind of warning and then start interrogating me about my personal life, yet I've heard nothing from you for months. Forgive if I'm confused. Is this just a random visit?'

Drakon shook his head. He had planned how he was going to present this. To somehow build it up and carefully cushion the impact. To make it sound as if it was just part of life and he was dealing with it. He hadn't been expecting to just come out and say it—or for the words to taste like bitter poison when he spoke them.

'No. This wasn't a chance visit. I intended to come here today. It's Niko,' he grated. 'He's dead.'

Lucy blinked in confusion for his words made no sense. Because Niko was Drakon's twin brother. The wilder version of Drakon. Niko was the unpredictable twin—always had been. The volatile twin. The one who made headlines for all the wrong reasons and had almost been expelled from school an unbelievable three times. But although Niko was reckless he was also full of life. Why, she remembered him as the kind of man who was positively *bursting* with life.

'What are you talking about?' she said and afterwards wondered how she could have asked such a naïve question, in view of her own experience. 'How can he possibly be dead?'

Drakon's face contorted with darkness and pain and that was when she knew he was speaking the truth.

'He died of a drug overdose,' he bit out. 'Last month.'

Lucy gasped, her fingertips flying to her lips, her heart crashing wildly against her ribcage as she wondered how she could have been so stupid. Didn't she of all people know that young lives could be cut down like a blade of grass being sliced by a tractor at harvest time? Had she thought Drakon Konstantinou was immune to pain and loss, just because he was one of the world's richest men and was always flying around the globe on his private jet, brokering deals to add even more dollars to his already massive fortune?

She wanted to rush over to him. To fling her arms around his tense body and comfort him, as she had comforted innumerable grieving relatives on hospital wards in the past. But that was the trouble with sex. It changed things. You could never touch a former lover and pretend it was impartial, even if it was. 'Oh, Drakon,' she said, in a low voice, and could see from his blanched features and haunted eyes that he was in deep shock. 'I'm so sorry. I had no idea. Please. Won't you sit down? Let me get you something.' She looked around rather distractedly, trying to remember what was in the ancient drinks cabinet. 'I think I have some whisky somewhere—'

'I don't want whisky,' he said harshly.

She nodded. 'Okay. Then I'll make you some tea. Strong tea with lots of sugar. That's what you need.'

To her surprise he didn't object, just sank into one of the fireside armchairs, which looked too flimsy to be able to deal with his powerful frame, and Lucy sped into the kitchen, glad to have something to occupy herself with. Something to distract herself from her racing thoughts. But her hands were shaking so much that the china was chinking madly as she pulled cups and saucers down from one of the cupboards.

Sucking in a deep breath, she waited for the kettle to boil, wondering why she hadn't realised right from the beginning that something was wrong. Hadn't she been taught to read the telltale signs of body language which might have suggested that here was a man mourning the loss of his only sibling? While instead she had been selfishly preoccupied with her own battered ego, reflecting on the fact that he'd dumped her after a long weekend of wild and totally unexpected sex. What did something like that matter in the light of what he'd just told her?

She made the tea and frowned as she picked up the tray, because a nagging question still remained.

Why *had* he told her?

Slowly she went back into the tiny sitting room, her head still full of confusion. He turned to look at her and suddenly Lucy was scared by the expression on his rugged features. By the stony look which made his black eyes look so hard and bleak and cold—eyes which said quite clearly *you can't get close to me*. Scared too by another instinctive urge to run over and hug him, wondering if she was using his heartache as an excuse to touch him again. Because hadn't she yearned to stroke his silken flesh ever since he'd set her body on fire and made her realise what physical pleasure really meant?

She poured tea, dropping four sugar cubes into his cup and giving it a quick stir, before placing it on a small table beside the fire. Then she sat down in a chair opposite him, her knees pressed tightly together. 'Do you want to tell me about it?' she questioned softly. 'About what happened to Niko?'

Talking about it was the last thing Drakon wanted, but if he was to get Lucy to agree to his demands it was unavoidable. And how hard could it be to do that? He was a master of negotiation in the business world—surely he was able to employ the same tools of demand, cooperation and compromise in his personal life if he were to achieve what it was he wanted.

'How much do you know about my brother?' he questioned.

She hesitated, shrugging her shoulders a little awkwardly. 'Not a lot. Once he left school he seemed to disappear off the radar.'

'*Neh.* That's a good way to describe what happened. He disappeared off the radar.' Drakon's voice grew distant and sounded as if it were coming from a long way off. But it was, he realised, with a jolt. It was coming from the past—and didn't they say that the past was like a different country? The Konstantinou twins, two black-eyed little boys, pampered like princes by a battery of servants yet overlooked by the wealthy parents who had employed those servants. They shared almost identical DNA and, for many years, few people could tell them apart, until they heard them speak. So similar in looks and yet so different in character. Sometimes they'd even been able to trick their own parents—but then, they'd lived such separate lives from their mother and father maybe that wasn't so surprising.

'Niko was the older of us—by just one and a half minutes—but those vital ninety seconds were all that were needed for him to be in line to inherit the family business. He thought he was going to be a very wealthy man—until the will was read and he discovered there was nothing left. All the money had gone.'

'How come?'

Drakon stared at her. Her bluebell eyes were a compassionate blur and for a moment he almost confided in her, until he drew himself short, reminding himself that certain segments of the past were irrelevant. He'd come here to talk about the future. 'The reasons don't matter,' he said, the words acrid on his lips. 'What is relevant is the way Niko coped with finding out the news, and the way he coped with it was with drugs. First it was a puff or two of dope at a party and then he started snorting cocaine, like so many of his buddies. But sooner or later, every addiction needs an additional boost because it isn't working any more.' His face twisted. 'And that's when he started on heroin.'

She didn't say anything. Had he expected her to? Had he secretly wanted her to come out with something trite and predictable so he could lash out as he had been wanting to lash out at someone for days now? He felt his jaw tighten as he continued with his story and yet somehow it was an unspeakable relief to unburden himself, because he hadn't really talked about this with anyone. Not even Amy. He hadn't dared. Had he been afraid that describing his twin's fatal weakness might somehow reflect poorly on *him*? Might hold up a mirror to the cold darkness in his own soul and the guilt which gnawed away at him because he hadn't been there for his brother when he'd most needed him?

'I didn't find this out until afterwards,' he ground out. 'Because he left Greece and kept his distance from me—from everyone, really—and resisted every attempt I made to meet up. I only realised afterwards that he wanted to hide the true extent of his drug habit from me. If I'd known I might have been able to do something, but I didn't know. I guess I was too busy trying to make my fortune. Trying to recover something of the Konstantinou name and reputation.' He sighed. 'But eventually, I heard that Niko was living in Goa and was in a steady relationship and I can remember thinking that maybe things might be different. Personally, I've never believed in the transformative power of love—but that didn't mean I wasn't hopeful it might work for Niko.' His mouth twisted cynically and there was a pause. 'Apparently they had a beachside wedding and then I heard that she'd had a baby.'

'B-baby?' she echoed.

Drakon saw the colour drain from her face but still he didn't say it. It was as if he needed to mould the facts into some sort of recognisable structure before he hit her with the big one. Was he hoping to build up an element of sympathy, so she would find it impossible to say no to him? 'He got in touch with me just after the birth, to tell me I was now an uncle. He…he asked me if I wanted to go and meet Xander for myself and I told him I would. So I scheduled in a trip to go and see them the following week and was hopeful that the birth of a healthy child might bring him the kind of fulfilment he'd been unable to find elsewhere. Maybe it would have done if he and his wife hadn't decided to celebrate in their own time-honoured way. Not with a bottle of champagne or a candlelit dinner, but a lethal cocktail of narcotics.'

Her face blanched even more. 'Oh, no.'

'Oh, *neh*,' he agreed grimly. 'My partner was on a business trip nearby and some instinct made me ask her to check on them unannounced.' He paused, suddenly finding the words very difficult to say. 'Their bodies were still warm by the time she got there. I got a local investigator to find out what he could, and a little searching revealed that Niko's wife was as hooked on illegal substances as he was.'

'Oh, Drakon. I'm so sorry.'

He shook his head. 'We spoke to the doula who'd been attending her throughout the pregnancy and the only thing I'm grateful for is that she must have retained some vestige of common sense, and was able to give up drugs for the whole nine months.'

She flinched, the words spilling urgently from her mouth. 'And the baby?' she demanded. 'What about the baby?'

'Is unharmed,' he supplied grimly. 'The life force is powerful. He is lusty and strong and with his Greek nanny now—safe and warm not far from here, in London.' He felt his mouth twist, as if recounting words he didn't particularly want to say. 'You see, Niko and his wife had named me as the child's official guardian and so he is living with me.'

She leaned forward, clasping her hands together

as if in prayer, an expression of earnestness on her face. But he could see indecision there, too, and she seemed to be choosing her words carefully. 'This is a heartbreaking story, Drakon—and I'm so sorry for your loss,' she breathed. 'But I'm still not quite sure why you're telling me all this.'

He stared at her. Was she really so naïve? Maybe she was. She'd certainly been *innocent* when he'd parted her thighs that hot summer evening and slid inside the unexpected tightness of her body. Though maybe he'd been the naïve one not to have realised that the wholesome Lucy Phillips had been untouched by another man. When he'd bumped into her in England she'd appeared almost invisible and the thought of seducing her couldn't have been further from his mind. And yet things had inexplicably turned sexual when he'd dropped in on her when she'd been staying on his island.

He remembered seeing her swimming in his pool, her strong arms arcing through the turquoise water in a graceful display of strength and power. Length after length he had watched her swim and when she'd eventually surfaced and blinked droplets of water from her eyes, she had looked genuinely surprised—and pleased—to see him. He shouldn't have been turned on by her plain and practical swimsuit but he had been, though maybe because he'd never seen someone of her age wearing something so old-fashioned. Just as he shouldn't have been unexpectedly charmed by the way she made him laugh—which was rare enough to be noteworthy. He'd found himself staying on for dinner, even though he hadn't planned to—and even though he'd told himself that her dress was cheap, that hadn't stopped him from being unable to tear his eyes away from the way the dark material had clung to her fleshy curves, had it?

Maybe it was inevitable that they had started kissing—and just as inevitable that they'd ended up having sex. The unexpected and unwanted factor had been encountering her intact hymen and realising he was the first man she'd ever been intimate with. At the time he'd been irritated by the fact she hadn't told him because, according to friends who knew about such things, taking a woman's virginity brought with it all kinds of problems—not least the kind of mindless devotion which was the last thing he needed. In fact, he despised it, for reasons which still made him shudder. His mouth hardened. He had enough difficulty keeping women at arm's length as it was, without some idealistic innocent longing for rose petals and wedding bells.

But his irritation had lasted no longer than it took to resume his powerful rhythm inside her. And she had surprised him. Not just because she had proved to be an energetic and enthusiastic lover who had kissed more sweetly than any other woman he'd ever known. No. Because she seemed to have realised herself the limitations of their brief affair and to have accepted the fact that he had ghosted her from his life afterwards. She hadn't made any awkward phone calls or sent texts carefully constructed in order to appear 'casual'. And if his abundantly healthy ego had been fleetingly dented by her apparent eagerness to put what had happened behind her, the feeling had soon left him, because it was entirely mutual. But it made him realise that in many ways Lucy Phillips was exceptional. Emotionally independent, a trained midwife and, thus, the perfect candidate for what he needed…

He felt his mouth dry as he studied her earnest face and the clothes which failed to flatter her curvy shape. It was hard now to believe that she had choked out her fulfilment as he had driven into her firm body or to imagine the way he had fingered her nipples in the blazing Greek sunshine so that they had puckered into tight little nubs just ripe for sucking. But when you stopped to think about it, *all* of this was hard to believe and he needed to present his case so that she would receive it sympathetically. Rising to his feet, he addressed her stumbled question as he slowly approached her fireside chair. 'I'm telling you because I need your help, Lucy.'

'*My* help?' she echoed, her bright eyes looking up at him in surprise as his shadow enveloped her in darkness. 'Are you kidding? How on earth can I help someone like you when you're one of the richest men in the world and I have practically nothing?'

'No, I'm not kidding,' he negated firmly. 'And, far from having nothing, you have something I need very badly. Niko's baby needs security and continuity. He needs a home and I'm in a position to offer him one. But not on my own. Not as a single man whose work takes him to opposite sides of the world and who has no experience of babies, or children. And that's why I'm asking you to marry me, Lucy. To be my wife and the mother of my orphaned nephew.'

CHAPTER TWO

LUCY'S MOUTH FELL open as she stared into the face of the powerful Greek billionaire, the flickering firelight illuminating the ebony and gold of his rugged features. She couldn't believe what Drakon had just asked her and his question made her feel as if she was taking part in a dream. An extra-surreal dream. But surely he wouldn't be looking so serious if he hadn't meant it. 'You want *me* to marry you?' she verified slowly.

He nodded—though his brief frown suggested he didn't quite agree with her choice of words. 'I do.'

Lucy shook her hair and her heavy ponytail slithered like a thick rope against her back. Wasn't it crazy— and sad—how, in life, timing was everything? If her brother hadn't been in the wrong place at the wrong time, he would still be here. And if Drakon Konstantinou had asked her this very question a few months earlier, her reaction to it would have been totally different. Because when she'd returned home after her brief excursion to his island home—high on a mixture of raging hormones and a heady introduction to multiple orgasms—she had prayed for a scenario just like this. She'd nursed the unrealistic fantasy that what she and Drakon had shared had been special. Super-special. She had longed for him to suddenly decide his life was empty without her and that he wanted them to make a go of things. Why wouldn't she, when he was like every woman's dream man—despite his undeni-able arrogance and detachment? When she'd always had a secret crush on him...

Of course that had never happened. He had cut her out of his life as abruptly as he had blazed into it again—at a school reunion where she'd been em-ployed by Caro's Canapés, the local catering firm for which she worked. In her plain green dress, she'd been serving sandwiches just before the pin-drop silence which had followed Drakon Konstantinou's entrance into Milton school's famous and historic hall. She re-membered the way all the other men had consciously or unconsciously pulled back their shoulders and sucked in their stomachs, as if to big themselves up or look taller. But it had been to no avail because the Greek tycoon had still dominated the vast room without even trying. Like a black star, dark brilliance had radiated from his powerful body and drawn every single eye to him. Yet for some crazy and inexplicable reason, he had been looking at *her*.

Lucy remembered blushing deeply as she'd offered him an egg and cress sandwich because she'd been acutely aware of the time, years ago, when he'd gashed his leg while rowing for the first team and, eager to be a nurse herself, she had been helping her mother, the school matron, in the school sanatorium. Drakon had been lying on a narrow trolley, with blood seep-ing from his gaping wound, and Lucy had thought

how much it must hurt as her mother had dabbed at
it with antiseptic. But he hadn't shown it. He hadn't
even winced, not once. She'd given him her fingers
to grip and he had opened his eyes and stared at her.
Stared at her with eyes as black as the night. A ripple
of something unfamiliar and exciting had whispered
its way down her spine and she had never forgotten
that feeling. She had been only fourteen at the time,
and Drakon a crucial three years older—it had been
Lucy's first experience of physical attraction towards a
member of the opposite sex and it had stayed with her,
all those years. Why, it had fired straight back into life
when she had extended the silver platter of sandwiches
towards him and met the velvety blackness of his eyes.

Was it her corresponding blush which had amused
him—which had deepened when he'd pointed out, in
his drawling Greek accent, that it was a rare thing to
see a woman blush these days? Or was it simply curiosity which had made him hang around as the reunion
was coming to an end, and the headmaster was im-
ploring him to join him and his wife for supper? But
Drakon hadn't stayed. Amid a torrent of thundering
rain, he had insisted on giving her a lift home in his
fancy car and naturally Lucy had been tongue-tied by
all that opulence.

It had been pretty scary to discover that her crush
on him was as powerful as ever, and slightly unsettling
that she couldn't seem to keep her gaze from straying
to the muscular thrust of his thighs. She remembered
the potent rush of warmth deep at her core, which had
made her feel both excited and a little bit embarrassed,
because she wasn't the type of person who usually

thought about stuff like that. She never really came across eligible men and certainly nobody of Drakon's calibre ever entered her life. Even the ones who were more her type tended to glance over her shoulder whilst chatting at parties, as if searching the room for someone more interesting to talk to.

Yet after the reunion, when the throaty car had slid to a halt outside her tiny riverside cottage, Drakon had turned to her and said, 'So how are you, Lucy? I mean, *really*?'

Was it the sense of what had sounded like genuine interest—something she suspected was rare for a man like him—which had made her blurt out everything which had been on her mind? Well, not *everything*. She'd missed out the part which explained why she'd given up her beloved job in midwifery—because the reasons for that made her feel even less of a woman, and who in their right mind would wish to do that in the presence of such a gorgeous man? Instead Lucy had found herself telling him about her brother in the army, who had lost his life in that awful conflict, just as her father had done in a different war before that. And how afterwards her mother had seemed to lose the will to live and had just faded away—like one of those dusky pink roses which bloomed in the lavish walled gardens of Milton school.

She remembered the deep frown which had crossed the tycoon's face as he'd studied her admittedly pale skin and told her that what she needed was a holiday in the sun. Had she explained that such luxuries were far beyond her grasp on her wages as a waitress, or had he just guessed? She wasn't sure. All she knew was that he had extended a careless invitation for her to holiday on his own personal Greek island.

'You actually own an island?' she remembered querying in disbelief.

'Sure.' He had glittered her a smile. 'And my house is empty a lot of the time. It's yours any time you want to use it.'

So she had gone. It had been an uncharacteristic response to what had probably just been a throwaway gesture on his part, but it had been too good an opportunity to miss. Although he had casually mentioned that his private jet was available, Lucy had scraped together enough money to fund a cheap flight to Athens instead and then caught the staff ferry to his private island of Prasinisos, with a pile of engrossing books to read. It had been the most impetuous thing she'd ever done and she wasn't sure what she had expected. She certainly hadn't expected Drakon to suddenly arrive on a glittering super-yacht the size of Jupiter later that day, when she was emerging from the swimming pool looking like a drowned rat. Nor for him to join her beside the aqua glitter of the infinity pool once she'd showered all the chlorine out of her hair and the fierce beat of the sun had made her feel all lazy and laid-back.

For a while she'd said nothing, because instinct had told her he was a man who valued silence, and gradually she had seen Drakon relax—something she'd suspected he didn't do very often. He'd shown her the faint scar from the gash on his leg which she'd helped her mother to suture all those years ago, and something about that distant memory had made them both laugh. She remembered their eyes meeting and something intangible shimmering in the air around them. Lucy had been inexperienced, innocent and slightly out of her depth—all those things, yes. But she had also been excited and eager for what had happened later, after a delicious dinner on the terrace once his housekeeper had gone home. For Drakon to fold her into his arms and kiss her and then kiss her some more. It had been as if her every dream had come true in that moment. As if her body had been poised on the brink of something very beautiful.

She'd thought he would quickly get bored with someone who wasn't at all experienced but her tongue's tentative exploration of his mouth had caused a low growl of pleasure to rumble up from his throat. He'd held her so tight that her soft body had moulded into the muscular hardness of his, so that when he had carried her off to his bedroom it had felt nothing but right. Even that slight awkwardness when he had stilled inside her and momentarily glared at her hadn't lasted longer than a couple of seconds.

The following morning she had woken naked in his bed and he had brought her dark coffee, which was thick and sweet, before taking her in his arms again, and the next few days had passed by in a sensual blur. He'd made love to her on the terrace, and in the cabin of his yacht as he'd sailed her round his island and showed her all the little bays and coves. He'd fed her grapes and trickled Greek honey onto a belly which had quivered as he'd licked it off.

And three days later it had all been over, without anything actually being said. There had been no awkward conversation or protracted farewells. He hadn't insulted her by telling her that his diary was too jam-packed for him to be able to see her again. He'd just given her a deep kiss, said goodbye and dropped her off at the airport by helicopter so at least she hadn't had to endure that rather bumpy ferry ride back to Athens. She hadn't heard a squeak from him since and, once she'd realised it wasn't going to happen, her hurt and disappointment had gradually faded into the recesses of her mind, because Lucy was nothing if not practical. She'd told herself to remember all the good bits and she'd tried not to have unrealistic expectations, because that way you could avoid hurt and disappointment as much as possible. She had been getting on with her life—her rather ordinary and predictable life—until the Greek tycoon had blazed back into it with the most implausible suggestion she'd ever heard!

'I can't believe you're asking me to marry you,' she breathed.

'Well, believe it,' he returned softly. 'Because it's true.'

'But why me?' she questioned, wishing that her heart would stop thundering. 'There must be a million women who would make a more suitable wife for a man like you.'

He didn't even pay her the compliment of pretending to consider her remark and certainly didn't bother to deny it, just answered with a bluntness which somehow managed to be supremely insulting.

'There are indeed,' he agreed. 'In fact, if I were to measure suitability in terms of sophistication and familiarity with my world, you would be right at the back of the queue, Lucy.'

She swallowed. 'You don't pull your punches, do you, Drakon?'

'Do you think I should?' he mused. 'I've always been of the mindset that life is too short for prevarication and Niko's death has only confirmed that.'

He paused and as his night-dark gaze shimmered over her, Lucy wanted to tell him not to look at her like that—yet the craziest thing of all was that she wanted him to carry on doing it and never stop.

'I've never wanted to marry anyone nor have children of my own,' he said. 'Despite the fact that I have a vast fortune just waiting for someone to inherit.'

'Why not?' she asked quietly.

His black gaze seared into her, as if he was deciding how much to tell her. 'Because I don't believe in love. It's something I've never felt nor wanted to feel. To my mind, love is nothing but an invention which seems designed to excuse the most outrageous forms of behaviour.' His black eyes narrowed. 'But now I have an heir whether I like it or not and, because I am a twin, this child almost completely carries half my genes. So in a way, I have a ready-made family. I may not have wanted or planned it but now that I have it, I will make the best of it because that is how I operate. Providing Xander with a suitable mother and giving him some sort of grounding is the least I can do to try to compensate for such a horrible start to his young life. And while you may not have much money or be familiar with the world's high spots, you have something which makes you extra-special, Lucy.'

'Really? And what might that be?' Lucy's heart quickened, though afterwards she would be ashamed of her needy desire to have him shower praise on her, because it didn't happen. Instead, he listed her credentials like an employer telling her why she had surprisingly beaten the other candidates.

'You're a trained nurse for a start,' he drawled, his Greek accent deep and velvety. 'A midwife as I recall, which makes you extra-suitable. And you are both pure and respectable, if what I discovered about you back in the summer was anything to go by. Once I started considering you for the role, I realised that your virginity was actually a great asset.'

He didn't seem to notice that his last remark had made her cheeks grow heated. Of course he didn't. He was talking *at* her instead of *to* her, wasn't he? He didn't really care about her thoughts and reactions— nor about the fact that he was making her sound like an upmarket brand of soap. To Drakon Konstantinou she was nothing more than a commodity.

'Rather than being a bit of a bore, which was how you seemed to regard it at the time?' she questioned rather snappily.

'Yes, you could put it like that,' he said, without missing a beat. 'Your purity now takes on an entirely different aspect, Lucy, and it has become important to me. It's an indication of the way you've lived your life. You haven't had a vast number of lovers before me, and such reserve is rare among women.'

'But what difference does my lifestyle make to what you have in mind?' she questioned. 'Why does it matter that I was a virgin?'

His mouth had hardened so that suddenly it resembled a savage slash across the lower part of his face and she could see coldness and calculation enter his black eyes.

'Because you will be able to lead by example. I want an old-fashioned woman with old-fashioned values and you are the perfect fit. This baby carries the genes of two addicts who were willing to put their own pleasure before his welfare,' he continued bitterly. 'Not only do I need to ensure that never happens again, I also need to stack the odds in Xander's favour from now on.'

Lucy didn't say anything. Not straight away. Not when he was looking so forbidding and so...*angry*— though she realised he was angry with his brother and not with her. She rose to her feet from the fireside chair because she felt at a psychological disadvantage having to stare up at him like that and it was making her neck ache. And she needed to put some distance between them. Some very necessary distance to get her thoughts in order. Away from the spell of his proximity and coercive weave of his words.

She walked over to the opposite side of the small room and stared out of the window at the river. The moon was beginning to rise and was forming a dappled silvery path on the darkening water and she could see that a cottage on the opposite bank must have put up their Christmas tree. She blinked as she stared at the glittering lights—rose and gold and green and blue— but felt none of the prescribed magic as she turned to meet Drakon's hooded gaze. 'Isn't the normal thing in these kind of circumstances to employ a nanny?' she questioned. 'Which you already have done, by the sound of it. You can afford to engage a whole battery of staff, Drakon. Why do you need a wife?'

He shook his head, like a man who had all the answers—but hadn't he always seemed like a man with all the answers? 'Obviously the child will need a full-time nanny and Sofia is eager to continue in that role,' he said, and paused. 'But that isn't the point, Lucy.'

'Isn't it?' she asked quietly.

'No.'

He shook his head and Lucy could see the bleakness in his eyes. She thought how *empty* his face looked. As if he'd been drained of all emotion so that he resembled some dark and forbidding statue. As if his body were composed of cold marble instead of flesh and blood, and a sudden trepidation whispered over her skin as she realised there was no real warmth in this man. 'I don't understand,' she breathed.

'Then let me make it clearer for you. I don't want this child to grow up in that kind of world—the adopted child of a single billionaire,' he bit out. 'I don't want him looked after by a series of employees with no emotional investment in his future, like I was. I don't want him sent away to school like I was. Xander needs a family. A real family.'

Lucy swallowed, wondering which of them was being naïve now. Did anyone truly know what a *real* family was—or did they all just rely on the slushy default version you saw in films, or read about in books, with people clustered round a fire, throwing their heads back in mutual laughter? Yet having a family was the bedrock of society, wasn't it? It was the dream which the majority of people aspired to, even if the reality was often so different. Was he really suggesting that the legal union of two people who had briefly been lovers could magically create some sort of fairy-tale household?

But then her mind began to focus on something else. On a single word the Greek tycoon had just uttered and which now lodged itself deep in her mind.

Xander.

Xander, his nephew and innocent little baby.

A motherless baby.

Lucy's heart clenched with a pain she should have anticipated because unwittingly Drakon had stumbled across her Achilles heel. The reason why she always felt as if something inside her was missing and incomplete. The one part of her life which could never be fulfilled, unless...

Her mouth dried.

Unless she was brave enough—or crazy enough—to accept the billionaire's bizarre offer. Because wasn't he offering her the magic-wand solution she had once yearned for in the form of instant motherhood? Her mind began to race. Could it work? Could she provide what little Xander needed—and in so doing gain for herself what she thought had been lost for ever?

Take it slowly, she told herself firmly.

Slowly.

'This sounds like a very long-term plan,' she suggested carefully.

'It is.' Some of the coldness had left his face and in its place she could see conviction. And persuasion. 'I'm talking endurance, Lucy. About putting a child's needs first and making a promise to each other that neither of us intends to break. About commitment and stability.'

'How can you be so sure you could find that with

me?' She stared at him. 'When you don't really *know* me. At school you were years ahead of me. I was just the school nurse's daughter who was allowed to take certain classes with the boys. Apart from those times when you were having the wound on your leg attended to, you didn't even notice me. We were just ships which passed in the night and, apart from that, we've only spent a few days together.'

'You think that time we spent on Prasinisos didn't provide me with the opportunity to discover something of what makes Lucy Phillips tick?' he enquired softly.

Lucy wanted to turn away from the mocking look in his eyes but that would be an immature response to a perfectly reasonable question. Because they *had* been intimate—and it would be hypocritical to pretend they hadn't.

'I can't deny we were lovers,' she husked. 'But physical intimacy during a mini-break on a Greek island is one thing. Real life is another. We're strangers, Drakon. How do you know I wouldn't drive you crackers before the first month was up?'

His eyes narrowed but Lucy couldn't mistake the brief flash of surprise which had gleamed there. As if he couldn't quite believe that she was prevaricating instead of instantly accepting his offer.

And wasn't there a part of her which couldn't quite believe it herself? Making out as if there were men lining up and asking her to marry them every day of the week!

'We would have to work at it, in the way that people with arranged marriages have always done,' he said. 'And we will be walking into it with our eyes open—

without any of the myths of love and romance which set people up for disappointment, and failure. If we refuse to have unrealistic expectations about each other, then we should succeed.' He slanted her a smile. 'Does that reassure you?'

Lucy thought how clever he was. And how controlling, too. That slow smile—she was certain—had been angled at her deliberately in order to pump up her heart rate and it had worked, hadn't it? Was that the main reason he was here—because he thought of her as passive? Wasn't it time to demonstrate that while she might be poor and unglamorous, that didn't necessarily mean she was a complete pushover? 'So what's in it for me, Drakon?' she questioned. 'What made you think you could turn up without warning and ask me to become your wife? Were you so certain I'd say yes?'

Drakon's eyes narrowed. He felt a certain responsibility towards her because he had unwittingly taken her virginity and had quashed his desire to see her again because he'd known he was capable of hurting her. He'd suspected that someone like her would be unable to cope with a commitment-phobe like him, even though he'd been sorely tempted to have sex with her again. But that had been back then—when his life had been free and unfettered. This was now, when he had an unexpected burden of responsibility to shoulder.

His mouth hardened. 'I had an idea you might be tempted.'

'Because?'

Would it be cruel to point out that without him a limited future inevitably beckoned for someone like her? But wouldn't any future be limited compared with the one he was offering her with all the money she could ever desire? He looked once again at her bare fingers. 'You don't show any signs of settling down,' he observed.

'Not at the moment, no.'

'So do you see yourself continuing to make ends meet as a relatively hard-up waitress?' he mused. 'Is that how you want the rest of your life to pan out?'

There was anger on her face now. And something which looked like pride. 'I don't just waitress. I actually help Caroline with all the cooking,' she declared icily. 'And she's indicated that she'd be prepared to let me buy the business when she eventually retires, which is what I've been saving up for. The waitressing is just a means to an end.'

'And that's what you really want, is it, Lucy? Resigning yourself to a life of relative poverty. Of a futile wait for Mr Right, perhaps—'

'Excuse me?' She pulled back her shoulders and glared at him. 'You think all women are just waiting around for a would-be husband to leap into their life?'

He gave a careless shrug. 'I'm saying that plenty of them are, yes—at least, in my experience. But if that's what you're hoping for, let me enlighten you. That man is just fantasy. He's someone who may or may not materialise,' he said softly. 'Whereas a rich man with whom you're sexually compatible—a man who really needs you—he's here. Right here.'

His words had got through to her, he could see that. Just as he could see the temptation which flickered in her blue eyes.

'And if I were to agree...' Her voice tailed off. 'What kind of marriage would you expect?'

Drakon heard the uncertain note in her voice but her darkening eyes told a different story. And suddenly he found himself being sucked into a vortex of erotic recall. He remembered the softness of her thighs and the untamed bush of hair which concealed her untouched treasure. For perhaps the only time in his adult sexual life, he had been momentarily astonished—and not just because she hadn't waxed—because what woman of twenty-eight was a virgin in this day and age? He remembered the soft gasp she'd given when he had entered her, the faint pain of her initial response quickly giving way to breathless murmurs of encouragement and then, to her first sweetly sobbing orgasm. And hadn't that felt sublime? Hadn't he experienced a deep satisfaction as she had choked out her pleasure against his bare shoulder, her ecstatic response filling him with a rush of primeval pleasure?

He'd made love to her countless times during those few short days—justifying his seemingly insatiable appetite with the assurance that he was simply enjoying introducing her to sex. But it had been more than that, even though he'd been loath to admit it then and was even less inclined to do so now. Her untutored eagerness had lit a strange yearning inside him—one which was being ignited right now.

He felt the exquisite throb of desire at his groin and heard the powerful thunder of his own heart. Maybe it was wrong to be thinking about sex at a time like this, but didn't they say the life force was at its most powerful during periods of grief and loss? Wasn't it nature's way of sustaining the human race, as well as reinforcing that, while his twin brother might be lying cold and dead beneath the hard earth, he, Drakon, was very much alive and at the mercy of his senses?

He began to walk towards her, noticing the instinctive tremble of her lips as he grew closer, but she didn't stop him, nor show any signs of wanting to. She just stood there, her blue eyes bright and questioning, her thick dark hair spilling out of the untidy plait which snaked down her back.

'I would expect the usual things which marriage entails,' he said huskily. 'Physical intimacy, for a start. I think that's one thing we both know we really do have in common.'

Distractedly, Lucy rubbed her toe against the rug, scarcely able to believe they were having this kind of conversation. Normally she didn't have to deal with anything more taxing than someone asking whether there were any gluten-free sandwiches available. Yet Drakon Konstantinou had just come right out and told her they were sexually compatible—him with a vast cast of ex-lovers and her with only one! She had no experience of such things but instinct told her that his words were true.

But was it *enough* for her to accept his offer of marriage? Enough for her to turn her back on her old life and enter a new one, which might be exciting but was tinged with uncertainty? With a father and a brother in the military she had grown up surrounded by uncertainty and she'd hated it. She'd longed for a safer world. A more predictable world. It was one of the reasons why she'd never really made waves in her own adult life. Why she'd always followed the rules and played safe.

Until she'd bumped into Drakon Konstantinou one balmy summer evening and the world had spun on its axis.

She knew she should say no. She should retreat back into her comfortable little world and try to forget the sexy billionaire and his bizarre offer.

But Lucy had been badly affected by what had happened to her family. In a few short years it had been wiped out as if it had never existed. Her father, brother and mother had all died in relatively quick succession. Orphaned and alone, she'd felt as if she had no real place anywhere. Sometimes she'd felt invisible. She still did. As if people were looking right through her. And all these feelings were compounded by the fact that she could never have children and be able to create a family of her own.

She stared into Drakon's rugged face, hope flaring inside her despite all her misgivings. Because the Greek tycoon was offering her exactly that. Something she'd once thought impossible but which, unlike him, she *had* wanted. An instant family. A baby to love and to care for. Her mouth dried. Could it work? Could she *make* it work? And by doing that give them both what they needed—he a wife and she a child?

She licked her lips. 'When do you need an answer by?'

'I don't see any point in waiting. I am a man who likes to settle a deal as quickly as possible. Now would be ideal.'

She shook her head. 'Now is too soon, Drakon. I

need a few days to process this. To mull over everything you've said and decide whether or not it could work. It's too big a consideration to just toss you an answer.'

His black eyes narrowed and in them Lucy could see speculation.

'Of course, there's another factor which needs to be considered. I'd hate you to overlook that, Lucy.'

She asked the question without really thinking about it. 'Which is what?'

He gave a slow smile. 'Use your imagination.'

The dip in his voice and the suddenly smoky light in his eyes made Lucy realise he was going to touch her and on one level she recognised that it was studied and manipulative. But it still worked, because Drakon knew how to press all her buttons. Even though an inner voice was urging caution, Lucy let him pull her in his arms to kiss her and, oh, she was hungry for that kiss.

So hungry.

Her fingers coiled around his broad shoulders as the voice of reason tried to warn her this was only going to confuse matters. But her body was refusing to listen to reason—its hungry demands silencing every sensible objection. Because this was amazing. Sweet sensations were flooding her body and her newly awoken sexual appetite—honed by five months of aching absence—made her think she might faint if Drakon didn't quell this sudden urgent need inside her.

His hand drifted up underneath her baggy sweater, his fingers encountering the shivering flesh of her torso before moving upwards to cup the straining mound of her breast. It was exquisite torture to feel her nipple pushing greedily against the lace of her bra, and all the while his lips were gently prising hers open. Exploring. Probing. Making her melt with the sensual flicker of his tongue. Making her writhe her hips in wordless appeal. She could feel the tension in his powerful body as he levered one powerful thigh between hers and it eased some of the pressure, even as it managed to build some more. She could feel the hardness at his groin. A hard ridge pressing urgently against the immaculate cut of his trousers, which told her graphically just how much he wanted her. She should have felt shy but that was the last thing she was feeling and Lucy knew that if the Greek had ripped off her jeans and panties before positioning himself where she was aching most, she would have taken him deep inside her.

'Drakon,' she choked out.

But her words seemed to shatter the spell as, abruptly, the kissing stopped. Moving his head away, he rocked back on his heels, inscrutable black eyes searching her face intently, and Lucy could see a nerve flickering at his temple. Had he decided he didn't want her after all? she wondered wildly. Had that rapid near-seduction been a demonstration of his power over her, rather than real desire? And did that mean he was about to withdraw his offer of marriage?

'Yes, I want you very much,' he said, scarily answering her unspoken question before directing a rueful glance at his watch. 'But now is not the time. Nor the place. Not when my car is waiting and I have a raft of meetings I need to attend. But it will keep.'

'K-keep?' she echoed.

'Neh,' he agreed, glittering her a sudden smile. 'I've

never been married before, Lucy. I've never wanted to be part of such a flawed institution, if the truth were known. But if I am to be your husband—which I fully intend to be—then there will be plenty of opportunity for lovemaking. And don't they say that hunger is the best aphrodisiac of all?'

All the time he was speaking, his fingertip was tracing a line along the edges of her lips and Lucy hated the way her mouth quivered in response. Just as she hated his arrogant assumption that she would be his wife when she hadn't given him her decision. 'But I haven't said I'll marry you yet. And I can't do that until I've met baby Xander,' she added firmly.

A look of calculation entered his black eyes. 'The key word is *"yet",*' he observed silkily. 'For it indicates that your acceptance is simply a matter of time. We both know that.' His black eyes glittered. 'Because you will marry me, Lucy. Not just because I can reward you with the things most people spend their lives craving, but because you are in a position to help a vulnerable little baby as no other person could do right now. But that's not all. You will marry me because you want me and the only way you're going to have me is by agreeing to become my wife.'

CHAPTER THREE

THERE WAS BARELY any room for the limousine to make its way down the icy lane and Lucy's heart was hammering as she locked the door of her cottage and made her way towards the luxury car. She looked around at the leafless trees and frosty bushes as if committing them to memory one last time—because who knew when she would be back?

Inadvertently she cracked through an icy puddle and mud sloshed onto her newly polished boots as Drakon's chauffeur opened the door of the car, her tentative smile being met with nothing more than a deferential nod. As she slid onto the back seat she could feel her anxiety grow and the doubts which had been bugging her for days threatened to overwhelm her. She thought about the way Drakon had kissed her and the way her body had responded so hungrily. She thought about his track record with women and her own miserable tally of just one lover. She thought about how detached and indifferent he could seem, except when engaged in some form of sensual contact and a very real fear washed over her as she realised she was entering territory which was completely alien to her.

You don't have to do this, she told herself. *It's not too late to pull out. Nobody's forcing you to become the Greek tycoon's wife. If he can't get you to look after his orphaned nephew then his money will buy him the best care in the world. It isn't your responsibility.*

For a split second she thought about jumping out of the car. About rushing back to the sanctuary of her cottage and emailing Drakon to tell him she couldn't go through with it. But then the limousine's powerful engine fired into life and they were on their way to London and suddenly it was too late for Lucy to change her mind. And wasn't the truth of it that deep down she didn't want to, for all kinds of reasons? It certainly wasn't the lure of the Greek tycoon's glamorous lifestyle which was calling to her. She'd seen enough rich boys at the boarding school where her mother had worked to know that money certainly didn't come with a guarantee of happiness. The thought of having a baby and a family of her own was the most powerful motivator, of course it was—but there was something else, too. Something which was much more intangible, and that was the way Drakon made her feel whenever he touched her. As if she were real. As if she were capable of things she'd never imagined she could do. It was a heady feeling but it was tinged with a danger she didn't quite yet understand.

All through the journey to the capital, she tried to relax, trying her best to keep her boots from smearing mud on the pristine leather interior. Not for the first time she wondered what had happened to one of her suede moccasins, which had mysteriously gone missing—and it was something of a relief to be able to think about something unconnected to Drakon as she tried to work out exactly what had happened to it. Once she had exhausted all possibilities she tried to concentrate on the landscape which was rushing past the tinted windows, but her busy thoughts ensured that most of what she saw remained a blur until they reached the centre of London. And that was when Lucy blinked in surprise, feeling as if she'd emerged from her countryside bubble to arrive in a city she scarcely recognised.

Because Christmas was all around and it was as if the entire city had been taken over by Disney. The big stores were shiny with tinsel and glitter and fake snow. Red-clothed Santas with fluffy white beards rocked manically as little children pressed their noses against the plate-glass windows. Past the giant tree on Trafalgar Square the luxury car purred and when they stopped at some traffic lights, Lucy opened one of the windows slightly so she could hear the carol singers who were collecting money for the homeless. Her heart clenched as she registered the first notes of 'Silent Night' because it always reminded her of her brother, and quickly she pressed the button so that the electric window floated up to blot out the nostalgic carol. Instead she focussed on the crowds of people who all seemed to be on a mission, hell-bent on buying gifts even though there were several weeks left until the big day.

There were plenty of things Lucy liked about Christmas. The lights. The colours. The music. The way usually inhibited people went out of their way to smile and say hello. She just didn't like the way it made her *feel*, because it seemed to emphasise all the things she didn't have. It was a time when you could feel extra-lonely if you lived on your own because most people seemed to have somebody, while she had nobody. It was when she most missed having a family. When she found herself feeling emotionally vulnerable—which wasn't a particularly nice sensation. Usually she tucked herself away with a large supply of chocolate and sobbed her way through just about every corny film which was showing on TV.

But this year was going to be different. Her teeth pressed down hard on her bottom lip and she gnawed away at it. And how. She had a wedding to organise and—this was the bit she still couldn't get her head around—she was going to be a Christmas bride. At least, that was the plan—although nothing had been arranged just yet, which was making the thought of marrying Drakon seem even more surreal than it already was. Excitement and dread flooded through her, yet the truth was that, despite her misgivings about becoming the Greek tycoon's wife, she had stumbled at the first hurdle. She had fallen in love with his orphaned nephew.

Her throat thickened as she remembered meeting the tiny baby—a meeting on which everything had hinged. She had insisted on Drakon being absent. Had she been afraid he would influence her? That he would distract her with his powerful presence and remind her of how much she still wanted *him*? She had expected objections from the powerful tycoon. She'd imagined he might wish to observe her first contact with his tiny nephew as a kind of interactive job interview, but to her surprise he had agreed to stay away. She'd been jittery with nerves—because the thought of holding a baby again after so long had thrown up all kinds of complicated emotions. Alone, she had waited in one of the reception rooms of Drakon's vast London apartment until the nanny had appeared with a snowy white bundle in her arms. Greek-born Sofia must have been in her fifties, though her step was spritely as she carried the baby towards Lucy.

And Lucy remembered the compassion which had washed over her as she'd stared down at Xander's tiny head and it had been pure instinct which had made her extend her arms so that she could cradle the infant close to her racing heart. She had been prepared for the pain which had speared through her at the thought that she would never hold a child of her own like this, but not for the instant bonding which had followed. Had it been provoked by tenderness for one who had lost so much at such an early age, or by the tiny starfish hand which had clutched her extended finger and melted her heart?

She had asked if she could give the baby his bottle and then cuddled him until he had fallen asleep. And soon after Sofia had taken Xander back to the nursery, Lucy's telephone had rung, as if it had been programmed to do so.

'Well?'

Drakon's question had been terse and to the point and there had seemed little point in prevaricating. Why pretend that this was anything other than a cold-blooded business arrangement?

'Yes.' Lucy's voice had been low but unfaltering. 'I will be your wife.'

'Good.' There was a pause. 'In which case, you need to pack a case and I'll send a car to collect you. Be ready tomorrow morning.'

'So soon?'

'What's the point of waiting, Lucy? Delay will serve little purpose.'

'But I've got three cocktail parties next week for Caro's Canapés which I'm booked to work at.'

'Leave that to me. I will arrange a suitable replacement.' His voice had dipped to become a murmured caress. 'I intend for you to become my wife as quickly as possible and I think we both know the reason for that.'

Lucy had opened her mouth to say something and then shut it again. Because didn't she want that too? Wasn't there a tiny part of her which worried that if they left it too long, Drakon might suddenly change his mind and realise that it was a completely preposterous idea to marry someone like her? And wasn't it crazy to realise how gutted she would be if that were the case? 'No, tomorrow sounds absolutely fine,' she said compliantly.

Which was why she was now on her way to Drakon's Mayfair apartment and her brand-new life. Trying not to feel like Cinderella as she perched on the edge of the limousine's soft leather seat and attempted to keep her muddy boots elevated.

Her heart was pounding as they skirted Hyde Park and drove towards the imposing modern block in Mayfair, which commanded a prime view of the city's largest park. Lucy peered out of the window, her heart missing a beat as she saw Drakon's imposing figure imprinted darkly against the glittering windows of the block. She blinked in surprise. He was waiting, she realised. Waiting for *her*?

He seemed lost in thought and hadn't noticed the car, giving Lucy the opportunity to study him unobserved. She thought that seeing him standing on the street made him seem even more of a stranger than he already was. She noticed a blonde wearing dark glasses and a fur coat do a double-take as she walked past him with a tiny white dog trotting on a red lead, though unfortunately the dog chose that precise moment to cock its little leg against a lamppost. Yet wasn't that the type of sleek woman he *should* have selected as his wife? Lucy wondered painfully, trying and failing not to drink him in with her hungry gaze.

On the cold winter day, he was dressed entirely in black and the effect was to make him dominate his surroundings even more than usual. The inky overcoat echoed the dark gleam of his eyes but his mouth was hard and unsmiling. He'd had his hair cut and the rock-star strands were now neatly trimmed in a style which seemed to emphasise all his olive-skinned beauty. Suddenly she realised he could make her blood sing even from this distance away, although the day was so cold and wintry. Being around him was like having a *fever*, she thought, clasping her fingers together so tightly that the knuckles cracked.

Some sort of notification must have gone off, for he slid his phone from his inside pocket and glanced down at it, then narrowed his black eyes to focus on the approaching limousine. Had he been forewarned that she was on her way, perhaps by his taciturn driver? In desperation, Lucy glanced down to see that her hands were shaking and a sudden shiver of trepidation whispered over her skin before she dared lift her head to meet his gaze. Was she imagining the faint flash of disapproval in his eyes as the car purred to a halt and he moved forward to open the door for her?

A cold gust of wind whipped through her as she stepped onto the pavement, acutely aware of the fact that her best coat was looking decidedly threadbare and that, although she'd spent an hour last night buffing up her boots, their newfound shine didn't hide the fact that they were old. She'd tried to do her best with her appearance but her resources were limited and even if they hadn't been—what *did* a poor girl wear when she was about to move in with her billionaire fiancé? She felt like diving back into the car and begging the driver to take her home, but somehow she managed to scrabble together a memory—an important thing she'd learnt on her very first day on the wards as a student nurse. And afterwards, whenever her mother had sunk into one of her deep depressions and Lucy had attempted to help her spirits up. *Keep it positive. Look on the bright side.*

'So,' she said brightly, tilting her chin upwards and managing a faint reproduction of a smile. 'Here I am.'

Yes. Here she was. Drakon tensed as he felt a rush of something he didn't recognise. Was it incredulity that he'd selected this woman to be his bride when she couldn't have looked like a more unlikely candidate if she'd tried? But he'd had no choice. And wasn't that the story of his life? he reminded himself grimly. That unwanted responsibilities were always waiting in the shadows to grab at him and to direct his life onto a path he had never intended...

Her big blue eyes were looking at him uncertainly and something made him dip his head to brush his lips over hers in a fleeting kiss, amused by her instinctive intake of breath and the sudden confusion of her expression, as if she hadn't been expecting him to embrace her so publicly. In truth, he hadn't been expecting it himself, but he found himself turned on by the fact she wasn't wearing any make-up and by the provocative tremble of her lips. Maybe he should take her inside and kiss her a little more thoroughly, so that she would lose that rather unflattering look of apprehension and replace it with one of passion instead.

'Let's go inside,' he said abruptly. Drawing away, he ushered her into the luxury complex, past the security guard who was regarding her with open curiosity.

'What about my suitcase?' she was saying as they reached the elevator and the doors slid open.

'What about it?'

'I've left it in the car.'

'The driver will bring it inside shortly. You don't have to worry about things like that any more, Lucy.' Rather impatiently, he pressed the button. 'You'll find my staff will deal with the more humdrum elements of your life from now on and you won't have to bother with logistics. So why don't you just concentrate on getting to know one of your new homes?'

'One of them?' she affirmed breathlessly.

The wave of his hand was careless. Sometimes he forgot that the extent of his wealth was remarkable to most people and he supposed he should be grateful that his new fiancée hadn't already tallied up all his properties with greedy anticipation. 'I have homes in New York and Athens as well as this one,' he drawled. My Greek island villa you have already seen, of course.'

'Of course,' she said.

He watched as she fixed her eyes imploringly on the bright red arrow indicating their progress towards his penthouse apartment, as if she was finding the confined space in the elevator claustrophobic. *You and me both,* he thought unwillingly, his attention drawn to the curves of her body, which her thin grey coat couldn't quite disguise. He could feel the pump of his heart and the throb at his groin and wondered whether he should rid himself of some of the frustration which had been building up inside him for days now. But thoughts of seduction were vanquished by the words which burst from her lips almost as if she hadn't planned to say them, her blue eyes suddenly darkening so that they looked as blue as a Grecian sea.

'I wasn't…' She drew in a deep breath. 'To be honest I wasn't expecting to see you until this evening. I thought you'd be working.'

Surely that wasn't disappointment he could hear in her soft English voice? A flicker of a smile touched the edges of Drakon's lips. Maybe there was more fire to Lucy Phillips than he had initially given her credit for. 'I had a rare window in my diary and I thought it might be less daunting if I was here to greet you myself,' he explained as the elevator reached the penthouse and the doors slid open.

'That's very kind of you.'

'Make the most of it. I'm not usually known for my kindness,' he informed her drily. 'Come on in.'

Obediently, she followed him into the reception room, and he thought how much she resembled a new member of staff as she stood nervously in the centre of his modern London apartment with its bird's-eye view over the park. But in a way, that was exactly what she was. As his wife, she would be fulfilling her prescribed role just as adequately as one of his chefs, or drivers, or housekeepers. And wasn't her trepidation one of the reasons he had chosen to marry her? She was both compliant and inexperienced and because of that he could mould her into the kind of spouse he wanted her to be, just as he would train up a new assistant.

'It's huge,' she commented.

'But you've been here before. When you met Xander.'

'Yes. That's right. But I only saw the nursery areas. I had no idea there was this other huge section.' She looked around, cocking her head to one side as if listening for something. 'Where *is* Xander?'

Drakon still wasn't used to having the baby around and he frowned, trying to remember. 'Sofia has taken him to the doctor for some sort of routine check. At least, I think that's what she said.'

She sucked in a deep breath. 'You didn't consider it might be better if I could have gone along as well? If I'm to be his, well, his…mother.'

Something unknown clutched at Drakon's heart like a vice. Was it anger that his brother should have treated his son with such a failure of care and cast him into the unwanted role of father? Or fear that he would be incapable of giving this child any true affection, as his own father had been unable to give him? With an effort, he pushed the bitter memories away—for what good would they serve him now?

'There will be plenty of time for you to play happy families, Lucy. First things first. Let me show you around properly and then I have a surprise for you.'

'I'm not crazy about surprises,' she warned him lightly.

'I think you'll like this one,' he promised.

Lucy thought how arrogant he sounded. Did that mean she was going to have to *pretend*? To smooth the way for their future marriage by showing him gratitude at all times? Would that be the grown-up way to proceed?

She began to follow him through the huge apartment, trying and failing to remember the precise configuration of the rooms. But she would quickly learn where everything was, she reassured herself—despite the fact that the entire ground floor of her riverside cottage would have fitted into one of the en suite bathrooms! One of the vast reception rooms led into a book-lined study, which looked more like a public library and contained leather-bound volumes in both English and Greek. There was an enormous kitchen with an adjoining dining room, three big en suite bedrooms on one side of the wide corridor, as well as the nursery suite on the other, which was completely self-contained.

'I've given you your own bedroom,' he said as his footsteps halted. 'I decided it would be more appropriate if we slept apart until the wedding. Something befitting the status of my relatively innocent fiancée.' His black eyes gleamed. 'That doesn't mean we cannot be intimate or imaginative, of course.'

'Oh?'

'I'll be right next door,' he informed her. 'It will be like a throwback to a different age. I cannot tell you how much the novelty of that appeals to me, Lucy.'

Lucy's breasts had grown heavy at his provocative words but her erotic recall was forgotten the moment he pushed open the bedroom door. Her lips fell open but she barely noticed the amazing view or huge bed, or the superb painting of a tiny fishing village which looked suspiciously like the one on his private island. All she could see were the piles of clothes which were *everywhere*, making the room look more like the changing room of an upmarket department store than a bedroom. There were sleek dresses hanging in front of the built-in cupboards and a gorgeous plum-coloured coat with a velvet collar. One of the cupboards was open and inside she could see colour-coordinated lines of beautiful silky shirts, and skirts which varied from pencil to flounce. Further along the rail were more casual clothes—cashmere sweaters which bore little resemblance to her own hand-knits and denim jeans which she was doubtful she'd be able to slide over her curvy hips. This must be the surprise he'd been talking about.

'I hope you like them,' Drakon said as she continued to stare at it all in silence.

Lucy forced herself to say something dutiful which wouldn't sound ungrateful, because there was no denying he must have gone to a lot of trouble. 'They're gorgeous. Did you—?'

'Actually, my partner chose them.'

'Your partner?' she questioned blankly and, although it was unconscious sexism on her part, she instantly imagined some strapping Greek male walking into a store waving a charge card.

'Amy,' he supplied, clearly oblivious to the sudden uncertainty in her voice. 'We've worked together for years.'

She wondered if he was aware of the emotional impact of his words, or of the exact way he'd phrased them—because didn't his relationship with his partner sound way more intimate and close than the one he had with *her*? Lucy could feel her heart punching against her chest in a way which was making her feel almost dizzy. 'I see. And does... Amy choose all your girlfriends' clothes for you?'

'Never. But then I've never been in a situation like this before. I knew your wardrobe was insufficiently versatile to be able to cope with your new role as my wife,' he said, clearly seeking diplomatic words to take the sting out of his statement. 'And I thought you'd be too busy packing to have the time to hit the shops.'

Was that so? Or just that he thought she would fail miserably at the task? That her lack of experience—and money—meant she'd be incapable of selecting her own clothes? But Lucy tried to be positive and take Drakon at his word. She had to be, or this simply wasn't going to work. And she would never have chosen any of these exquisite clothes—not in a million years. She wouldn't have dared purchase items which individually probably cost more than she earned in a month. The question was whether she'd be able to change or return any without embarrassment if they turned out not to fit.

On a nearby chest she could see a deep drawer which was partially open and, sucking in a breath, she walked over and pulled it wide open to find it filled with the most provocative lingerie imaginable. Sexy thong panties were lined up beside balcony bras. Silk stockings and lacy suspender belts lay side by side and Lucy blinked at them in disbelief, sudden ice rippling down her spine. 'Please don't tell me your partner choose *these*?'

He shook his head and laughed. 'Of course not. I bought these myself. It happens to be the most enjoyable shopping trip I've done in years, if you must know. Do you like them?'

Lucy continued to stare at them as she considered his question. On the one hand, of course she did. This was the kind of underwear she'd never imagined herself wearing, not in her wildest dreams. It was impossible not to like such exquisitely made garments, nor to imagine the amount of work which must have gone into making them, but… She turned to him, blinking her eyes rapidly. 'How on earth did you know my size?'

He shrugged. 'I guessed.'

'You guessed,' she repeated slowly. 'Because you have such a comprehensive knowledge of a woman's body that you instinctively know what size bra she wears?'

'I'm in the ship-building industry, Lucy. Learning about dimensions comes with the territory.' A smile curved the edges of his sensual mouth. 'The shoes were a little more difficult.'

'The shoes?' she questioned blankly as the expansive wave of his hand indicated rows of high-heeled shoes and butter-soft leather boots she hadn't even noticed before. She wondered what on earth he was doing as he bent down to retrieve something from underneath the bed, and was momentarily taken aback when he produced a suede moccasin and waved it in the air—like a magician plucking a rabbit from a top hat. 'That's my shoe!' she declared.

'I know.' He gave slow smile. 'I picked it up from that pile by your front door so I could get your size right, on the day I asked you to marry me. It isn't really a winter shoe, so I didn't think you'd notice it had gone.'

It took a couple of seconds before Lucy could bring herself to speak and when she did her words came spitting out like bullets. 'I *did* notice, as it happens. I don't actually own enough pairs of shoes not to realise when one goes missing.' She glared at him, still not quite believing what he'd just told her. 'So let me get this straight. You thought you'd go ahead with some modern-day enactment of Cinderella's slipper and I'm supposed to coo with delight in response?'

'I certainly had hoped for something a little more enthusiastic than your current reaction,' he offered drily.

'Well, please don't bother in future. Like I said, I'm not the biggest fan of surprises. In fact, don't bother with—'

But her sentence was destined never to be completed because Drakon had pulled her into his arms and was kissing her. Kissing her so thoroughly that all the breath left her lungs. And Lucy let him. No, that wasn't quite true. She actively encouraged him. Was it lack of oxygen which made her so instantly yielding? Which made her gasp out a note of breathless approval as his mouth roved hungrily over hers, before darting her tongue into his mouth as if it were a weapon? Or was it simply that she was so *incensed* by what he'd done—by his arrogance and control—that she felt as if she'd been taken over by a different kind of desire? So that very quickly the kiss became something it had never been on Prasinisos. This wasn't soft and searching but punishing, and hard. It was driven by frustration—that he had been so high-handed about overhauling her appearance and given someone she'd never met *carte blanche* to play such a key role in changing it. But there was physical frustration, too, gnawing away inside her like some alien creature she had no idea how to handle. She wondered if sex would release some of the tight frustration which was coiling inside her like a compressed spring. Whether now was the time to tell him she didn't want his *partner* buying her clothes for her. That she wasn't just some kind of doll who could be dressed up for his approval before she was permitted to be seen in public.

'I don't know why we're fighting about clothes, Lucy,' he said unevenly as they broke away to drag oxygen into their air-starved lungs. 'Since my expressed preference is to see you not wearing anything at all.'

And wasn't it pathetic how thrilled she was to hear that husky compliment? As if she was only just beginning to realise that, despite her somewhat homely appearance and complete lack of fashion sense, Drakon

Konstantinou really *did* fancy her. But that was one of the reasons she was here, Lucy reminded herself. Her midwifery training wouldn't mean a thing without the white-hot chemistry which seemed to combust whenever they touched.

She felt blindsided by the sense of something which, having been awoken, now needed urgently to be fed. Was that why she let him kiss her again and to deepen it with provocative intimacy, so that she moaned softly into his mouth? And something about that moan made him lever her up against the wall, his face dark and inscrutable as he looked down at her. She could sense the tension which was making his powerful body seem as tight as a strung bow and, where they were touching, her skin felt as if it were on fire.

His fingers were unbuttoning her grey coat and unashamedly roving beneath her sweater and when he jutted his hips forward like that, she could feel the hard column of his erection pressing against her. Beneath her thick denim jeans the molten slick of desire made itself known and Lucy longed for him to touch her there. His fingers were whispering over the cool skin of her torso, moving down towards the top button of her jeans, and she shivered as he popped it open then slid her zip down with a dexterity which suggested he must have undressed millions of women before.

But suddenly Lucy saw herself as an outside observer might see her—all windswept and rumpled with the Greek tycoon's fingers burrowing their way inexorably towards her panties. Why, she hadn't even taken her coat off! She'd only been in his apartment for ten minutes and all they'd done was to fight and kiss and now he was about to take it one step further. If she didn't put a halt to this then before she knew it, she would be pressed up against that wall with Drakon thrusting deep inside her.

She pressed her hand against his chest, feeling the powerful pound of his heart beneath her palm. 'We need to stop this right now.'

'Oh, Lucy. That's not the message I was getting a moment ago,' he drawled.

Well, it's the m-message you're getting now,' she said, unable to iron the tremble from her voice. 'I need to freshen up before Sofia comes back with the baby and to…'

'To what?' he questioned mockingly as her words tailed off.

Lips pressed together, she gave him a determined smile. 'To unpack my case and settle in. And to be honest, Drakon…' She hesitated. 'I think you're right about having separate rooms, but let's do it properly, shall we—with no sneaking around the corridors at midnight? Maybe we *should* wait until we're married until we have…"

'Sex?' he supplied, his eyebrows arching in disbelief. 'Is that what you're trying to say?'

She could feel hot colour flooding her cheeks and, although she realised she could be accused of having double standards, wasn't it better this way? Because what if her earlier doubts came true and she drove him crazy—wouldn't it be easier to draw a line under the whole thing if they *hadn't* become lovers? Easier to walk away if she hadn't had a second distracting taste of physical intimacy? And it would do Drakon good to demonstrate that he wasn't the one making all the rules, and she wasn't going to be totally submissive. To show him that she might have agreed to this marriage of convenience but that didn't make her into some sort of *puppet*.

'That's exactly what I'm trying to say,' she agreed primly.

Still he waited, as if she was going to suddenly turn around and tell him she was joking—as if no woman in her right mind would refuse the opportunity to fall into bed with him at the earliest opportunity.

And Lucy wouldn't have been human if she hadn't enjoyed the brief look of disbelief which flashed from Drakon's ebony eyes when he realised she meant every word she said.

CHAPTER FOUR

LUCY AWOKE TO the sound of a baby's cry and instinct made her sit bolt upright in bed, her heart clenching with painful recognition. Hunger, she thought, as she listened some more. Funny how you could still recognise the different nuances of an infant's cry even though it had been so long since that sound had been part of her daily routine.

Heavy-eyed after a restless night, she got out of bed and it took a few seconds for her befuddled brain to realise she wasn't tucked up in her cosy riverside cottage, but in the fanciest bedroom she'd ever seen. Her new home. The vast Mayfair apartment where she would live as wife to one of the world's most powerful men. Above her head, a chandelier glittered like a shoal of falling diamonds and silk rugs lay strewn over a pale wooden floor, which felt deliciously silky against her bare feet. Grabbing her dressing gown, she knotted it tightly around her waist. It was actually her old dressing gown which she'd brought with her from home because it seemed that her luxury replacement wardrobe didn't cater for a sensible garment you could throw on first thing in the morning to cover up your pyjamas and feed a baby in. *Presumably because once she was married she would no longer be wearing pyjamas.* Running her fingers through her hair to tame its tousled wildness, she set off towards the nursery.

The crying had stopped by the time Lucy got there and she was greeted by a scene of perfect domesticity. Sofia was sitting on a yellow sofa giving Xander a bottle while soft nursery rhymes played gently in the background. It felt a little strange for Lucy to be standing in her nightclothes in front of someone she'd only met a couple of times but the middle-aged nanny merely looked up and gave her a friendly smile as she entered the room.

'Good morning, Lucy,' she said. 'Did you sleep well?'

'Very well, thank you,' said Lucy with more politeness than truth—because nothing was more boring than hearing someone relate the story of what a bad night they'd had. She certainly didn't want Sofia quizzing her about the reasons for her restlessness. *Reason,* she corrected herself silently. One reason alone—all six feet three of him. 'You should have woken me.'

Sofia shook her head. 'Drakon said you were to be left undisturbed.'

Drakon. Lucy started at the mention of his name and she thought—how pathetic is *that*? Had her heart missed a beat because she'd resisted his sexual overtures when she'd arrived yesterday and been haunted by tantalising dreams about him ever since? Or because it was still difficult to believe that the gorgeous billionaire would soon be her husband and that this was now her reality? A reality brought home by the stilted dinner they'd shared last evening, presided over by his stern-faced housekeeper, Zena—a meal which had kept being interrupted while Drakon had dealt with one international phone call after another. He'd been talking to someone in New York when eventually Lucy had excused herself and his absent wave of farewell as she'd headed off to her bedroom had spoken volumes. He hadn't followed her and she hadn't really expected him to, because instinct told her that a man like Drakon would never beg a woman for intimacy when she had told him it wasn't going to happen. She'd lain there listening until eventually she'd heard him heading for bed, freezing with hope and expectation as his footsteps had paused outside her door, before moving on. As an introduction to life in the fast lane, it hadn't exactly felt welcoming. Or maybe he had just been making a point…

She stood in the doorway watching as Sofia fed the baby and suddenly felt almost redundant. With a touch of anxiety she licked her lips and looked around, but the room was pristinely tidy. 'Is there anything I can do? Some dusting, or tidying up?'

'No, honestly, I'm fine. It's all under control. Drakon employs an army of people to do the housework for him. He's going down for a nap shortly but you could do the midday feed if you like. But only if you have time before you go out for lunch,' Sofia amended hastily.

Lucy maintained her bright smile even though she was aware that her voice sounded brittle. 'I wasn't aware that I *was* going out for lunch.'

Sofia's eyes crinkled in a smile. 'Apparently. Zena

told me. The car has been ordered for you. Lucky you,' she added, in her perfect but heavily accented English. 'It will inevitably be somewhere grand.'

Lucy hoped her expression didn't give away her feelings as she returned to her bedroom and tugged off her dressing gown. Whether or not the restaurant was grand was completely beside the point. It was one thing to agree to a marriage of convenience, she thought furiously as she stood beneath the fierce blast of the shower. But quite another when she was being treated a convenience. Did Drakon think he could just move her around like a vacuum cleaner? How come the housekeeper and the nanny knew she was going out for lunch, when it was a mystery to her?

She dried her hair and, for the first time, tried on some of the new clothes which had been chosen by his business partner, Amy. Last night at dinner she'd stubbornly insisted on wearing one of her own dresses, still needled by the fact that Drakon had asked someone else to kit her out for her new role in his life. Yet hadn't her defiance backfired on her, so that she'd been left having to endure the entire meal feeling somewhat *less than*? Her navy shirt-dress dress was her go-to favourite but there was no doubt that the fabric looked cheap against all the unrestrained luxury of Drakon's home and Lucy was certain his housekeeper had been looking down her nose at her, as if wondering why someone like her was associating with the impeccably clad tycoon. Hadn't the same question crossed her own mind more than once as the evening had progressed?

So just go with the flow, she told herself as she rifled through the colour-coordinated rows of garments before pulling out a long-sleeved dress in silk chiffon. The soft violet hue was the colour which sometimes tinged a late sunset and, admittedly, a shade she would never have thought of choosing for herself. The delicate fabric floated to just above the knee and made her waist look positively *tiny*, and she teamed it with a pair of shoes higher than anything she'd ever worn before. Did the added height make her assume a rather awkward gait? Was that why the middle-aged housekeeper did a double-take as Lucy cautiously picked her way into the dining room for breakfast?

'Good morning, Dhespinis Phillips,' said Zena.

'Good morning, Zena.' Lucy sat down at the table and gave the housekeeper a nervous smile. 'Um…is Drakon…?'

'The master went to the office at seven this morning, but he left you a note,' said Zena, indicating an envelope which was propped up in front of a vase of flame-coloured roses. 'I will bring you some breakfast.'

'Thank you.'

Lucy thought about the housekeeper's words as she picked up the envelope. The master. It was an oddly archaic term of address yet it seemed scarily suitable. Because Drakon *was* the master, wasn't he? The master of all he surveyed. At least that was the impression he gave, with his cabal of loyal staff, his enormous wealth and his different homes dotted around the world. Was he expecting to become *her* master once they were wed— was she to obey him in all things, as the marriage ceremony used to demand but which most modern couples now rejected? And shouldn't this be something they discussed before she allowed him to slide that gold ring on her finger?

Slitting open the envelope, she pulled out a single sheet of paper, realising that this was the first time she'd ever seen Drakon's writing. It was exactly as she would have imagined it to be. Angular black lines slashed over the thick writing paper. Succinct, forceful and strong. A reluctant smile curved the edges of her lips. Just like him.

My car will pick you up at 12.25. We'll eat lunch at the Granchester for reasons which will quickly become evident.

Mysterious as well as autocratic, she thought as she drank some inky Greek coffee and picked at a bowl of iced mango, before getting up to leave.

She spent the next hour exploring the sprawling apartment and studying some of the books she found in the library, before going to the nursery to give the baby his feed. But at least her interaction with Xander cheered her, and as he glugged greedily on the teat she buried her nose in his silky hair, remembering how much she loved tiny babies and how much she'd missed them. And this baby would soon be her *son*. The child she had always longed for and never thought she'd have.

But she couldn't stem the dark doubts which began to crowd into her mind as she winded the infant and laid him in his crib. He was so cute, with his black eyes and matching hair—a miniature version of his father's identical twin brother. What if she fell hopelessly in love with this little infant and her marriage failed, as so many marriages did, despite Drakon's determination for that not to happen? Because he couldn't control everything, could he, no matter how much he tried?

He'd told her he didn't believe in love and that he'd never been in love—but who was to say that the thunderbolt wouldn't one day hit him, as it had hit so many cynical disbelievers in the past? In that scenario, wouldn't she become an also-ran in Xander's life? The woman with no blood ties with no real claim on the child who could be dispensed of as carelessly as you would yesterday's newspapers. Lucy sighed, knowing she mustn't think like that because nobody was ever given any guarantees in this life—you just had to do the best you could in the circumstances.

She was nervous as she snuggled herself into the cashmere coat with the velvet collar and slid into the back of the waiting limousine, and even more nervous when the car drew up outside the landmark Granchester Hotel after a ridiculously short journey from the apartment. Outside the impressive building, she could see an enormous Christmas tree, topped with a huge golden star and smaller gold and silver stars which dangled from the abundant branches. The doorman hurried forward to open the door for her and Lucy gingerly made her way into the gilded foyer in her new shoes, her heart missing a beat when she spotted Drakon, with his back to her, standing beside another decorated fir tree—almost as big as the one at the front of the hotel.

Dark, broad-shouldered and powerful, he seemed oblivious to the stares he was attracting from the other guests and she wondered whether something must have alerted him to her approach. Why else did he suddenly turn around? He was mid-conversation on his phone but his eyes narrowed and his words seemed to die away as she approached and, abruptly, he cut the call. Something about the way he was looking at her was making her feel breathless and excited and scared all at the same time and Lucy found herself resenting his effortless power over her.

'Lucy,' he murmured as he helped her slide the coat from her shoulders. 'You're here.'

'Yes, I'm here. Though I could have walked in less time than it took to drive!'

'I don't think so. Not in those shoes,' he commented wryly, his gaze travelling down to her feet and lingering on them for longer than was strictly necessary.

'You don't like them?' she asked, berating herself for needing reassurance but asking for it all the same.

Drakon heard the genuine doubt in her voice and, unusually, he was surprised—searching her face for signs of disingenuousness and finding none. Was she out of her mind? Didn't she realise that every man in the place was staring at her as if she'd just tumbled down from the heavens? Of course, she didn't. Because she was totally without guile, he realised. An innocent who stood out from the women he usually mixed with. But she looked *incredible*. Having slipped the coat from her shoulders, he saw the filmy dress, which hinted at the firm flesh which lay beneath, and in those spike-heeled shoes... He swallowed. Didn't her calves look ripe for stroking and her ankles made for wrapping around a man's neck?

'I like them very much,' he said unevenly. 'In fact,

there's a term which is commonly used to describe shoes like those but I don't think that now is the right time to introduce it into the conversation.'

Predictably, she blushed and Drakon felt a powerful beat of lust, which made him wonder why he'd arranged to meet her here, in one of the most public venues in the city, rather than exploiting the intimacy of his nearby apartment. *You know why,* he thought grimly. Because she had firmly stated that they weren't going to have sex until they were married and he was in no doubt that she meant it. Just as he was aware that he was in part responsible for her old-fashioned stance.

He frowned. He'd thought he'd tantalise her by offering her a separate room, thinking that *interludes* of pleasure would keep her on her toes. More than that, he liked his own space and was used to it because he'd never shared a bedroom full-time with a woman before. He'd thought he would use the opportunity for some extended personal space before things changed once they were married.

Yet Lucy had neatly turned the tables on him by telling him she thought they should wait until after the wedding before being intimate again. He sighed with frustration and anticipation—tinged with a grudging sense of admiration, because he couldn't think of another woman who would have refused to have sex with him.

And if that was the way she wanted to play it, why not go along with it? He had chosen her because of her pliability but the fact that she was now showing some token resistance made this arranged marriage of theirs seem a little less predictable. In a way, it amused him to let Lucy Phillips think she was calling the shots, because he could have broken her self-imposed sexual embargo any time he wanted. He knew that and he suspected she knew it, too.

The pupils of her eyes were huge and dark and he could sense the sudden tension in her body as she met his gaze, as if silently acknowledging the inexplicable chemistry which was sparking between them. He'd never seen her looking so sleek and so sexy. He'd never imagined she would scrub up this well. The tremble of her lips kick-started something indefinable inside him and a lump rose in his throat. Drakon swallowed, certain that if he reached out to whisper his fingertips over the pulse which fluttered so wildly at the base of her neck, or snaked his hand around her impossibly slender waist, she would do the predictable thing, and melt against him with a hunger which matched his.

But leaving aside the fact they were in a public space, it would be wrong to act on hormonal impulse. He would use restraint because this was too important a deal to jeopardise with sexual impatience. And if he was being honest, wasn't it turning him on to an unbearable pitch at the thought of being made to wait—he who'd never had to wait for a woman in his life? True, she might be playing games with him—possibly in an attempt to make him fall in love with her—but that certainly wasn't going to give him any sleepless nights. She would soon discover he was immune to the ruses women employed and was not in the market for 'love'. All he cared about was that Lucy Phillips was going to make the perfect mother to his adopted son and the exquisite sharpening of his sexual appetite in the meantime was simply a bonus.

Touching his fingers to her back, he guided her towards the Garden Room restaurant. 'Come on. Let's go and have lunch.'

They walked along a long corridor, where golden baubles and scarlet ribbons were woven into the seasonal greenery which festooned the walls, and he watched as she looked around and drank it all in.

'What an amazing hotel,' she exclaimed. 'It's enormous!'

'You've never been here before?'

'Funny you should say that, but no,' she answered, dead-pan. 'Five-star hotels aren't my usual stomping ground on one of my rare visits to the capital. I've seen photos of it, obviously.'

'I thought we could get married here,' he offered casually.

'Here?' she said, coming to an abrupt halt just before they reached the restaurant entrance and nearly losing her balance on the spike-heeled shoes.

'You really don't like surprises, do you?' He put out an arm to steady her. 'Why shouldn't we? It's a very famous wedding venue.'

'I know it is! Don't film stars and princes choose it for their nuptials?'

'I don't keep tabs on celebrity weddings unless I happen to be a guest at them,' he drawled. 'But Zac Constantinides, the owner, is a friend of mine, so he's given us a date when it was supposed to be shut. As a favour, you understand.'

'Of course,' she said faintly.

'It's a perfect solution, especially this close to Christmas. So what do you say, Lucy? Apparently, there's an in-house wedding planner who'll do most of the donkey work for you.'

Lucy registered his puzzled expression as she hesitated. Was he expecting her to gush her thanks, or swoon about the sumptuousness of the venue, instead of standing there chewing her lip in a state of nervous anxiety? But she was having difficulty getting her head round the idea of someone like her standing up in a place this grand and making her wedding vows.

But what was the alternative? Surely she could overcome her nerves enough to get married in one of the world's most glamorous venues—especially if she was marrying such a high-profile man. And wouldn't the wedding co-ordinator take away some of the stress?

'You had something else in mind?' he prompted, when still she said nothing.

Lucy shook her head. 'You don't mind the fact that it will be a very *public* wedding?'

'You think I want to hide the fact away? I'm Greek, Lucy,' he said simply. 'And we Greeks like a good party.'

'Okay,' she said, speaking as quietly as possible in order to eliminate any telltale tremble of nerves. 'In that case—why not?'

'Not the most rapturous reaction I might have hoped for,' he observed drily. 'But I suppose it will have to do. Come on. Let's eat.'

The maître d' greeted him with easy familiarity as he showed them to a table which offered a perfect view of the winter garden, with its icy fountain and dark red branches of dogwood.

'Are we celebrating anything in particular today, Mr Konstantinou?'

'We certainly are. Ask the sommelier to bring my fiancée a glass of Dom Perignon rosé, would you, please, Carlos?'

There was a split-second pause and, when he spoke, Carlos's voice sounded faintly strangulated. 'Certainly, sir. And for yourself?'

'Just water, thanks.'

Lucy waited until they were alone before she spoke. 'That man looked as if he'd just been hit by a sledgehammer when you described me as your fiancée.'

'He was probably surprised, *neh*. I have a reputation which precedes me.'

'What kind of reputation?'

He gave a wolfish smile. 'As a man who has never wanted to settle down. A man who was fundamentally opposed to marriage. Maybe I was unconsciously drawing a line in the sand, to demonstrate that, from now on, things are going to be very different.'

Were they? Lucy wondered distractedly. But how different? A glass of champagne was placed in front of her but she stared uninterestedly at the fizzing pink bubbles before lifting her eyes to Drakon. 'I suppose you've brought loads of women to this hotel in the past? Probably to have lunch in this very restaurant before taking them to bed?'

His black gaze was very steady. 'I'm not going to lie to you, Lucy. I was never promiscuous or indiscriminate but I'm thirty-one, single and, yes, of course I've slept with women during that time. Why wouldn't I? The evidence is everywhere if you care to look for it—because you can find out pretty much anything online.' He leaned forward, across the starched linen of the tablecloth. 'But I'm hoping you won't bother because I'm being perfectly transparent with you. I see no point in pretending to you, or rewriting history. You may have been a virgin when we hooked up, but I most certainly was not.'

'So why announce our engagement to someone you don't really know? Was that really necessary?'

'I think so. Carlos is perfectly aware how these things work.' He gave a flicker of a smile. 'He'll mention it to someone, who'll mention it to someone else. The press will get to hear about it and there will be a diary piece—only by then it will be old news.' There was a brief pause. 'Like I said, it draws a line in the sand and discourages any hopeful overtures from ex-lovers.'

His statement was more matter-of-fact than arrogant and Lucy told herself it shouldn't have bothered her, but it did, and she was taken aback by the hot flash of jealousy which pulsed through her. But of *course* he would have plenty of exes eager to return into his life. Hadn't she been pretty keen to see him herself when she'd returned from Prasinisos, forever glancing at her mobile phone and wondering if he would ring? Which, of course, he hadn't.

And that was what she needed to remember. The one fact which should never be far from her mind. That she would never have seen Drakon Konstantinou again if his brother and sister-in-law hadn't decided to go on a narcotic-fuelled bender and leave their baby son with no parents.

'Did Xander have any other relatives?' she asked suddenly. 'Apart from his mother?'

He shook his head. 'I put an investigator on the case. Niko's wife was adopted as a baby, but had been estranged from her family for many years. There were no living blood relatives, so Xander will have no connection with the past.' His expression grew shuttered. 'And it will be better for him in the long run. Much better.'

'In your opinion.'

'It's my opinion which counts,' he said cuttingly. 'And what I say goes. And I'd rather my adoptive son wasn't in the grip of people I don't know. People who might influence him to follow the same sorry path as his parents.'

Feeling faint, Lucy gripped the stem of her champagne flute, but she didn't lift it to her lips. She was afraid that her hands would tremble too much and she would spill it all over the perfectly starched tablecloth. Because it wasn't just the things Drakon had said which freaked her out, but the way he'd said them. He'd sounded so…*ruthless*. As if you could take the parts of somebody's life which you didn't like and simply wipe them out—like airbrushing a photo or altering something on your camera phone. But if he'd sounded ruthless it was because he *was*, she reminded herself. She should forget that at her peril. Suddenly she was glad that she was going to be there for baby Xander. Glad she would be able to fight his corner, because surely he needed someone there for him when Drakon started being even more high-handed than usual.

Eventually she felt calm enough to take a sip of wine, which eased some of her tension, and beneath the table she stretched out her legs, her new pointy shoes touching what she thought was the leg of the table, but Drakon's mocking eyes informed her that she'd made direct contact with his calf. Hastily, she jerked her foot away and his gaze grew more thoughtful.

'So why don't you like surprises?' he asked suddenly.

It was a question she hadn't been expecting, and if she hadn't been so blindsided by everything which had happened in the last twenty-four hours Lucy might have glossed over it—because why revisit pain when you didn't have to? But Drakon seemed to have an uncanny knack of getting her to open up. He'd done it on the night of the school reunion and he was doing it again now. She wondered if it was because he'd known her so long ago, in those days when she'd had a mother and a brother and hadn't been such a lost soul. And surely if they were planning on spending the rest of their lives together, he needed to know some of the things which made her tick. Only some of them, mind. A twist of guilt seared her heart and she stared down at her fingernails before looking up to meet the searching gleam of his eyes. 'I guess I just associate surprises with unpleasant things.'

'What kind of things?'

'Oh, you know.' She shrugged her shoulders restlessly. 'All the stuff which comes with having family in the military. The heavy knock at the door, or the ring of the telephone late at night. The men in uniform who stand on your doorstep with grim faces as they prepare to give you the news.' News which rocked the foundations of your world and made you realise nothing was ever going to be the same again. Yet hadn't it been those experiences that had provided the lessons which had enabled Lucy to ring-fence her emotions and keep herself safe from pain? Which had forced her to build barriers around her heart so she could never be hurt like that again? She folded her lips together. Wasn't that one of the *good* things about agreeing to marry a man like Drakon—that he had spelt out he didn't do love either? He had his own emotional barriers in place and that made them equal in a totally unexpected way. He could never hurt her because she would never let him get that close.

And the bottom line was that he didn't want to get close.

'That must have been tough,' he observed.

'Life is tough, Drakon—as I'm sure Xander would tell us if he were able to speak.'

He nodded, his eyes still searching her face, as if he was seeing something he hadn't noticed before. 'I don't want any more children,' he said suddenly.

'I'm sorry?'

'More kids.' His voice was rough. 'One is my limit and if you want more—'

'I don't,' she said quickly, as relief washed over her. 'I think children should only ever be conceived in love and we've both agreed that isn't what is driving this marriage of ours.'

His nodded slowly, his eyes narrowing. 'There's something else we haven't addressed,' he said softly.

Her brow creased. 'Which is?'

'The ring.'

'The ring?' she repeated.

'An engagement ring. It's fairly traditional in most cultures, as far as I'm aware. Surely you must have been expecting one, Lucy? I thought all women had preferences about what kind of jewels they'd like in this situation.'

'No, Drakon, all women do not—at least, not those of us who live relatively normal lives. I have better things to do with my time than drool about diamonds.' Recklessly, she took another mouthful of champagne— a much bigger one this time—which really went to her head. *Serves you right,* she thought dazedly as she carefully replaced the glass on the table. 'I'm astonished you didn't ask your partner, Amy, to select one for me as she did my clothes,' she said, in an acid tone she'd never heard herself use before. 'Or maybe she already has?'

He shook his head. 'The answer is no on both counts. She couldn't have done even if I wanted her to because she's flown out to Singapore on business.'

'Gosh. How will you be able to manage without her?' she questioned, the lingering effects of the wine still evident in her unusually flippant tone.

'Amy's absence certainly makes me realise how hard she works.' Almost carelessly, he slid a small box across the table. 'I bought this for you myself, so if you don't like it you're at liberty to change it.' As Lucy continued to stare at it, he lowered his voice into a murmured command. 'Stop looking at it as though it were an unexploded bomb. Open it.'

With faltering fingers she did just that, and it was a

measure of just how glitzy the world in which she now found herself that Lucy realised she was expecting to see a whacking great diamond, or an emerald the size of a gull's egg. Because wasn't that what billionaires usually bought for their future brides, especially if it was an arranged marriage? Some huge chunk of glittering gemstone which would be way too big for her finger and look like paste on someone so unremittingly ordinary.

But as she flipped open the box to reveal a ring, it was to discover that Drakon had surprised her and in a way she almost wished he hadn't, because it made her feel quite breathless. Set in embellished gold was a square-cut sapphire the indefinable colour of a spot of ink dropped into a beaker of water, which glittered in the pale winter light that streamed in through the windows. It was delicate, unusual and beautiful. The most beautiful ring she had ever seen.

'What made you choose this?' she questioned shakily.

He shrugged. 'The jeweller asked me what colour your eyes were.'

Lucy's heart raced and a strange, restrictive dryness in her throat made it difficult for her to speak as for one split second she allowed herself to sink into a fantasy of longing. 'And you remembered?'

'It's hardly neuroscience, Lucy. I only saw you a couple of days ago.' His slightly impatient look was followed by a dismissive shake of his head as he picked up his menu. 'Come on. Let's order. I have a meeting this afternoon.'

CHAPTER FIVE

STANDING IN ALL her wedding finery and trying not
to let her nerves get the better of her, Lucy waited in
the anteroom of the grand ballroom where her marriage to Drakon was about to take place. Tightly, she
gripped her bouquet, which contrasted so vividly with
the snowy whiteness of her dress. Scarlet roses flared
like beacons amid the lush greenery and a sprig of
mistletoe had been playfully added at the last minute
by the Granchester's in-house florist, as a nod towards
the fact that it was almost Christmas.

Donna, the wedding planner, had arranged for carols to be piped through the hotel's sophisticated sound
system because 'everyone loves Christmas carols'. But
if the seasonal songs were supposed to be soothing
or comforting then they had failed in their mission
because Lucy's brow was clammy and her heart was
racing beneath the heavily embellished dress which
she'd been persuaded into against her better judgment.
She'd wanted something simple. Something plain, in
ivory—an outfit she didn't have to think about, rather
than something which would wear *her*. But the dress
designer had explained that a room as grand as the

Granchester ballroom needed a gown to stand out among all the lavish fixtures and fittings. Something which would fill the makeshift aisle rather than getting completely lost in it. Which was why she was wearing jewel-encrusted white silk satin, with an oversized veil cascading down her back, looking as if a tipper truck had just offloaded a ton of sequin-sprinkled meringue.

Her throat felt like dust and her lips were dry and she kept thinking, *Surely this isn't how a bride is supposed to feel?* Lost and displaced and alone. Wondering what she'd let herself in for and whether she'd been a fool to accept the Greek magnate's offer of marriage. But how did she *expect* to feel, when the hectic preparations for the imminent ceremony seemed to have done nothing but emphasise the huge differences between her and her billionaire bridegroom? Especially since, after citing a busy work schedule, Drakon had absented himself from all the arrangements—except for providing a list of guests he wished to be invited, which hugely outnumbered her own.

'So it's definitely just *five* guests on your side?' The wedding planner had clearly been puzzled as she'd looked at Lucy expectantly, as if waiting to be told there'd been an elemental mix-up in the numbers and she'd missed off a nought.

Lucy's smile had stayed firmly in place. 'That's right.'

'Okay… Well, if you're *quite* sure…'

She supposed it wasn't conventional for the bride to be so sparsely represented but Lucy had been strong in her determination only to have people there who meant something to her. Wasn't this wedding fake enough already without her shipping in a load of guests just for show? Her parents and brother were dead and her only other living relative was Auntie Alice, who lived in Australia and had been unable to make the wedding this close to the holidays. And it wasn't as if she and Drakon had already formed lots of friends between them as a couple, was it? They'd barely spent more than a couple of hours together at a time during the frantic run-up to the big day.

And whose fault was that?

Hers and hers alone. Her determination to keep their sleeping arrangements separate until after the ceremony had given Drakon free rein to throw himself into his work and he had been out at the office from dawn to dusk. Why, he hadn't even asked her a single question about what they'd be eating at the wedding breakfast!

Caroline, her boss from Caro's Canapés, was going to be in attendance—as well as two of the other waitresses, Judii and Jade. A heavily pregnant Patti, her best friend from midwifery days, was also going to be there—along with Tom, her new husband. And they all loved her, Lucy reminded herself fiercely. They would be rooting for her even if her sudden decision to marry a man they'd never heard her mention had perplexed them. She didn't even have anyone to give her away, but had been loath to go searching for someone suitable. Tom had kindly offered to step in but Lucy barely knew her best friend's husband. Which was why she would be walking towards Drakon completely on her own.

Donna stuck her head round the door and gave her a thumbs up. 'Ready?'

Lucy touched her fingers to the pale glittery veil which rippled down her back, and nodded. She just needed to remember the special Greek traditions she'd been taught and which were to be incorporated into the day. They would eat sugared almonds at some point and people would attempt to pin money to her dress. After their wedding rings had been blessed, they would be placed on their fingers three times—to symbolise the unity of their entwined lives.

And during all this she would try her best not to feel like a hypocrite.

'I'm ready,' she whispered.

The double doors were opened with a flourish and all Lucy could see was the long walk which lay ahead, decked on either side by chairs festooned with yet more greenery and slivers of golden ribbon. Everyone turned to look at her and she clutched her bouquet even tighter, aware that even in here Donna had gone over the top with the Christmas theme, but she hadn't wanted to come over as some sort of Grinch by telling her not to bother. Yet somehow the gloriousness of the occasion was starting to feel overwhelmingly poignant. Tall candles of scarlet flickered patterns of transparent gold onto the gilded walls and silver stars dangled on spangled strings which hung from the vaulted ceiling. The sound of a carol being sung by a single boy's voice in Greek was making Lucy want to blink her eyes against the unwanted threat of tears and she hoped she didn't need to blow her nose during the service because she didn't have a handkerchief.

And there was Xander, fast asleep in the arms of his nanny, Sofia. Darling little Xander, whom she'd fed and played with that morning before she'd left for the hotel, wondering if Drakon ever intended to be anything other than a father in name. Because the man who was supremely confident in all things seemed wary of the innocent child he had adopted. She could count on the fingers of one hand the times she'd seen him hold the baby and she'd found herself wondering if she should try to bridge the distance he seemed to have constructed between himself and Xander. Was it her place to even try?

She began to walk with small steps—partly because she was terrified of toppling over in her spiky heels, but also in an attempt to quell her spiralling nerves as she saw her Greek bridegroom standing beneath an arch of Christmas roses.

As the music heralded her arrival, he didn't turn to look at her and although Lucy told herself it was easier not to have to face the enigmatic glitter of his eyes, it was also daunting to be confronted by his imposing back view. She gazed at his powerful body, clad in a dark suit which accentuated his broad shoulders and muscular limbs. A body which very soon…

No. She wasn't going to fret about her wedding night or give into the nebulous fears which had been bugging her. She wasn't going to start worrying that their time on Prasinisos had been an aberration—a peculiar one-off, fuelled by sunshine and novelty.

Because what if she disappointed her new husband on the first night of their honeymoon? What if the reality of an arranged marriage had somehow extin-

guished the passion they'd shared before? Wasn't that
another reason why she had been secretly relieved to
maintain separate rooms until the wedding—because
she'd been afraid of being put to the test, and failing?

At long last she reached the fragrant green arch and
Drakon turned around and stared down at her. He took
her trembling hand in his and suddenly this became
about much more than whether this was the craziest
thing she had ever done. Suddenly Lucy felt breathless
with longing as Drakon's strength seemed to radiate
from his powerful frame, his black eyes crinkling in a
way which reminded her how long she'd known him.
Surely that counted for something. Surely they could
make this work if they worked at it.

'Okay?' he mouthed.

She gave a quick nod. 'I think so.'

'You look beautiful.'

'Th-thank you.'

Her voice sounded tremulous, Drakon thought as
the celebrant began to intone the words. And her face
was as white as her dress. He stole another glance at
her, aware that his compliment had been dutiful rather
than genuine because this dazzling creature didn't look
a bit like Lucy. The huge dress swamped her and the
sequin-spattered veil did not seem to sit well with the
simple country image she'd always projected. And her
fingers were cold. As cold as the gold band which, moments later, he slid onto her finger. He looked down
at a similar band which now gleamed unfamiliarly
against his own olive skin. He'd never worn a ring before and it felt heavy and alien.

'I now pronounce you man and wife.'

The finality of the words shattered his thoughts like a spray gun and Lucy's blue eyes were blank as she looked up at him, almost as if the whole ceremony had happened without her realising it. *You and me both, agape mou*, he thought with a black-humoured sense of identity.

'You may now kiss the bride.'

Drakon slid his arms around her waist and bent towards her, aware that the kiss was mainly for the benefit of the watching congregation. He hadn't kissed her since that afternoon when she'd arrived at his apartment and, as a consequence, his desire for her had reached a level of intensity he'd never experienced before. For days it had been heating his blood and gnawing at his senses with a remorselessness which had left him barely able to think straight. It had tortured him. Tormented him. But hadn't he almost *enjoyed* the boundaries she'd primly put in place, which had heightened his exquisite anticipation of tonight's consummation? Strange to think that this most unlikely candidate was the first woman who had ever denied him anything. Which was why he didn't make this a real kiss. He didn't dare. He was afraid that once he'd started he wouldn't be able to stop. That he would pin her down to the ground and rip that monstrous dress from her body—contemptuously tossing aside the tattered satin to touch the soft flesh beneath. He gave a brief nod as he brushed his lips over hers, in nothing more than a swift acknowledgement that the deal was done and dusted.

But he was aware of the disappointment which flashed through her eyes as he pulled away from her.

And something else, too. Something which looked almost like *fear*, as the applause of the assembled guests echoed up into the gilded arches and they walked into an adjoining room to sign the register. Was it the sudden inexplicable need to quell that fear which made him whisper his fingertips against her waist, so that she relaxed a little?

'All done,' he said.

She nodded. 'I guess so.'

'So how does it feel to be Mrs Konstantinou? Kyria Konstantinou,' he amended as they made their way towards the desk, where the registrar was waiting.

'Slightly weird,' she admitted. 'Probably about as weird as it feels for you to have taken a wife, but no doubt we'll get used to it.'

Her brisk words were reassuring. Drakon had wondered if she would expect him to recite affectionate words he didn't really mean—saccharine statements which would leave him with a bad taste in his mouth. But if she was prepared to treat this marriage as nothing more than a business merger with benefits—what could possibly go wrong?

'I suggest the best way of getting used to it is by having as early a night as possible,' he said smoothly, scrawling his signature on the wedding licence and strangely pleased by the blush which flared in her cheeks. 'Since tomorrow I'm taking you on honeymoon.'

She blinked at him—unaccustomed mascara making her eyes look huge and smoky. 'We're having a honeymoon?'

'Isn't that traditional?' he murmured as his finger

trailed over her pearl-encrusted sleeve. 'As traditional as your white gown and veil? You'll enjoy it, Lucy. I thought we'd fly to my island for the Christmas Eve celebrations.'

'You mean Prasinisos?

He smiled. 'At the last count, Prasinisos was the only island I owned.'

She pushed the waterfall of white veil back over her shoulder. 'I never really thought about going to Greece at Christmas time.'

'You thought my homeland neglected the winter holiday entirely?' he challenged mockingly. 'Or that it only comes to life when you can dip your sun-baked body into the wine-dark sea?' He gave a soft laugh. 'Then you must be prepared to have your mind changed.'

'And what about Xander?' she asked tentatively. 'What's going to happen to our…son?'

Drakon frowned. His son. It was a word he had so far avoided using because it had been strange to think of himself as a parent. It still was. Every time he looked at the helpless infant, he could feel a cold fear clench at his heart, which made him turn away. But while nobody could accuse him of being falsely demonstrative, surely she didn't think him uncaring enough to drag the infant halfway across the world and back for a couple of days? He narrowed his eyes. 'The child's presence is unnecessary,' he said. 'And the journey will be too much.'

'But it's Christmas!'

'And you think a baby of less than three months will miss out on opening his presents?' he demanded.

'Please don't put words in my mouth, Drakon!'

'Then stop being so emotional. We will be gone for just three nights and then we will be back home in Mayfair.'

'It just feels… I don't know… It feels weird to leave him behind.'

'You'll get used to it. That's why we employ a loyal and caring nanny. Now, wipe that frown from your face and let's go and greet our guests. My godfather has travelled here from Honolulu and I really want you to meet him.'

With a heart which felt suddenly heavy, Lucy followed Drakon back into the ballroom to the sound of loud clapping and people crying, *'Opa!'*

Smiling at the guests, she tried to shake off her worries about guilt she'd felt when the celebrant had talked about them extending their family and her gaze had dropped to stare at the gleaming marble floor. But she'd told herself that none of his words were relevant, not in their case—and there was no need to feel guilty. Drakon didn't want any more children, so the fact she was unable to give him any was neither here nor there.

Her heavy train slithering like a giant white snake behind her, she accompanied her new husband to the far end of the crowded ballroom, where his godfather was holding court. A handsome, silver-haired property magnate in his early sixties, Milo Lazopoulos was charming as he bent to kiss her on each cheek. The adoring crowd around him instantly dispersed, leaving the two men to speak briefly in Greek before Drakon excused himself and disappeared. Putting her bouquet down on a nearby table and finding herself alone with his godfather, Lucy was forced to address Milo's probing line of conversation once the traditional pleasantries had been dispensed with.

'I thank heaven that Drakon has stepped up to the plate and taken on the responsibilities left behind by his brother.' Milo shook his head. 'It was a terrible business. A terrible end to all that golden promise Niko was born with. To lose everything because you want to stick a needle in your arm. I just can't understand it.'

'They say that addiction is an illness,' said Lucy quietly. 'So perhaps we should feel compassion for him.'

Milo's gaze was piercing. 'Drakon tells me you used to be a nurse.'

'That's right.' Lucy nodded. 'A midwife, actually.'

'Which means you are well equipped to take on a young baby,' he observed.

'I'm going to do my very best.' She wondered what else Drakon had told his godfather. That they had agreed to a loveless marriage which was more of a business arrangement than anything else?

'But you left midwifery?' Milo continued.

'Not everyone stays in the job for life,' she commented gently.

'Because it was too distressing?'

There was a pause and Lucy could hear the loud beat of her heart hammering beneath the embellished bodice of her wedding dress. He was insightful, she thought, as well as being blunt. There were distressing aspects in every field of nursing, of course there were. But she wouldn't be telling Milo about her real reason for leaving the profession. Or Drakon, come to think about it. There was no need to, she reminded herself painfully. 'Something like that,' she agreed.

Something about her guarded reply made Milo's eyes narrow. Was he aware of her misgivings and did this make him decide that his interrogation had been a little on the harsh side? 'You seem the perfect choice of wife for my godson, Lucy. Someone calm and solid. A safe harbour after all those years of him resisting all forms of commitment. Funny, we always thought he'd…' His words came to an abrupt halt as he plucked two glasses of champagne from a passing waitress and handed one to Lucy. 'Let me be the first to toast the beautiful bride,' he said, the fine lines which edged his black eyes crinkling into a smile as he held his goblet aloft. *'Na zisoun!'*

But Lucy could be insightful too and as she chinked her glass to his she wondered what he wasn't telling her. 'Always thought he'd, what…?'

She could see speculation flashing in Milo's eyes, as if working out what she would or wouldn't be able to tolerate. But she kept her gaze firm and steady, willing him to tell her the truth. Because this was a marriage based on truth, wasn't it? Not fairy tales or fantasy.

He shrugged. 'We always thought he might marry Amy.'

Lucy nodded, recognising the name immediately. Of course. Amy. Drakon's business partner—and the woman who had bought his prospective bride a wardrobe of beautiful new clothes. The elusive Amy who was currently in Singapore wheeling and dealing and had apparently been unable to make the ceremony. She'd wondered if Amy's explanation of back-to-back meetings had been true, or whether it had been too painful for her to watch Drakon take another woman as his bride. Lucy hoped her expression didn't give her feelings away as insecurity began to pump through her veins. Instead, she aimed for the calmness she'd always been able to project even in the most trying circumstances—and this was hardly up there with those, was it?

'We haven't actually met,' she said, managing to produce a smile from somewhere.

Milo turned his head as there was some sort of commotion over by the double set of gilded doors and a murmur went up around the ballroom. 'Well, I think that's just about to change,' he said.

Lucy followed the direction of his gaze in time to witness the entrance of the most beautiful woman she had ever seen. The rich emerald material of her slinky dress provided a luscious backdrop for the shiny hair which spilled over her narrow shoulders like melted dark chocolate. Her lips were as red as the berries in the garlands of holly and people were crowding around her making spontaneous whoops of joy—their behaviour in marked contrast to the wariness they'd displayed when introduced to Lucy.

Amy's dark eyes were searching the room until they alighted on the bride and Lucy felt her heart give a great lurch as Milo spoke.

'Here's Amy,' he said quietly. 'And she's heading this way.'

CHAPTER SIX

'DON'T LOOK LIKE THAT,' Drakon instructed softly.

'Like what?'

'Like a sacrificial lamb all poised and ready for slaughter. Close the bathroom door, *agape mou*, and come over here so that I can take off your wedding dress as quickly as possible and make love to you, as I have been badly longing to do for so long.'

But Lucy felt paralysed and unable to move. Struck by unwanted fears and an apprehension which was making her limbs feel awkward and heavy. She was trying to blame it on the long day—on the tension leading up to the ceremony itself and the supreme weight of her heavy gown—but deep inside she knew the real cause of her anxiety.

She licked lips which had grown as dry as bone. Because she'd met Amy. She hadn't wanted to, but she'd liked Amy. She'd liked her very much. Her warm American voice had sounded both friendly and genuine. She'd found herself wishing that Amy had chosen her wedding dress because she was a damned sight sure it would have been more flattering than the one she'd ended up wearing. Remembering Milo's words,

Lucy had even found herself wondering why Drakon hadn't married the stunning partner who'd been with him for years—when she seemed so beautiful and confident and fitted into his world much better than Lucy ever could.

Her confidence had been battered by the meeting but somehow she had managed to survive the toasts and the dancing before Drakon had whispered that it was time for them to slip away. And now she was standing nervously in the honeymoon suite of the Granchester Hotel, about to begin her married life with a man she didn't really know.

She swallowed, removing the fragrant garland of roses and the attached veil from her head and placing both on a nearby table. Should she ask if he still wanted to go through with this? If seeing Amy had made him realise what a dumb thing he'd done by marrying someone like Lucy Phillips? Because if he *had* changed his mind then perhaps they could still get the marriage annulled before they actually consummated it. She was certain that was legally possible and it would certainly be a mature thing to suggest. She opened her mouth to speak, but no words came. All she could feel was the rush of hot colour to her cheeks.

'Still she stands there like a frightened lamb, which makes me realise I shall have to come to you instead, my blushing bride.' Drakon's words were cajoling as he began to walk across the marbled floor towards her, but he moved with the stealthy intent of a dark panther who had just spotted its helpless prey. He had removed his jacket and tie and undone the top buttons of his dress shirt and, with his olive skin glowing and black hair ruffled, he looked relaxed and supremely poised. Unlike her, who was feeling completely over-dressed and had started trembling violently, despite the warmth of the room.

He reached her at last and touched his fingertips to her cheek, slowly trailing their tips downwards until they reached the quivering outline of her lips. He bent to brush his mouth over hers in a slow kiss, before raising his head to look at her, his eyes still narrowed speculatively. 'Don't look so scared, Lucy,' he murmured. 'There's no reason to be. I mean, it isn't as if we've never done this before, is it?'

But never as man and wife, thought Lucy desperately—the sweet magic of his kiss fading as the enormity of her actions hit her. People said getting married needn't change anything but of course it did—otherwise, why would anyone bother? Because she wasn't just starry-eyed Lucy Phillips any more—the virgin who'd had a crush on him since for ever. Now she was the billionaire's wife and mother to his son—and suddenly she felt like an imposter. 'It just feels…different.'

'Then maybe we should stop overthinking it and just rely on our senses to do the work for us. What do you think? Turn around,' he said softly, without waiting for an answer.

She'd actually thought he couldn't bear to look at her anxious face but realised he wanted to undo each tiny hook of her wedding gown, his fingertips tiptoeing enticingly over her sensitive flesh. As the corseted bodice came apart and the cool air hit her skin, Lucy closed her eyes and silently practised different ways of asking the questions which had been plaguing her throughout the reception.

Tell me about Amy. How long have you known her? Have you ever made love to her? Or wanted to?

But Drakon's lips were following in the wake of his fingers. They were whispering over her back and trailing over her quivering flesh as he formed a featherlight path of kisses from neck to waist. Her skin flowered into goosepimples wherever he touched her and against her lacy bra, she could feel the insistent pushing of her nipples. Lucy sucked in a shuddering breath as he turned her around to face him again. The gleam of desire in his black eyes made something clench deep inside her and she wondered if she had taken complete leave of her senses. How could she possibly shatter the mood by asking him about another woman at a time like this?

'Now,' he murmured. 'Why don't we get rid of this dress completely?'

She heard the rueful note in his voice and was instantly on the defensive. 'You don't like it?'

He smiled as he traced a slow finger along the modest neckline of her very traditional gown. 'I thought it was perfectly appropriate for the entrance of my beautiful bride, but looser and freer is what I have in mind for what happens next.'

He slid the embossed satin of her gown over each shoulder and let the entire confection fall to the ground before effortlessly lifting her from the vast canopy of stiffened petticoats, until she was standing before him in just her white lacy underwear, hold-up stockings and spiky white high-heeled shoes. Slowly, he studied her and his black gaze felt as if it were scorching her skin where it lingered. 'Much better,' he said, and his voice was unsteady. 'Though I'm now feeling a little overdressed. Any ideas how we might redress the balance, Lucy?'

Lucy felt suddenly stricken with shyness as she lifted her fingers to his chest. Was he wondering what had happened to the uninhibited person she'd been back in the summer when he had awoken her sexuality and her appetite for him had been wild and untamed? She was wondering the same thing herself. But back then it had felt as if she had nothing to lose, while now the stakes seemed significantly higher. Yet wasn't she in danger of sabotaging their union before it had even started if she wasn't careful?

So snap out of it. Enjoy your wedding night with your gorgeous new husband. Make this so good he'll never want to look elsewhere for his pleasure.

'I have some idea,' she murmured. 'Let me help you out of this shirt.'

She was so nervous she could barely undo the first button, but as soon as she made contact with his skin all her reservations melted away like honey left out in the midday sun. How could she have forgotten just how beautiful he was? His olive skin gleamed with health and vitality and hungrily she ran her gaze over all that hard, honed muscle. Her fingers drifted over his hair-roughened chest and Lucy heard him expel a shuddered sigh as she slipped the shirt from his shoulders and it slid to the ground. Which just left his trousers. She swallowed. It was easy to see how huge and taut his erection was, straining against the fine material, and her cheeks grew hot as she dropped her head to his shoulder.

'Oh,' she whispered against his neck, shy once more.

'Anyone would think you'd never seen me in such an intimate state before.'

She swallowed. 'It seems like a long time ago.'

'It seems like that to me, too,' he agreed raggedly as he tugged at the belt of his trousers and swiftly bent to remove the rest of his clothes, his black eyes opaque with lust as he straightened up again. 'I've never had to wait for a woman like I've waited for you, Lucy. And it has been an exquisite kind of torture, do you realise that?'

Was it the thrill of the unknown which was making his voice dip with such husky intent as he unclipped her bra, so that her breasts sprang free against his bare chest? Did novelty alone account for the tense shudder which ran through his big body as he tugged her panties down over her thighs and kicked them impatiently away, before dextrously disposing of her high heels and filmy stockings so that they ended up in a white heap on the floor? Lucy didn't know and, right then, she didn't particularly care because he was lifting her into his arms and carrying her over to the bed, laying her down in the centre of the vast mattress like a willing sacrifice. His gaze moved down over her body. He stroked his fingers over her breasts, her belly, her hips, his narrowing eyes noting the restless wriggle of her bare bottom against the duvet. And then he smiled.

'Want me?' he questioned softly.

'You know I do,' she whispered.

He lay down on top of her, pushing her hair back from her flushed face before bending his head to kiss her. And as Lucy opened her eager lips to meet his, she felt a powerful wave of emotion rushing through her. Because *this* was the bit she remembered best. The sensation of his flesh pressing against hers. The long, drugging kisses and entwining of limbs and the feeling that this was somehow *meant* to be. Eagerly, she touched him back, and he moaned softly as she stroked him, and for a while they both seemed content with a rapt and silent rediscovery of each other's bodies. And then suddenly the tempo seemed to change. Drakon's body became taut as he captured her arms above her head and held them against the pillow, before pressing his mouth to her nipple so that she could feel the warmth of his breath against the erect skin.

'Oh,' she gasped softly.

'I love your breasts, Lucy,' he said huskily. 'They're so damned…big.'

As if to illustrate his pleasure, he began licking what felt like every inch of her, making her squirm with helpless delight. And meantime his hand had slipped between her legs and was spreading open her thighs, one finger thrumming urgently against her creamy heat so that Lucy's head fell back against the pillow. His rhythm was blissful and relentless—it rocketed her straight up to the stars and she came very quickly, her body arching beneath his hand as the spasms clenched low in her belly and then reverberated through her body like a sweet, spent storm. And when at last her eyelids fluttered open, it was to meet the black gleam of his penetrating gaze.

'And I like watching you come,' he observed throatily. 'I like it when your body goes rigid and you make those gasping little sounds at the back of your throat.'

These were starkly sensual statements which only an hour ago might have had her blushing like a schoolgirl, but not now—not when satisfaction was flooding through her still-pulsing body. Yet despite the intense pleasure which had transformed her, it wasn't enough, Lucy decided. Not nearly enough. Because she was no longer just some random woman he'd ended up having unexpected sex with on his private Greek island. She was now his wife and she wanted him to make love to her properly. She wanted him inside her. Badly. Reaching her arms up around his neck, she pulled his head down, and as his lips met hers a restless heat begin to rise inside her once more. She heard him give a low laugh as his tongue slipped inside her mouth and he began to circle his hips in a provocative demonstration of his arousal, until she thought she would go crazy with longing.

She realised he was rolling away from her and, for one illogical moment, wondered if her earlier fears had materialised and he was actually having second thoughts about consummating the marriage. But his reasoning was far more pragmatic than that. He was reaching for something on the bedside locker and Lucy swallowed when she saw what it was. A condom. Of *course* he would wear a condom. She could feel faint hysteria—and fear—spiral up inside her, because he'd told her he didn't want any more children and he was just making sure that wouldn't happen. He wasn't to know that protection was completely unnecessary in her case, was he?

'Drakon?'

His eyes were smoky with lust as he turned round. *'Ti?'*

'I'm… I'm on the pill.'

He smiled approvingly as he dropped the condom back on the nightstand. 'What excellent planning, my clever wife,' he murmured. 'That's exactly as it should be.'

Hysteria began to build again. Should she tell him she'd been on the pill for years because of her endometriosis? But by then he was rolling back towards her, pulling her into his arms with a groan of feral hunger, and Lucy could feel his naked hardness touching against her moist heat. He bent his dark head and was kissing her with a thoroughness which was making her heart want to burst out of her chest, because when he kissed her like that it felt like a fairy tale. And why would she risk destroying that by talking about her tragic gynaecological history at a time like this, when none of it related to their marriage plans?

'Now,' he breathed as he eased himself inside her. *'Evge!* You are so tight, Lucy. So very tight, my sweet little virgin.'

'But I'm not…' She gasped as he began to drive up deep inside her. 'I'm not a virgin any more.'

'Always,' he contradicted as his body took on an exquisite rhythm. 'Always to me.'

Did his raw words intensify her pleasure? Possibly. Again, Lucy came very quickly and so did he—and all her fears about the amazing chemistry they shared being some sort of fluke were banished. Afterwards she lay sleepy and sated in his arms but she felt him stir almost immediately and they did it all over again. And again. They did it so many times that she lost count and she must have dozed off, because the next thing she knew she was being woken by the sound of Big Ben chiming out midnight. But as the last chime faded into the night, Lucy knew she had to ask him the question which was still gnawing away at her— because otherwise wouldn't she just keep torturing herself with fevered imaginings?

She waited until he had poured two glasses of champagne and brought them back to bed, but her own drink lay untouched on the nightstand as she glanced over at Drakon's autocratic profile. He had picked up his phone and was reading something off the screen and Lucy cleared her throat, trying to make her words sound as nonchalant as possible. 'You seem very close to Amy,' she observed.

'Mmm…' he said absently as he put the phone back on the locker, screen side down. 'We've known each other a long time.'

Make it casual. All you're doing is finding out a bit more about him and the people in his life.

She tried to keep her voice bright but her words sounded as forced as the last bit of toothpaste you tried to squeeze from the tube. 'So how did you first get into partnership with her?'

There was a pause as he turned to look at her, his black gaze mocking. 'You really want to talk about this right now?'

Of course she didn't. She wanted him to put his

glass down and pull her into his arms and tell her he was starting to fall in love with her, but that was never going to happen, not in a million years. And in the meantime she had to face down her nameless fears or allow them to grow. To grow and run the risk of dominating her thoughts and ruining her relationship, even if it was a relationship which fell short of her dreams. 'I'm just interested,' she said blandly. 'And as your wife, it's useful if I find out as much as I can about you. There's loads about your past which is a mystery to me.'

Drakon took a sip of champagne and leaned back against the bank of feathered pillows. He didn't particularly feel like talking—but the sex had been so damned hot that he was feeling unusually accommodating towards his new bride. 'Me and Amy,' he mused. 'I guess it was one of those lucky meetings.'

'Sort of...star-crossed?' she ventured casually.

He shrugged, wondering why women always complicated things—or was she just trying to impress him with overblown quotes from Shakespeare? 'I don't know about that,' he said, a little impatiently. 'We were both working at the same office in Hong Kong and one night I decided to ask her out for dinner.'

'Because you fancied her?'

Drakon frowned. She might have been a virgin until very recently, but surely she wasn't *that* naïve? Because Lucy was practical. A practical and realistic woman who'd experienced her own share of bad stuff. Surely one thing which could come out of this unplanned marriage was the ability to be completely honest with her, because wasn't honesty the quality he valued above all else?

'Who wouldn't fancy her?' he questioned, barely registering the way she flinched, because by then his jaw had tightened with the memory of those turbulent days. 'I was in a bad place,' he admitted. 'My father's will had just been read to reveal that he'd basically blown the entire Konstantinou fortune during his lifetime. And my brother had gone ballistic when he'd discovered there was nothing left for him to inherit.'

'And you must have been disappointed to discover that you'd lost your own expected share of the family fortune?' she suggested.

He shook his head. 'That would never have been the case. The laws of primogeniture meant that, as the eldest son, Niko would have inherited everything.'

'And you never minded that?'

'Of course I minded! I'm not some sort of saint, Lucy.' His mouth twisted into a hard smile. 'But I'd resigned myself to my fate a long time earlier. And underneath it all, I discovered I was less like my father and more like my grandfather, who had worked his way up from the bottom to the very top. I knew I could make my own way in the world and that's exactly what I was doing. I'd been to university and got myself a decent degree and was a petrochemical engineer, working for a big company in the Far East.'

'But employees of big companies don't tend to make billions of dollars,' observed Lucy slowly. 'They don't own private jets or private islands or spend hundreds of thousands of pounds on last-minute weddings in luxury hotels.'

'No, they don't. And that's where Amy came in.' Drakon's voice became thoughtful. 'She was a geologist—the best geologist I've ever come across. After she'd explained she wasn't interested in me romantically, she told me that she'd seen the potential for oil on one of the Indonesian islands, but didn't have the wherewithal to explore it. And that's where *I* came in.' He paused. 'I believed in her passion and enthusiasm and my gut feeling told me she was onto something big. I'd just received a huge bonus from the company but I was growing bored and frustrated with working for someone else. I told Amy I was prepared to back her hunch but that we needed to really go for it. So we chartered a small company to do the drilling for us, and within six months we'd struck oil.' He took another sip of champagne and sighed. 'Best feeling in the world,' he reflected.

'I'm sure it was,' she said woodenly.

He turned to look at her. The rosy flush which had made her skin glow after a rapid succession of orgasms might never have happened, for her face was as pale as it had been just before she'd taken her wedding vows. He felt a flicker of irritation, because surely irrational mood swings had no place in what they had both agreed was to be a purely functional marriage. 'Is something wrong?' he questioned coolly.

Lucy wanted to jump up from the bed and rail at him for his insensitivity. To tell him that yes, of *course* there was something wrong. It was the first night of their honeymoon and not only had he confided that discovering oil was better than having sex with his new bride—he'd also confessed that the gorgeous Amy had once turned him down!

But one thing puzzled her more than her very natural feminine outrage at his reaction. Because Drakon was a determined and charismatic man who attracted women like ants to honey. Who was to say that Amy mightn't have lived to regret her impetuosity in refusing a relationship with someone like him—especially once he had decided to adopt Xander?

'So when Xander was orphaned, you weren't at all tempted to ask Amy to marry you, just in case she'd changed her mind?' she questioned slowly. 'Seeing as how you know each other so well and clearly get on.'

He narrowed his eyes and seemed to be running something over in his mind because it took a moment or two before he answered. 'That was never going to be on the cards, because I needed not just a mother, but a wife in the fullest sense of the word.' There was another pause. 'Amy's gay, Lucy,' he said eventually. 'She explained that at the time. She just hadn't come out to her family about it yet. She still hasn't. Like I said, you were my first choice. My only choice, really.'

Lucy supposed he must be paying her a compliment but somehow it didn't feel like one. Somehow it felt like being second-best and that wasn't such a great way to start married life. She turned to pick up her champagne glass but the fizzing bubbles only seemed to emphasise the flatness of her mood, when she realised that Drakon was sitting up in bed and pointing out of the enormous picture windows opposite.

'Will you take a look at that?' he exclaimed softly, his Greek accent velvety and pronounced.

She turned to follow the direction of his gaze, where the dazzle of the city was just visible through the bare branches of the trees—but that wasn't what had caught the tycoon's attention. It was the giant snowflakes which were tumbling from the sky like acrobats, turning golden in the bright light which streamed from the hotel windows.

'It's snowing,' said Lucy dutifully, trying to replicate his wonder since she supposed it was rare to see snow in Greece. But the irony of this final fairy-tale aspect to her Christmas wedding didn't escape her.

She was lying in a rumpled bed, having had mind-blowing sex with her stunning bridegroom, while outside the world was magically turning white. It was like something out of a movie.

But just like a movie—none of it was real.

CHAPTER SEVEN

THE PRESS WERE out in force next morning when the newly-weds left the Granchester Hotel in a flurry of flashbulbs. Drakon's hand was pressed lightly against Lucy's back as he guided her through the scrum of photographers and she looked up at him in gratitude just as the flash went off. And that was the photo which made the online edition of Britain's biggest tabloid. Lucy Konstantinou, standing by the giant hotel Christmas tree with shining eyes and snowflakes on her nose, while Drakon looked down at her with something indeterminate written on his hard and handsome face.

On the way to the airfield Lucy insisted on stopping by the apartment to check on Xander, but the baby was fast asleep and Sofia was assembling a new interactive baby mat with bells and squeaky cushions, for when he awoke. The nanny had looked up when they'd walked in, a question creasing her eyes, as if surprised to see them. Almost as if this unscheduled stop was as unwelcome to her as it had been to Drakon.

'Satisfied?' her new husband had demanded as the limousine had pulled away from the kerb and Lucy had nodded before staring out of the window at the falling snow, feeling kind of *extraneous*. Not a real wife, nor a real mother either, it seemed.

There were photos of them boarding the plane at Northolt, where the fields surrounding the airstrip were soft and white and more clouds of snowflakes swirled from the sky. There was even a shot from inside the wedding reception—though it was a mystery who had taken it—in which she and Drakon had been feeding each other hunks of creamy wedding cake.

Nobody would have guessed from that laughing image that at that precise moment Lucy had been in an agony of self-doubt about Amy and her place in Drakon's life. Yet now that fear had been banished and they were just about to begin their married life together and everything should be just fine and dandy, shouldn't it?

Shouldn't it?

Cosseted in the luxury of Drakon's plane, Lucy scrolled down the newspaper website past all the pictures. *English Nurse Marries Greek Billionaire!* ran the headline, and she found herself wondering why newspapers seemed obsessed with stereotypes.

Her smile was wry. Or maybe they were simply more perceptive than she gave them credit for. Perhaps they had homed into her dreamlike state before, during and after the ceremony—and managed to work out for themselves that this all felt as if it were happening to someone else, not her.

The jet flew them straight to Prasinisos and once Drakon had dismissed the flight attendants, he pulled her into his arms and started to kiss her. And wasn't it strange how sex could melt away your misgivings? Because the only thing she seemed able to rely on was her body's reaction whenever Drakon touched her. It had only been a few hours since they'd last made love but already she was hungry to feel him inside her again. To feel him and taste him and shudder out her pleasure as he filled her with his thrusting hardness. Inside the plane's master bedroom, he peeled off her clothes with care, as if he were slowly unwrapping a Christmas present, and he laughed when she tugged at his clothes with more eagerness than finesse.

'Are you going to rip my shirt off, Lucy?'

'If you could be bothered to help me with the buttons that wouldn't be an option.'

'Or maybe I'm enjoying being the passive object of your desire?'

'You? Passive? I don't think so.'

'I don't think so either,' he growled, pushing her back on the bed to bury his dark head beneath her thighs, so that she had to bite at the knuckles of one hand to prevent herself from shouting out her pleasure. Eventually he moved back up her body and thrust deep inside her and she could feel the shimmering of another intense orgasm waiting in the wings. Afterwards she repaired her hair as best she could but her cheeks still had a fiery glow as the plane touched down on his private island.

It felt strange to be back. Last time Lucy had visited Prasinisos had been for an unexpected freebie weekend when it had been impossible not to be overawed by the beauty of Drakon's exclusive home. But she'd also been aware of how broke she was in comparison to her wealthy host—a difference which had been brought home when his driver had been sent to meet her, widening his eyes before quickly composing himself.

That same driver was here today—Stavros, his name was—but there was no such look of bewilderment on his face. Maybe he didn't even recognise her as the same woman. Why, when she'd looked into the mirror this morning Lucy had barely recognised herself! Her designer clothes were exquisitely cut and hugely flattering and she knew that the cost of her shoes and handbag had been eye-wateringly high. She *looked* expensive and felt expensive—as if she had every right to be married to one of the world's wealthiest men. But inside she was the same Lucy, wasn't she? The woman who was not really a complete woman, married to a man who seemed indifferent to love and emotion.

But unless she wanted to ruin this honeymoon, she was going to have to put a lid on her insecurities. To learn how to manage and adjust them. She had just married the most amazing man and was about to experience the holiday of a lifetime and she owed it to them both to make the very best of it.

Drakon was quiet as they drove up the rugged path towards his cliff-top villa past the dramatic outcrop of rock which some people said resembled a man's face. He could feel the tension of the last few weeks leeching from his body, and not simply because of the post-sex endorphins which were lingering after that amazing mid-flight encounter with his new wife. No. It was a sense of achievement which now prevailed because it had all worked out exactly as he'd planned. He'd pulled it off. He had gained a suitable mother for his baby nephew and all he needed to do now was to play the part of contented newly-wed with conviction. Still, if the first twenty-four hours of married life were anything to go by, that shouldn't be too difficult. Leaning back against the leather seat, he gave a small smile as Lucy's excited voice broke into his reflection.

'Look! Over there. What's that, Drakon?'

He narrowed his eyes in the direction of her pointing finger. 'It's a peregrine falcon. Never seen one before?'

'I'm not sure. And if I did I wouldn't know what to call it.'

'Call yourself a country girl?' he teased.

'As you know, I only live an hour outside London, which is hardly rural isolation,' she protested as she leaned forward to get a better look at the falcon. 'Wow. That's amazing. So fast and so graceful.'

'And so deadly,' he commented, deadpan. 'To small mammals, at any rate.'

'I suppose so.' She turned to look at him. 'And the sea is very blue. Do you suppose there's any chance of going swimming?'

Drakon thought how wistful her voice sounded and was reminded of the first time he'd seen her here— with her body ploughing through the azure waters of his pool. 'It's December, Lucy,' he reminded her gently.

'And people in the UK swim in all weathers,' she informed him. 'In the newspapers recently was a photo of a woman in Scotland who had to smash her way through the ice with a pickaxe before she could go for her daily swim.'

He laughed. 'I'm not sure I'd trust you with a pickaxe. We'll see. But not today. Today I have only one thing in mind and that's to take my beautiful wife to bed as quickly as possible.'

Lucy wanted to object. To tell him not to say things like that because she wasn't beautiful and they sounded dangerously romantic and she was afraid of getting sucked into a vortex of false promise, which would make her long for things which were never going to happen. Because flattering words didn't really mean anything, did they? They were just words.

They reached the palatial villa where all the staff were lined up to greet them and it was only after she had shaken everyone's hands that Lucy noticed the giant decorated tree which was glittering in one corner of the vast sitting room which led off the marbled foyer.

'I didn't know you had Christmas trees in Greece,' she said wonderingly as she gazed at lush branches strewn with stars and fairy lights.

'On the contrary, we love them. Sub-zero temperatures aren't obligatory,' answered Drakon with soft mockery in his voice. 'On Christmas Eve the children sing carols and carry model boats painted gold and decorated with nuts. And we give presents, of course.'

Lucy thought about the modest gift she had tucked away for him in her suitcase and realised how humble it would appear in this lavish setting, as Drakon led her upstairs to the vast bedroom which overlooked the Mediterranean. The room was full of bright light and winter sunshine but she found herself glancing around nervously, and her voice was diffident when she spoke. 'It looks…*different* in here.'

'It is.' The sweeping movement of his hand indicated the pristine linen adorning the king-size bed, as well as a soft new shade of grey on the walls. 'I decided to have the room redecorated before you got here.'

She was silent for a moment. 'Oh? And why was that?'

'Does it matter why?'

Lucy tried to stem the question but she couldn't. Afterwards she would try to justify it by reasoning that she needed to know exactly where she stood, but perhaps it was more like worrying a healing cut on your finger and inadvertently making it bleed again. 'I think so,' she said lightly. 'Aren't we supposed to be honest with each other now we're married?'

There was a pause. 'I just thought it would be good to start afresh, with a completely clean slate.'

'You mean, we'll be using sheets which haven't been slept in by any other woman?'

He winced. 'If you like.'

She nodded, hating the completely unreasonable urge to cry which was making her eyes prickle. She knew the reality because he'd painstakingly spelt it out for her in London, just so there could be no mistake. He'd explained that he hadn't been sexually indiscriminate but, even so, of *course* he'd had plenty of lovers before her. And why *shouldn't* he? *She* was the freak, not Drakon. She was the woman approaching thirty who'd never been intimate with anyone until she'd melted into the arms of her Greek lover.

'But won't you miss it, Drakon?' she forced herself to question huskily. 'The variety of having all those different lovers? Though maybe I'm being presumptuous in assuming there won't be any in the future.

We've never discussed whether this is going to be an open marriage before now, have we?'

Drakon could hear the bravado in her voice and admired her outspokenness, knowing that few women would have been so matter-of-fact about such a tricky subject. Until he reminded himself that her candour was only possible because neither of them had any real emotion invested in the relationship. And that was why this marriage had a chance of succeeding—*because* there were no unrealistic expectations of love. And if she wanted honesty, didn't he owe her that? His mouth hardened. Of course he did. Especially when he found lies so detestable.

'I thought I'd made it clear that I would pledge to you my sexual loyalty,' he said coolly. 'Because I know how destructive infidelity can be. I'm not planning on having anyone other than you as my lover, Lucy, because sexually you thrill me in every way.' He sucked in a deep breath. 'But right now I'm having difficulty talking because the desire to pin you down on that bed and lose myself deep inside your body is pushing everything else from my mind.'

'Then what are you waiting for?' she questioned shakily.

He could hear the relief in her voice as he walked towards her, enjoying the instinctive darkening of her eyes as he unbuttoned her coat and hung it over the back of a chair. 'You seem to be wearing rather a lot of clothes,' he complained as he bent to unzip her knee-high boots.

'It was s-snowing when we left the Granchester, if you remember,' she breathed, perching on the edge of the bed as he slid the soft leather over each calf.

'Well, it isn't snowing here.'

She lifted her hips accommodatingly to allow him to slither her skirt over them. 'Does it ever snow on the island?' she queried conversationally.

'I didn't bring you here to discuss the damned weather,' he growled. 'We're not in England now.'

He undressed her efficiently and though on some level he registered the fine fabric and cut of her new clothes, it was the naked Lucy which made his senses soar like the peregrine falcon which had swooped through the sky on the journey here. His fingers skated over her big, pale breasts and traced featherlight paths over her arching ribcage and although he was rock-hard and eager to thrust deep inside her, he made himself wait. As he slowly kissed her belly and licked a teasing line downwards, he lifted his head to look at her.

'You've waxed,' he observed, one demonstrative finger circling the satin-smooth skin of her inner thigh. 'I noticed it last night but was a little too...*preoccupied* to mention it.'

'Drakon!'

'You want to be intimate in all ways?' he mused. 'Or do you want always to behave like a virgin and talk like a virgin?'

She shook her head. 'The...the wedding dress designer advised I get it done.' She gasped as his finger dipped lower. 'She said she thought...less is more—'

'Except concerning the application of sequins, of course,' he commented drily as he moved over her.

He made it last as long as he could—which was precisely long enough to allow them both to choke out their almost simultaneous pleasure. The second time he took it more slowly, enjoying Lucy's cries of wonder as her nails dug into his shoulder. When eventually they fell asleep, the setting sun was blazing through the huge windows so that the interior of the bedroom resembled a coral furnace. And when they woke, diamond-bright stars had been dusted over the clear, night sky. Drakon clicked on a lamp to see Lucy struggling to open her eyes, her nut-brown hair spread like satin over the pillow.

'What time is it?' she enquired sleepily.

'Dinner time.' He glanced over at his wristwatch. 'At least, it will be soon. Spiro was in the process of preparing a wedding feast and if you want to shower—'

'I do. I won't take long.'

'Take as long as you like. This room has two bathrooms.'

She nodded and rose from the bed but she didn't lean over and kiss him and, for Drakon, it felt as if all the intimacies of the previous few hours hadn't happened. As if she'd filed them all away under Sexy Lucy and gone back to being Sensible Lucy. He told himself he liked it that way. That it would be easier if they compartmentalised their lives like that all the time. But then she went and spoilt it all.

'Drakon?'

Something in the way she said his name warned him, for it contained that curious note of emphasis which women made whenever they were about to start prying. Perhaps hoping to distract her with the sight of his ever-present desire, he pushed back the rumpled duvet and got out of bed. 'What?'

But she deliberately kept her gaze fixed on his face,

not his groin. 'Earlier on, when you said...when you said you knew how destructive infidelity can be... Were you talking about your own experiences?'

He made no attempt to hide his displeasure. 'Does it really matter?'

'I think it does, yes. Did someone cheat on you?'

In a way, yes, though not in the way he suspected she meant. 'Go and have your shower, Lucy.'

'But—'

'I said *go*.'

He went into the second bathroom and stood beneath the fierce jets of the shower before quickly shaving and dressing and hoping Lucy would have had the sense to forget it and move on. But when eventually she'd finished getting ready—standing in front of him in a velvet dress the colour of the night sky outside the window—he could see that look of stubborn determination still on her face.

'Are we going to talk about it?' she questioned.

'About what?' he said, deliberately misunderstanding.

'About the infidelity you were referring to earlier.'

'It's nothing.'

'Doesn't sound like nothing to me. And weren't you the one who suggested the necessity of intimacy in this relationship?'

It was a clever twisting of his own words and Drakon felt trapped—but he could hardly storm out of the room and tell her to go to hell, could he? Not on the second night of his honeymoon. 'Is this what they taught you to do at nursing school, Lucy?' he demanded. 'To keep digging and digging until you got your answer?'

Biting back an exclamation of impatience, he walked over to the dressing table and extracted a pair of golden cufflinks from one of the drawers. But he was aware that he was playing for time and he suspected Lucy was aware of it, too. He could sense her watching him, and waiting—but the overriding feeling he was getting from her was one of compassion rather than prurience. And suddenly Drakon found himself wondering why he was so intent on keeping his memories locked away, because it wasn't as if anything he told her was going to affect the practical nature of their relationship, was it?

Slowly, he slotted the second cufflink in place so that it lay flush and gleaming against the cream silk. Mightn't it be a relief to confide in her something he'd only ever discussed with his mother? His mouth twisted. His lying mother. He felt the knot of pain in his gut tighten as he turned back to face his new wife.

'Okay.' He watched as she sat down on the end of the bed, her eyes fixed unwaveringly on his face, and it was only then that he began to speak. 'You're probably aware that I grew up in extreme luxury?'

She gave a short laugh. 'There were no poor boys at Milton school, Drakon.'

He nodded. 'No. I guess there weren't,' he agreed thoughtfully. 'My father was the only child of an extremely wealthy man, but he didn't follow my grandfather into the business. In fact, he'd never worked—he just lived off the profits of the company which my grandfather had painstakingly built up from scratch. Maybe the fact that everything had always been handed to him on a plate and the lack of purpose in his life were what lay behind what I was to later discover were his fundamental lack of self-worth and low self-esteem. But from the outside, at least, things looked perfect. He married my mother, who worshipped the ground he walked on, which only made his sense of entitlement all the greater. Everything she did was for my father. It was my first experience of unconditional female adoration, though it certainly wasn't to be my last. She spent the majority of her time completely pre-occupied with her appearance. Trying to stay young. Trying to fight nature's natural progression with one surgical procedure after another. By the time she was in her forties, her face was so cosmetically altered that she could barely move her mouth to smile.'

'And what was she like towards you—and Niko?'

'We were superfluous to requirements. In short, we got in the way.' His mouth twisted. 'When Niko and I were seven they sent us away to school in England, and after that I felt as though I had two very different lives. My life in England and my life in Greece. But every time I went home on vacation, I could sense things weren't right. I remember the atmosphere as being incredibly *tense*. I knew the marriage wasn't happy, but since I had no idea what a happy marriage looked like, I just accepted it. But things seemed to be getting worse and every time I asked my mother if anything was wrong she would just fob me off and tell me everything was just fine. Tell me that my father was nothing less than a genius and it was none of my business.'

'But it wasn't fine?' she interjected, into the silence which followed.

He gave a bitter laugh. 'You could say that. Behind the scenes everything was breaking down at an unbelievable speed. She knew that and she must have known how the outcome of the decline would impact on all our lives but she lied to me.' His voice grew silent for a moment. 'But it wasn't until my father's death that it came out just how comprehensively she'd lied. One sordid fact came spilling out after another—and the bubble which had been the perceived perfection of Konstantinou family life burst in the most spectacular way.'

'How?'

He didn't answer straight away and when he did, he winced, as if he had just bitten into something sour. 'I learned that for years my father had been entertaining a series of high-class hookers. Women who indulged him in whatever depravity was his current favourite and, from what I could gather, there were plenty of those. In turn he indulged them with whatever took their fancy—anything ranging from large diamonds to fancy apartments. He became a regular at the world's biggest casinos and high-rollers like him always attract a following of low-lifers. As a result, the business was in tatters and there was barely anything left. It wasn't what Niko had been led to believe would be his inheritance and that was the beginning of his descent into addiction. That was when he disappeared. I should have done something,' he added bitterly. 'I should have prevented it.'

'But what could you have done, Drakon?' she questioned urgently. 'Because I'm getting the feeling that you're shouldering most of the blame here.'

Drakon clenched his fists as familiar feelings of anger and frustration pulsed through him. 'Because by then I had some idea how commerce worked and could have helped,' he bit out. 'I could have found some sort of rescue package to have halted the decline of the company, or implored my father to seek help. If my mother had told me the truth instead of pretending nothing was wrong, then I could have done everything in my power to turn it around.'

She shook her head. 'But sometimes the best will in the world won't make people do what you want them to do!' she said, holding the palms of her hands towards him in silent appeal. 'Even if you'd known about it, your father might have blocked all your attempts to save the company—he might still have chosen his life of depravity. Sometimes you're powerless to do anything except sit back and watch while other people make their own mistakes, and there's absolutely nothing you can do about it.'

But Drakon shook his head, closing his heart and his ears to what she was saying. 'I don't do powerless, Lucy,' he said. 'Not any more. That's something you need to know about me. Maybe the only thing.'

His words tailed away as the bells from the village church began ringing out and he could hear the sound of the children beginning to sing the traditional *kalandra*, but Drakon found himself unable to feel any sense of joyful celebration as he glanced down at his watch.

It was Christmas Day.

CHAPTER EIGHT

PUSHING ASIDE THE festive wrapping paper, Lucy felt her eyes widen as she pulled a circlet of glittering diamonds from the dark leather box. 'Oh, Drakon,' she said.

'Do you like it?'

'How could anyone not like it?' she questioned shakily, slipping the bracelet over her wrist and holding it up in the air so that it sparkled like a ring of rainbows in the winter sunshine. But the truth was that it felt too expensive. Too impersonal—and nothing like the ink-spot sapphire which he'd picked out himself. She wanted to know who'd chosen it but she also didn't *want* to know, for fear that it might have been Amy or one of his assistants. And in the meantime—how humble was her own little present going to look in comparison to this?

A little awkwardly, she walked over to the Christmas tree and bent to retrieve the gift she'd placed there earlier. 'It's not very much,' she said as she handed it to him.

'I'm sure it will be perfect,' said her new husband, his voice carrying the bland reassurance of someone who was impossible to buy for.

But she saw his face change as he pulled out a small picture from within the neat folds of holly-strewn paper.

'You don't like it?' she questioned anxiously as he stared at it in silence.

'I... It's a line drawing of Prasinisos,' he said slowly, lifting his head to look at her. 'Where on earth did you get it?'

'I found it in London just before the wedding. There's a tiny shop in an arcade close to Leicester Square station which specialises in maps and drawings of small islands. I couldn't believe it when I saw it there. You haven't already got it, have you?'

He shook his head as he turned it over, his thumb caressing the worn leather frame, and an odd kind of smile touched the corners of his lips. 'No, I haven't got it.'

'I know it's only—'

'It's not *only* anything,' he corrected, almost fiercely. 'It's probably the most personal gift anyone has ever bought me. And now I think I'd better thank you properly, don't you?'

Lucy smiled and bit her lip. 'If you like.'

'I really did think you might have learned to stop blushing by now.' He gave a low laugh and she felt as if she'd just won the lottery. 'Come here.'

It was a Yuletide like no other Lucy had ever experienced, but then she'd spent so many of them on her own these past few years that maybe she had simply forgotten what it was like to celebrate. For lunch they sat down to a festive feast which had been prepared for them by Spiros, the chef. There were shiny crackers and napkins embroidered with stars on the table, and shiny *christopsomo* bread, which was traditionally eaten on Christmas Day. The delicious loaf was flavoured with cinnamon, oranges and cloves and Drakon told her that it translated literally as 'Christ's bread'. Afterwards, they ate lamb with salad and a delicious walnut-covered cake called *melomakarono*—which was also traditional.

After retiring to their bedroom for a sex-jammed siesta, Drakon drove her to his favourite cove, a curving crescent of deepest blue, and Lucy kicked off her shoes immediately, feeling the pale, soft sand between her toes as she gazed out at the glimmering horizon. 'I'd love to go for a swim,' she said, a little wistfully.

'It's way too cold.'

'I guess.' She sighed. 'Anyway, it's pointless wishing because I haven't brought my costume.'

'And because only a crazy person would swim on a day like this.'

Lucy stared out at the sapphire water on which the winter sunshine was dancing in undulating lines of liquid gold, telling herself that this might be Greece but it was still winter and Drakon was probably right—only a crazy person would want to swim on Christmas Day. Yet something was compelling her to take to the water and she couldn't work out if it was just a sense of feeling so intensely alive, or the powerful sense of hope which had been building up inside her since their plane had touched down on Prasinisos. Because despite her initial misgivings about the trip, this felt as if it was rapidly turning into a proper honeymoon. Not just the sex, which had been perfect as always—but because Drakon had revealed a chink in his steely armour and allowed her to look inside at the man beneath. He had confided stuff about his family which made her understand him a little better and didn't that spell only positive things for their future together?

He was standing silhouetted against the shoreline, his black hair ruffled and the light breeze blowing at his linen shirt, which was tucked into a pair of faded jeans, and he looked so utterly gorgeous that a thrill of pleasure ran through her. Was that what made her feel so uninhibited? Why she suddenly peeled her sweater over her head and dropped it on the sand, before starting to unbutton her jeans?

His black eyes narrowed as the denim slid to the sand. 'Now what are you doing?'

'What does it look like?'

'You're not planning on going *skinny-dipping* are you, Lucy?'

She registered his tone of mocking incredulity and forced herself to focus on her smile rather than the goosebumps which greeted the removal of her jeans. 'Why not?' she queried innocently as she unclipped her bra and wriggled out of her knickers. 'Didn't you say you owned this beach and nobody ever came near it?'

She relished the look in his eyes as she turned to pound across the beach and ran into the water. She was too intent on forcing herself to plunge straight beneath the icy depths to take any notice of what Drakon might be doing, but she was curving her arm into a powerful front crawl when she realised he was swimming right beside her, black hair plastered to his head like a seal, his naked body gleaming olive-gold underneath the water. In silent acknowledgement of his unspo-

ken challenge, Lucy set off, racing in a line parallel
to the shore, and gave it everything she had. She was
the strongest female swimmer she knew, but it wasn't
nearly enough to beat her powerhouse of a husband.

He made it look so effortless and was barely out
of breath when eventually she swam into his waiting
arms, and he laughed against her wet neck and kissed
it over and over again as she wrapped her legs around
his back. The exercise had given her immunity against
the chilly sea and it felt perfectly natural for Drakon's
hands to begin a sensual exploration of her body beneath the surface of the water. And perfectly natural for her to do the same to him. His mouth was on
hers—it tasted salty and cold and her nipples were like
bullets as they pressed into his chest. A small butter-
fly beat of awareness at her clitoris was making itself
insistently known and he gave a small groan of pleasure when she curled her fingers around his hardness.

'I want to do it to you now,' he whispered.

'Then do it,' she whispered back.

He covered her mouth with his seeking lips and Lucy's brain just went to mush. His lips were on her neck
and then her breasts. His hungry fingers were parting
her aching folds and as he nudged his moist tip against
her, she tightened the grip of her legs around the jut
of his hips. She gasped with pleasure as he made that
first thrust, tilting to accommodate the huge width of
him, and the angle of his penetration made her gasp
some more. She came very quickly, glad he was supporting her buttocks as he choked out his own fulfilment, and she could feel the rough rasp of his jaw as

his head sank against her shoulder, his mouth pressing against her wet hair.

'I never thought I'd make love in the sea,' she said, once she could trust herself to speak again.

'And your verdict?'

'It was...*okay*,' she said, and he laughed.

'Just okay?'

She shrugged.

'Then maybe I'd better do it to you again,' he growled with soft intent and Lucy only pretended to run away from him.

Afterwards they swam back to shore and dressed with numb fingers, hastily pulling clothes onto their still-damp bodies. But any coldness was forgotten the moment they got back to the heated car where soft blankets were stashed on the back seat and Drakon must have arranged for Spiros to make a thermos of creamy hot chocolate, lightly laced with brandy, which they drank from a shared cup.

'Drakon?'

'Mmm?'

'Did you...did you *plan* this?' questioned Lucy suspiciously, surveying him across a cloud of steam.

'The outing?'

'The sex.'

There was a pause. 'Put it this way, I like to cover every eventuality.' The smile he gave her was automatic but suddenly Drakon found himself looking away from her searching blue gaze to stare at the horizon ahead. He swallowed, still reeling from the intensity of what had happened back there in the water. Not just because it had been outside—he certainly wasn't a secret exhibitionist craving to be observed *in flagrante*—and he'd meant what he said when he'd told Lucy that his beach was completely private.

No. It wasn't that. It had more to do with the closeness he'd felt when their bodies had been locked together in that urgent, underwater coupling. Almost as if they'd been part of the same body. It had felt... *unsettling.* Disturbing. It had brought with it echoes of the past. Of things happening which were outside his control—and that was a feeling he'd vowed never to replicate. More than that—hadn't he felt the twist of something unknown in his heart when she'd held her face up to his and he'd started to kiss her? There was something about her sweet enthusiasm which was difficult to resist and that wasn't the only thing about her which was dangerous. Somehow she'd manged to peel away some of the defensive layers which were such an intrinsic part of his make-up. He'd talked about stuff he usually kept locked away and in the process she'd made him feel as if she'd burrowed inside his head.

He felt his skin icing as he started up the engine and the four-by-four ascended the cliff road, past the rocky outline of the man's face. Well, it wasn't going to happen again. She wasn't going to get any closer than she already had and maybe he needed to show her that, once this honeymoon was over. Despite the thoughtfulness of her Christmas present, which had affected him in a way he hadn't been expecting, it didn't actually *mean* anything, did it? This was never intended to be anything more than a marriage of convenience and it was pretty *inconvenient* to have a wife who was always prying like that. He was silent on the drive back to the villa and glad when his phone started vibrating the moment they entered the complex and he could excuse himself to deal with a phone call from one of his brokers in New York.

'I'm not sure how long this will take,' he called to her, over his shoulder.

'No worries. Honestly, I'm fine.' The dreamy note in her voice hinted at inner satisfaction. 'Take as long as you need,' she called back.

Left alone while Drakon retreated to his glass office, Lucy wandered around, feeling deeply content. It felt almost as if she were *floating*. As if she were walking on air. She didn't even mind her new husband shoehorning in a little work, despite his avowed intention to put business on the back burner during their honeymoon. Who cared if he'd succumbed to a call from his busy empire when this brief time together had exceeded all her expectations? When their interactions as a couple had filled her with the tentative hope that they shared a basic compatibility which could grow, if they nurtured it—and that maybe this marriage could become more than she'd ever dreamed it could be.

She texted Sofia, who informed her that Xander had discovered the use of his hands while they'd been away and had been trying to grab the soft toys attached to the sides of his cot.

Lucy texted back.

Sounds very advanced for a seven-weeker! Can't wait to see you both tomorrow. X

And it was true. She couldn't. Funny how you could bond with a tiny baby, even when you didn't realise it was happening. Even when it wasn't your baby. Couldn't they become a *real* family, she wondered hungrily, even if it was a somewhat unconventional family?

She glanced up as Drakon returned, his expression slightly preoccupied as he walked into the room. 'Is everything okay?' she questioned.

'Mmm?' He glanced across the room at her as if he had only just noticed she was there. 'I'm going to have to deal with a conference call a little later.'

'Oh? Must you?'

'Yes, I must,' he said smoothly. 'I'm afraid it can't be helped.'

It was disappointing. Of course it was—and part of her wanted to ask him to put whatever or whoever it was on hold, so they could enjoy every last second on the island. But Lucy was made of stronger stuff than that. She might have sometimes resented the military life in which she'd grown up, but being an army brat had taught her how to be strong and resilient. She needed to remind herself why Drakon had married her. Mostly because he wanted a mother substitute, but hand in hand with that went his own need for a supportive wife. She had to look on anything else as a bonus, rather than with any sense of entitlement.

'That's okay,' she said. 'I might do some packing so we aren't rushing in the morning.'

And that was how Lucy spent the last evening of her honeymoon. She took a long bath and washed all the sea water out of her hair. Then she packed her case and started reading a previously unopened novel she'd brought with her.

And though it was difficult to empathise with a woman who found herself marooned in a snowy cottage on Christmas Eve with a brooding stranger—*why on earth had she set out for the cottage when the weather forecast had been so atrocious?*—Lucy gave it her best shot.

At least Drakon made it down in time for dinner but he ate more perfunctorily than with any obvious signs of enjoyment and refused Spiro's home-made baklava, which made the chef go into a slight sulk. Only at bedtime did things settle into an agreeably familiar pattern, when her new husband took her to bed. He pulled the duvet over them like a private snowy tent and began to kiss her, and all the faint frustrations of the evening were forgotten. He made love to her very quickly, as if he were seeking some sort of release—but Lucy wasn't going to analyse that either. She just revelled in the elation which pulsed through her veins afterwards. Because this was bliss. Being in Drakon's arms was like finding her own tiny piece of heaven. Through heavy-lidded eyes she studied his profile, his skin silvered by the moonlight which flooded in from the windows, his indifferent expression giving nothing away.

'Did you sort all your business out?' she questioned.

He frowned. 'Are you really interested in talking about that right now?'

Was that censure which underpinned the hint of mockery in his voice? 'I thought you might want me to show some interest,' she said, a little defensively.

'Well, I don't. At least, not in that. Only in this.'

Lucy's head fell back against the pillow as he gave a featherlight flick of his tongue against her nipple and she squirmed when he licked some more and his hand crept down between her thighs. And although warm desire flooded through her, it was followed by a feeling of frustration which had nothing to do with the physical. Because this was a familiar pattern with Drakon, she recognised. He used his physicality to distract her from subjects he had no desire to pursue. And it worked. Every time. That was the magical yet ultimately infuriating thing about her husband. That he had the power to manipulate her. To use sex to quieten or console her—and there didn't seem to be a thing she could do about it.

They left the island at noon the following day and arrived in London just as dusk was falling and the Christmas lights in the city were starting to glow in the fading light. Inside the lobby of the luxury apartment block shone a glittering tree she'd barely noticed before the wedding—and this evening it seemed to symbolise a faded air of festivity which echoed her own increasingly flat mood. In the elevator she badly wanted Drakon to kiss her but he was busy looking at his phone and Lucy knew she needed to ruthlessly prune any romantic fantasies instead of allowing them to grow. They'd had a great honeymoon. So what? That didn't change anything, did it? That didn't mean he'd suddenly started to care for her, did it? Yet she had started to care for him even more than she'd done before. That was the truth of it.

Be careful, Lucy, she thought. *Be very careful.*

The elevator doors slid open and she walked straight into the apartment, where a smiling Sofia was waiting with Xander in her arms. The baby was dressed in a green sleepsuit covered with red-nosed reindeers and Lucy felt a welling up of something hard in her chest which took her breath away as she cradled the infant. He was so tiny and helpless and…she'd missed him, she realised with a wrench. Had Drakon missed him too? she wondered, turning her head to speak to her husband.

'Drakon? Look. See how he's…' But Lucy realised she was talking to an empty space. That Drakon had slipped from the room without a word and, from the fading sound of his conversation, it appeared he was already on the phone to somebody.

She tried not to let it bother her as she played with the baby. She bathed him and fed him and sang a crooning little song she remembered from those long hours of night duty when she'd worked in the neonatal unit at St Jude's hospital. She gave Sofia the evening off and, once Xander was asleep, Lucy changed into a dress she'd never worn before. Before she'd met Drakon, she would never have dared. Silky scarlet jersey clung to her hips and the slashing V neckline gave an uncharacteristic glimpse of shadowed cleavage. Spikyheeled black shoes with scarlet soles completed the outfit and she styled her hair into a fashionably messy topknot which the Granchester hairdresser had showed her how to do.

Zena had prepared a meal which she'd left for them and Lucy was just lighting tall candles in the dining room, when Drakon walked into the room. The top two buttons of his shirt were undone and she could see the faint darkness of chest hair, which arrowed downward in a beguiling path. He hadn't changed since they'd arrived back from Prasinisos, she realised, narrowing her eyes. He must have been on the phone all this time. He was looking around the room, taking in the holly-strewn centrepiece with tall silver candles which adorned the table and the bottle of champagne which protruded from an ice bucket.

'This all looks very…festive,' he observed, with the air of a man who had just been told that his dentist was about to make an unscheduled visit.

'Doesn't it?' Lucy said brightly. 'Zena must have gone to a lot of trouble and it's still…well, it's still Christmas.'

He turned his attention to her outfit. 'Is that why you're dressed like the personification of seasonal sex in your Santa-red dress?' he questioned huskily. 'Because you want me to unwrap you?'

Lucy swallowed as her nipples tightened in time to his slow scrutiny. 'I don't see why not,' she whispered. 'We might no longer be on honeymoon, but that doesn't mean we can't still make love after dinner every night, if you want to, which I'm rather hoping you do.'

'Who knows what either of us will want? This is still all very new—to both of us.' He picked up the champagne bottle and began to tear the foil from its neck. 'Let's just take it one day at a time, shall we, Lucy?'

His voice was soft but entirely devoid of emotion, and as she looked into the unfathomable darkness of his eyes Lucy wondered whether he intended his words to sound more like a threat than a promise.

CHAPTER NINE

DRAKON SAT BACK in his chair and twisted the stem of his wine glass between his fingers as he studied his wife who was sitting opposite him in the large dining room of his Mayfair apartment. Candlelight flickered over the polished table and over the dark, coiled gloss of her hair. 'Did I mention that I need to go to Singapore tomorrow?' he questioned.

Lucy looked up from her bowl of Greek lemon chicken soup, her spoon suspended in mid-air. 'No, you didn't.' A frown criss-crossed her brow. 'Tomorrow? Just like that? Without any kind of warning?'

'That's business, Lucy.'

'It seems to be a very demanding business.' She hesitated. 'When you always seem to be working.'

He shrugged. 'Billion-dollar empires don't just happen without someone putting in the legwork.'

'It would be nice…' her voice trailed off and, once again, she seemed to be picking her words carefully '…if you could spend a little more time with your son.'

Drakon felt a flicker of irritation because that felt almost like a criticism, and it was not in her remit to criticise him. But why not placate her when he was

going away tomorrow, by wiping that look of uncertainty from her face? 'That will happen,' he said.
'When things are a little quieter.'

She looked unconvinced and maybe he couldn't
blame her for that because, in truth, his heart was not
engaged in fatherhood. He could see her hesitating,
worrying her teeth into her bottom lip as if she was
trying not to say something, but she said it all the same.

'Do you *have* to go, Drakon?'

She tried to keep the question casual but in this she
failed because it was a refrain he'd heard from women
countless times over the years and Drakon tensed—
because didn't her words almost *justify* his intended
trip? Didn't they reinforce what he suspected was her
growing emotional dependence on him and make him
aware of the subtle ways she was trying to steer him
away from his work? But she had to understand that no
way was he going to take his eye off the ball, because
he'd seen what could happen if you did. He was still
his own boss and a man who answered to nobody—not
to his adopted baby and certainly not to his wife—and
the sooner she realised that, the better.

Steeling his heart against the reproach in her eyes,
he shrugged. 'I'm afraid I do,' he answered coolly. 'I
don't know if I mentioned that we're trying to extend
our oil refinery—'

Her voice sounded stiff. 'No, I don't believe you
did. You don't exactly encourage me to keep up with
what's going on in your empire, do you?'

Ignoring the underlying complaint in her question,
he picked up a piece of home-made pitta bread. 'Amy
hasn't been able to get anywhere with the government.

She keeps coming up against opposition—she suspects it's because she's a woman—and I really do need to be there.'

'Of course you do.' But Lucy put her soup spoon back down on the plate, her appetite suddenly deserting her. Was that because, although Drakon was going through the motions of *sounding* apologetic, the anticipation in his voice suggested he really wanted to go off on a last-minute trip to the Far East? And wasn't the truth of it that he probably felt trapped in a marriage he'd never really wanted?

Because the honeymoon was over. At least, that was how it seemed to her. Within twenty-four hours of returning to London from Prasinisos, life had picked up a new routine and Lucy realised just how much time she was expected to spend on her own. Drakon had resumed what she was to discover were his habitual twelve-hour days at the office, leaving her at home with Xander, Sofia and the rest of his large contingent of staff.

She took to rising deliberately early in order to eat breakfast with her husband before he left for the office, knowing he wouldn't return until dinner time. Because what was the point of being married if you never got to see the man you'd married? At least when she was pouring strong coffee and offering him a croissant—which he would invariably refuse—she felt as if she was going through the motions of being a married woman. But only at night did she feel like a real wife, when Drakon undressed her and took her into his arms. When he made her cry out with disbelieving pleasure as his lips and fingers and tongue opened up her senses. Her breasts would grow full and aching—her nipples pebbling into tight little bullets as he grazed at them hungrily with his teeth. She opened her legs and took him deep into her body, his hard heat filling her and making her feel, well... complete. Was it crazy to admit that was the effect he had on her? Suddenly she could understand all those things she'd read about successful sex—as if some kind of transformational magic had taken place between two people.

Afterwards she would lie in his arms, her ear pressed close to his chest, listening to the dying thunder of his heart. Their legs would still be entwined and she could feel the sticky trickle of his seed on her thigh as she longed for him to say something—*anything*—which would make her understand just how he really felt about her. But there was nothing—which made her conclude that he felt nothing. Inevitably, he would fall asleep straight away, leaving Lucy lying there, her eyes adjusting to the mysterious shadows which seemed to be lurking in the corners of the vast room. Was this how it was going to be from now on, or was there a possibility that their incredible physical closeness might eventually lead to some kind of emotional bond?

The signs weren't promising. At times, she still felt like something he had acquired—in the way he might acquire a new yacht. One morning he presented her with a credit card—a shiny platinum affair which glowed against the starched white linen tablecloth, as he slid it across the table towards her.

'What's this?' she questioned blankly.

'Surely you can work that out for yourself, Lucy.'

'A credit card?'

'I thought you'd be pleased. You need your own money,' he added, in response to her blank stare.

'But how can it possibly be my money when I haven't earned it?'

It was a naïve question and maybe she deserved the answering elevation of his brows.

'You could work a million hours a week and never earn a fraction of what I do,' he said, his gentle tone not quite taking the sting out of his words. 'You shouldn't have to come to me every time you want to buy something. What if you want to get yourself a new car? Or redecorate the apartment? Put your own stamp on it. That kind of thing.'

Her own stamp. Lucy gritted an automatic smile as she poured him a cup of the strong black coffee he seemed unable to function without. His statement would have been funny if it hadn't been so sad. Because how could she possibly make her presence felt when her brilliant billionaire husband dominated everything and everyone around him? She had no desire to change a beautifully decorated home just for the sake of it—because that would be a terrible waste of money and that wasn't the way she had been brought up. But she was certainly going to have to find something to do with her days, other than help Sofia look after Xander.

Xander.

A lump rose in her throat. The child she was loving more with every day which passed. Was it knowing that he was going to be her *only* child which made her feelings for him so fierce and fundamental? Sometimes when Drakon was at the office she found herself staring down at the infant lying sleeping in his crib. The infant still largely ignored by his adoptive father—unless you counted the perfunctory kiss Drakon sometimes planted on his head if ever his return from the office managed to coincide with Xander being awake, which wasn't often.

Sometimes Lucy found herself wondering if he timed his arrival home deliberately, to make it so. If he was determined to keep his distance. Why, even on Sundays—Sofia's and the rest of the staff's day off—the workaholic tycoon didn't go out of his way to bond with his baby son, did he? He still managed to absent himself for long periods of time, going out for a sprint around Hyde Park and returning covered in spatters of mud with his black hair clinging in damp tendrils to his neck. Or holing himself up in his home office to read through long contracts with horribly small print.

True to his word, Drakon went to Singapore the very next day and was gone for two weeks. Two whole weeks with phone calls his only method of communication. He blamed their sporadic nature on the time difference between London and Singapore and maybe that was true. But to Lucy it felt as if they were a million miles apart, rather than six and a half thousand. All he seemed to want to talk about was how brilliantly the talks about extending the oil refinery were going. He even sent a photograph of him and Amy sitting in some plush restaurant in the famous Botanic Gardens of the city, having dinner with a load of government ministers. Lucy felt as if he were standing on the deck of a ship which was moving further and further away from her. And all she could wonder was whether this was how it was going to be from now on.

'So, when are you coming back?' she asked.

'Tomorrow lunchtime. I've asked for the plane to be ready at midnight.'

Lucy spent the day trying to contain her state of excited expectation, but at the appointed hour she heard her phone ringing, rather than the welcome click of Drakon's key in the lock.

'Where are you?' she said as his name flashed up on the screen.

'*Agape*, forgive me.' He paused. 'A last-minute meeting was scheduled with the trade and industry minister.'

'And you had to be there?'

'Yes, of course I did,' he said coolly. 'Do you have a problem with that?'

Too right she did, but Lucy held back from saying so because the sensible side of her knew she was being unreasonable, while instinct told her she was only going to make matters worse if she turned this into a battle. Yet Drakon was worth fighting for, wasn't he? For Xander's sake mostly, but for hers too.

Because no matter how much she tried to tell herself it shouldn't be happening, her feelings towards the man she'd married were growing—feelings which had never been part of their marriage deal. Unstoppable emotions which had been nurtured during their brief honeymoon and taken on a life of their own. She tried blaming it on her lack of experience, convincing herself that a woman who'd reached the age of twenty-eight without ever having sex would be in danger of mistaking physical pleasure for something else. Something which felt uncomfortably like love. And she didn't want to love Drakon. The last thing she could afford to do was to waste her emotions on a man who'd told her right from the start that he didn't believe in love. Because that would be a self-destructive course and would detract from something she *could* do. Something positive and good—which was to strengthen the bond between father and son.

Because if Drakon wanted their marriage to endure, which was what he *said* he wanted—then he couldn't keep the baby at arm's length the whole time, as he'd been doing until now. She didn't think he was necessarily being unkind to Xander. It was just that he didn't know *how* to love him because he had no experience of parental love to fall back on. Maybe he had to learn to be a good father another way, and maybe she could help…

So just do *it,* Lucy thought to herself. *It's no good complaining about the state of your life if you don't do anything to try to improve it.*

She spun into action that same day, signing up for family membership at the local gym which she sometimes passed on her way to the park. Mayfair didn't run to budget gyms so the one she joined was eye-wateringly expensive, but it did have the benefit of a super-sized swimming pool. She tried it out a few times—in fact, her hair was still damp when Drakon arrived back from Singapore, his black eyes faintly bemused as he saw the drying locks of hair clouding around her shoulders.

'What's all this?' he questioned as she went into his arms to kiss him.

'I've joined a gym.'

'That's good,' he said absently as his phone began to trill in his pocket.

She made no further mention of it until the following Sunday morning, just as Drakon replaced his empty coffee cup and told her he was going to read through a new contract in his study, but Lucy shook her head, feeling her heart pounding nervously in her chest.

'I'd much rather you didn't.'

There was a split-second pause. 'I'm sorry?'

'Not today, Drakon. I wonder…' she licked her lips '…would you mind coming swimming with me and Xander instead?'

'Swimming?' he demanded. 'Don't be ridiculous. At his age?'

'They can start lessons as early as four weeks,' she informed him calmly. 'In fact, he's had a couple at the new gym already but they've got a class this morning and it would be nice to have some company.' She sucked in a deep breath. 'I think you might enjoy it. And before you trot out all the reasons why that's not possible—can I just ask what's the point of being one of the world's most successful men if you take less time off than the average factory worker?'

Drakon met her resolute expression and felt a flicker of mild irritation at the fact that she was so openly defying him. Yet he couldn't fault her logic, no matter how much he'd like to be able to. In fact, there was little about his new wife he could fault—and hadn't that been the biggest revelation of all? She was…

He studied her.

She was *surprising*. She was like the first soft shimmering of spring after the harshness of winter. Like a welcome sea breeze which whispered over your skin on the hottest day of the year. Her skills as a mother had never been in question because Drakon had known exactly what he *didn't* want from someone taking on that particular role. His mouth hardened. He'd wanted someone as unlike his own mother as possible—without her brittle exclusion of her own children, and her all-encompassing absorption in her philandering husband, and her preoccupation with her own appearance. He'd wanted someone soft and caring and honest and true. Someone with a heart and someone with a conscience—and Lucy had ticked all those boxes, and more.

He swallowed. Much more.

He hadn't been expecting her to keep surprising him as a lover, nor imagined he would find it difficult to drag himself away from the seductive sanctuary of her arms each morning. Sometimes he would even find himself glancing at his watch at the end of a working day and itch to get away, but he forced himself to work as late as he'd always done, because independence was key to his success. Wasn't that one of the reasons why his Singaporean trip had provided such a welcome relief and the space he needed? Because no way was he ever going to rely on another human being and open himself up to pain.

Yet Lucy wasn't asking for the world, was she? She

wasn't demanding emotional reassurance, or expecting him to bolster her unrealistic dreams about marriage. She simply wanted him to accompany her while she took the baby swimming. Not the biggest ask in the world.

'What time do you want to leave?' he growled.

'In about an hour.'

'I have a couple of calls I need to make first.'

'Of course you do,' she said, with a smile which somehow niggled him.

The gym was only a short walk away, reached through an oasis of a garden square which was new to him, but then, it was a long time since he'd taken a walk in London just for the sake of it. Feeling like a man who had just emerged from a long sleep, Drakon heard the unmistakable sounds of birdsong coming from the bare branches of a tree, before peering down at a carpet of snowy white flowers whose white tips were pushing their way through the grass.

'Snowdrops,' said Lucy as she followed the direction of his gaze.

'I know they're snowdrops,' he snapped.

He was slightly disconcerted to discover mixed changing rooms at the upmarket gym—he hadn't been in *any* kind of changing room since uni—and by the way Lucy thrust a pair of impossibly tiny armbands at him.

'Could you put these on Xander?'

He looked at them with a frown. 'Can't you do it?'

'Well, I *can*, of course—but I thought you might like to.'

What could he say in response? That he had no desire to do so? That the thought of touching the baby filled him with dread because he was so impossibly tiny? Especially as a nearby blonde was openly listening into their conversation, her eyes devouring him in a predatory way he hadn't come across in a while. Was that because he never really looked at other women any more, other than to compare them unfavourably to Lucy? He shot the blonde a glance before disdainfully averting his gaze. She was practically falling out of some skimpy bikini and he thought how much sexier his wife looked, clad in a sleek one-piece which hugged her toned curves.

He turned back to the task in hand and stared down at the tiny baby who was now cradled in the crook of his arm. It was a nerve-racking experience to slide on the armbands and he wanted to lash out at Lucy for making him do it, when he looked up and met the soft understanding shining from her blue eyes.

'You're doing just fine,' she said softly. 'Babies are stronger than they look and all dads feel funny at first. I've seen men the size of mountains looking completely lost when confronted with a newborn. You just need to do it more often. You know what they say. Practice makes perfect.'

But Drakon could hear his heart pounding. Pounding in a way he didn't recognise. Xander was wearing a hooded little towel which made him look like a miniature caped crusader, but nothing could detract from his vulnerability, despite the fact that he was over three months old now. Drakon stared into black eyes framed by impossibly long lashes. He had his father's eyes. Niko's eyes, he realised with a wrench. But they were *his* eyes too, for hadn't he and his twin brother been identical, sharing almost the same DNA? He stared down again at his adopted son and something inside him turned over and started to melt.

And that was how it started. Insidiously at first, but with gathering force—like the fierce Meltemi wind which blew through his homeland every summer—Drakon began an emotional connection with the child he had adopted.

He tried to deny it. To convince himself his life wouldn't change in any way because he didn't want it to change. He would play the part of husband and father, yes. That had always been part of the deal. But he would play it from a suitable distance, for that was how he operated. He was there to support Lucy in her role of mother, because that was her primary role. At times he'd started to wonder whether she truly understood and accepted the boundaries within their relationship, then something happened which made it clear he was going to have to spell it out for her.

The episode in question occurred when he was returning from a day trip of meetings in France and found his limousine waiting for him at the airfield. Unusually, the chauffeur remained in the driving seat and Drakon opened the rear door himself, to discover Lucy sitting on the back seat waiting for him—a vision in a silky dress which matched her eyes and suede high-heeled shoes in exactly the same colour.

'Hi,' she said.

'Hi,' he said, his eyes narrowing as some unknown fear clouded his heart. Something to do with Xander, perhaps? 'Is something wrong?' he demanded.

'No, nothing's wrong. I just thought it would be fun to come and meet you for a change.' She crossed one pale, stockinged leg over the other and tilted him a smile he'd never seen her use before. It was a slightly nervous smile but also kind of...*predatory.*

His senses were on instant alert as he got in beside her, noting the tense atmosphere inside the tinted interior of the car. He could see that she'd floated up the soundproofed and darkened screen which separated them from his chauffeur, so they were in a private world of their own. As the powerful vehicle pulled away she leaned forward to kiss him, guiding his hand up her skirt to illustrate the fact that she wasn't wearing panties. Before too long she had unzipped him and was straddling him, easing herself slowly down onto his rigid length and riding him as if they were in some kind of erotic rodeo. He felt compromised and manipulated but his desire for her was so intense that he had no choice other than to submit to her sexy ministrations. Even when inside her he tried to hold back—to make her wait for what he knew she wanted—but suddenly his seed was pumping out and he was moaning softly against her mouth.

It was undoubtedly the most stimulating homecoming he'd ever experienced—possibly because it was so unexpected. It was hard to believe this was the same blushing virgin he'd seduced on his Mediterranean island, and that disturbed him almost as much as this sudden reversal of control. He'd chosen her for her suitability and purity. Didn't she realise that he had chosen her because he had wanted a mother for his son? If he'd wanted a vamp, he would have married one.

'So what was all that about?' he demanded, once he'd got his breath back.

She paused in the act of smoothing down her rucked skirt before looking up, and he was caught in the teasing crossfire of her bluebell eyes. 'You didn't like it?'

He didn't respond to the feigned innocence in her voice. 'I didn't say that. I just wondered if there was any particular reason for such a mind-blowing homecoming and whether this is something I should expect every time I take a flight in future?'

Something in the repressive tone of his voice sent a shiver down Lucy's spine. He was looking at her with a stony expression in his black eyes, which somehow contradicted his passionate response, and she felt a worm of worry wriggling away inside her. Should she tell him the truth? Should she confess she'd been concerned he might find too much domesticity and fatherhood stultifying and she wanted to reassure him that she intended to remain as exciting a lover as possible? But that might let too much light into her occasionally paranoid thoughts and make what had just happened seem almost...*predictable*. Surely it would be better to allow a little mystique to prevail. To keep her gorgeous husband on his toes and ensure he'd never get bored and want to walk away from her, because that was something she couldn't bear to contemplate.

Still a relative novice to the game-playing of romance, she flicked him a smile. 'You'll just have to wait and see, won't you?'

'I guess.'

But her attempt to engage him again fell disappointingly flat for he picked up his briefcase and began rifling through it, effectively dismissing her. Quickly Lucy looked out of the window, terrified her gaze would betray her feelings, though he wasn't actually looking at her. But if he was…

She swallowed. If he was then mightn't he recognise that she was falling in love with her Greek husband, even though she knew there was no way he would ever return those feelings? Even though he now seemed to be in a strange kind of mood after she'd plucked up enough courage to travel to the airfield to seduce him. She never knew what was going on inside his head, because he rarely told her. Sometimes she felt as if they were growing further apart rather than closer, despite their cohabitation. Yet when he relaxed enough to let his guard slip…didn't she adore the man who existed behind the brittle exterior he'd formed to protect himself? The man who'd suffered such a loveless childhood, which meant he kept all his emotions locked away. And didn't she cherish a hope that his feelings for his son were growing—and would continue to grow if she could help facilitate that?

But it was hard to communicate with someone who was increasingly absent and Lucy's growing sense of insecurity was fuelled by Drakon jetting off again. This time he was travelling to Indonesia with Amy and communication filtered down into the usual snatched phone calls, squeezed in around the time difference. Lucy kept herself busy with Xander and that was always a pleasure. A growing pleasure. With every day which passed the baby was growing more and more aware and when she went in to him each morning, she was rewarded with the sunniest of smiles. Sometimes he nuzzled his silky little head against her neck, and Lucy felt a pure joy which was almost *painful* in its perfection. He was just gorgeous. The most gorgeous little baby in the world.

She had just put Xander to bed, sung him a small medley of lullabies and was standing beside the crib watching him when she heard an almost imperceptible sound by the door and glanced up to see Drakon standing silhouetted there. Lucy's heart leapt with instinctive longing but when he made no move to join her, she crept from the nursery to find him waiting for her in the corridor. After days of absence, his powerful body looked especially muscular and virile, though the expression on his dark face seemed much sterner than usual.

'How long have you been standing there?' she whispered.

'Long enough.'

'I wasn't expecting you back until Friday.'

'I know. I tried to ring a short while ago, but you didn't pick up.'

'I was bathing Xander.'

'So I see.' He smiled then. 'Your hair is damp.'

Self-consciously, she patted the dishevelled strands. 'I'd better go and tidy up. Don't you want…to say goodnight to Xander?'

He shook his head. 'I don't want to risk waking him. I'll see him in the morning.' There was a pause. 'Would you like to go out for dinner tonight, Lucy? Just the two of us. I thought we could try that new Italian restaurant in Knightsbridge.'

'I'd love to,' she said, a little breathlessly. 'I'll go and get changed.'

'Why don't you wear that green dress you had on the other night?' he suggested carelessly, his words fading away as he walked towards one of the dressing rooms.

Lucy hurried away to get ready, wondering if she was just imagining that Drakon's mood seemed…*different* tonight. Had something happened during his business trip to Indonesia? Had he met a woman and realised how constrained his life was by marriage to someone he was only with because it happened to be *convenient*? Was that why he had asked her to wear her admittedly on trend but least sexy dress, with its high ruffled neck and knee-length skirt?

She was silent in the car on the way to the restaurant but Drakon seemed too preoccupied with his own thoughts to notice. And it wasn't until they were seated at a table at the far end of the discreetly lit eatery in Knightsbridge, with two Bellini cocktails sitting in front of them, that she plucked up courage enough to ask him. Because hadn't he seemed more distant than usual, ever since that time when she'd surprised him at the airport in the back of the car? Moistening her lips with the tip of her tongue, she stared into the dark gleam of his eyes.

'Is something wrong, Drakon?'

He paused for long enough to magnify all her unspoken fears. Long enough for her heart to begin pounding painfully hard in her chest. But what he said next made Lucy's heart pound even louder.

CHAPTER TEN

'I WANT US to have another baby, Lucy.'

Lucy's fingers dug into the linen tablecloth as she struggled for words which wouldn't seem to come. 'What…what did you say?' she croaked.

He leaned forward. Close enough for her to reach out and touch his gorgeous face and on some instinctive level Lucy was tempted to do just that, knowing in her heart that in a few minutes' time such a move would inevitably repulse him. Because wasn't this the moment she'd been waiting for? The moment she had been secretly dreading?

'Another baby,' he repeated. 'A child of our own.'

'A child of our own,' she echoed dully.

'Neh.' His black eyes glittered. 'It makes sense.'

'Does it?'

He didn't seem to register the wobble in her voice and Lucy was grateful that her hair was successfully concealing the prickles of sweat which were beading her brow.

He nodded. 'Of course it does. Perfect sense.'

'B-because?'

He sucked in a deep breath before the words came

out in a rush, as if he'd prepared them before say-ing them. 'Because Xander needs a brother or a sis-ter. I don't want him growing up in a world occupied solely by adults. I want him to have someone to play with. Someone to keep him company. Someone who is there for him, fighting his corner. I want us to be a real family. To give him the brothers and sisters he needs, which might help erase the terrible start he en-dured at the beginning of his young life.' He paused, and his black eyes had suddenly grown very intense. 'And you are such a good mother that I think you need a child of your own to love and care for, as you have loved and cared for little Xander. Don't you, Lucy?' His mouth quirked into a reflective smile. 'Something more worthwhile to keep you busy, rather than hav-ing to put on silk stockings to come and meet me at the airport.'

Lucy stared at him in dismay, and not just because he was making her sound like some kind of amateur hooker. Because this was the moment she'd dreaded. The moment she'd prayed would never come. But in the long run, mightn't it all be for the best? Couldn't admitting the bitter truth she'd nursed for so long pro-vide some sort of catharsis for them all? Drakon had said he wanted a real family and she wanted that too. Couldn't she show him that what they already had could be enough, if they were prepared to work at it? With an effort she composed herself, acutely aware of the fact that they were in a public place.

'Perhaps we should order first,' she said.

He narrowed his eyes. 'Some men might be of-fended by your preoccupation with dinner,' he observed, with a flash of mockery. 'Are you so hungry that you can't wait a moment longer or do you just want to make me suffer by making me wait for your answer?'

It was more the fact that she could see the waiter hovering in the background and Lucy didn't want him coming over and disturbing them when she was in the middle of her story. The story she wished above all else she didn't have to tell. Just as she wished that Drakon had worded his proposal with more affection and that he wanted more children for reasons which had to do with love, rather than expediency. But it was point-less wishing for the impossible. She knew that better than anyone. With cold dread, she cast her eye over the menu and chose something which would take ages to prepare and then attempted to speak as if she actu-ally cared about it. 'Why don't we have the chateau-briand, to share?'

'If that's what you want.'

If only he knew that the only thing she wanted could never be hers. Lucy spoke quickly to the waiter and, once the order had been given, clasped her hands to-gether as if praying for a courage she wasn't sure she possessed.

'Drakon. There's something...' Her voice trembled. 'Something I haven't told you.'

His body tensed—as if her tone was warning him that what she was about to say wasn't just some un-discovered quirk of character. 'Oh?'

She sucked in a deep breath but the air which made its way to her lungs was scorching her airways. 'I can't give Xander the brothers and sisters you want for him,' she husked, 'because I'm…'

Go on. Say it. Say those two painful words which you've never quite been able to get your head around.

'I'm…infertile.'

There was total silence as he sat back in his seat and Lucy searched his face for some kind of reaction. But there was none. His enigmatic features were as unreadable as they'd ever been, and somehow that felt much worse than open pain, or anger.

'Have you known about this for long?'

The conversational tone of his voice gave Lucy the hope she needed and she nodded. 'I found out while I was nursing. It's one of the reasons which made me leave midwifery. I found it…' She swallowed as she tried to convey some of the pain she'd felt—not just the physical pain of endometriosis, but the emotional pain of knowing her womb was always going to be empty. 'I found it increasingly hard to be around pregnant women and babies. Every day when I went into work, I was reminded of what I could never have.' She searched his expression but still she could pick up nothing from his hard-featured stillness. 'It's one of the reasons I never really had any boyfriends before you, because most of the time I only felt like a shell of a woman.'

And now the cold words which began to fall like stones from his lips gave her a clue as to what he was feeling.

'But you didn't think it was pertinent to tell me all this before we were married?'

'I meant to. But we didn't really know each other

back then, did we? It's not the kind of thing you just casually drop into the conversation with a virtual stranger.' She licked her lips. 'And it didn't seem relevant, because you said you didn't ever want children of your own.'

'But things change, Lucy,' he ground out. 'We're both intelligent enough to realise that. People change their minds all the time. I would like to have been given the choice instead of having it taken away from me, without my knowledge.'

Lucy shook her head, but it didn't change the fact that her throat felt as if someone were pressing their fingers against it, making it almost impossible to breathe. But she needed to breathe. To try to explain how it had been. How it had felt. 'A couple of times I intended to tell you—but the right time never seemed to come up,' she said. 'The preparations for the wedding were so intense and all-consuming that I never found the opportunity to start a conversation about it.'

'You could have made the time,' he said repressively.

Her head was hurting and so was her heart. 'She could sense that he didn't understand and she wanted to make him understand. 'Did you ever see that film about Queen Elizabeth I—the one which won all the awards?' she questioned suddenly.

'*What?*' he demanded, his dark look of accusation momentarily morphing into one of perplexity.

'The English Queen was almost completely bald, and she hid her baldness beneath a lot of elaborate wigs,' she rushed on. 'But they said that anybody who had seen her in her true state could never look at her in quite the same way again. That she remained permanently ugly and scarred in the mind's eye of the beholder. And that's how *I* felt, Drakon. I didn't want you to look at me as less than a woman. As some barren creature only to be pitied. I wanted you to continue to desire me and want me.'

He gave a short and bitter laugh. 'So you lied to me?'

'I did *not* lie!' she protested. 'The subject never came up.'

'Oh, but you did. It was a lie by omission—and deep down you know that, Lucy.'

She stared at him, unable to deny his bitter allegation.

'It was a lie by omission,' he repeated with quiet force, his face a blur of rage. 'In fact, I don't think I've ever met a woman who *doesn't* lie. It seems to be stamped into their very DNA. I learnt it first from my own mother, almost as soon as I'd left the cradle, and I've been having it reinforced on a regular basis ever since.'

Lucy heard a note of *triumph* which edged the cynicism in his voice as their meal was brought to the table, and she watched in excruciatingly tense silence as the meat was carved into neat slices and heaped onto their plates.

'I guess in a way this has made you happy?' she ventured, once the waiter had gone.

'Happy?' he echoed. 'Are you out of your mind?'

'Not at all. This must be a self-fulfilling prophecy for you,' she said slowly. 'You don't like women and you don't trust them—you never have. And I've just given you yet another reason to hate us as a sex.' She sucked in a deep breath. 'The only thing I can say to you, Drakon, is that I'm sorry. And if I could have the time back, I would do it differently.' She could hear her voice starting to wobble. 'Except that then you might never have wanted me and I would never have become your wife and learned to love you as I do.'

'Love?' he queried disdainfully. 'You think I want your tainted love, Lucy? That I want to spend the rest of my life with a liar?'

Lucy recognised that their marriage was hanging precariously in the balance. That a delicate line as fine as a spider's web was all that lay between happiness and loneliness. One clumsy move and it would all be lost. Yet surely what they had discovered together was worth fighting for. Fighting with every single breath in her body. 'But we're all capable of lies by omission. Of fashioning reality to look like something quite different,' she pointed out quietly. 'Even you, Drakon.'

'What the hell are you talking about?'

'I'm talking about your close friendship with Amy. So close that even your godfather told me he thought the two of you would get married and so did everyone else. And before you remind me that Amy's gay— surely that's all part of it. She hasn't come out, for whatever reason—so it probably suits her very well to have people speculate on the true nature of her relationship with her business partner.' She took a sip of her cocktail and felt the champagne and peach juice foam against the dry interior of her mouth.

'That's different,' he snapped.

'Is it?' she questioned quietly. 'Oh, Drakon.' Her voice was filled with a deep sadness which she couldn't seem to hold back. 'Can't you ever forgive me? Can't we just put all this behind us and start over—now that everything's out in the open?'

But she got her answer instantly as he rose to his feet, towering over her and the table, his muscular shadow seeming to swallow her whole.

'I'll tell you exactly what's going to happen now,' he said quietly. 'I'm going to pay the bill and leave. And then I'm going outside to catch a cab. You can take the car.'

'I don't want your damned car!'

'Really? Then how are you proposing to get back to Milton tonight?'

'To Milton?' she repeated blankly, blinking her eyes at him in sudden confusion. 'You mean, back to my cottage?'

'Of course that's what I mean! Where else did you think you'd be spending the night, Lucy? Do you really think I want you in my home in the light of what I've just learned?'

'Drakon...' Lucy felt as if she had fallen down a deep well only to discover there were no footholds to allow her to get back up again. She had expected his censure, yes, and his condemnation, too. Deep down she'd felt as if she deserved both those things. But surely not such an instant and outright rejection, which felt so final and so *permanent*.

'What did you *think* was going to happen after this astonishing revelation, Lucy?' he demanded cruelly. 'That we would just go back to Mayfair and pretend nothing had happened? That we would make love and carry on as normal?'

She shook her head as a pair of dark eyes and a silky head swam into her mind. 'But what about Xander? What's going to happen to our son?'

'Xander has a nanny—and a father,' he said coldly. 'We don't need you, Lucy. Perhaps we never did. I will arrange to have your stuff sent to the cottage—'

'Please don't bother. Keep it!' she said furiously. 'I won't be able to wear those kinds of clothes in Milton, anyway!'

'That's entirely your decision. Oh, and I don't think I have any further use for this, do you?' he added contemptuously. She saw him twist his gold wedding band from his finger before letting it fall with a tiny clatter onto an unused side plate and fixing her with a final withering look. 'Obviously I will make sure your settlement is generous, provided you agree to a swift, no-claim divorce. I don't think there's anything else, do you? Other than to say goodbye.'

He turned and made his way through the restaurant, oblivious to the curious eyes which followed him, and Lucy wondered if she would be able to manage that same degree of insouciance. But most of all she wondered just how long she would be able to keep the hot flood of tears at bay.

CHAPTER ELEVEN

Don't forget Xander's check-up appointment at the clinic tomorrow. Sofia already knows but thought you might like to accompany them. L

DRAKON STARED AT the text message from his estranged wife which had just appeared on his phone and his brow creased in a frown. It wasn't the first he had received—all to do with the welfare of his son, he noted, and all signed off with Lucy's initial and not a single endearment.

Initially, he'd been surprised that she'd bothered contacting him, given the unceremonious way in which he had dumped her at the Italian restaurant. But wasn't that a mark of Lucy's soft and caring nature—that she wouldn't allow hurt pride to stand in the way of her concern for the baby she had mothered so beautifully? Another stab of the pain pierced relentlessly at his heart. The same damned pain which had been plaguing him since her departure. Fury and denial rose up inside him in a hot and potent mix. He kept telling himself it wasn't *her* he missed—it was her presence as Xander's mother which was making him feel so remorselessly uncomfortable.

And an inner voice mocked him every time that thought came into his head, because deep down he suspected it wasn't true. For a man so enamoured of the truth, wasn't he falling short of his own high standards? Because hadn't Lucy taught him how to relax around his son, so that now he felt completely confident whenever he cradled little Xander in his arms? Yet it hadn't always been that way. A lump rose in his throat and his heart began to pound. Before Lucy had come into their lives, the realisation that he must adopt his orphaned nephew had lain heavy on his heart. It had been a task he had been prepared to undertake—but Drakon's attitude had been reluctant. Not any more.

He stared down at the sleeping infant and his heart clenched. These days he embraced fatherhood with a sense of immense satisfaction and with something else, too. Something he'd never thought he'd feel towards Niko's baby—and that something was love.

Restlessly, he left the nursery and moved aimlessly through the Mayfair apartment which had felt so vast and so empty since his wife had moved out. He missed her in his bed at night—and the hard, physical ache which greeted him each morning bore testimony to that.

Just as he missed talking to her over breakfast and dinner and swimming with her in the Greek sea on a winter day when surely no sane person would have swum.

He had the services of the best nanny in the world

and the wherewithal to find another any time he wished. He had an address book practically overflowing with women who would be eager to provide him with whatever consolation he required.

He drew himself up short, reminding himself that he didn't *need* consolation—because that would imply that he was grieving for something and he wasn't.

Really, he wasn't.

Of course she missed him. That was only to be expected. But it was *Xander* she missed, Lucy convinced herself fiercely. She certainly didn't miss his pig-headed father. And of course it was weird being back in her tiny riverside cottage and waking up alone every morning, without the warm and muscular body of Drakon stirring beside her in more ways than one. But she would get over it. She had to. And all things passed eventually—some just took longer than others.

At least she'd got her job back. She had telephoned Caroline and had a brief and uncomfortable conversation. Her mentor and employer had diplomatically agreed not to quiz her about the reasons for the end of her brief marriage and Lucy had gone back to work as a waitress. The jobs were busy and distracting—which was probably a good thing—and she tried her best to pin on her brightest smile, hoping it would conceal the pain of missing the family life she'd so nearly become a part of.

One night she put on her pale green uniform and went to work at a large house outside the town, handing out canapés to the guests of a local landowner whose daughter had just got engaged. The whole affair seemed destined to mock Lucy, from the moment she was diverted to enter the house via the back door and told to tidy up her hair, to someone impatiently dismissing her and her tray, as if she were a large fly who had just landed on a piece of sushi and started laying eggs. She'd forgotten how patronising the rich could be, when you were in a position of domestic servitude. The newly engaged woman was flashing her massive and rather vulgar ring and, stupidly, Lucy found herself thinking about the discreet ink-spot sapphire which was tucked away at home with Drakon's discarded wedding band, which she had snatched up before leaving the restaurant, and wondering whether she ought to send both back to her estranged husband.

The moon was high in the sky by the time she left the party and, although transport home was included, Lucy had no desire to sit on a steamy and overcrowded minibus, especially as she was always the last one to be dropped off. Despite the ever-present drizzle, she set off to walk along the familiar roads and lanes, pausing briefly by a small footbridge, to watch the dark gleam of the water as it flowed beneath her. Because the river never changed, she thought gloomily. It had been the same all through her life and would be the same once she was dead and gone.

An unfamiliar sense of melancholy washed over her as she brushed past a low-hanging branch of wet leaves on the final approach to her cottage and tiny droplets of water showered over her. And then she nearly jumped out of her skin as a large figure loomed out of the darkness, her instinctive fear quickly replaced by an intense feeling of longing as she identified the late-night intruder.

Drakon.

Drakon Konstantinou, in all his towering and muscular beauty. Her heart twisted with pain and regret, but indignation was a far healthier reaction and that was the one she clung onto. 'What the hell do you think you're doing, jumping out of the shadows like that?' she demanded. 'You gave me a fright.'

'And what are you doing walking back alone at this time of night?' he returned furiously. 'Anything could have happened to you!'

'I can't think of any fate worse than my former husband turning up unannounced like this!' she retorted. 'What are you doing here, Drakon—have you come to gloat?'

Despite the darkness of the night, Drakon could see the fury spitting from his wife's eyes and his heart sank. Because this wasn't what he had planned. He'd thought she'd be home and he'd be able to talk his way into the cosy comfort of her small cottage within minutes. But the place had been in darkness and he'd been walking up and down this damned riverbank for hours, his tortured mind conjuring up pictures of where she might be, especially since her phone had been switched to silent and she hadn't bothered to return any of the calls he'd been making all evening.

Yet could he blame her for being so angry?

No, he could not.

Rarely in his life had he been forced to admit that someone else had the higher moral ground, but he did so now, repeating the same words he'd used when he'd turned up on this very same spot a few months back, asking her to marry him.

'Can I come in?'

'No, you can't. Contact me through my lawyer.'

He frowned. 'Have you got a lawyer?'

'Not yet. But I will. At least I suppose I will—isn't that what people do when they're going through a divorce?'

'I don't know, Lucy, because I've never been married before and I don't want a divorce.'

'Well, I do! I can't think of anything worse than—' She stopped abruptly, as if his words had only just sunk in, and eyed him suspiciously. 'What do you mean, you don't want a divorce?'

'There's no qualifier to that statement,' he said drily. 'I just don't.'

'Well, I do.'

He sucked in a deep breath as he read the defiance on her shadowed face. 'We can't have this conversation on the doorstep.'

'We seem to be managing perfectly well, so far.'

'Open the door and let's go inside, Lucy,' he said gently. 'Your hair's all wet.'

Lucy wanted to shout at him. To tell him not to adopt that silky tone which made her think of all the times he'd cradled her after they'd made love and made her feel so cherished and protected and wanted. Because all that stuff had been an illusion. It had withered and died at the first test, hadn't it?

Yet she recognised it would be immature to send him away when he had come all this way to see her. They needed to deal with this situation like adults.

He probably wanted her to promise not to give her side of the story to the press—as if she would dream of hanging out all her heartache for the world to see. And besides... She glanced nervously at the look of determination which was making his jutting jaw look so formidable. She swallowed. He didn't look anything like a man who would accept being turned away.

'Oh, very well,' she said crossly. 'But this had better not take long.'

She made him wait while she lit a couple of lamps and put a match to the fire because the temperature in the room was positively arctic. Then she took off her comfy black work shoes and shot him an acid look as she lined them up next to the others in the hallway. 'I'm assuming you won't be spiriting away any of my shoes this time?' she questioned sarcastically.

But he didn't rise to the bait. Instead he walked over to the window and stared outside, his head bent and shoulders suddenly hunched, like a worn-out fistfighter on the brink of defeat who was about to make one last stab at victory. 'I just want to say that I'm sorry, Lucy,' he said, and when he turned round Lucy was shocked by the ravaged expression she could read on his rugged features.

'It doesn't matter,' she said woodenly.

'Oh, but it does. It matters a lot. It matters more than anything else in the world that you realise how bitterly I regret the things I said to you that night.'

She shook her head, because hadn't her nurse training taught her always to see the other person's point of view? 'It doesn't,' she repeated, as generously as she could. 'We all say things we sometimes regret when we're angry. Or even when we're not angry. It's okay, Drakon. Honestly.'

'No, it's not okay,' he flared. 'It's anything but okay. Stop trying to be kind and reasonable, even though those are the very qualities which drew me to you in the first place.'

'Stop talking like that and just tell me why you're here, Drakon,' she demanded, her voice trembling with anger, because she didn't need to know these things. In fact, weren't they making the situation even worse?

'I'm here because I miss you, Lucy,' he bit out. 'I miss you more than words can ever say and in every way—physically, mentally and emotionally. And Xander misses you, too.' He shook his head. 'I can't believe I didn't even let you say goodbye to him.'

'But Xander has a nanny,' Lucy put in fiercely, because it wasn't fair for him to do this to her. To put her heart through the wringer all over again, only to leave her high and dry. 'As you told me on the night we parted. Just as you told me you couldn't tolerate a woman who had lied to you. And as for not saying goodbye to a baby of that age—what difference would it have made? Xander is too young to have realised what was going on and it would only have upset and confused the baby and Sofia.'

'But that wasn't why I did it,' he persisted. 'Why I wouldn't allow you to go to him.'

'No. I realise that. You did it to punish me because I had failed to live up to the image you'd created of me as your ideal woman.' She drew in a deep breath. 'Because that's the truth of it, isn't it, Drakon? You'd put me on a pedestal and that's where I was expected to stay. The nurse. The virgin. The mother. And you didn't like it when I blurred those roles, did you? When your good girl became a good-time girl and seduced you in the back of the limousine, you could hardly hide your dismay. You couldn't bear to accept that I had flaws, just like everyone else—or that I was a real person with real needs. Maybe if you hadn't been so intent on perfection, I might have had the courage to tell you I was infertile before. But I didn't want to risk you not marrying me,' she admitted huskily, because what did she have to lose now? 'I had an opportunity to do just that when we first discussed it, over lunch in the Granchester that day, when you presented me with my engagement ring.'

'But you didn't?' he questioned slowly.

'No, I didn't. You didn't ask why I didn't want children of my own and I was glad you hadn't, because in that moment I was living the dream and I didn't want to wake up from it. And like I said, we didn't really know each other—there was no expectation that we would ever care for each other—so why would I confide something so intensely personal?'

There was silence for a moment and when eventually he spoke, his voice was very low. 'What if I were to tell you again that I'm sorry for what I did and that I care very much? What if I were to tell you that my life has been empty without you and that I love you and want to spend the rest of my life with you and our son?'

Lucy couldn't prevent the surge of hope which flooded into her chest, but she quashed it and forced herself to ask the question which still hung between them, like a dark spectre. 'But you want more children, Drakon!' she declared, her voice shaking. 'That hasn't changed. You want more children and I can't give them to you.'

'I wanted more children with you,' he corrected sombrely. 'And if that isn't possible, then I will count my blessings and be content with the family I've already got. All I'm asking is for another chance, Lucy. To show you that I mean what I say. To love you in the way that you deserve to be loved.'

Lucy stared at him as those two words resonated more than any others. *Another chance.* How could she deny him that, even if she wanted to? Because how many people would give everything they owned for one more chance? Her brother would have liked the chance to have dodged that stray sniper's bullet—and if that had happened, her mother would never have faded away, like the blowsy roses which grew in the walled garden at Milton school.

She swallowed, knowing that this was the biggest and most important decision she'd ever had to make. If she accepted Drakon's offer, she would be taking a risk and she had never been a natural risk-taker. But what was the alternative? To turn him away and say goodbye? Yes, she might get hurt if she stayed with him—that was a very real possibility in every single relationship—but wasn't she being given the opportunity to spend the rest of her life with the only man she had ever loved? And wouldn't the hurt of turning him away transcend any other pain she'd ever known?

Because Lucy had glimpsed a world without Drakon in it and it was a bleak one. And maybe this place in which they now found themselves was the best place of all. One where all the barriers and fears with which they had surrounded themselves had crumbled away and all that was left were two people who loved each other and wanted to be together. She clasped her hands together as if in prayer and looked at him with all the tenderness she had never dared show before.

'Yes, Drakon,' she said softly. 'Yes, to everything you ask of me. Because I love you, too. I love the man I see beneath the hard layer you present to the world—and I'd like the world to see more of him.'

He nodded as he took a step towards her. 'Just know one thing, Lucy.' His voice was shaking as he pulled her into his arms and buried his face against her hair and she could feel his powerful body trembling. 'That I won't ever let you down. Not again.'

But Lucy knew that already, in the only place which mattered.

She knew it in her heart.

EPILOGUE

'YOU'RE NOT COLD?'

'Cold?' Lucy smiled up at Drakon. His arm was protectively clasped around her shoulders and she thought how handsome he looked in his dark dinner suit and black bow tie. 'Not at all. Mainly because I'm wearing thermal knickers.'

'Are you joking?'

'Of course I'm joking, darling. Do you really think I would have passed over all that deliciously decadent lingerie you bought me for Christmas in favour of a pair of sensible pants? And besides…' She snuck a glance at the jewel-studded wristwatch she'd also found nestling at the bottom of her stocking a week earlier. A delicate watch with ink-spot sapphires he'd had made specially. 'It's not long to wait until the fireworks.'

Her husband's black eyes gleamed as he studied her. 'Do you know how much I love you, Lucy Konstantinou?' he questioned softly.

'I think I've got a good idea. Just so long as you understand that the feeling is completely mutual, my darling. *S'agapo.*'

Noting Drakon's nod of contentment at her increasingly confident use of Greek, Lucy took the opportunity to look at the lavishly dressed guests who were milling around, drinking champagne beneath the fairy lights on the roof terrace of the Granchester Hotel as they waited for midnight.

'People seem to be having a good time,' she whispered. 'Don't you think?'

'Mmm,' he said, more concerned with dipping his head to brush his lips over the fall of her hair. 'The best time in the world, but of course—the moment I'm most looking forward to is when the fireworks are over and I can take you along to the penthouse suite to continue our own, very private party.'

'I'm looking forward to it, too,' said Lucy. 'Though I'm still not quite sure why we're staying the night here, when we only live down the road in Mayfair and have a car at our disposal.'

'I thought you might enjoy sleeping in the same bed we occupied on the first night of our honeymoon.' His mouth quirked. 'Or not sleeping, as the case may be.'

Lucy gave a contented sigh. 'You are a very romantic man, Drakon Konstantinou—as well as being an exceedingly sexy one.'

'I do my best. Because I gather that's what you like.' He whispered a fingertip over her waist. 'Am I right, *agape mou*?'

'Irrefutably,' she purred.

It was New Year's Eve and Drakon had thrown the party to end all parties to celebrate the discovery of a new oil field, which was being mooted as the biggest find in almost a century. And although Lucy sometimes mused that he really didn't need to earn any more money, the philanthropic arm of his empire had benefited in so many ways that she couldn't really complain. Her husband had taken over the entire hotel and the evening was—apparently—the hottest New Year ticket in town. Movers and shakers had flown in from pretty much every country in the world, as well as Hollywood actors and international sports stars, whose arrival was thrilling the growing crowds who had gathered outside behind the roped-off barriers.

Everyone who'd been at their wedding was here. Caro and her husband, as well as Lucy's two waitress friends, Judii and Jade. Patti and Tom were enjoying their first outing since the birth of their second child. And Amy was there too, with her not-so-new partner and proclaimed love of her life. Lucy smiled. When she and Drakon had decided to give their marriage another go, he had arranged a meeting with Amy. Gently, he'd explained to his business partner that the smokescreen of their close working relationship must necessarily end, because he intended travelling a lot less in future and spending more time with his family. Perhaps his words had galvanised her into action, for Amy had taken Michelle to meet her parents and told them she was in love. And in the end, perhaps her parents had recognised that their daughter's happiness was more important than a prejudice which they simply had to learn to let go of.

Lucy sighed as she stared up at a clear and starlit sky, which boded well for the eagerly awaited fireworks. What a long time ago their wedding seemed now, and how the years seemed to have flown by in

the time it took to blink your eye. Three whole years—
and back then she'd been so scared. A trembling mass
of nerves in her too-fancy dress as she'd walked down
the aisle towards a man she'd never stopped wanting.
She'd never for a moment imagined she'd get love and
devotion from someone who made no secret of having
a heart of stone. But Drakon's heart wasn't made of
stone, she'd realised. These days she would describe it
as a heart of gold—for he had learnt to show his love,
not just for her, but for their darling little Xander, who
flourished with each day which passed.

'Something is different about you,' Drakon said, his
velvety voice breaking into her thoughts.

Lucy turned her attention away from the star-
spangled sky to study the ruggedly handsome face
of her husband. 'What do you mean, *different*?'

He shrugged. 'You've been…thoughtful all day,'
he said slowly. 'And your face has a kind of radiance
about it which I've never seen before.'

How perceptive he was, Lucy thought, and savoured
the moment before telling him what she still couldn't
quite believe herself. 'I'm pregnant, my darling,' she
said softly. 'I'm having your baby, Drakon.'

He stared at her without comprehension and it was
several dazed moments before he could speak. 'But
you said—'

'That I had endometriosis and because of that I
was infertile, yes. That's what I was told. So when
I started getting symptoms of pregnancy, I thought
it must be something else. But when I saw the doctor this morning, she confirmed what I hardly dared

dream. She told me that miracles do happen, and this is ours, Drakon—our very own miracle.'

Drakon felt a lump rise in his throat and the hot spring of tears at the backs of his eyes as he put his arms around her and held her tightly against his beating heart. Not for the first time, he wondered what he had done to deserve a wife like Lucy. A woman who had been prepared to take on an orphaned baby and to love the helpless tot without condition, just as she loved him. She had forgiven her sometimes irascible husband his many transgressions and taught him the things in life which were truly important, and the most important of these was love.

'I discovered that myself on the day I met you again, my love,' he said gruffly. 'Although it took me a long time to realise it.'

She pulled back from him. 'Realise what?'

'That miracles really do come true. Sometimes they are right in front of your eyes…you just have to let your vision clear for long enough to see them properly.'

'Oh, Drakon,' she said shakily.

The first chime of Big Ben rang out and the guests began counting down the seconds towards midnight. Trumpets sounded and streamers were popped and people started to sing as the final chime faded away. But as one year merged seamlessly into the next and a kaleidoscope of fireworks exploded on the London skyline, nothing came close to the burst of joy in Drakon's heart as he held Lucy tightly in his arms, and kissed her.

* * * * *

CONFESSIONS
OF A PREGNANT
CINDERELLA

ABBY GREEN

This is for Austin, Gary and Billy.
You guys are my heart.

CHAPTER ONE

LAZARO SANCHEZ SURVEYED the glittering ballroom of one of Madrid's most exclusive hotels. A hotel that he owned. Satisfaction and anticipation coursed through his veins. This moment...was huge. His whole life had been building to this, to standing here in front of his peers.

But they hadn't always been his peers. These people wouldn't have recognised him as the semi-feral teenager who'd roamed and lived on the streets. Hustling to make a few euros by washing car windows at traffic lights; showing tourists how to beat the queues into museums and galleries; eating out of bins when he couldn't afford to buy food.

The familiar burn of injustice and rage burned low in his gut when he recalled those desperate days. He'd run away from his last foster home when the father had cornered Lazaro in the bedroom and started taking his trousers down.

Lazaro had jumped out of the first-floor window.

From the age of thirteen he'd fended for himself.

The cruel irony of it all was that Lazaro hadn't been orphaned, or abused by his parents so badly that he'd been removed from their care, like other kids who'd ended up in the foster homes. He'd been abandoned into the system by his parents. And, actually, his father was in this very room right now. Not that he would ever look him in the eye. Or admit he was his father—even under duress.

As for his mother, he'd only ever seen her a handful of times in his life, from a distance.

The reason for that was because Lazaro Sanchez was the illegitimate result of an affair between two members of two of Spain's oldest and most respected and revered families. The closest you could get to royalty without being royal.

The only way he'd found out about his parentage had been through a mixture of fluke and happenstance. A careless social worker had left his file unattended one day and he'd seen his birth certificate and memorised his parents' names. When he'd investigated them afterwards nothing had come up. They were fake names.

Then, while changing foster homes at the age of about twelve, he'd been dozing in the back of the car as two social workers had driven him to the new home. He could still remember seeing one of them glance behind, to check if he was sleeping, and then, as if she hadn't been able to sit on the information any longer, whisper to the other social worker the rumour about who his real parents were.

Lazaro had clamped his eyes shut completely and frozen solid in the back of the car. Even at that age he'd heard of the Torres family and the Salvadors. They were two of Spain's most important and wealthy dynasties, with lineages stretching back to medieval times.

When he'd had a chance he'd looked them up for more information. And even though it had been just a rumour he'd *known* as soon as he'd seen a picture of his father when he'd been Lazaro's age. They were mirror images. And he'd inherited his mother's unusual green eyes.

He'd taken to stalking the palatial properties belonging to the Torres family and the Salvadors in an exclusive suburb of Madrid. Watching them come and go. Seeing his half-siblings. One in particular was an older boy on his father's side—Gabriel Torres. For some reason, Lazaro had fixated on him...perhaps because they were relatively close in age.

One day he'd seen them all sitting in a restaurant in the

centre of Madrid, celebrating his half-brother Gabriel's birthday.

Lazaro had waited outside, and when they'd emerged— the women wearing designer dresses and dripping in diamonds, the men in bespoke suits—Lazaro had darted forward and planted himself in front of his father and Gabriel.

'I'm your son!' he'd announced, shaking with adrenalin as he'd looked up at the towering man, aware of his half-brother beside him, looking at him as if he was an alien.

It had all happened so fast. Men had appeared from nowhere and Lazaro had found himself face-down in the dirt in an alleyway beside the restaurant. His father had hauled him up by the hair and spat into his face.

'You are no son of mine—and if you ever come near me or my family again you will pay for it.'

That was when Lazaro's ambition had been born. The ambition to one day be in a position where he was *literally* touching shoulders with them. Where they would have to look him in the eye. Where he would taunt them with his presence—with the knowledge that he had thrived and survived in spite of their attempts to excise him from their family histories.

And here he was, in the same room as his father and his half-brother Gabriel—with whom he was embroiled in a bitter and ruthless battle to take over one of Madrid's oldest indoor market buildings and redevelop it into a new space.

His half-brother Gabriel still refused to acknowledge that Lazaro could be his brother even though—

'Lazaro?'

He looked to one side to see the reason why both his father, his half-brother and other peripheral members of both his birth families were all in the same room.

Leonora Flores de la Vega.

With her exquisitely beautiful face, long black hair, dark

grey eyes and a willowy body that curved in and out in all the right places, she was arguably one of the most beautiful women in Spain.

And one of the most well-connected.

Her family might have no money—in fact that was one of the reasons for the marriage—but their name was as old and venerated as the Torres or Salvador families. And that was priceless.

Hence the reason why Lazaro wanted to marry her. It would bring him another step closer to the inner circle that had always been shut to him, no matter how many millions he'd made. It would bring him another step closer to making his family squirm. Another step closer to ultimate acceptance.

'Are you all right?' she asked. 'You look very fierce.'

He forced a smile and held out a hand to Leonora. She slipped her hand into his and Lazaro closed his fingers around hers. *Nothing.* Not even a twinge of response. But then he wasn't marrying her for their chemistry. He was marrying her for something much more enduring. Securing his own legacy. Forcing those who would ignore him to acknowledge him and respect him. Finally.

'Yes, fine…just a little preoccupied.'

He saw her glance across the room to someone or something, and a faint tinge of colour came into her cheeks. She bit her lip.

'Are *you* okay?' Lazaro asked.

She always seemed so composed, unruffled, it was strange to see her suddenly look a little flustered. Distracted.

She looked back at him and smiled. 'Yes, I'm fine.'

He tightened his fingers around hers. 'I'm glad you agreed to marry me, Leonora. I think we can have a good marriage. I think we can be…happy.'

A shadow seemed to cross her face, and her smile

faltered for a second, but then she said brightly, 'Yes. I hope so.'

Lazaro realised at that moment that he hardly knew this woman. He'd sought her out because of who she was, and they'd dated a few times—chaste dates. He liked her. And it was no secret that her family were in dire financial straits. He'd seen an opportunity to silence the critics of his playboy reputation *and* move that bit closer to where he ultimately wanted to be.

When he'd suggested she marry him, and in so doing pay off her family's debts, she'd said yes.

He let go of Leonora's hand and slipped his arm around her back, resting a hand on her hip. An intimate move. A proprietorial move. *And still nothing.* Not even a trip in his pulse.

He told himself again that attraction wasn't everything. Lust was a base emotion. No one in this milieu married for lust. He was living proof that they married for other, far more practical reasons and kept their lust hidden. Secret. He wasn't like them. He had more control.

Suddenly his conscience pricked hard and a picture formed in his mind. A memory, to be precise. A memory that had been haunting him with increasing and irritating frequency. As if the closer he got to making a commitment to Leonora the louder his conscience got.

Which was ridiculous. He had no reason to feel guilty.

Don't you? asked a snide voice. *So why can't you stop thinking about her?*

'Her' was a woman he'd met just over three months ago. In another city. Before he'd become engaged to Leonora. A petite woman. With long, unruly red hair. Freckles covering nearly every inch of her pale skin. Small plump breasts with tight pink nipples. A surprisingly curvy body. Russet curls at the juncture of her legs. He'd spread her there, opening her up to him, her glistening folds...

'Lazaro—'

He looked at Leonora, shocked at the vividness of that memory and the effect it was having on his body. Which was galling when the stunningly beautiful flesh-and-blood woman beside him couldn't arouse even a heightened sense of awareness.

She was smiling, but he could see it was forced. 'You're hurting me.'

Instantly Lazaro became aware of his hand, digging into the flesh at her hip. He relaxed. 'I'm sorry.'

A sense of shame engulfed him. And anger. That woman had been no one. His conscience pricked. Okay, so he'd wanted her more than he could remember wanting any other woman in a long time, but it had just been a moment out of time. In another city. Where people didn't see him and whisper behind his back.

'Isn't that Lazaro Sanchez? They say he used to forage in the streets for food. Didn't he used to be in a gang?'

That woman—the stranger—hadn't had the faintest clue who he was. And it had been refreshing. It had made the intense and immediate attraction between them even more compelling. And explosive.

She'd been a virgin. *A virgin.* The words resounded in his head, still having the power to shock him. He hadn't expected that. And it had led to the most erotic experience of his life...

Leonora was handing Lazaro a glass of champagne now, and he shook his head slightly, as much to rid himself of unwanted and disturbing memories as anything else.

'Your advisors are making motions that it's time to make the announcement. Ready?'

Lazaro excised all thoughts, memories and images of that woman from his mind and looked into the eyes of his future wife. The woman who would open the last doors for him into a world that had been denied him from the day of his birth.

'Yes,' he said, clinking his glass to hers with a melodic chime. 'Let's do it.'

Skye O'Hara was feeling nauseous. *Literally.* And she also felt sick with nerves. Not a good combination. A cold clammy sweat lay over her skin, and it had only got worse since she'd slipped into the jaw-droppingly beautiful ballroom, with its gold-panelled walls and massive crystal chandeliers.

She'd never seen so many beautiful *tall* people in her life. Or such finery. Glittering sheaths of dresses. Tuxedoes. Acres of smooth honey-hued skin, making her feel even more pale and wan. Golden lights everywhere. It even smelled exclusive. The kind of scent that couldn't be bottled. It was wealth.

She'd dressed in a white shirt and black skirt to try and fade in with the staff. Put her unruly hair up in a tidy bun on her head. No way would she have had the wherewithal even to remotely attempt to look like one of these people. For a start she was about a foot too small, and the only redhead in sight. And she had freckles. A physical imperfection people like this would eliminate on sight, no doubt.

She craned her head, going up on tiptoe to try and see further into the room. To see where *he* was.

Her hand went to her belly where the reason for much of her nausea resided.

And then she saw him in the distance. How could she not? He stood head and shoulders even above these giants. His dark blond hair was still just the right side of too long, and still messy. Stubble emphasised the hard line of his jaw. And his mouth…

She couldn't see it from here but she could remember

it. Sculpted and firm. *Hot.* She remembered how it had felt on her bare skin…closing over her…

A gap formed in the crowd and now she could see all of him.

Her heart pounded as she drank in every long and lean inch of his six-foot-three-inch frame. Tall and broad-shouldered. Golden. Gorgeous. The sexiest man she'd ever seen. The first man she'd ever thought of as *sexy.* And consequently the first man she'd ever slept with.

He was wearing a white tuxedo jacket with a white bowtie. Black trousers. He stood out effortlessly…a little bit different from everyone else. As if he couldn't contain some elemental part of himself even in this civilised milieu.

Elemental. That was what it had been like that night. Wild. Visceral. Unbelievable. Unforgettable.

Skye's hand tightened on her belly. Unforgettable in more ways than one.

A woman came up to her with a stern look on her face. Staff, not a guest, wearing a black uniform dress. Just as Skye was about to panic that she'd been caught out, the woman handed her a tray full of glasses of champagne and told her to stop wasting time. Relief flooded Skye. Her disguise had worked.

She took a deep breath and started to move closer through the crowd to where *he* stood. Lazaro Sanchez. She'd looked him up on the internet the day after their night together—and nearly had a heart attack when she'd realised that he was a seriously wealthy and influential financier, with an extensive real-estate portfolio. A household name in his native Spain.

And he was also a renowned playboy. There had been acres of photos of him with a veritable stream of beautiful women. It had stung more than a little to know that she'd been naive enough to fall for his smooth charm. That what had happened between them must have merely been a blip in his normal routine. A forgettable night among many. And it had stung even more that she didn't resemble any of his usual women, so evidently he'd only slept with her because she'd been a bit...different.

And now... Now he was about to announce his engagement to the most beautiful woman in the world. Skye could see her standing beside Lazaro, with his arm around her waist.

They looked good together—both tall, lean. Her dark hair was sleek and pulled back, and she wore a red strapless dress. A slim classic column that clung to every perfectly proportioned curve and oozed sophistication and elegance.

For a second Skye faltered. She put the tray down on a nearby table for fear of dropping it. Should she have come here to do this?

She lamented again the fact that she hadn't been able to get to Lazaro before this event, but it would have been easier to get a message to the Pope. She'd been blocked and shut out at every turn.

What right did she have to interrupt this momentous moment? The announcement of his engagement to this Glamazon?

Because you're pregnant with his baby and he needs to know, reminded a cool voice in her head.

Just then there was the sound of someone tapping on glass, which cut through the buzz of chat in the room. Everyone fell silent and turned to where Lazaro and his fiancée were standing on a raised dais.

Skye felt even more sick now. Had he been involved with her when they'd slept together three months ago? Had he known he would be getting engaged?

She saw the cordon of security men near the couple. Fearsome-looking individuals. Skye could see what would happen—they'd announce their news, and suddenly they'd be thronged, and then they'd be whisked off to some secret location.

This was her only chance to get his attention. She had to take it. She couldn't have it on her conscience that he didn't know she was pregnant. That their one *amazing* night together had had repercussions.

And his fiancée deserved to know the kind of man she was marrying, if they had already been involved while he'd been seducing Skye in another city.

Lazaro cleared his throat. He savoured the few seconds before he spoke, aware of every eye turned their way. His father, pretending he didn't know this was his illegitimate son, about to make an announcement. His half-brother Gabriel was scowling and looking even more brooding and forbidding than he usually did.

'Thank you all for coming here this evening…'

Lazaro looked at Leonora and smiled. She wasn't looking at him, though, she was looking into the crowd, slightly transfixed. There was a flush in her cheeks. He exerted a tiny bit of pressure on her waist and she glanced at him and smiled. But it was strained.

Lazaro ignored the prickling sensation over his skin. Last-minute jitters.

'I know it's hardly a surprise to many of you, as it's already appeared in *some* papers…' here there was a ripple of laughter '…but it gives me great pleasure to formally announce that Leonora Flores de la Vega has consented to be my wife. Invitations to the wedding will be sent out shortly.'

Lazaro lifted his glass of champagne, about to make a toast to his future wife, when a voice shattered the expectant hush.

'Wait! Stop!'

It took Lazaro a second to realise that people weren't

looking at them any more. They were all looking to his left-hand side at something. Or someone.

He glanced around to see that two of his security team were holding back a woman. A petite, red-haired woman. Who looked familiar. *Too* familiar. He noticed the details dispassionately, as shock flooded his system to see her *here*, not just in his memory.

Her blue eyes were huge and slightly wild-looking. Her hair was up in a bun, with tendrils of red and gold falling down around her heart-shaped face. Determined chin. Small straight nose. Full mouth currently in a thin line. White shirt…black skirt.

He could see the white of her bra under the material. The press of her breasts against the fabric. He'd cupped those breasts in his hands, rubbed his thumbs across her deeply sensitive nipples. She'd shuddered against him when he'd touched her there.

Heat flooded his body.

Suddenly the shock galvanised him into action. He let go of Leonora and made a move towards the woman, as if he knew what was about to happen and thought he could stop it. But, no. Before he could reach her, her voice rang out again—loud and clear. The fact that she spoke in Spanish was a detail he didn't even absorb fully.

'You need to know something. I'm pregnant. With your child.'

For a long moment nothing seemed to happen. There was a shocked stillness in the air and everyone was frozen. Even the security men holding her arms seemed to go slack.

She was looking directly at Lazaro, and suddenly it was as if everyone else had disappeared and it was just them in the room.

She said in a quieter voice, in English, 'It's true. I'm pregnant…and it's yours.'

Skye O'Hara. That was her name. She'd been a waitress in the restaurant where he'd had dinner after a business meeting in Dublin. He'd noticed her as soon as he'd gone in—something about her, the way she moved and interacted with people, had caught his attention. Which was unusual, because nothing much distracted Lazaro these days. But there had been something very refreshing about her. Open. Unaffected. Natural.

She'd been dressed much as she was now. Her clothes utterly banal. Not designed in any way to entice a man. And yet she had. With her petite figure and soft curves.

She'd served him. Pulling a pen out of the bun on the top of her head, flipping over her orders pad to a new page before looking at him. And that had been the moment. *Zing.* Lazaro had felt it like a thunderbolt. Instant heat and sexual awareness.

And so had she, judging by the flush on her cheeks and the way her eyes had widened.

Lazaro's razor-sharp brain kicked into gear. There were members of the press in this room. His doing. To ensure maximum coverage of his moment of triumph. If he instructed his men to kick this woman out on the street the press would hunt her down, and he could already see the headlines and the lurid sob-story.

He had no doubt she was just capitalising on the fact that she'd realised who he was. She was on the make. He needed to contain this situation, defuse it and salvage what he could of this evening.

He put down his glass and stepped down from the dais and went over to her, taking her arm in his hand. It felt very slender. 'What the hell do you think you're doing here?'

She went white. He ignored the prick of his conscience. He'd forgotten how petite she was.

She stuttered. 'I came…to…to tell you… I couldn't reach you any other way…we didn't…you didn't…we didn't exchange numbers…'

He'd given her his card when he'd asked her to join him for a drink. But she'd left it in the wastebasket in the hotel room the following morning.

Her show of independence the morning after—her determination to go even after he'd offered to order up breakfast—had obviously been an act.

He could still see her, backing away in her skinny jeans and a loose jumper falling off one shoulder. Her hair down and wild. She'd looked like an art student. She'd looked thoroughly bedded. And he'd wanted her *again*.

He'd just come out of the shower with a towel around his waist to find her leaving. 'Where are you going?' he'd asked.

She'd looked up as she'd slipped on her shoes. He could still recall how her eyes had devoured him, lingering on his chest. Making him hard again.

'I should leave... It's okay. I know how these things go. I know this was just a one-off. You're not from here.' She'd waved a hand at the very rumpled bed and a flush had tinged her cheeks. 'And I really wasn't expecting this...'

She'd been a virgin.

Lazaro had felt a moment of panic at the thought of her slipping out through the door and never seeing her again. Impulsively he'd said, 'Stay. I'll order breakfast. There's no need to rush.'

She'd looked torn for a moment. And then she'd shaken her head. 'No, I have things to do. I have to leave.'

She'd turned around and walked to the door and then stopped and looked back over her shoulder. Her hair had been like a bright flame down her back.

'Just...thank you. I wasn't expecting what happened to happen. I wasn't expecting to meet someone like you. But it was lovely.'

And then she'd slipped out through the door and Lazaro had stood there, stunned and very aroused, for long minutes. *'It was lovely.'* Not something any woman had ever said to him before after a night of passion so intense he was surprised they hadn't burnt the suite to ashes.

That memory mocked him now. It had all been an act. Clearly. And this had been her endgame. He'd been an idiot.

He took his hand off her arm and spoke to his men. 'Take her to the office and keep her there until I give further instructions.'

He didn't look at her again, just turned away towards the crowd. And, to Leonora, who was looking at him with wide eyes, cheeks leached of colour. He stepped back up onto the dais, not sure which fire to put out first.

He faced the crowd and held up his hands, forcing a smile. 'I'm sorry for that interruption. It's being dealt with.'

He was about to say that there were no grounds for what she'd said—*'I'm pregnant...and it's yours'*—but then he recalled that exquisite moment when he'd been poised to thrust inside her tempting body and he'd realised he wasn't protected.

'Are you protected?' he'd asked her.

She'd said breathily, 'It's fine...please, just don't stop.'

Self-recrimination blasted him. *She could be telling the truth.*

He looked at Leonora, who was backing away now, staring at him as if he was a monster. He stretched out a hand. 'Leonora, please...let me explain.'

She stopped moving. Her face was pale. 'Is it true?'

Lazaro couldn't deny that it *might* be true, so he said nothing.

Leonora interpreted his silence. She shook her head. 'I can't agree to marry you—not now.' She cast a wild-eyed look around them and then said with quiet desperation, 'How could you do this to me? In front of all of these people?'

She turned and stepped down from the dais and all but ran to the nearest exit.

There was no sound at all for a long moment. And then came a slow hand-clap from the crowd.

Lazaro turned around to see his half-brother Gabriel moving forward through the crowd. Clapping. A smirk on his face. Lazaro's hands bunched into fists at his sides.

'I really didn't expect this evening to be so entertaining, Sanchez. I have to hand it to you. If anyone knows how to make a reputation sink even lower into the gutter it's you. But, frankly, I've better things to be doing than witnessing your lurid domestic dramas.'

Before Lazaro could articulate a response Gabriel strode out of the room, in the same direction as Leonora. And, as much as he wanted to go after him and punch that smirk off his face, Lazaro knew he couldn't. Not here, not now.

He turned back to face his audience. The crowd *he* had assembled to share this moment of ultimate acceptance. No one would meet his eye except one man. His father, at the back of the room. He had a mocking look on his face as if to say, *You tried and you failed to be one of us.*

This moment, which should have been the pinnacle of his success, had turned into a farce. All because of a woman. *And himself.* Because for one night he'd let himself be ruled by lust and had thrown caution to the wind.

He should have known, after the life he'd lived, that he would suffer the consequences for any moment of weakness.

These people could afford to be weak. But not him. Not ever him. And he'd just proved that his desires were as base as theirs…that he didn't, in fact, have more control.

Skye sat in a square box of a room, More like a storage cupboard, really. The burly man who had put her in here had just brought her small knapsack and her coat from where she'd left them in the cloakroom. She'd come straight here from the airport.

The adrenalin was still pumping through her system. Okay, so she'd got her message across. She hadn't intended on the dramatics, but it had been impossible to try and contact Lazaro Sanchez from Dublin. He had more rings of security and assistants than a head of state. And at every step she'd been stonewalled.

It hadn't helped that she'd thrown away the card he'd handed her when he'd asked her to join him for a drink. She'd not seen the point in keeping it, and hadn't wanted to torture herself by knowing she had his phone number.

She'd been searching on the internet for another way to try and contact him when she'd seen the news that he was due to announce his engagement at an exclusive gathering at the Esmeralda Hotel—one of Madrid's finest.

Before she'd lost her nerve she'd booked a cheap return flight. She'd travelled in her work uniform, hoping that it might help her blend in with staff. Which had worked only too well.

He was to be *engaged*. Yet he'd slept with her.

She'd always thought she was a good judge of character, but evidently lust had rewired her normal instincts that night three months ago.

He'd asked her to stay for breakfast the following morning and she'd been so tempted. He'd been standing there in nothing but a short towel. Massive chest bare and still damp from the shower. Dark hair dusting his pectorals and then narrowing into a line that dissected his six-pack before disappearing under the towel.

Skye stood up, suddenly restless. And hot. Thankfully the nausea had subsided slightly. Her morning sickness was acute at the moment, and mainly in the early part of the day, but the doctor had told her it should subside soon. If she was lucky.

Pregnant. She stopped pacing and put her hand on her belly.

She'd tried to contact her mother to no avail. She was somewhere in India at an ashram, with little or no communications. Not an unusual scenario. But even without her mother's advice Skye hadn't felt a moment's hesitation about keeping the baby.

Even though, she'd always wanted a different life for herself than she'd had as a child. Being dragged all around Europe as her mother had followed one whim after another. Or one lover after another. She'd had Skye when she was eighteen, and most of the time Skye had felt more like the adult than her bohemian but very lovable mother. Yet here she was, only a few years older than her mother had been, and quite possibly about to become a single mother too.

She'd always vowed that if and when she had children she would be in a committed relationship and their existence wouldn't be rootless. It would be secure and stable.

Suddenly the door opened again and Skye whirled around, her heart jumping into her throat. But it wasn't *him*—it was the burly security guard.

'You can come with me now.'

As much as Skye might have preferred not to go, she knew she had to see this through.

The man led her to a staff elevator and they ascended to the top floor. The doors opened onto an unremarkable corridor and the guard opened an unremarkable door. He led her into a small utilitarian kitchen and then into a very plush suite, with jaw-dropping floor-to-ceiling windows and views over Madrid.

This must be the penthouse suite, and she'd just been brought through the service kitchen.

Her face grew hot with humiliation.

The man led her to a vast open-plan space, with couches dotted around glass coffee tables. Vast canvases of modern art hung on walls. Low lighting imbued the space with golden light but made it no less intimidating.

And there he was. With his back to her. No jacket. Just his shirt and trousers.

He turned around, but Skye couldn't see his expression from where she was. Probably a good thing. She could see that his top shirt button was open and his bow-tie hung askew, as if pulled apart roughly.

He dismissed the guard with a few curt words and Skye heard the door snick shut behind her.

And then, in a lethally soft voice which was worse than if he'd shouted at her, he said, 'What the hell do you think you're playing at?'

CHAPTER TWO

SKYE DID HER best not to show how intimidated she was. She walked further into the room, even though her legs felt suspiciously rubbery.

Lazaro Sanchez looked unbelievably tall and imposing. He fitted the vast space around him and the spectacular views of night-time Madrid through the windows.

Had his shoulders always been so broad? His legs so long?

She could see that he was furious. Livid. A million miles from the charming urbane man who had seduced her that night.

You were a very active participant, pointed out a snarky voice in her head.

She could see a muscle pop in his jaw, as if he was gritting it. But in spite of his palpable anger she could still feel his affect on her. As if a million nerve-endings were firing to life. Her whole body humming with awareness. Liquid electricity running through her veins.

When she'd met him in the bar of that Dublin hotel after he'd issued her an invitation to join him, she'd said, 'I don't do this sort of thing…meet random men in bars. And I haven't come here for something…anything…' She'd blushed profusely, feeling as gauche as a sixteen-year-old.

He'd just smiled sexily and pulled out a chair for her. 'Let's just have a drink, hmm?'

That felt like a very long time ago now.

She swallowed. 'I'm sorry…about downstairs. I wouldn't have done it like that if I'd been able to contact you through normal channels. I did try calling your offices—several of them, in fact—but no one would pass on a message. Not when I said it was personal.'

'Not good enough.' He folded his arms.

Skye flushed. 'When I read the news about your engagement announcement, I thought it would be the best opportunity to get close enough to tell you.'

He arched a brow. 'How convenient that this *opportunity* also maximised your impact by ensuring you'd be splashed all over the tabloids.'

Skye frowned. 'Tabloids?'

Lazaro's mouth thinned. 'Don't pretend ignorance now, after that stunt. You knew damn well the press would be there.'

Her conscience pricked when she thought of the look of horror and shock on his fiancée's face. 'I thought… I made a judgement that the only way I'd get your attention would be to do…what I did.'

Lazaro was grim. 'Well, you have my attention. You assured me after our night together that you understood "how these things go". Were you lying?'

'No.' Skye choked out, but her conscience pricked.

She could recall how tempted she'd been to indulge the fantasy and stay a little longer the following morning. But the memory of her mother falling in and out of lust and love had come back to haunt her, and Skye had been too terrified to give in to the urge to linger, when everyone knew one-night stands never went anywhere.

'I meant what I said that morning. Obviously I wasn't aware that…that something had happened.'

Namely, a baby.

Now he sounded accusing. 'I asked if you were protected and you said, "It's fine". You lied.'

Skye bit her lip. All she could remember was the desperation she'd felt in that moment for him to join their bodies. For him not to stop. She'd never been so desperate for anything in her life. But, even so, she hadn't completely lost her mind.

She shook her head. 'I really did think it would be okay. I thought I was at a safe place in my cycle.'

He made a dismissive noise. 'How do I even know you're pregnant? You don't *look* pregnant.'

Skye didn't know whether to be flattered or dismayed that her growing belly wasn't obvious. She put her free hand there. 'I am pregnant. I had my three-month scan last week, to confirm that everything was okay. That's why I waited till now... Sometimes things happen...'

There was a heavy silence as he digested that, and then he said, 'How can you be certain I'm the father?'

Skye was immediately indignant. 'I've had sex *once*— with you. No one else.'

They'd had sex twice that night, actually. But Lazaro wasn't about to issue that reminder, because those X-rated memories were far too vivid and recent as it was.

He saw a dull flush rise up under her pale skin and felt a corresponding jump in his pulse. His blood was running hot, but he told himself it was anger, not lust.

He looked at the small pale hand that rested over her still flat belly. It was almost impossible to accept the revelation that she was pregnant. *With his child.*

As someone who had been abandoned at birth by his own parents, and who had been thrown around the foster care system most of his young life, he had a jaundiced view of the bond between parents and children to say the least. And yet the thought of her having that scan without him made him feel disturbingly conflicted. As if he'd missed out on something.

He'd always vowed that if he did have children he would do his best by them and not abandon them. He would give them a better life than he had known. But he certainly hadn't expected to have to think about it yet.

Even with Leonora he would have expected at least a few years to elapse before they talked about children.

He was still reeling from what had happened. The sudden and swift fall from grace.

Ha! sneered an inner voice. He'd come close to grace— that was all. Maybe it was something that would elude him for ever. Like the ultimate acceptance he craved.

He'd gone after Leonora but she'd disappeared, and he'd known it would be futile anyway. She'd told him it was over, and in her world that kind of public humiliation couldn't be forgiven. It really was over. And so he'd come up here. To try and deal with the situation. With *her.*

Skye put her bag and coat down at her feet. She straightened up and her expression was contrite. Before he could stop himself Lazaro was struck again by her natural beauty. The scattering of freckles across her nose and cheeks. *Innocent.*

She said, 'Look, I promise I didn't intend to tell you like this. I really believed it was the only way. I didn't mean to upset your fiancée.'

Lazaro didn't believe this faux sincerity for a second. 'She's not my fiancée any more. The engagement is over.'

Skye seemed to go even paler. 'If she loves you then maybe you can work this out—'

Lazaro emitted an involuntary laugh and held up a hand, stopping her words. 'Love? There is no such thing as love. We weren't marrying for love. That's not how this works.'

Skye looked genuinely perplexed. 'Then what were you marrying for?'

He shrugged minutely, this line of questioning making him uncomfortable. 'Because it made sense. Because she would have helped me to get where I need to be and I would have helped her.'

'That sounds so…cold.'

'I would have said efficient, myself. Marriages based on such nebulous notions as love rarely last.'

Hesitantly she asked, 'Were you together when we… met?'

'No. It happened…just afterwards.'

Lazaro felt even more uncomfortable when he recalled how the intensity of his experience with Skye had left him feeling hungry for more, but also very wary. He was not looking for grand passion in his life. He was looking for acceptance and respect. And he needed a woman who would help him achieve it. A woman from his father's world and the right side of it.

Leonora Flores de la Vega had already been on his radar—he'd seen her at a few events and had always been intrigued by her aloof manner. The way she always seemed slightly apart from the crowd. It had resonated with something inside him—perhaps the part that was still ostracised despite his success.

But he had to concede now that meeting Skye had spurred him on to ask Leonora out. As if that night with Skye had spooked him. Made him realise that he had a voracious hunger inside him that he'd never acknowledged before. He'd wanted to forget that he'd acted totally out of character for a moment. Put their extraordinary chemistry down to a fluke happenstance.

But it hadn't been a fluke because he could feel it again now. An inexorable pull to this woman. A sizzling in his blood. A growing urgency to touch her again. Damn her.

'Oh.'

Skye looked away for a moment and the irritation he was feeling at this woman's effect on him showed in his curt response. 'What does that mean? *Oh.*'

With visible reluctance she looked at him again. 'Well… I'm very different to her. You looked good together. I can see why you chose her to be your wife.'

It was as if she could see into his mind. His skin prickled. She was right. Skye O'Hara couldn't be more different from the very tall and svelte Leonora. But her petite curvy body and fresh-faced prettiness had a far earthier appeal to his libido than Leonora's cool elegance. Leonora had never connected with that part of him.

In fact Skye was like no other woman he'd ever been with, and yet she'd been the one with whom he'd connected most viscerally.

She said, 'Well, maybe this has done her a favour. Everyone deserves to be loved.'

Inexplicably, Lazaro felt an ache deep inside him. He quashed it brutally. 'Don't be so ridiculously sentimental. *You* caused this to happen by interrupting a private and exclusive gathering.'

'Not that private or exclusive if the press were there,' she pointed out.

Lazaro ground his teeth. 'We are not here to debate the issue.'

She bent down then, and picked up her bag and coat. 'No, we're not. I came to tell you that I'm pregnant, and now that I have I'll leave.'

She moved as if to walk out and then stopped, looking around at the maze of doors leading off in different directions.

She turned around, sheepish. 'Can you tell me the way out, please?'

Lazaro shook his head, as much in negation of her question as to check if he was hearing her correctly. But she looked deadly serious.

Remembering how quickly she'd slipped out of his grasp once before, he went over and caught her arm, leading her over to a sofa, saying grimly, 'You don't get to deliver a bombshell, wreck my engagement and then walk out the door like nothing's happened. Sit down. You're not going anywhere.'

Skye should have known it wouldn't be so easy. Of course a man like Lazaro Sanchez—so important that it was impossible to get in touch with him like any normal mortal—wouldn't just let this go. And she had to concede that this had to be a huge shock for him. As much as it had been for her, and she'd had three months to absorb it now.

As if it was paining him to ask, he said, 'Do you want something? Tea? Coffee?'

Skye appreciated the fact that he patently didn't want her there but was being forced to be civil. 'Maybe a glass of water?'

She was also starving. This was usually the best time of day for her to eat, when she could keep it down, but she didn't think Lazaro was about to order her a club sandwich and fries—her current craving.

He came back from the drinks cabinet and handed her a glass of water, which she accepted gratefully. He had a glass of something for himself that looked like brandy or whisky.

He went and stood in front of one of the windows and Skye felt awed. He really did look like a titan. Master of his universe.

'You must have known who I was,' he said.

Skye looked at his back. 'Excuse me?'

He turned around. 'You knew who I was and you targeted me.'

Skye stood up, incensed, water splashing unnoticed from her glass to the rug on the floor. 'I beg your pardon? You walked into *my* restaurant and sat in *my* section.'

Now he flushed, and a bolt of heat went straight to

Skye's groin because it reminded her of his flushed face after they'd made love. He'd looked so...*sexy*.

She sat back down again. 'You didn't tell me your name until you gave me your card and asked me to meet you at your hotel.' She winced inwardly. It sounded so sordid when she said it like that.

'You would have had time to look me up then—maybe that's why you decided to meet me...when you knew it was worth it.'

'Maybe I didn't look you up,' Skye shot back. 'Maybe I decided to go because you were the sexiest man I'd ever met and I knew if I didn't go I'd regret it.'

She stopped and bit her lip, aghast at what had just tumbled out of her mouth.

She lifted her chin. 'I will admit that I looked you up the following day. And then I realised that you were... someone.'

It was a ridiculously ineffectual way to describe a man who had become a self-made millionaire by the time he was twenty-five after setting up his own hedge fund. He'd since become a billionaire, by diversifying into the real estate market. His signature move was buying up old decrepit buildings in up-and-coming areas and restoring them.

'So that's when you decided to take advantage of the situation?'

Skye stood up again. 'Unbelievable as it might seem to you, my life plan wasn't actually to get pregnant at the age of twenty-two.'

'Oh? And what was it then? To become the manager of that restaurant?'

'That's not fair. You have no idea who I am or what I want.'

Lazaro took a step towards her and said with an infuriatingly smug tone, 'On the contrary. I think we established pretty effectively what you wanted that night.'

Skye's cheeks were burning now, her hand gripping the glass hard. 'There were two of us in that room, and as I re-call it any *wanting* was pretty mutual.'

He gritted his jaw at that. 'Why did you really come?'

'To tell you. Don't you want to know that you're going to be a father?'

He studied her for such a long moment that Skye fought not to squirm, and then he shook his head.

'You're not just here to impart this news out of the good-ness of your heart.'

Skye struggled to hold on to her temper. 'You are being incredibly negative. Would you really have preferred that I didn't tell you? That you had a child out in the world that you knew nothing about?'

To her surprise he blanched slightly at that, and then his face became shuttered.

'*If* you are pregnant, and *if* the baby is mine, then of course I want to know about it. I'll admit it's not something I was prepared to deal with quite yet, but no child of mine will want for the lack of a father.'

His eyes glowed with an intensity that caught at Skye in-side. She realised then that she hadn't seen anything about his parents in the information she'd found about him online, and she wondered about that now. But before she could say anything else a wave of dizziness took her by surprise and she swayed on the spot.

Instantly he was at her side, taking the glass out of her grip, a hand around her arm. 'What is it? You've gone as white as a sheet.'

She was trembling. 'I think I need to eat something...'

'When was the last time you ate?'

Skye just wanted to sit down. 'Breakfast?'

If you could call a banana and a croissant that had later made its reappearance in the airport toilet breakfast.

Lazaro made a rude sound and led Skye over to a chair

to sit down. He handed her the water. 'What do you want to eat?'

She hated being weak and vulnerable like this. She'd wanted to come and face Lazaro, give him the news and then walk away with her head held high, knowing she'd done the right thing.

'Maybe a sandwich? And some fries?'

He went over to a phone and made a call.

When he came back Skye said, 'Thank you. I'm sorry. I really didn't intend to cause such an upset and I didn't intend taking up your time like this.'

He looked at her and put his hands on his hips—which only drew Skye's attention to that lean waist.

'So you were going to come, drop your bombshell and then leave?'

Skye winced at his thunderous expression. 'I just wanted to let you know. I don't expect anything from you. Maybe once the news has died down you can repair things with your fiancée…' She saw his expression darken even more and corrected herself. 'Sorry, *ex*-fiancée.'

He dismissed that with a wave of his hand. 'I told you— Leonora won't have anything to do with me after this.'

In fairness, Skye had to admit she had looked like a nice person. A person who didn't deserve to be upset in public like that.

Her insides cramped with remorse. She hadn't handled this very well at all.

Just then a chiming sound rang through the room, and Lazaro sent her a dark look before he went to the door. He came back with a tray. On it was a plate covered with a silver dome.

'Come into the kitchen.'

Skye dutifully followed Lazaro, trying not to notice the sexy athleticism of his stride. Or feel hurt that he was going to take her into that utilitarian kitchen to eat—probably for fear she'd drop crumbs all over his pristine suite.

He must have been staying here in order to make the announcement. Perhaps he'd even planned on spending the night here with his fiancée. Celebrating their engagement. It was certainly romantic enough, with its stunning views of Madrid laid out around it.

Then Skye stopped on the threshold of a kitchen she hadn't seen before. It certainly wasn't the one she'd been led through. This one was massive, and had state-of-the-art appliances and a sleek modern finish. There was a dining table and chairs by one window. Lazaro was putting the tray down and taking off the silver dome to reveal a very fancy-looking sandwich and fries.

Her mouth watered. She went over and sat down.

'I thought I came up through the kitchen?'

Lazaro looked slightly discomfited. 'I asked them to bring you up that way to avoid the paparazzi.'

'Oh.'

She said *'oh'* a lot. Lazaro watched, half-fascinated, as Skye tucked into the sandwich and fries with little self-consciousness. Watching a woman eat, he realised, felt like a curiously intimate thing to do. Especially when most of the women he spent time with chased a lettuce leaf around their plates.

He got another glass of sparkling water and put it down on the table. She glanced at him and wiped her mouth. Her cheeks were tinged pink as she said thank you.

They'd gone pink like that when their eyes had met in that small restaurant near his hotel in Dublin. And they'd gone even pinker when he'd asked to her join him there for a nightcap when she finished work.

She'd said *Oh* then too.

'Oh… Wow… I don't think that's a good idea.'

'Why not?'

'Because I don't know you. You could be anyone.'

He'd handed her a card from his jacket pocket. A platinum-embossed card, with his name and contact details. He'd said, 'It's not proof I'm not a serial killer, but I can assure you I'm not. I'm just asking you to meet me for a drink at the bar…a chance to get to know one another a little better.'

She'd looked at him with those huge blue eyes that seemed to hide nothing. 'But what's the point?' she'd asked.

Lazaro had surprised himself by saying, 'Haven't you ever done anything totally spontaneous for no good reason but just because you want to?'

He'd also surprised himself with how much he'd wanted her to say *yes*. He'd expected her to jump at the invitation— as most women would—but she'd seemed genuinely torn.

Eventually she'd said, 'Okay…maybe.'

And so he'd sat in that hotel bar, waiting for a woman. And for the first and only time in his life he hadn't known if she'd show up.

And then she had.

He could still recall seeing her standing in the doorway, in skinny jeans and that tatty jumper, half-falling off her shoulder. Holding a slouchy bag. It should have been the moment he'd realised he'd gone a bit crazy, but her long red hair had been down, and tumbling wildly over one shoulder, and an intense hunger had bitten into him so acutely that he hadn't even been able to stand to greet her.

'Thank you for that.'

Lazaro broke out of his reverie and saw Skye pushing the now empty plate away from her. He couldn't recall ever seeing a woman actually finish her food.

'Where are you staying?' he asked.

She went pinker and avoided his eye. 'I hadn't actually got as far as booking anywhere. I saw a hostel at the train station when I came in from the airport, I'm sure I can get a room there.'

Lazaro's gaze narrowed on her, his voice heavy with sarcasm. 'You didn't plan on staying and you've booked no accommodation? Did you even book a return flight? Or were you hoping that perhaps this little stunt might induce me to take you into my bed again, where you could ensure you became pregnant?'

Skye had been avoiding his eye, embarrassed at having been exposed in her lack of planning for this, but now her head snapped around so quickly she almost got whiplash.

For a long moment she couldn't speak, she was so incensed. And then she stood up, trembling with emotion. 'You are the most unbelievably cynical person I've ever met. I'm not here to fleece you, or to seduce you, Lazaro. I couldn't care less about your wealth or your fancy hotel suite—'

'Apartment.'

'What?'

'This is my apartment. I own the hotel.'

'Oh.'

He owns the hotel. Of course he does.

Suddenly feeling overwhelmed, Skye made a move back to the living area, searching for her bag and coat.

'Where are you going?'

She found them and picked them up. She turned around. 'I'm going to go and find somewhere to stay. My return flight is early in the morning—because, as I told you, I'd just planned on giving you this information. *Not* staying. Leaving. Which I'm going to do now. Goodbye, Lazaro.'

Before she could turn to go Lazaro came and stood in front of her. He was shaking his head.

'You're not going anywhere. You're staying here tonight and then we'll discuss where to go from here tomorrow.'

Skye's head was feeling fuzzy from tiredness. 'But I'm due at work tomorrow night…'

'If you are pregnant with my child—and let's say I give you the benefit of the doubt until we can prove the baby is mine with a DNA test—then you'll be staying right here in Spain.'

Skye's mouth opened and closed. Opened again. 'That's crazy. You can't order me to stay here.'

'*If* you're carrying my child, as you claim you are, then, yes, I have a right to be involved in its future—and in yours too.'

Skye felt panicky. 'In its *future*. When he or she is born. Anything could happen between now and then.'

'And in the meantime you're going to run yourself ragged waiting on tables, staying in hostels and living in God knows what kind of place.' He frowned. 'Where *do* you live?'

Skye felt defensive. 'In a perfectly nice basement apartment in Dublin.'

She felt guilty when she thought of the mould on the damp walls of her bedroom. And the malfunctioning gas cooker. And the fact that her area turned into a kind of war zone at night. But she was fine. They knew her face so they left her alone.

Lazaro made a sound as if he could read her thoughts. 'If you're working as a waitress then I know what kind of place and area you can afford, and I don't want the mother of my child putting herself or my child at risk.'

Skye's hand automatically went to her belly. 'I would never do that.'

She had to admit to herself, though, that she had had misgivings about how she would cope on her tiny salary and in a cold and damp apartment.

He took her bag and coat out of her hands before she could stop him. 'You'll stay here this evening and tomorrow we'll go to see my physician and confirm your pregnancy. Then we'll have another discussion.'

Anger and a feeling of impotency made Skye say, 'You can't just upend my life like this. I have a job. A home. A life.'

He arched a brow. 'I can't upend your life? Like you just upended mine?'

CHAPTER THREE

SKYE HAD HAD no answer to Lazaro's killer response. It had shut down her anger and her justification for leaving because she *had* done that. She had come here and created this situation and now she had to deal with it.

So she'd agreed to stay. For now.

He'd shown her into a huge bedroom and said, 'Make yourself comfortable.'

For a while she was too afraid to move in case she left a mark on the pristine carpet, which felt like walking on a cloud, or the silk upholstery of the furniture. Everything was in tones of white and light grey. Sleek and modern lines. Elegant and classic.

She looked at the huge bed warily, but eventually the feeling of grime on her skin got to her and she realised she couldn't risk getting the sheets dirty.

She went into the bathroom and gasped. It was almost as big as the bedroom. With a slate wet room shower and bathtub big enough for a dozen people. Two sinks. Its soft lighting was very kind to her, making her look less washed out than she felt. But she knew it was just an illusion.

She stripped off and stepped under the shower, almost groaning out loud as the powerful jets of warm water pummelled her skin. Her hair usually took an age to dry, but she couldn't resist the urge to clean that too, massaging her scalp with the most delicious-smelling shampoo.

Afterwards she went back into the bedroom with a towel

wrapped around her head and a voluminous terry cloth robe dwarfing her body. She was tired, but too restless to sleep after everything that had happened, so she curled up in a large armchair and looked out over the view of Madrid under a starry sky.

She wondered if Lazaro was devastated by losing his fiancée. He hadn't seemed too upset about it. But then he'd said their marriage hadn't been based on love. He appeared to have an aversion even to the notion of love.

And she hated to admit that a small part of her had been relieved to hear that his relationship with his fiancée hadn't been a love match.

The night she'd spent with Lazaro had been so...*cataclysmic*. It had touched Skye emotionally far more than she liked to admit. The morning after she'd wanted to stay more than anything. But she'd known it would only be prolonging the inevitable. Even before she'd known the extent of who he was she had known that Lazaro Sanchez wasn't a man who struck up a relationship with a waitress after a one-night stand. It might have gone into a two-night stand, but that would have been it.

Anxiety knotted her belly and she had to consciously breathe in and out to unravel the tension. Her mother's voice came into her head. *'We're human beings, Skye, not human doings. All you can do is focus on the present moment. Nothing else exists.'*

Her mother would always smile radiantly at that, and her New Age pronouncement would usually be followed by one of her customary spur-of-the moment decisions to move city/country/job. Basically, as soon as somewhere had just started to feel like home they'd moved.

But in one way she was right. Skye couldn't do much right now but submit to Lazaro Sanchez's decree. He was the father of her baby. Even if he didn't believe her.

He could have thrown you out on her ear and refused to listen to you, an inner voice pointed out.

Okay, so she hadn't exactly given him much choice, but it had been her only option. And, even though she wished there had been some more discreet way of doing things, she didn't regret informing him that he was going to become a father.

She'd never had the chance to know her own father. It was the one thing her mother had always been uptight about—Skye's father's identity. She'd eventually revealed the truth that she wasn't sure *who* her father was. She'd been at a party...there had been two guys...she didn't even remember their names...

Skye's mother had actually come from a very wealthy background, but she'd been rebellious and artistic. Her family had cut her off after news of her pregnancy had emerged, and that was when she'd taken up the life of a hippy nomad. Her pride had refused to let her contact her family again. Pride and—as Skye had realised over the years—immense hurt that she'd been rejected by them.

Family. Skye sighed deeply. She had a very jaundiced view of family, considering the way her mother's had treated her, and yet that had never stopped her dreaming about a family of her own. A family that was rooted in one place. Secure. Stable.

When she'd found out she was pregnant, as much as the timing was seriously off, she'd felt a huge urge to nest. Put down roots. And telling Lazaro Sanchez about his child had been a part of that. She wanted to be settled when she had this baby, and to have some kind of communication with Lazaro so that her child would grow up knowing where it was from and who its parents were.

She wanted her child to see the world, as she had, but with the knowledge that he or she always had a home to return to.

Skye felt a wave of weariness steal over her. She let her head drop back into the deep cushions and closed her eyes. She'd snooze, just for a minute, and then she'd get up and sort out her few paltry belongings.

Lazaro stood looking down at the sleeping woman for a long moment. He'd wanted to check that she was okay, but she hadn't answered his knock on the door so he'd opened it. He hadn't seen her immediately and for a moment had thought she'd gone—back the way she'd been brought in. Through the service entrance.

He hadn't liked the spurt of panic…

But then he'd seen her. Curled up. Dwarfed by the chair. Fast asleep.

Her head was resting on her shoulder. The towel on her head was almost falling off. He couldn't deny how she made him feel. Hot. Aching. Even now, when she was all but covered up. He just had to imagine her naked under the shower and his body went into meltdown.

She also made him feel livid, for appearing like a genie to rob him of his moment.

Basta! He bent down and slid his arms under her legs and her back, lifting her up. She didn't even stir, she was so deeply asleep. She was light. Fragile.

Pregnant.

When Lazaro put her down on the bed the towel slid off and her damp hair fell in a sprawl around her head, a splash of red against the white linen. She looked utterly innocent and guileless.

His conscience pricked. She *had* been innocent—a virgin. Would she have jumped into bed with someone else so quickly?

Everything inside him rejected the notion.

When Skye had said she'd struggled to get hold of him he'd had to concede that perhaps she was telling the truth.

He recalled seeing his card in the bin of that hotel suite, and he could remember the sensation of disbelief. No woman—ever—had missed an opportunity to gain access to Lazaro's inner circle.

But he did have a rule that no one unknown was allowed to contact him. Especially women. She would have been an unknown to everyone else but him. No one knew about that night. Because he had been in Dublin. He wasn't on the paparazzi's radar there.

He remembered something else from that night. When they'd sat down for a drink in his hotel bar he'd asked her why she'd decided to come.

She'd looked at him a little embarrassed, but also with something almost defiant, and said, 'Because I've never met anyone like you. And you're right. Sometimes it's good to be a little spontaneous.'

He'd looked back at her. 'You're refreshingly honest.'

She'd frowned at him as if he was crazy. 'Why wouldn't I be? What do I have to hide?'

Something heavy settled in Lazaro's gut. The truth was that she didn't come from his world, where cynicism and mistrust went hand in hand. She was most likely telling the truth. But still, he'd be a fool not to confirm it for himself. And he'd be an even bigger fool to throw all caution to the wind and assume she wasn't up to something just because of a feeling in his gut.

When Skye woke the following morning she was disorientated. She was in the most comfortable bed she'd ever slept in—except she couldn't remember falling asleep in it… Because she hadn't. She'd fallen asleep in a chair.

She came up on her elbows and felt the towel behind her on the pillow. She groaned. Her hair would be a disaster today. And how had she ended up in bed? She was under the covers, but still wearing the robe…

Her face grew hot at the thought of Lazaro carrying her to the bed. But he must have. He must have come in. And watched her sleeping. And then he'd picked her up.

Her insides knotted, and not entirely with anxiety. With awareness.

She couldn't hear any sounds coming from outside the bedroom but the sun was up. She got up, and after a quick wash, and trying to tame her hair as much as possible, she dressed and took a deep breath before venturing out into the suite—the *apartment*.

She found Lazaro in the formal dining room. He was sitting at one end of a long table with breakfast laid out around him and a stack of papers. His legs were stretched out under the table and he was dressed in a blue pinstripe shirt and dark trousers. Hair damp from the shower. Jaw clean-shaven.

And she felt a tug of desire deep in her belly.

He looked up, just as a woman Skye hadn't seen before bustled into the room, carrying what looked like a coffee jug.

She greeted Skye. *'Buenos dias.'*

Skye murmured hello back and went over to the table, feeling shy and self-conscious in the only change of clothes she'd brought with her—her habitual uniform of jeans and a loose top…sneakers. She'd always veered towards a tomboyish style, but she'd never been so aware of it than now, when she was in front of this man.

The woman—his housekeeper?—left them alone again. Lazaro put down the paper he was reading and raked her up and down with those vivid green eyes, heightening her sense of exposure.

'No fake waitress outfit today?'

Skye blushed guiltily. 'I wore my work clothes as I figured they might help me blend in with the staff at the hotel.'

It wasn't as if she could have hoped to blend in with the guests!

Lazaro made a rude sound which only reminded her of the audacity of her actions and the dramatic consequences. Suddenly she felt sick.

She gripped the back of a chair. 'I've said I'm sorry about how it happened.'

Lazaro frowned. 'What's wrong? You've gone white.'

The dreaded nausea was rising. Skye managed to garble something unintelligible before she sprinted from the room, back to her bathroom, and made the toilet just in time.

She groaned as she sensed a presence hovering nearby. 'Leave me alone, please. It's fine. It's just morning sickness.'

He didn't leave. 'You have this every day?' He sounded horrified.

Skye might have laughed if she'd been able to. She literally couldn't possibly reach any lower in Lazaro Sanchez's eyes right now, with her head inside a toilet bowl. Whatever desire he'd felt for her would be well and truly gone after this little episode.

To her relief the sickness soon dissipated and a damp facecloth came into her vision. She took it. It was warm. She wiped her face and pulled herself up, going to the sink to rinse her mouth out.

She didn't want to see herself in the mirror, knowing just how wan she'd look.

Lazaro was standing in the doorway looking slightly shell-shocked.

'I'm sorry about that. I've no control over when it comes, but it passes pretty quickly. And the doctor said it shouldn't last into the next trimester.'

Lazaro still looked shocked, so she said, 'It's a perfectly normal part of pregnancy.'

'Do you think you can eat something?'

Skye nodded. That was the thing. Not long after her morning sickness she was usually ravenous.

She followed him back into the dining room and he said something to the housekeeper, who sent Skye a sympathetic look before disappearing again.

Skye sat down and saw her passport was on the table. She picked it up and looked at Lazaro accusingly. 'What are you doing with my passport?'

He poured himself some coffee, and her, and then looked at her, totally unrepentant. 'Skye *Blossom* O'Hara?'

Skye flushed and reluctantly divulged, 'My mother was...*is*...a bit of a hippy. Hence Skye and Blossom.'

'Is she in Ireland?'

Skye shook her head and took a sip of the strong coffee, relishing its warmth soothing her insides. 'She's in India. In an ashram. I haven't managed to track her down and let her know about the baby yet.'

The housekeeper returned at that moment, with a selection of breads, eggs and pastries, and Skye smiled her thanks, relieved that Lazaro hadn't asked about her father. When she glanced at him, though, he was looking at her with an arrested expression on his face.

She wanted to divert his attention from her. 'What about your parents?' she asked. She had a sudden thought and her hand stilled in the act of picking up a croissant. 'Were they there last night?'

He avoided her gaze, and seemed to hesitate before saying very curtly, 'I don't have a relationship with my parents.'

'Oh.'

He looked at her. 'You say that a lot.'

'Do I?'

'Yes. You do.'

'Well, if it's annoying you I can always leave.'

The thought was immensely appealing—to get away from this man's far too disturbing orbit.

He shook his head. 'Oh, no, you don't get to walk away so easily.' He looked at his watch as he stood up. 'We have an appointment with my doctor in an hour—we'll leave in forty minutes. I'll be in my study till then, making some calls. Finish your breakfast.'

Skye watched him walk around the table. 'Are you always so bossy?'

He didn't stop, nor did he look at her. 'Always. Be ready to go in forty minutes.'

Skye breathed out when he'd left the room, her insides unknotting marginally. His scent lingered, musky and masculine. She marvelled to recall how charming he'd been when she'd first met him. Presenting a far more benign façade to the world.

To a woman he'd wanted.

Right now Skye wondered if she'd ever see that charming side of him again. It seemed not very likely at all.

'Well, Ms O'Hara, I can confirm that you are indeed pregnant.'

Skye sent a look across the doctor's office to Lazaro, who was staring straight ahead.

She answered the doctor. 'Thank you.'

'And I called your own doctor, who has confirmed that the three-month scan shows that everything is progressing normally.'

Lazaro interjected. 'She was sick this morning…it was pretty intense.'

The doctor glanced at Skye, who shook her head. 'It was fine. Just the usual morning sickness.'

'Which should hopefully dissipate now, as you go into your second trimester.'

'Yes, that's what I've been told,' Skye said, not sure

whether to be heartened or annoyed by Lazaro's concern about her morning sickness.

She could imagine that it might look scary, and no doubt he wasn't used to seeing the women he consorted with display such basic bodily functions in front of him. The thought almost made her smile. *Almost.*

They were wrapping up the appointment when the doctor said, 'I'll have my secretary book you in for a scan when you're about twenty weeks along.'

Skye opened her mouth, about to tell the doctor that she wouldn't be here then, but Lazaro spoke before she could.

He said, 'I'll have my assistant set up the appointment, but thank you.'

They were in the back of Lazaro's chauffeur-driven car before Skye could round on him. 'You shouldn't have let that doctor think I'll still be here when I'm five months pregnant. There are perfectly good doctors in Dublin.'

Lazaro was looking at his phone. He said, 'What's your address again?'

Skye reeled it off, not sure why he wanted to know.

After a few seconds he handed her the phone. She could see an image of her street, and the building her apartment was in. She winced. It didn't look good. The houses on either side were boarded up, and there was a huddle of young guys near the steps down to her flat. It looked as if a package was being passed from one guy to the other. Not to mention the piles of dumped rubbish.

'This *is* where you live?'

Skye nodded, and said defensively, 'It's not that bad. One of the houses is actually being renovated now.'

Lazaro wasn't impressed. 'So it's turning from a drug pick-up corner into a construction site?'

She didn't answer.

Just then Lazaro's phone rang and he took the call. It was something about a building he was investing in, in Venice.

They were pulling up outside the hotel again when he terminated the call and got out, coming around to open her door for her.

When they were back in the penthouse apartment he led her into the living area and turned to face her, his hands in his pockets.

'So, are you telling me you plan on living out your pregnancy in that hovel? And is that where you would bring the baby home to?'

Skye felt cornered and defensive. 'Not everyone is lucky enough to grow up living a mile above the streets, Lazaro. People have babies all around where I live and they survive and thrive. It's not a ghetto.'

He looked grim. 'I didn't grow up living "a mile above the streets". Far from it, actually. I know exactly what those kind of areas are like, and what goes on there, and there is no way any child of mine is being brought into the world in a place like that.'

Skye was caught by what he said, but now was not the time to be distracted. She fought to retain her composure. She'd already missed her flight. 'Well, I'm sorry, but that's all I can afford. It's good enough for me and I'll make sure it's good enough for my baby.'

'*Our* baby.'

Her heart thudded against her breastbone. 'You believe me, then?'

The doctor had informed them that her ultrasound confirmed her due date, and it tallied with the date they had spent the night together. Pretty irrefutable proof of Lazaro's paternity. But he'd been totally expressionless when the doctor had said that, so she wasn't even sure if he'd heard.

Lazaro sighed heavily. 'Well, apart from what Dr Rubén said about the due date, there were two of us there that night and I had no protection with me. It was my responsibility more than yours.'

Skye was a little taken aback at this admission. 'I really did think it would be okay…but I was wrong.'

'When the baby is born we'll do a DNA test to confirm paternity, but until then I'm treating this as my child.'

Skye flinched minutely at that. He was prepared to believe her and take responsibility, but he wouldn't totally trust her until he could prove it emphatically. She guessed that in his shoes, with his vast wealth, it made sense. Still, as someone who took people as they came and trusted her gut judgement about them, she found it stung not to be trusted.

'I've missed my flight. I called work earlier, and they've excused me for today, but I have to be back tomorrow or I'll lose my job. I need to buy another flight back today. I know you don't like where I live, Lazaro, but all I can do is try and find somewhere else when I go home.'

With a housing crisis in the country Skye didn't hold out much hope of finding anywhere else she could afford, but there wasn't much more she could do.

She'd turned away to go and get her things from her bedroom when Lazaro spoke from behind her.

'Have you listened to a word I've said?'

Skye stopped, and turned around. Lazaro looked incredulous.

'Going back to that flat and that job is not an option. Not now. I have a responsibility to you and to this baby.'

Skye put a hand on her belly, as if to protect it. 'But you've said you won't believe it's yours until we do a DNA test.'

Lazaro waved a hand. 'That'll just be a formality.'

He shook his head and moved towards her. Skye's body tensed against her inevitable reaction. How galling that she should still want him when he was probably looking at her and wondering how on earth he'd lost his mind that one night in Dublin?

'I have to go down to my estate in Andalucía tomorrow, to take care of some business. You'll come with me and stay there for a while, until we figure out a long-term solution. Everything has changed now, Skye. You're pregnant with my child and I'm going to be involved one hundred per cent.'

Lazaro watched the expressions flit across her expressive face. It was fascinating. It was one of the things that had drawn him to her in the first place—every emotion laid bare for the world to see. Not a usual occurrence in women of his acquaintance. Leonora had been like a sphinx...

Right now Skye's emotions were running through anger, frustration and something he couldn't quite decipher. Not resentment... Impotency?

He knew he was in a position of power here, and he wasn't afraid to use it if it meant that he could keep her where he could watch her, try to see if he could salvage anything from this situation *and* take care of his child's future.

It struck him then. The equanimity with which he was taking this news of becoming a father. Because it didn't feel *real*.

Maybe he was still in shock. Maybe if Skye had looked pregnant...

He suddenly had a mental image of her body growing and ripening with his baby. It was curiously vivid and provocative. Provocative enough to make him say curtly, 'The truth is that you have to face the fact that your life has changed as much as mine has. We are both responsible for this and we're in it together. How that will pan out remains to be seen, but for now your place is here. Correct me if I'm wrong, but it doesn't appear as if there's a whole lot tying you to Dublin. You have no other family?'

He saw her wince slightly at that, and pushed down the twinge of his conscience.

She shook her head. 'No, it's just me.'

Why did Lazaro suddenly feel like a heel? And also, more disconcertingly, a strange tug of resonance? He, too, was pretty much alone in the world. Always had been. He trusted very few—only one or two people. A couple of friends he'd made along the way.

Her chin came up, and her eyes were sparking with blue fire. They looked like bright sapphires.

'I do have a life, you know. I'm an independent person. The only reason I will consider your suggestion to stay here is because it'll be for the good of the baby—but don't assume that I'll say yes just because you don't like what I do or where I live. You have no jurisdiction over me and I could have just as easily decided not to tell you about this baby. But I did.'

To Lazaro's surprise, Skye picked up her handbag and put it over her shoulder.

'I'm going to go out to a coffee shop and take a little time to think things over. Then I'll let you know what I plan to do.'

He was too stunned to say anything as she turned and walked out through the door, her bright red hair falling down her back. And then she was gone.

Lazaro looked around him. He saw her passport was still on the table and something eased inside him. She might try to run but she wouldn't get far.

He went over to the window, restless. He had to consider what she'd just said—that she could have easily not told him he was to be a father. Cynically, he didn't believe that for a second—not when she knew he was worth so much. But at the same time he had to concede that there were plenty of instances where men *weren't* informed of their fatherhood. And the thought of a child of his, out there in the world unbeknownst to him, made his blood run cold.

His whole life he'd cultivated a deep and abiding anger at

his parents for doing what they had. Essentially disposing of him like an unwanted package. That anger had driven him and fuelled him to achieve and to succeed—which he had done, many times over.

But he was honest enough to admit that his anger masked a deep hurt that they'd abandoned him to save their own reputations and precious legacies. So, no matter what happened now with Skye and this baby, they would always be a part of his life. He would never visit the same treatment on his own flesh and blood.

Last night might have been an unmitigated disaster, and it had derailed his plans, but once he'd dealt with Skye and the future of their child he was confident he would get things back on track.

The fact that he wanted her was a weakness he would not indulge again.

As if to taunt his resolve he saw her emerging from the lobby of the hotel, some twenty floors below him. She lifted her face to the late-summer sun and her hair glinted bright red. He watched her pull it up into a careless topknot and saw more than one man do a double-take as they walked past.

Lazaro's eyes raked over her slim form. The perfectly proportioned curves. She truly was a million miles from Leonora's classically elegant beauty, but his hands had never itched to trace Leonora's body.

It was Skye he'd been thinking of even as he'd prepared to commit himself to another woman. *Her* curves he'd thought about...*her* pert breasts—

Basta.

He stuffed his hands into his pockets.

He'd never envisaged marrying for lust, or for any emotion. Those things were dangerous. Those things were not controllable. And Lazaro knew he needed to be very controlled in all he did because he would always be held to a higher standard than anyone else. Because the people whose opinion he cared about would want to see him fail.

Blissfully oblivious to Lazaro's tangled thoughts, Skye pulled sunglasses from her bag and set off towards the coffee shop across the road, looking for all the world like a carefree student.

Who had just been given a golden ticket for life, Lazaro surmised grimly. He refused to believe she wasn't aware of just how powerful her position was.

She disappeared into the coffee shop and he had to curb the urge to go after her. Instead he made a call on his phone, and after a few seconds saw one of his men go and take up a spot near the café.

He was fairly sure she wouldn't disappear, but he wasn't taking any chances.

Skye had been sitting there for so long that she was beginning to get looks from the staff. She knew Lazaro hadn't been happy with her just walking out. When a man like that said, *Jump!* everyone around him usually asked, *How high?*

Skye's mother had dated a millionaire for a while. Skye mostly remembered him for the yacht he'd had moored in Cannes. And for how much fun she'd had exploring the town with the kids she'd met from the surrounding streets and the children of the marina workers.

Skye remembered that he had been a nice man, if not very interested in her. The relationship hadn't lasted long, though. He'd wanted her mother to commit, and as soon as she'd started to feel stifled and controlled they'd left.

Skye had learnt from an early age not to get attached to anyone. The first few times when she and her mother had lived somewhere and then left suddenly it had devastated her to leave her friends behind, or adults she'd become close to. The secret was never to allow anyone to get too close.

The fact that Lazaro had managed to sneak under her

guard to such an extent that she'd let him be the first man to make love to her was not something she wanted to investigate. She told herself that it had been purely physical... that her virginity had been weighing on her. It had been something she'd wanted to get rid of and he'd happened to come along when she was ready. That was all.

Liar, whispered a voice.

She ignored it.

But she'd never been in this kind of situation before—where, no matter what happened between them, Lazaro would be in her life for ever, thanks to this baby growing in her belly.

She told herself she wasn't afraid of getting emotionally attached to Lazaro. Their one night of crazy passion had clearly been an aberration, and the man had told her he didn't believe in love. She was too smart to risk losing her own heart. That had been packed up tight a long time ago.

All that was important now was the baby. And she had to admit that he did have a case. She didn't have ties to Dublin. No more than to anywhere else. She didn't have extended family. And her job was a decent one, in a good restaurant, but it was hardly putting her on the ladder to get anywhere.

In truth, she'd really just needed to get some space away from Lazaro. Put her thoughts together. Make him see that she wouldn't just follow his orders like some kind of robot.

Her skin prickled and her pulse-rate quickened even before she saw him. *Damn,* said a little voice in her head. She looked up and there he was. Standing in the doorway, uncaring that he was blocking it. Scanning the room from behind dark shades.

His head stopped moving when he spotted her. He took the shades off and Skye could have sworn she heard every woman and most men in the place sigh audibly as he cut a swathe through the line of people waiting for their coffee.

He sat down opposite her, long legs stretched out, trapping her. 'Had enough time to think? You've been here for an hour.'

Skye scowled at him. And then she admitted defeat. 'I have thought things through, yes. And I'll go along with your suggestion. For now. Because I think it's best for the baby. After all, we need to get to know one another.'

A wary look came into his eyes at that. *Intriguing,* thought Skye.

He leant forward. 'I'll have an assistant go to Dublin to sort out your apartment and pack things up. We can put your furniture et cetera into storage and ship everything else.'

She flushed. After a lifetime of travelling light, all her worldly possessions could fit inside two large suitcases. 'I really don't have that much, and the furniture belongs to the landlord.'

'Fine. I'll have one of my PAs come round this afternoon to go through with you what needs to be done.' He stood up. 'Ready?'

Skye felt seriously disorientated for a second. She hadn't imagined things would move in this direction or so swiftly. She'd thought she'd be back in Dublin by now, dealing with the huge life-change coming down the tracks towards her.

And then Lazaro held out a hand, and Skye's chest tightened with a surge of emotion she couldn't control. For a second she had the sensation that she wasn't alone. For the first time in a long time. It was seriously disconcerting. And seductive.

Very quickly, though, she told herself that it didn't mean anything. A lot had happened and she was feeling vulnerable.

Skye ignored Lazaro's outstretched hand for fear that touching him would expose her in some way and stood up, saying, 'I'm fine, thanks.'

She preceded him out of the coffee shop and back into the sunshine.

He stopped at the entrance to the hotel and said, 'I have to go to my office for a couple of hours. I'll send one of my PAs over. We leave for Andalucía tomorrow morning.'

'Okay.'

Without looking at him, Skye went inside and back up to the apartment. Once Lazaro's PA arrived, and she gave him instructions on how to pack up her Dublin life, she knew she was officially handing herself over to someone else.

After living at the mercy of her mother's whims for so long, Skye's independence was very important to her. But now— She put a hand on her belly. Lazaro was right. She didn't have just herself to think of any more. There was a baby on the way. And that baby had to come first. In this, at least, Skye would be different from her mother, who had only ever thought of herself.

At that moment Skye heard a ringing sound, and plucked her mobile phone out of her bag. She saw the name on the screen and smiled ruefully, before answering. 'Hi, Mum…'

CHAPTER FOUR

'NEVER BEEN ON a private jet before?'

Skye refrained from rolling her eyes at the question. 'Funnily enough, no. It's not something most mortals experience, believe it or not.'

They'd taken off from a small airfield outside Madrid about thirty minutes before and were now high in the sky over Spain. Skye glanced at Lazaro and instant heat sizzled under her skin. He was dressed more casually today, in dark trousers and a dark grey polo shirt. The muscles in his arms bunched and moved under his golden skin as he read the newspapers.

In an effort to try and hide how annoyingly compelling she found him, Skye picked up one of the papers. The woman on the front page looked familiar... She was wearing a red dress and she was being helped into a car by a very handsome if slightly grim-looking man. And then she realised who and what it was and her insides contracted.

'What is it?' Lazaro asked with a sharp tone. 'You've gone white again. Are you going to be sick?'

Skye shook her head. Actually, today was the first day she hadn't had morning sickness. She wished she hadn't picked up the paper now. But it was too late.

She held it across the aisle to Lazaro, saying nothing. The headline said it all: *Humiliated fiancée Leonora Flores de la Vega finds comfort in the arms of Gabriel Ortega Cruz y Torres.*

He took it, and Skye watched as his face became hard. He said something in Spanish. A curse. And then he looked out of the window.

'I'm sorry,' said Skye in a small voice.

Even if he hadn't loved Leonora, it had to hurt that she was already seeing someone else. Lazaro turned back and Skye was shocked at the anger on his face.

'You need to stop apologising. What's happened has happened. It's not your fault Gabriel Torres is taking advantage of the situation to stick the knife in. I can't say I'm surprised.'

'Who is he?'

Lazaro made a sound halfway between a laugh and a growl. 'See that land down there?'

Skye looked out of her window and saw nothing but lots and lots of brown landscape. Mountains. Gorges. Small villages. 'Er…yes…but I'm not sure what I'm meant to be looking at.'

'It doesn't matter. What you're looking at is most likely owned by Gabriel Torres and his family. They own half of Spain—and that's only a slight exaggeration.'

Feeling her way in this sudden air of frostiness, she said, 'So he's some kind of…rival of yours?'

Lazaro emitted a curt laugh. 'Something like that. Yes.'

'And you think he's seduced Leonora just to get back at you?'

Lazaro looked at her. 'It's just the kind of thing he would do.'

Skye's insides twisted. 'That's awful. Poor Leonora.'

Lazaro shook his head. 'She knows who he is. She's not stupid—she comes from that world too… He might have done this to get back at me, but if she went with him it's because she wanted to.'

'And that doesn't bother you?'

Skye couldn't imagine that it wouldn't. Her insides

twisted even harder when she thought of how she had felt to see Lazaro standing beside Leonora in that beautiful ballroom.

He said, 'After what I did to Leonora, she can do as she pleases. She doesn't owe me anything.'

'I owe her an apology.'

Lazaro looked at Skye. He lifted a brow. 'I don't think you're someone she wants to hear from right now. Or me.'

'I guess not...'

Skye had turned her face away from Lazaro. He marvelled that she'd looked genuinely contrite. Anxious. As if she really cared about Leonora, who was a complete stranger to her.

He relaxed his grip on the paper in his hand and forced himself to look at the picture again. It had been taken that night, outside the hotel. Gabriel had his arm protectively around Leonora as he helped her into his low-slung sports car. He was looking directly down the lens of the paparazzi's camera, as if to send a message to Lazaro: *You had no right to try to marry your way into our world, Sanchez.*

Lazaro threw the paper down, a feeling of impotent fury boiling in his gut. Gabriel Torres was a thorn in his side. A constant reminder that he would never be fully accepted. A reminder that his parents had thought so little of him that they'd handed him over to complete strangers to bring up, uncaring if he lived or died.

He glanced moodily at Skye. It should have been Leonora accompanying him to his estate this week. He'd been planning on showing her his land. And yet he knew that if she was sitting on the other side of the plane right now he wouldn't be feeling this constant hunger. Like an ache. He wouldn't be sparring with her. They would be having a perfectly civil conversation that would never delve beneath the surface...

And as Lazaro thought of that now he instinctively went to loosen the tie at his throat—except he wasn't even wearing a tie.

Something struck him then. Was he *relieved* that the engagement had been blown apart? Obviously not in the way it had happened—he could have done without the press attention. But, yes…there was a grudging sense of relief and he hadn't expected that.

Right now Skye couldn't have provided a more stark contrast to Leonora Flores. She was dressed in what seemed to be her default style, skinny jeans and yet another loose colourless top. A faded pink bra strap was visible. Her hair was haphazardly up, with soft golden-red tendrils falling around her face. Small straight nose. Full mouth. Those freckles that danced across almost every exposed bit of skin.

Lazaro cursed silently and had to adjust himself as his body responded.

Suddenly Skye looked at him and her face flushed. She touched her hair. 'What is it? Is something wrong? Why are you looking at me like that?'

Irritated to have so little control of himself around her, he said, 'Like what?'

'You're scowling at me.'

Lazaro had literally never been in this situation with a woman he desired. He was known for his charm. For his easy-going manner which hid a far steelier persona. The reason he'd been so successful was largely in part because people underestimated him. They got punished every time.

Suddenly Skye stood up. She was pale and Lazaro noticed she was trembling.

'Look, I've said I'm sorry about how this worked out, and I know that I'm not the woman you would have chosen to be here with you, but we're in this situation now and we have to make the best of it. I know you hate me because of what happened, and I know you wish I was *her*, even if you didn't love her, but I'm me and I'm here…and I'm sorry.'

She looked left and right, visibly distraught, searching for somewhere to go. Lazaro's insides clenched. He put out a hand and caught her arm just as the plane hit some turbulence, putting her off balance. She landed in Lazaro's lap with a soft *oof*.

Suddenly every coherent thought went out of Lazaro's head as he became very aware of Skye's curvy body nestled intimately into his. *She fitted him.* She looked equally stunned. There was no space between them. Her short sharp breaths whispered close to his mouth.

Somehow one hand was on her waist and his other hand had found its way to her head. Her hair tumbled down over her shoulder with a mere flick of his fingers. She smelled of crushed roses—and something much earthier.

He stretched his fingers over her waist, unable not to trace the delicious curve. And then he gave in to the primal need beating inside him and pulled her even closer, crushing her soft breasts against his chest, covering her mouth with his.

Fire. Skye was on fire. Burning up from the inside out. One minute she'd wanted to get as far away from Lazaro as possible and the next she was in his arms and melting all over. Melting into him. Her mouth was opening under his, allowing him access so he could sweep inside and take her even deeper.

It had been like this the night she'd met him in his hotel. He hadn't even kissed her before he'd asked her to go up with him to his room. And yet she'd gone with him. It had been crazy. Totally out of character. But she'd been burning up after talking to him, after looking into his eyes. Aching to know what it would feel like to have him touch her. Kiss her.

He was the first man she'd ever craved intimacy with. The first man she'd ever let past the carefully erected walls that protected her from getting too close to people.

Since they'd met again there had been no indication that he still desired her, but now it was all she could feel—and along with the desire racing through her system was a rush of something that felt awfully like relief.

She welcomed the desperate press of his fingers into her waist, tugging her top up so that he could touch her bare skin. Every nerve tingled…her breasts ached.

Her arms were wrapped around his neck. If she could have climbed into his skin she would. She was desperate to experience that conflagration again. The exquisite release he'd wrung from her body, leaving her spent and sated beyond her wildest dreams. She'd never been so…at peace. Still. Safe.

She had felt as if she'd been travelling for a long time and finally found her harbour.

That disturbing recollection broke her out of her trance.

Skye pulled back from Lazaro abruptly. Every part of her body protested as she put space between them. Her heart was pounding. He looked at her, his eyes a stormy dark green. His hair flopped messily, *sexily*, onto his forehead.

She scrambled back and stood up, unsteady on her feet as she looked down at the carelessly sprawled body and the expression on Lazaro's face that spoke of how utterly *usual* it was that a woman would fall into his arms—literally— expecting to be pleasured to within an inch of her life.

The fact that her whole body was throbbing and it was taking her so long to speak only compounded her humiliation.

Eventually she got out, 'I am not some convenient plaything for you to use when you want to vent your frustration.'

Lazaro's body tensed and he sat up and forward, green eyes flashing. 'Believe me,' he gritted out, 'there's nothing *convenient* about this or how you make me feel. It would be a whole lot more convenient if I felt nothing when I looked at you.'

Ignoring the voices in her head that told her to just walk away and regain her composure, Skye asked, 'What do you feel when you look at me?'

He raised a dark blond brow. 'I think we've answered that question pretty effectively.'

This was uncharted territory for Skye. She was a novice when it came to dealing with a consummate playboy like Lazaro Sanchez. He was eyeing her now the way a lazy cat might look at a terrified cornered mouse.

Something caught her peripheral vision and she saw the air stewardess coming out of the bathroom at the other end of the plane. Skye garbled something incoherent and fled in that direction, seeking escape from that far too knowing and cynical green gaze.

When she reached the bathroom the woman in uniform looked shocked and said, 'Miss O'Hara, there's a private suite and bathroom for your convenience at the other end of the plane—you don't need to use this one.'

Skye's face was burning at the word *convenience* and she said, 'This is fine, honestly,' and locked herself inside the small space.

She sat on the closed toilet seat and berated herself. *Stupid...no self-control.* She'd just shown herself up to be totally gauche and inept. Lazaro Sanchez must be wondering what he'd ever seen in her. He clearly resented every second that this desire flared between them.

Skye stood up and gasped when she saw herself in the mirror. Her hair was down and in a mad tangle over one shoulder. Her face was pink. Her mouth was swollen. Her eyes were glittering. Her nipples stood out like two hard pebbles against the thin material of her top.

Angry all over again at her lack of control, she scraped

her hair back and into a tight knot. She splashed cold water on her wrists and face and emerged only when she looked slightly less ravished.

When she came back down the plane and saw Lazaro engrossed in something on his laptop she avoided looking anywhere near him and slipped into her seat.

Lazaro was aware of every minute move that Skye made—which was incredibly irritating because she appeared to be a fidgety person. He'd not even looked at her on her return from the bathroom, telling himself that if he didn't then he wouldn't want to stand up, throw her over his shoulder and take her to the bedroom at the back of the plane and finish what they'd started.

But not looking at her was nearly worse. He could smell her subtle scent. Recall only too easily how sweetly her mouth had opened under his. Still feel the curve of her waist under his hand...the press of her breasts against his chest.

He pushed aside his laptop with a sound of frustration and anger and finally gave in to the urge to look across the aisle, fully expecting to see those huge blue eyes staring guilelessly back at him.

But she wasn't looking at him. She was asleep. Her legs were tucked up underneath her. Her head was against the pulled-down blind on the window. She'd rolled up a blanket as a pillow. She was frowning in her sleep, and her lips moved as if she was saying something.

It reminded Lazaro of how, after they'd made love, she'd draped herself over him, one leg entwined with his, one arm across his chest. As if to hold him down.

With any other woman, at any other time, he would have felt claustrophobic. Stifled. Trapped. But with her he'd found himself almost...enjoying it.

She'd made little noises—sleep-talking. Gibberish he hadn't been able to understand. And then she'd woken with a start, and he could remember how her eyes had focused on him and the way they'd widened as she'd obviously remembered where she was and what they'd been doing.

Just from that look he'd become as hard as a rock, and she'd felt him and smiled shyly. That was when they'd made love for the second time.

Lazaro cursed silently and looked away. He never thought of ex-lovers like this. He never dwelt on the past. Always on the present moment and the future. The future he wanted to create. Like a phoenix rising out of the ashes of his ignominious past.

This was just a bump on the road to that future. He would treat this situation as he would anything that got in his way—as a problem to be assessed and dealt with in the most expedient way possible. Skye and the baby…this very inconvenient desire he felt…he vowed that none of it would hold him back.

How she and the baby would figure in his life going forward was something he would have to deal with, but first he'd get Skye settled and then do some serious damage control on the last forty-eight hours of his life.

All Skye could see was acres and acres of sunflowers. They were driving up a long winding driveway under a cerulean blue sky and Lazaro was at the wheel of a sleek four-by-four.

He made a gesture to the sunflowers. 'We make sunflower oil here. And we also have vineyards. I'm working on a sherry and some red wines. We hope to produce something with this harvest of grapes.'

The scenery was breathtaking—the sheer expanse of the land around them with the Sierra Nevada mountains rising majestically in the distance. They turned a corner and Skye gasped as the driveway opened out into a huge courtyard in front of a two-storeyed white building in the old colonial style.

It was very green and lush. Lazaro pulled the car to a stop by the front door and got out. Skye opened her door and hopped out before he could come round—she was being a coward, avoiding any possibility of touching him.

She relished the heat of the late-afternoon sun. She'd always loved summer in southern Europe.

Lazaro was waiting for her by the front door, which was open, and Skye walked over, very conscious of her casual attire, feeling very underdressed for this majestic place.

There was a stone over the doorway that proclaimed *Hacienda Armonía*. She said out loud, 'Estate of... Harmony?'

'You speak Spanish?'

Skye avoided Lazaro's eyes. She shrugged. 'A little.' She was actually practically fluent, but she wasn't sure if she wanted to invite his laser-like gaze and inevitable questions.

They passed through the main hallway and then into an open central courtyard set in the middle of the *hacienda*. Skye's mouth dropped open as she turned around in a circle, taking in the cobblestones and flowering plants everywhere. A colourful bird darted nearby. It was idyllic.

She followed Lazaro as he showed her through to a terrace at the back of the *hacienda*. It bordered formal gardens and a swimming pool was tucked behind blooming bougainvillea plants in vibrant purples and pinks.

'Señor Sanchez!'

They both turned to see a middle-aged woman approaching them with a worried look on her face. She spoke rapidly, exclaiming that they were earlier than expected.

Skye watched with interest as Lazaro took the woman's hands in his and calmed her down, telling her not to worry. The woman smiled. There was genuine warmth between them.

He turned to Skye, and some of that warmth faded. She felt it like a chill breeze over her skin.

'Skye, I'd like you to meet Almudena—my housekeeper. She lives in the gate lodge with her family, and her husband oversees the farming and gardening and general maintenance.'

Skye stepped forward and extended her hand. *'Mucho gusto.'*

Almudena smiled. *'El gusto es mio.'*

Skye could feel Lazaro's eyes on her, assessing her. To her relief he said, 'Almudena will show you to your room. When you've rested we'll have dinner on the terrace.'

'Okay.'

She was relieved to have a moment to gather herself, out of Lazaro's immediate orbit. The effect of that kiss on the plane still lingered in her blood. She felt too exposed around Lazaro. Not sure of who she was any more. He scrambled her brain.

Lazaro watched Skye disappear up the stairs with a beaming Almudena, who had obviously taken to her. Skye seemed to have that effect on people. He'd seen her interact with her customers in the restaurant the night they'd met and had witnessed the effect of her sunny disposition on them.

He'd wanted her to look at him like that. And then, when she had, he hadn't been prepared for the effect. Or how it would make him feel to see her treat everyone the same. Even if there had been a palpable electricity between them that had elevated their bond beyond the merely polite.

A vivid memory flash of how it had felt to slide into her hot, tight body came back to him, and Lazaro cursed. Their interaction had been far from polite...

He turned away from where he was standing, looking into space, and strode back into the *hacienda* and to his study. He switched on his computer and reminded himself of what his priority here was: damage control.

Skye had showered and changed into the black skirt she'd brought with her and worn that first night, and a clean long-sleeved top. They were all the clothes she had with her, and she tried not to feel too self-conscious.

She wandered downstairs and began exploring the gardens, which were filled with surprises. She found a hammock stretched between two trees in one corner. A table inlaid with mosaics and stone seats strewn with coloured cushions in another corner. There were lounge beds dotted around the place, and several lined up by the pristine-looking swimming pool.

It was decadent and luxurious. And totally peaceful. Hacienda Armonía, indeed.

It seemed slightly incongruous when she thought of Lazaro and the man she'd discovered when she'd looked him up online. This didn't seem like the habitat of a ruthlessly ambitious and driven playboy. There wasn't a sound except for the crickets and planes far above in the sky, travelling to the other side of the world.

It was so peaceful—

'Here you are.'

Skye turned around to see Lazaro strolling towards her, dressed in a fresh white polo shirt, open at the neck, and faded jeans. Every provocative line of his powerful body seemed to be moulded and emphasised by his clothes, and she found it hard to breathe for a moment.

How had she ever caught his eye?

His hair was damp. He'd obviously had a shower too. That reminded Skye of watching him emerge from the bathroom at that hotel in Dublin, with nothing but a towel slung around his narrow hips.

She turned away from *that* view and back to the less

provocative one. He came and stood beside her. 'You have a beautiful property,' she gabbled. 'It's so peaceful. Do you come here often?'

She winced at that. *Gauche, much?*

'Not as often as I'd like.'

'Has it always been in your family?'

Lazaro made a slightly choked sound. 'Hardly. I bought it about nine years ago.'

Skye realised that she knew next to nothing about his family, and that whenever she touched on his past he made some sarcastic comment. She turned to face him. 'Where are your family?'

Lazaro placed his hands on the stone wall of the terrace. His jaw tightened. 'They're in Madrid.'

'But they weren't there the other night—at the hotel.'

'My father and half-brother were, actually.'

Something cold prickled over Skye's skin. Lazaro's face showed no emotion. 'You said you don't have a relationship with them.'

'I don't.'

'Why?'

He waited so long to answer that Skye thought he was going to ignore her, but then he said, 'Because I am the result of an illicit affair between two members of Spain's oldest and most celebrated families. They abandoned me at birth into the social care system. I was an inconvenience for them—a stain on their whiter-than-white reputation.'

'Oh.'

He looked at her then, and she was surprised to see a glimmer of humour in his green eyes.

'*Oh.* Your favourite word.'

She made a face, but inside her heart was beating hard as she thought of the significance of what he'd said. 'What happened to you?'

Lazaro turned around and rested his back against the

wall. His face was hard. 'I bounced around foster homes until I realised I'd be safer on the streets. That's where I got the most invaluable part of my education.'

The fact that she'd judged him for having a privileged life mocked her now.

She thought of something else. 'That guy... Gabriel... the one who was in the paper...'

He went very still beside her. 'He's the half-brother I mentioned—on my father's side.'

'Does he know he's your half-brother?'

Lazaro made a face. 'He chooses not to acknowledge it.'

Skye was about to say *oh* again and bit her lip. 'I'm sorry that that happened to you. It wasn't fair.'

'No, it wasn't fair. But it's made me who I am today.'

Skye would have preferred not to sink any lower in Lazaro's estimation, but after what he'd just told her she felt compelled to blurt out, 'My father was never on the scene either.'

He looked at her.

'That's why it was so important to me that I told you about the baby. I don't want him, or her, growing up fatherless if I can help it.'

Just then Almudena appeared, to tell them dinner was ready, and Skye followed Lazaro to where a table had been set under a trellis of abundant bougainvillea.

She sneaked glances at Lazaro as they ate their starter of a light salad. He looked so self-contained. So urbane. She could barely imagine what he must have been like *before*.

Curiosity got the better of her, and when Almudena had served the main course Skye asked, 'How did you go from living on the streets to all of...this?'

He arched a brow. 'You didn't do your research on the internet?'

Skye blushed again. 'I didn't read everything.'

Mainly just the headlines about his billionaire playboy status.

He shrugged. 'I was noticed one day, outside a museum. I had found a way to get tourists in through a back entrance and was charging them less than the official fee.' He sat back, cradling a glass of wine in his hand. 'One of the tourists was impressed with my entrepreneurial skills and it turned out he was a successful businessman, moving to Madrid for work. He offered me a job. I was something of a maths genius, which I think I get from my father's side. They are a family of bankers. One opportunity led to another and I just made the most of it.'

Skye could understand where his ambition stemmed from now. His tenacious will to succeed.

They ate in silence for a while, and then Lazaro put down his napkin. 'I've arranged for your things to be packed and sent from Dublin—they should arrive here tomorrow. I'll have to return to Madrid tomorrow. Something has come up with a project I'm working on. I'll come back at the weekend.'

Skye wasn't entirely dismayed at the thought of some time to get her breath back, away from Lazaro's disturbing presence. 'And then we'll discuss plans going forward?'

'Yes.'

'Good. Because I'll need to find a new job—and somewhere to live that meets your exacting standards.'

Lazaro had to admit he was taken aback by Skye's apparent desire to get back to her life. She wasn't looking at him as she spoke. She was eating with the same single-minded absorption that she'd had the other night. Unselfconsciously.

She was wearing another shapeless long-sleeved top which, thankfully for his rogue hormones, wasn't falling off one shoulder. And, if he wasn't mistaken, the same black skirt she'd been wearing that night in the hotel. Quite possibly the same skirt she wore to work as a waitress. Flat shoes. No make-up. Her hair was down and the setting sun burnished it copper and gold.

She was economical in her movements. Precise. She wasn't remotely interested in seducing him. And yet he was sitting here, his body in a permanent state of heightened awareness just from being near her. Since she'd stormed into his life the other night he had been constantly on the cusp of full-blown arousal, if not actually aroused. Like this afternoon, on the plane.

He couldn't deny she had an effect on him unlike any other woman. Take just now, for instance. He rarely, if ever, spoke of his past or his family—with anyone. And yet with little or no provocation he'd told Skye more than most people knew. Only close confidants and the people actually involved knew of his parentage.

They weren't so dissimilar. He sensed that her life with a single parent hadn't necessarily been easy. She certainly hadn't grown up with a silver spoon in her mouth. And she wasn't looking for hand-outs. *Yet.* Lazaro had seen too much and was too cynical to trust that Skye didn't have an agenda. After all, if he proved the baby she was carrying was his she'd be set for life.

Suddenly he felt the urge to push her, to see how she would react. Almudena cleared away the plates and he said, 'What do you see happening, Skye?'

'What do you mean?'

'I mean, are you hoping for some kind of permanent arrangement?'

She looked at him as if he was speaking in tongues, but Lazaro didn't let it fool him.

'We won't have a relationship beyond coming to an arrangement for our child,' he said.

* * *

Skye was fighting to keep her expression neutral even as hurt mixed with pride in her gut. Clearly he hadn't welcomed the reminder of their explosive chemistry when they'd kissed on the plane. And she certainly did not need to expose her susceptibility again.

'I couldn't agree more,' she replied. 'I don't need you to tell me I'm not someone you'd want a relationship with. Clearly I'm not well-connected enough, or beautiful enough. But, I am the mother of your child, and I'm prepared to do what it takes to come to an agreement.' The feeling of hurt made her add impetuously, 'For what it's worth, you're the last man I'd want to be with. You're far too cynical and obsessed with social standing and money.'

Skye immediately felt bad—especially when she thought of all he'd been through. She was pathetic. But she couldn't bear to hurt anyone. Even someone who seemed as impervious to hurt as Lazaro.

He said, 'If this is a game, Skye, you should know that I don't respond well to manipulation. You'd be better off laying your cards on the table now, so we can come to an agreement.'

Her sense of guilt dissipated in the face of his cynicism. 'I don't play games, Lazaro. I wouldn't know how. If it wasn't for this baby growing inside me I'd almost wish I'd never met you, but I refuse to regret the consequences of that night. You're not the only one who has had their life turned upside down, so if you think I'd sign up for a repeat performance of that night or anything like it then you've another think coming.'

Skye stood up and walked off the terrace, passing a stunned-looking Almudena, holding two plates of what looked like dessert. She garbled something in apology and went straight to her room.

Once she was there she paced back and forth, angry for

letting Lazaro get to her like that. There was no sense of satisfaction in having got the last word in—she didn't care for herself, but she cared for their child, who would grow up no doubt held at some remove while Lazaro got on with his super-successful life. It was Skye's job to ensure their child wasn't pushed aside and forgotten about.

She'd known the man was cynical, even if she hadn't known of his background. His whole demeanour screamed *jaded*. It was one of the things that had intrigued her about him—the fact that such an obviously world-weary man was attracted to her, who couldn't be more his opposite.

Skye had managed to retain a fairly sunny outlook on life, in spite of her own experiences. Only she knew about the walls she'd erected over her lifetime that protected her from letting anyone get too close.

Except once again Lazaro had proved how flimsy those walls were. He, uniquely, got to her. Got under her skin. And that made him very dangerous.

As for how she felt about him, and the way he made her body sing whether she liked it or not, that was just something she would have to deal with.

She told herself that by the time he returned to discuss the future, she'd be feeling more in control.

Lazaro was used to women storming away from him—usually after he'd told them their liaison with him was over. But this was different. He'd never felt an urge to go after any of them and yet he'd had to physically restrain himself from following Skye.

Her words rang in his head: *'If you think I'd sign up for a repeat performance of that night or anything like it then you've another think coming.'*

Another novelty. And he had to admit that her words stung. That night had been the most erotic experience he could remember in a long time. If ever. Not to mention their kiss earlier.

Lazaro thought of another man being the first to awaken her innate sensuality and his hand gripped his wine glass so tight that he had to relax for fear of breaking it. He looked at the sweet dessert that Almudena had left on the table but his appetite had fled.

His carnal appetite, however, was alive and burning him up inside.

Emitting a curse, Lazaro got up and went inside. He was in control of this situation and he was *not* at the mercy of his libido.

CHAPTER FIVE

Two weeks later

'SO HOW EXACTLY were you planning on handling this situation, hmm?'

Lazaro scowled at his best friend, Ciro Sant'Angelo, whom he'd met up with in Rome to discuss a business proposition.

Ciro was holding up an Italian tabloid with a grainy picture of Skye from that night at the hotel on its front page and the screaming headline: *Pregnant with Lazaro Sanchez's baby—but where is she now?*

Ciro threw down the paper on his desk. Tall, dark and handsome. He would have been the quintessential Italian god, if it wasn't for the jagged scar that ran down his right cheek, giving him a dangerous air. It was the result of a kidnapping he'd endured some years before.

He said now, 'My friend, I don't think you need me to tell you that you're looking at a lifetime commitment even if you don't marry this mystery woman you won't tell me anything about.'

Ciro's words rubbed up against every jagged edge inside Lazaro. Along with his conscience, which reminded him every day that Skye was still waiting at his *hacienda* and that for the past two weeks he'd leapt on every opportunity to delay his return. He did not like this *need* he had to see her again.

'Why would I marry her? She's completely wrong for me.'

'Maybe because she's the mother of your child?' came Ciro's dry response.

Lazaro looked at his friend. 'Just because *you've* let a woman brainwash you—'

'Do *not* speak of Lara that way. Not even in jest.' Ciro's expression turned dark in an instant. Tension crackled in the air.

Lazaro's insides clenched. This wasn't *him*. He never provoked his friend. Lazaro had picked Ciro up off the floor—literally—after the woman he'd loved had betrayed him. But now they were back together, and Lazaro had been a witness at their wedding only recently.

He'd never seen such absorption and passion between two people. It had unnerved him as much as it had caught at something inside him. Something deeply shut away and hidden. He couldn't imagine ever letting himself be that vulnerable in front of another person. Not to mention dozens of people at a wedding.

And that was another reason why he'd avoided going back to the *hacienda*. Skye touched on too many things inside him. Emotions he'd never explored before and had no intention of exploring now.

Ciro said, 'Actually, I have some news.'

Lazaro looked at his friend, who said with a smile, 'Lara's pregnant. Three months.'

Now Lazaro felt like a total heel. He went over and embraced his friend. Then stood back. 'I'm really happy for you and Lara. You deserve this happiness.'

His friend looked him in the eye. 'Thanks… But so do you, you know.'

A couple of hours later, on his private plane en route back to Madrid, Lazaro was looking out of the window broodingly, thinking of Ciro's words.

So do you...

Did he? It was an abstract concept for Lazaro, the notion of happiness. He'd always imagined it would come the moment he stood in a room in front of the people who had shunned him when they would have to acknowledge his presence and his success. Acknowledge that he was one of them.

He'd almost had that moment. But his own careless actions had precipitated his downfall.

An image of Skye's heart-shaped face came into his head...that soft mouth. Instantly his body responded. He cursed.

His phone pinged and he took it out, looking at the email one of his legal team had just sent him. And as he took in the contents his body temperature went from hot to icy. She was doing it again. Drawing attention to herself. And him. Making him a laughing stock in the process.

He called the air steward and said, 'Tell Philippe we have a route-change. I'd like to go straight to Andalucía.'

Skye twisted her hair up onto her head and kept it in place with a long paintbrush. She'd found a great spot on the upper floor of the *hacienda* to work—an empty room that led up to the roof, with huge windows and lots of light. A natural studio.

She picked up a piece of charcoal and looked at the photo propped nearby and smiled. She was doing what she loved most. Capturing people on paper. And it was fulfilling two purposes—giving her the means to make enough money to buy herself a flight home, and stopping her dwelling on the rage she felt for Lazaro Sanchez, who had gone to Madrid two weeks ago and left her behind like some unwanted baggage.

But as she stood in front of the makeshift easel and the blank piece of paper now, instead of drawing the face in the photo she started drawing another one that was seared into her memory like a brand. One with beautiful symmetry but hard lines. One with a world-weariness etched into every pore, but also a curious vulnerability.

After a few minutes of frantic sketching Skye stood back. It was Lazaro. Laid bare. Or, she realised in that moment, how she felt about him laid bare.

A surge of panic rose up from her gut, along with rejection of the very notion that she could be feeling anything for him. Especially after the last two weeks.

But she had to acknowledge painfully that even if they'd never met again, if she'd never fallen pregnant, she would still have held him up as an impossible standard that no other man could ever hope to reach.

Skye quickly moved the sketch of Lazaro into her folder and took out a clean piece of paper. She broke out in a cold sweat at the thought of him ever seeing it, because as far as she was concerned it screamed out how she felt about him.

Just then she heard a noise, and every tiny hair stood up on her body. She looked around and there he was. Dressed in a three-piece suit and looking as pristine as she felt dusty and dishevelled. She might have thought he was an hallucination if the physical effect on her body hadn't been so immediate and visceral.

An intense rush of emotion rose before she could control it. Anger and relief. All mixed with desire. She felt an urge to rip that suit from his body, to expose the elemental man she'd met in Dublin. The man who had torn her world apart.

The man who had abandoned her for a fortnight.

Lazaro stepped into the room and said, 'What the hell do you think you're doing?'

Skye took a breath to compose herself, all of a sudden very conscious of her jeans and vest top. Of the paintbrush keeping her hair in place. She probably had streaks of charcoal on her face.

She said, as coolly as she could, 'I'm sketching. Almudena said it was okay to come up here and use this space.'

'Sorry,' Lazaro said, coming closer and not sounding sorry at all. 'I should rephrase that. Why have you been in the local town's market square doing portraits of people like a common hustler?'

Skye fought to control her tumultuous emotions. 'I've been doing portraits to make some money. It's a good spot to drum up business.'

Skye could see the anger turning his eyes a vivid green, and the tautness in his jaw, but she refused to be intimidated.

'And why on earth are you doing that?'

'To make enough money to buy a flight back to Dublin.'

Something caught his eye behind her and he went over and picked up the photo she'd printed out. He looked at her, holding it between thumb and forefinger as if it was toxic. 'What…who is *this*?'

'It's a commission. The man's daughter wants me to sketch a portrait for his birthday. He's eighty. A beautiful soul.'

Lazaro put the picture down and drew his phone out of his pocket. After a couple of seconds he handed it to her. She saw some grainy pictures of her in the square, smiling at someone and accepting money.

She winced inwardly. These were paparazzi shots.

The headline screamed: *We Found Her! Forced to make a living on the streets, even though the father of her baby is Lazaro Sanchez, one of the richest men in the world!*

Skye handed the phone back, refusing to feel guilty. 'I had no idea there were paparazzi here.'

Lazaro held up his phone. 'For all I know you called them. When you should have been calling *me*, to let me know you wanted to leave. Instead you've created a public sensation—*again*—while looking like a student.'

Skye put her hands on her hips. Hurt and anger was an explosive mix in her belly. 'Well, I'm sorry that I don't meet your high sartorial standards, but I'm afraid that with limited means and an even more limited wardrobe this is as good as it gets. And,' she continued hotly, 'do I need to remind you of how hard you are to contact? I *tried* calling you, but when I realised after week one that you'd obviously decided to leave me to my own devices, I knew I had to take care of myself.'

Colour scored along Lazaro's cheekbones, but it brought her no sense of satisfaction. It only reminded her of how he'd looked in the throes of making love. Flushed cheeks, glittering eyes and an intensity on his face that had transformed him from gorgeous into seriously— *Stop it!*

'I did *not* call the paparazzi,' she said. 'Was it always your plan to get me out of Madrid and away from polite society, so that you could hide me away like something unwanted on the bottom of your shoe?'

Lazaro's conscience pricked hard. He had hoped that by bringing her here the whole situation might somehow magically fade away. But the gods were laughing in his face at his paltry efforts to control this situation.

Desire for Skye pulsated through his blood in hot waves. He could see where the top button of her jeans was undone, to accommodate her growing belly. And from where he stood he could see the tantalising swell of her cleavage in the dip of that ridiculously flimsy vest. It looked more voluptuous.

He'd been to two functions in the past two weeks where he had been surrounded by sleek and coiffed women, and yet *this* one made his blood surge like no other. Even dressed like this.

Skye stuck her chin out. 'I don't think this is going to work. Frankly, I have better things to be doing than languishing in this luxurious outpost, waiting for the moment you deem it fit to return like an overlord.'

Lazaro watched in disbelief as she put the photo and the blank piece of paper that was on the easel into a leather folder and then walked away.

She was almost at the door when he heard, coming from deep inside him, *'Stop!'*

She stopped. And turned around. Her expression was part belligerent and part something else far more ambiguous. It unnerved him. He was transfixed by her ability to stand up to him. It was absurdly refreshing in spite of everything.

He was also mesmerised by the passionate expression on her face. Her flushed cheeks.

He'd closed the distance between them before he'd even made the conscious decision to move.

Her eyes were like bright jewels. Tendrils of golden-red hair fell around her face and he had a dark suspicion that a paintbrush was the device being used to hold the unruly mass precariously on her head.

There was an inferno inside Lazaro, burning away any rational thought. He'd been right to avoid coming back here. She stirred up too much for him.

He could have handled it if it was just desire—he knew how to deal with that and it never lasted. But she stirred up other things as well. Things he didn't want to deal with. And yet he couldn't let her walk out of this room.

Skye was talking. '…one more day and I'll have enough to fly home. I'll be out of your hair and I'll let you know when the baby is born, okay? We can meet then and decide what to do. But this…' she waved a hand around her '…this is not working.'

She was about to turn away again when Lazaro reached out and caught that hand. 'Wait—please.'

Skye stopped breathing at the rough tone in his voice. He was barely holding her hand, yet it felt as intimate and provocative as if he'd kissed her. It was caught up in the air in his, as if he was about to pull her into a dance.

She looked at him and saw a million things in those mesmerising green eyes. Anger and affront that she'd dared to stand up to him. But also *heat*...the same heat she felt rushing through her veins right now in a dizzying rush.

Tension crackled between them, but now it was a different kind of tension. She could still feel the anger thrumming through her system—anger at him for coming into her life so cataclysmically, sending her and it spinning off in a new direction. But, treacherously, all she could think of were those long nights of X-rated dreams. Waking feeling cold and bereft—which was ridiculous. She'd slept with this man once.

Twice, reminded a wicked inner voice.

Her anger was turning into something much more dangerous and volatile. Anger at how he made her feel, at how easily he could seduce her just with his presence. She didn't want to want him—she wished she could just walk away and reclaim her independence—but that was fading into insignificance in such close proximity.

All she could see were those deep pools of green. That savagely beautiful face. He tugged her towards him. She wanted him so badly that she was trembling with the effort it took not to show it.

'Lazaro—'

'Skye—'

They both spoke at the same time and stopped. Time had trickled to a stop. The air was still. Nothing moved and there was no sound. Only an intense need.

Skye couldn't even recall what they'd just said.

He laced his fingers with hers and a pulse throbbed deep between her legs. He was holding her so lightly she could have resisted. But she didn't want to. Through the fog of need clouding her brain she felt an urgent desire to expose the man under the civil façade. To somehow restore the balance of power. To punish him.

He shook his head and spoke almost as if to himself. 'What do you do to me, *bruja*?'

Skye answered without even thinking. 'I'm not a witch… I'm just me.'

For a moment neither one moved. And then something snapped. She didn't know who had moved first, but it didn't matter because she was in his arms, and his mouth was on hers, and she was twining her arms around his neck, straining to get as close as possible.

Her folder fell to the floor unnoticed.

He was kissing her like a man possessed. Thoroughly. Expertly. And Skye was kissing him back with all the pent-up frustration and anger of the last two weeks.

She felt feral. She wanted to rip Lazaro's suit off and find the man who had awoken her with such devastating skill.

When he broke off the kiss to take her hand she said nothing. She was afraid she wouldn't be able to speak anyway. Her heart was hammering out of her chest, her vision was blurry, legs wobbly.

He led her down the stairs to his bedroom. He pushed the door open and brought her into the cool interior. Open French doors led out to a balcony that Skye guessed must look out over the back of the property, taking in the vista of gently rolling hills covered with vines.

She'd had two weeks to contemplate that view, every evening as the sun set over the horizon, turning everything golden and orange. Her anger returned—fuelled by her desire.

Lazaro pulled her towards him and put his hands on her waist, which was already a little thicker than it had been a couple of weeks ago. She might have felt self-conscious, but the intensity in his eyes burnt it away. It sent a rush of renewed desire through Skye's body and between her legs, where she felt achy and hot.

He asked, 'Are you sure you want this?'

Skye wasn't sure about a lot of things, but she was sure of this. She wanted Lazaro with a ferocity that might have scared her if she'd been feeling more rational. She wanted to drive him to the edge of his control…see him lose it.

She didn't nod, or say a word. She just answered by putting her hands underneath Lazaro's jacket and pushing it off his shoulders. It fell to the floor with a soft thud.

He responded with a sexy tilt to his lips. It made Skye want to scowl but she was too hungry.

He caught her face in his hands and angled her up to him, before covering her mouth with his and throwing them both over the edge of the simmering tension between them and into the fire.

Skye was vaguely aware of Lazaro lifting her arms so he could pull her flimsy top up and off. Then his hands were on her back, smoothing up and down, tracing the contours of her body, undoing her bra. Her breasts were freed and she sucked in a breath when his mouth closed over a tight, sensitive peak.

She speared her hands in his hair, holding him there as he administered the same exquisite torture to her other breast. Everything was so heightened she felt she might blow there and then, but he pulled back and Skye opened her eyes, unable to focus for a moment.

His waistcoat and shirt were still closed. His tie perfect. She needed to ruffle that smooth surface. She snapped open buttons and pulled apart his tie, feeling feverish. When his chest was bared she sucked in a breath. He was pure magnificence.

She spread her hands across his chest, dislodging his shirt and waistcoat, pushing them aside and pulling them down his arms. They fell to the floor and now they were both naked from the waist up.

Urgency sizzled in the air. Lazaro reached for Skye's jeans, pulling down the zip and tugging them over her legs. She stepped out of them and watched with a dry mouth as he undid his belt and opened his own trousers, discarding them and his underwear with brutal efficiency.

Skye drank in his naked form. All six foot plus of perfectly honed male. Even though he should look vulnerable, being naked, she saw nothing but pride and strength.

Her gaze dropped to where his erection was thick and hard. A bead of moisture dewed the head. He took himself in his hand, moving it up and down slowly. Skye had never seen anything so erotic in her life.

'Lie on the bed,' Lazaro instructed.

Skye wasn't even sure how her legs were still working. It was a relief to do his bidding. Lazaro's green eyes blazed with heat as he looked at her body, all the while his hand moving up and down that proud column of flesh.

She was overcome with the desire to do something for the first time in her life but was far too shy. She wanted to know how he would taste in her mouth…on her tongue.

Oblivious to her fevered imaginings, Lazaro came onto the bed and moved between her legs. He dispensed with her underwear the same way he had his own—efficiently. She was panting, almost begging, as he looked down at her. And then, gently, he pushed her legs apart. She felt nothing but intense desire as she watched him lower his head to press kisses along the insides of her thighs, before coming closer and closer to where the very core of her pulsated with pleasure/pain.

When his mouth touched her there, his tongue flicking out to explore her slick folds, she almost bucked off the bed. He put his hand on her belly, holding her still, and his other hand under her buttocks, angling her so that his tongue and mouth could push her right over the edge of the cliff she was clinging to, shattering her into a million tiny shards of pleasure so exquisite she was barely aware of him seating himself between her legs.

He entered her in one smooth thrust on the last ebbing wave of her orgasm. Skye had no time to recover, but she found she was already greedy for more pleasure, clutching his buttocks, winding her legs around his waist. She could feel her inner muscles clamp around him, as if loath to let him go ever again, as his powerful body surged in and out in a timeless rhythm.

This was *more* than she remembered, if possible. Maybe it was just pregnancy hormones heightening every sensation, but Skye didn't think so. It was Lazaro, uniquely. And his effect on her.

Lazaro was in heaven and hell simultaneously. He was in heaven because no woman had ever had this effect on him, and hell because he hated this sense of being out of control. Tasting her essence, feeling the contractions of her orgasm against his mouth and tongue, had almost been the death of him.

He drove deep and hard into the snug embrace of her body, but even as he did so any illusion of taking back control was fast unravelling. Her breasts rubbed against his chest and she clasped desperately at his buttocks. He lifted her thigh, holding it over his hip, and he could see how she bit her lip and entreated him with her eyes to have mercy…to let her fly.

Only when he saw that she was as crazed as he felt did he push her over the edge and let his own pleasure rush through him in hot waves so powerful he couldn't hold on to any semblance of control any more.

He was undone.

When Lazaro woke it was late afternoon. Skye was draped over his body, much as she had been in Dublin. And once again—disconcertingly—it didn't make him feel claustrophobic.

At that unwelcome revelation he extricated himself from her embrace. She made a sound but then turned on her side away from him, not waking. Lazaro stood up and looked down at her body, his eyes roving over the dips and curves, wondering what it was about her that got to him so uniquely and turned him into some kind of primal animal he didn't recognise.

It was only small comfort to know that Skye had been similarly affected.

He'd never had a lover like her before. He'd never known a woman to give herself so fully and passionately. Most lovers he'd had had been obsessed with making sure their body was angled a certain way, never fully letting go.

When he'd seen Skye in that room earlier, a moment before she'd noticed him, she'd been standing sideways, her profile illuminated by the sun. In particular he had seen that small rounded belly. For the first time since she'd told him she was pregnant he'd felt the reality of it punch him in the gut. It had made him dizzy for a moment.

He'd told her he wouldn't touch her again. And yet within minutes of arriving back at the *hacienda* he'd been devouring her like a man crazed with lust. He'd forgotten why he was so angry with her. He'd forgotten everything.

But now he remembered.

Damage control.

This was a situation that he couldn't run away from— as had just been made painfully clear.

Lazaro went into his bathroom and turned the shower

on to cold. He gritted his jaw as the icy needles slammed into his body, willing the cold water to douse the lingering heat in his body.

He told himself that the fact that they had chemistry was something that could no longer be denied or ignored. And perhaps it was a good thing—because when he told Skye his plans for the future he wouldn't be afraid to play dirty if he had to.

She would submit to his will. She had to. She owed him.

It was dusk when Skye woke from the deepest slumber she could remember in months. She felt disorientated, and it took her long seconds to get her bearings and realise she wasn't naked in her own bed. She was naked in Lazaro's bed. And then it all came rushing back, along with the after-effects of pleasure. Aching muscles. Tender parts of her body.

The room was empty, just one low light casting shadows. Skye groaned. She'd been so angry with Lazaro for leaving her here, and yet within minutes she'd been climbing him like a tree and all but begging him to make love to her.

He'd told her that it wouldn't happen again. That their relationship wasn't about *this*. But clearly there was a force between them stronger than his will and her better judgement. It was little comfort to know that he was as affected as her. He must resent her for it.

Skye got out of the bed and picked up the detritus of her clothes, her face burning when she thought of how desperate she'd been to get naked. She pulled on her jeans and top and tiptoed back to her own room, stripping off again and diving straight under a hot shower. As if that could wash away her humiliation.

After drying and plaiting her hair, to keep it out of her way, Skye dressed in clean jeans and a top, flushing again when she thought of how Lazaro had been so scathing about her attire.

She hated to admit it, but he'd got to a very secret part of her that had always felt conscious of not being more feminine. She'd noticed the women who came into the restaurant sometimes and envied their sense of style. Women like the impeccably coiffed Leonora Flores de la Vega.

Enough. Skye scolded herself for the uncharacteristic self-pity. She knew she had to face Lazaro again some time, so she forced herself to go downstairs, where an enticing smell of cooking food was drifting from the kitchen.

When Skye reached the entrance hall the massive front door was open. There was only the faintest of breezes on the warm Andalusian air. It was so beautiful here. Peaceful. One might be forgiven for forgetting that there was a greater world out there, full of strife and turmoil.

Skye had often wondered if her mother's wanderings were an endless search for peace... The real world had never bothered Skye too much—she'd learnt at an early age how to adapt to her surroundings and make the best of a situation, no matter where they were. But she'd always wanted to settle down one day and know she didn't have to keep moving.

She'd thought she'd done that in Dublin—but now look at her. *Like mother like daughter.* No, she assured herself. *Not* like mother like daughter. She would offer her child a stable life, no matter what it took...

At that moment Almudena came into the hall and smiled at Skye, who flushed guiltily as she wondered if Almudena knew where she and Lazaro had been all afternoon.

The older woman said, 'Lazaro is in his study. He's asked that you go to him before dinner.'

Skye smiled and said, *'Gracias,'* feeling butterflies erupting in her belly as she approached the half-open door of Lazaro's office. She heard the low rumble of his voice and knocked lightly before entering.

He was on the phone and saw her, gesturing for her to come in, terminating the conversation as he did so.

Skye automatically said, 'Sorry, I didn't mean to disturb you.'

He shook his head and stood up. 'You didn't. Come in.'

Skye ventured further in, noting his worn jeans and the polo shirt that emphasised his powerful physique. She hoped her face wasn't as red as it felt.

'Did you want to discuss something?' she asked.

Lazaro went over to a drinks cabinet, turned around, 'Would you like a drink?'

'Maybe just some water?'

After a few seconds he handed her a glass. She saw that he had a drink for himself—something that looked far more potent than water. For a second she envied him.

She took a sip to try and cool her blood.

He went back around his desk and gestured. 'Please... sit down.'

So polite. As if the previous hours hadn't happened. Still, if he could act cool then so could she.

She went over to the chair, but just before she moved to sit down she saw something on the desk and the glass in her hand nearly slipped out of her nerveless fingers. Her sketches.

She put down the glass with a clatter and leant forward, gathering up the sketches and stuffing them back into her leather folder. She looked at Lazaro. 'How dare you go through my things.'

Lazaro, supremely unconcerned, sat down and looked at her. 'Please, sit.'

She ignored him, hugging her folder close, praying silently he hadn't seen *that* sketch. 'You had no right.'

Lazaro looked at her for a long moment, as if trying to

see inside her head, and then he surprised her by saying with a note of grudging respect, 'Your portraits are good. Really good.'

Skye was so stunned she sat down. 'Thank you.'

'Where did you study?'

'I didn't. I'm self-taught.'

Lazaro stood up again, as if he couldn't contain his own energy. He paced to the window and then turned around, hands in his pockets. 'You don't appear anywhere—not at any schools…universities.'

Skye frowned. 'You looked me up?'

'You're carrying my child. I'm a wealthy man and I know next to nothing about you.'

You know how to make my body sing.

Skye shut that thought down. 'I could say the same about you.'

Lazaro didn't look happy about the fact, but he said, 'Nevertheless, if you do an Internet search on me plenty of information will appear.'

This was said with a complete lack of hubris. He was just stating the facts.

Skye said, 'Are you accusing me of setting you up by getting pregnant? I thought we'd been through this.'

Lazaro folded his arms. 'You've said you're not motivated by money but, let's face it, no matter what, if that child is mine, you've hit the jackpot.'

Skye held the folder over her belly, as if to stop the baby hearing him. 'He or she *is* your child—and that is a horrible thing to suggest.'

Lazaro shrugged. 'It's true.'

The depth of his cynicism rubbed Skye raw—especially after what they'd shared that afternoon. She stood up, emotions bubbling over. 'You could have just asked me, you know. I don't have anything to hide, and I'm not here to extort money out of this situation.'

He gave her that hard look again. 'Everything tells me not to believe you, but I actually think you might be telling the truth.'

'You mean your cynical nature tells you not to believe me,' she pointed out.

Lazaro spoke in Spanish. 'You understood me when I said *bruja*. And I've heard you speaking Spanish with Almudena. Where did you learn to speak it so fluently?'

Skye felt ridiculously and irrationally guilty. 'My mother and I had a somewhat nomadic existence. We lived all over Europe and the Middle East at one point or another. I found it easy to pick up and retain languages…probably a survival technique. If I ever did enrol in a school it was never long before we moved again. I taught myself the basics of everything and picked up stuff along the way. That's probably why you couldn't find me listed anywhere.'

'Why did you move so much?'

Skye shrugged one shoulder, desperately wanting to avoid Lazaro's penetrating gaze, but not wanting to show him any vulnerability.

'My mother was always enticed by the new and the shiny—whether it was the promise of a job or a new lover.' She saw something on Lazaro's face and said fiercely, 'She was a good mother. I knew I was loved and I was always secure, no matter how much we moved around. She made sure of that. But I don't want that lifestyle for my child. One of the things I wanted most when I was growing up was a home…one place. Somewhere I knew was mine, that I could come back to.'

Lazaro stayed silent.

He wasn't used to feeling a sense of affinity with anyone, but Skye's words had struck a chord deep inside him. When he was younger he'd used to stand outside the palatial properties belonging to his mother and his father and his half-siblings, envying the very solid roots that they took for granted. That envy had nurtured his ambition to be successful. To be accepted.

The fact that Skye had been through a very different yet somehow similar experience was disconcerting. She hadn't had it much easier than he had, and yet she appeared to hold no grievance, just a wish to do things differently. She also appeared not to have a cynical bone in her body.

At that moment Almudena knocked on the door to tell them dinner was ready.

Lazaro's focus came back. He couldn't let a fleeting sense of affinity derail his ultimate ambition.

He gestured to the door. 'Shall we?'

CHAPTER SIX

SKYE COULDN'T DENY she was relieved at the interruption. She didn't enjoy being under the spotlight of Lazaro's exacting questions.

She walked out to the terrace, where the table was set. Candles flickered and silverware shone against a pristine white tablecloth. It was an undeniably romantic setting and yet, despite what had happened between them that afternoon, Skye couldn't imagine that Lazaro appreciated the effort. He didn't strike her as the romantic type.

It made her wonder how he'd been with his fiancée.

Skye felt a pang of conscience and impulsively asked, as Lazaro took his seat opposite her, 'Have you talked to Leonora?'

Something fleeting crossed Lazaro's face, but it was gone so fast Skye couldn't decipher what it meant.

'No, I haven't spoken to her. Why do you ask?'

Skye played with her napkin. 'I just feel bad... I'm sorry that she was embarrassed like that. I hope she's not too upset.'

Lazaro took out his phone and after a few seconds handed it over to Skye, who looked at it and gasped.

The headline read: *Gabriel Ortega Cruz y Torres weds Leonora Flores de la Vega in an exclusive and private wedding at the family estate in Madrid.*

Skye gasped and looked up. 'They're *married*? How is that even possible?' She handed the phone back.

'For Gabriel Torres pretty much anything is possible.'

Skye suspected that the same could be said of Lazaro. 'Does Leonora know that Gabriel Torres is your half-brother?' she asked.

Lazaro's face was totally expressionless, but Skye could see a tightness in his jaw. 'Hardly—he doesn't acknowledge it himself. I didn't think he'd go to these lengths to get back at me.'

'Maybe he really likes her.'

Lazaro shot her a look. '*Like?* Like and love are not emotions people from Gabriel and Leonora's world indulge in. She comes from his world and she needs money. I'm sure they came to some arrangement.'

'That's so…cold.'

'That's reality.'

Almudena arrived then, with their starter, and Skye started eating the delicious asparagus and ham. She could enjoy food again without fearing its reappearance the following morning, as the morning sickness that had blighted her first trimester appeared to be over. In fact, she was feeling better than she'd felt in a long time.

Hmm… said an inner voice. *I wonder why?*

A lurid image of her body entwined with Lazaro's came into her head and she cursed it silently, not even looking his way in case he saw something on her far too expressive face.

'You eat every meal with a single-minded absorption I've never seen in anyone else.'

Skye looked up, and finished chewing her last mouthful of asparagus, trying not to feel as if he'd just compared her unfavourably to every woman he'd known.

'I learnt early to appreciate whatever was put in front of me, because sometimes it was a long time between meals.' If her mother had suddenly decided to jump on a train and go from Paris to Prague. Or Berlin…

Lazaro regarded her, cradling a wine glass in his hand. 'How can you be so *un*-cynical? You hardly had a more secure start in life than I did.'

Skye shrugged. 'My mother was trusting—probably far *too* trusting—but we generally had good experiences. People looked out for us...for me. And, even though my mother's way was scatty and unconventional, I knew I was loved and that she would do anything for me.'

'Except stop moving around?'

Skye looked at Lazaro, surprised at his perspicacity and at the dart of hurt it provoked. Because she'd often wondered that herself.

She smiled a small smile. 'Except that. When I was seventeen we were in London, and I had a job in a hairdressing salon. When she announced that she wanted to move on I told her I was staying. I was earning money and I got a room-share in a flat with a friend. That's when I stopped moving around.'

He arched a brow. 'You know how to cut hair?'

Skye nodded. 'It's a useful skill to have.'

Once again she cringed inwardly, thinking how different this line of conversation must be from what he was used to. If Leonora Flores was anything to go by, Lazaro's usual women oozed class and sophistication. They didn't have obscure skill sets like Skye, thanks to her unusual upbringing.

'And where does your talent in drawing come from?'

'Not my mother...she couldn't draw a stick-man to save her life.' She shrugged self-consciously. 'I don't know... maybe my father? Whoever he is.'

Almudena arrived with the main course. Lazaro was surprised. He hadn't even noticed her taking away the starter plates.

He found Skye genuinely...interesting. Which was a novelty when not many people interested him or surprised him.

He could recall sneaking into art galleries when he was a teenager, standing transfixed in front of massive majestic canvases. He could imagine that Skye had done the same thing. Both of them had been on the margins of society for different reasons. And yet she didn't seem to be consumed by greed for what she might have missed out on as her birthright.

'Your father could be a millionaire,' he pointed out.

She shrugged, unconcerned. 'He could. Equally he could be a pauper—or dead.'

Lazaro sat back. 'Are you really telling me you couldn't care less?'

She looked at him. 'I don't deny I'd like to know who he is…maybe even talk to him…but as for what he has? That means nothing to me. Because it's who you are underneath that counts.'

Lazaro might have thought she was messing with him if she hadn't sounded so genuine. 'A nice sentiment,' he said. 'But somehow I don't think it's that simple.'

She looked at him, a fork full of Almudena's signature *paella* halfway to her mouth. She actually managed to give him a pitying look.

'Maybe some day you'll find that your cynical world view isn't all it's cracked up to be.'

Lazaro watched her eat and thought to himself that that was highly unlikely.

They finished the meal in a surprisingly convivial silence. Skye said thank you to Almudena when the woman cleared away the plates and brought some sweet pastries and coffee.

When they were alone again Lazaro said, 'There's something we need to discuss.'

Skye sat up straighter. 'Yes…there is. I know you're not happy with where I'm living in Dublin, but maybe I can find a new place and then—'

Lazaro was shaking his head. 'You're not going back to Dublin.'

Skye felt frustration rise at his matter-of-fact tone. 'What are you proposing, then? To leave me here and drop in when it suits you?'

To have mind-blowing sex? snarked that little inner voice.

Skye ignored it and said hurriedly, 'Or maybe you're going to set me up somewhere that's conveniently on the sidelines of your life with your child?'

Lazaro looked at her. 'If you think you're someone who can be easily *sidelined* then you do yourself a disservice.'

That kept Skye quiet. She didn't think he'd meant it as a compliment. She had the distinct impression that he wished she was more easy to sideline.

'So what *are* you suggesting?'

Lazaro stood up and walked over to the wall that separated the terrace from the gardens. She couldn't stop her gaze roving over his broad back and down to the slim waist and powerful buttocks. He turned around and she shifted her eyes up, feeling a guilty burn under her skin.

'What I'm suggesting is that we get married. It's the only viable option right now.'

It took a second for his words to sink in, and when they did Skye shot up from her chair. 'Is this because we had sex?'

'It's because you're pregnant. And until we can prove irrefutably that I'm the father the world believes that I am.'

Something suspiciously like hurt lanced Skye. 'But you still don't?'

His jaw clenched. 'It's not that I don't—just that I'm not naïve enough to believe something I can't prove.'

Skye walked over to the wall, but kept a distance of a few feet between her and Lazaro. 'I'm not going to marry you—that's a preposterous suggestion.'

'Is it? Really? The fact is that we had a night together which has resulted in consequences that will affect both our lives for decades to come, and we need to face those consequences. Together.'

The implacable tone of his voice, and the way he seemed to be prepared to sacrifice himself for the sake of keeping up appearances, even while resenting her for it, sent panic into Skye's gut.

'You've admitted you're not prepared to believe you're the father till you get evidence, so why would you want to make such a public commitment to a woman who may or may not be the mother of your child?'

His jaw clenched again. 'Because the press won't rest in their hounding of you—and us—until I do. I'll be pilloried for not supporting my pregnant mistress. I don't have the luxury of hundreds of years of legacy-building to withstand that kind of negative press attention.'

'But I'm *not* your mistress,' Skye wailed.

If she hadn't fallen pregnant she would only have ever been a one-night stand to this man. A dim memory as he got on with his life with his perfect wife. That stung far more than she liked to admit.

'Let's face it,' she said, trying to hide the insecurity she felt and hated. 'I would never have been a mistress of yours. What happened between us was out of character for both of us, brought on by extreme—'

'Chemistry,' he supplied, sounding grim.

Skye got hot, thinking of how that chemistry had manifested itself a few hours ago. 'Whatever. I just don't think it's necessary to overreact and make a commitment for the sake of it.'

He folded his arms and shook his head. 'You don't get it, do you?' He kept going before she could respond. 'You are fast becoming a household name here in Spain. I can guarantee you that right now people are looking you up, trying to delve into the most secret details of your life. You can never just fade away again. Not as long as people think you're the mother of my baby.'

Skye frantically racked her brains for a solution. 'I'll say I made it up. To get money out of you... Or because I was jealous of your engagement.'

Lazaro shook his head. 'It's too late. I've done all the damage control I can, but the only option going forward is for us to marry. And soon. Within the next week.'

Skye's legs turned to jelly. She had to grip the wall beside her as something occurred to her. 'Is this because your half-brother and ex-fiancée got married? You want to get back at them? I'm not a pawn, Lazaro.'

'No, it's not because of them. I'd decided to do this before I saw that they'd married.'

The only thing convincing Skye that he was telling the truth was, well, why would he lie? He didn't need to.

'You can arrange it that quickly?'

He nodded. 'I have contacts. We can do it here, in the nearest town. A civil service.'

The speed at which this situation was morphing out of Skye's control was dizzying. 'What if I say no? You can't force me to marry you.'

'You're the one who has said it's important for you to live your life differently. To give your—*our* child a secure and stable future. Settled. I can offer you the life you never had with your mother. And, what I experienced, there's no way I'll abandon my child.'

The reminder of how much they had in common made Skye feel emotional, when it was the last thing she wanted to feel. But he was right. She *did* want to offer her child a stable life. And a father.

'What would...? How would this work?'

'The way I see it happening is this: we would marry for a period of up to five years—enough time to get you and the child settled, establish a base that suits us both and that gives our child a solid start in life—and then we would separate amicably and arrange joint custody. I would always be in my child's life, and he or she will know who its father is. I can promise you that. My own father treated me like a dog in the street. I want more for my child—just as you do.'

Skye absorbed his words. 'This is a lot to think about…'

Lazaro looked at her for a long moment. 'On some level you must have been prepared for this when you decided to come to Spain to tell me about the baby. You can let me know what you decide in the morning, but we both know there's only one solution here…the right one.'

He turned and walked away, leaving her standing there feeling as though her guts had been pulled out and squeezed.

Was he right? *Had* she been prepared for this when she'd come to Spain? *No.* She'd never imagined this. She'd never thought for a second that he would commit to her like this. Offer her a life. Her *and* the baby. She'd never imagined that he'd still want her.

Her conscience struck her. *But had she fantasised about this?* That was another thing entirely. And, to her shame, on some level she knew she had. Not that he would marry her, but that he would want her.

She turned to face the view blindly, not seeing the dusky lavender-hued sky. She could only see inwards, to a rushing kaleidoscope of images—meeting Lazaro for the first time, that passionate encounter, interrupting his engagement and incurring his wrath, then earlier, and now this ultimatum.

Because that was what it was.

Skye shivered. She had seen many facets to this man, but ultimately this was who he was: a ruthless billionaire whose main focus was in protecting his reputation and his business at all costs. Skye and the baby would only ever be by-products.

She had to surmise bleakly that even if he had married Leonora, she would have suffered a similar fate. Because Lazaro clearly wasn't interested in forging personal connections or creating the kind of family unit Skye had always yearned for.

She was glad she hadn't told him the full extent of her dreams and aspirations. She'd exposed herself enough as it was.

Skye had a sleepless night ahead of her. Not because she didn't know what to do, but because she knew she only had one option.

The following morning Lazaro heard a noise and looked up from where he was reading his tablet at the breakfast table on the terrace. Skye was standing there, looking pale and incredibly young. He was surprised to notice how tense she was. He put the tablet down and sat forward, pulling out the chair at his right. He had the very distinct impression that Skye might bolt at any moment.

'Come, sit down.'

He cursed her for his sleepless night. Knowing she was just down the hall had been torture.

Her hair was down and fell over her shoulders in long, damp, curly skeins of red and gold. She must have had a shower. Promptly he was rewarded with an image of water sluicing down her naked body. He shifted in the seat, irritated that she had this power over him.

She wore jeans and another non-descript T-shirt, and suddenly Lazaro wanted to see her draped in silks and satins.

Still she hadn't moved. He was about to speak again when she blurted out, 'I'll do it. I'll marry you.'

Something unclenched inside him, and he didn't like to acknowledge that it was a sensation of relief.

He stood up. 'Come with me. I have something for you.'

He walked back into the house, aware of her light, clean scent. He went into his study and to the safe, took out a small box.

He handed it to Skye, who was still looking pale. Something about her apparent fragility made him feel both irritated and something far more disturbing: protective.

He told himself that it was a natural biological reaction to the woman who was carrying his child.

Skye took the box. She still couldn't believe that she'd said yes to Lazaro's non-proposal and he'd barely changed expression. She cursed herself. What had she been hoping for? Tears of gratitude? He was only marrying her because he wanted to protect his reputation.

And give you and the baby a secure start, reminded her conscience.

She opened the royal blue velvet box and sucked in a breath when she saw the ring. It was a round pink diamond in a gold setting, with smaller white diamonds either side. Unusual. Not what she would have expected from someone like Lazaro.

She loved it.

She touched it and it sparkled. 'It's beautiful.' She looked at Lazaro. 'You knew I'd say yes?'

'I was prepared.'

Skye wanted to ask him if he'd picked it out himself but was too superstitious. If he had it would mean something, and if he hadn't it would mean something.

'Here—give it to me.'

She handed the box back to Lazaro and he took the ring out. He caught her left hand and lifted it up.

As he placed the ring on her finger Skye was saying, 'It probably won't fit—'

But it did. Perfectly. And it looked right on her finger, suited her skin tone.

She pulled her hand back, suddenly very aware of Lazaro holding it and their close proximity. But Lazaro didn't let go.

She looked at him, thinking, *If he kisses me now I'm not going to be able to hide—*

Hide what? asked that voice.

But he didn't pull her closer. He said, 'This ring...it's just a symbol. You know it doesn't mean anything, right? What there is between us...it's just physical. I don't want you to confuse passion with emotion.'

Skye pulled her hand back again and this time tucked it behind her back. She forced herself to hold Lazaro's gaze. 'I learnt not to get attached to people when I was growing up, as we were always moving. And as for love...? I saw how crazy it made my mother—constantly searching for something she couldn't find—so you really don't have to patronise me. I'm under no illusions.'

Lazaro looked at her, as if searching for something, but then he seemed to relax visibly and he said, 'Good. We're on the same page. I wouldn't want you to get... hurt, Skye.'

Irritation sparked inside Skye at his arrogant pronouncement, and she welcomed it as an antidote to feeling so powerless and vulnerable in this situation. 'I've had long years of practice in not letting people hurt me, Lazaro, but don't be so sure that you're immune. You might just find that you're the one liable to be hurt here.'

The tension dissipated as Lazaro smiled—one of the first really genuine smiles she'd seen. He looked younger. More carefree. More beautiful. *Lord.* If he smiled like that on a regular basis she wasn't sure her walls of defence wouldn't start to crumble. So much for her lofty words...

He caught her arm and started to walk her out of the study. 'I think I'll survive,' he said.

Suddenly Skye longed to see Lazaro brought to his

knees—all that pride and arrogance in tatters around him. She imagined herself standing over him, triumphant and smiling…

He obviously saw something in her face and said, 'What's so funny?'

And her smile faded because she knew it was a scenario about as likely to happen as a sudden snow shower over the Andalusian vineyards in summer.

'Nothing,' she said.

'Let's get some breakfast—we've got lots to plan now.'

A couple of days later Skye was looking reluctantly at herself in the full-length mirror in her bedroom at the *hacienda*. She was surrounded by women, the chief of whom stood back now and said, 'Very elegant, Miss O'Hara. Perfect for your wedding day.'

Skye's hair had been pulled back and she wore a cream shift dress overlaid with chiffon. It came to just below her knee and had an empire line. Her bump seemed to be growing daily now, but she was still at that stage where she didn't look obviously pregnant yet. There was a light coat to go over the dress, a shade darker. Slightly golden in hue. There were sheer tights and cream satin shoes with perilously high heels.

The woman gave her a last once-over and then instructed her assistants to put the wedding outfit away carefully. Then she looked at Skye and said ominously, 'Now for everything else.'

'Everything else' was a veritable wardrobe of clothes for all and any occasion. Daywear—beautifully cut trousers, shift dresses, delicate silk shirts. Evening wear—cocktail dresses and long gowns that Skye overheard the stylist say they'd have to adjust for her petite size. There were clothes to accommodate her in every stage of pregnancy. There was also underwear, shoes and jewellery.

She was relieved to see some jeans in the mix—maternity and regular. So her own identity wouldn't be erased completely.

Then she was taken into the local town to a beauty salon, and subjected to a range of procedures ranging from pleasant—massage—to downright sadistic—a bikini wax.

As she sat under the hands of a hairstylist at the end of the day, having been waxed, buffed and pummelled, Skye thought of what Lazaro had asked her the other morning after breakfast.

'Why did you say yes?'

She'd answered, 'For all the reasons I told you, and also because I never even knew my father's name. By giving our child your name, he, or she, will never have to wonder where he comes from, like I did.'

Skye had been surprised at how emotional she'd felt when she'd said that to Lazaro. She'd spent so many years wondering who and where her father was. What he did. What his name was. She could at least give that to her child—a name.

Skye's focus came back to the salon, where the hairdresser was saying something about trimming her hair by an inch or two. She made a noncommittal noise of assent.

A little while later the hairdresser beamed at Skye and held up a mirror so she could see the back of her head. Skye smiled weakly, not recognising herself.

This was her life now, and she had to get used to it.

Lazaro saw Skye arrive back from the salon in town and for a second almost didn't recognise her.

She was sleek and polished. Her hair was straight and gleaming red and gold, bouncing around her shoulders. She wore a bright blue shirt-dress with a gold belt around her still slim waist and gold gladiator-style sandals. Gold hoops swung from her ears.

Instinctively he moved from his office to meet her in the hall. Her scent reached him—except it wasn't her scent. It was too heavy for Skye…too flowery.

'You're back.'

She turned, and he saw the tell-tale way her eyes widened on him before she shuttered her expression.

'Yes. I'm back.' She struck a pose with her hand on her hip. 'The new improved me—like it?'

Lazaro wasn't sure he did at all, and that revelation was very disconcerting. He felt like mussing her up…putting his hands in her hair to bring back its unruliness. He lamented the fact that make-up was hiding the smattering of freckles across her nose and cheeks.

But as she stood before him now there was no denying what had been hiding in plain sight under her tomboyish uniform.

He said, with a rough tone in his voice that he couldn't hide, 'You're beautiful.'

Instead of feeling pleased with the compliment, Skye wished she hadn't opened her mouth. She felt deflated that he liked her like this. Because she didn't feel like herself. And yet Lazaro approved of this version of her, if his obvious approval was anything to go by.

He said, 'I've got a copy of the pre-nuptial agreement in my office, if you want to come and look it over?'

'Oh.'

Lazaro's mouth quirked and Skye fought not to scowl at him. She followed him into his office.

'Please, sit,' he said. 'Do you want something to drink?'

Skye sat down, seriously intimidated by the thick document she saw. 'Um…just some water, please.'

She pulled the papers towards her and started skimming over the words.

Agreement between the parties... Skye Blossom
O'Hara... Lazaro Sanchez...to agree to be married
for a minimum of five years...or until such time as
they mutually agree to part...

There was a section on matters pertaining to the baby, how custody would be agreed in the event of a divorce. And there was another section on money. Skye's jaw dropped.

Lazaro, who was pacing near the window, stopped. 'What is it?'

Skye pointed at the page where there was an amount listed—an annuity for her when they divorced, and if she remained faithful during the marriage.

Lazaro came closer and looked down. He stepped back, a strange look coming over his face. 'What? It's not enough?'

Skye sputtered, 'It's ridiculous!'

Lazaro's expression turned hard. 'It didn't take long for your true colours to emerge.'

Skye stood up, outraged. 'Not because it's too little! It's too much! It's about as much as the national debt for a small country. It's obscene. Do you have *any* idea what most mortals survive on in a week, a year?'

Lazaro fought back the cynicism which told him she was lying. She had to be. He gritted out, 'Of course I know what most people survive on. I survived on a lot less myself for years.'

She immediately looked contrite. 'I forgot…sorry.'

'It's because I know how hard and undignified it is to live on nothing that I've vowed never to be in that position again—and as the mother of my child, you certainly won't be.'

'Okay,' she said, sitting down again. 'I get that. But this is too much. I can survive on a fraction of that. And it's not *my* money. I'd feel weird living off you.'

'It's not just you, though—it's you and my child.'

Suddenly Skye felt sad to think of a time when it would just be her and the child now inside her, getting on with their lives while Lazaro dipped in and out. But he was so busy, so in demand, how could it be any other way?

'Still, once a child is clothed and fed and educated, it really doesn't need much else. It's too much.'

After a long moment he conceded. 'Okay, we can renegotiate that bit. Is there anything else? You should really have a solicitor look it over. I can recommend someone impartial.'

Skye shook her head. 'No, it's fine. You've been very fair, and the custody arrangements are in the best interests of our child so I've no argument there... Just give me a pen and I'll sign.'

Lazaro got a pen and made some notes to say she wanted to renegotiate the settlement monies, and then turned to the last page and handed her the pen. She signed without even looking at the rest of it. Then she put the pen down and stood up again.

'Is that all?'

'So eager to leave?'

Lazaro had asked the question lightly, but Skye had the impression he was actually a little hurt. Nonsense. Lazaro Sanchez was impermeable. She was dreaming. In truth, she wanted to throw herself into his arms and beg him to make love to her again, but there was no way she would ever reveal herself like that.

'I want to go up to that room and work on my sketch of the old man. I promised his daughter I'd get it to her before the weekend.'

When he was silent for a moment Skye thought he was about to tell her she couldn't do the sketch, but then he said, 'I have to go to Madrid, actually—today. And I won't be back until the wedding. The stylist and her team will help you get ready on the day. We'll leave for Venice after a small breakfast reception here.'

'Venice?'

Lazaro nodded. 'I have some events to go to and some business to take care of there—a building I'm acquiring. We can double it up as a honeymoon.'

Skye panicked at the thought of being in such a beautiful place with the most intoxicating man she'd ever met. And if there were social situations how on earth could she hope to match up to the kind of people she'd seen that night at the engagement party?

'But it's a fake marriage—do I *have* to go there with you?'

Lazaro had never met a woman who made him so hot that every time he looked at her he wanted her, but who also couldn't wait to get away from him at every opportunity.

The fact that she preferred to sketch some old stranger rather than—

Rather than what? sneered a voice. *Rather than spend time with you?*

Lazaro didn't think. He reached for Skye, and just touching her was instant heat. He brought her flush against his body, saw her pupils dilate, colour flood her cheeks. The silk of the dress was a flimsy barrier between their bodies.

'You want me, don't you?' he asked, even as he could feel the tremor of reaction in her body. He had to hear her say it. She couldn't deny it. But she wanted to—he could see that.

'You know I do.'

Something inside him howled with gratification. He bent his head and fused his mouth to hers, the cushiony softness of her lips almost undoing him. He willed her to open up to him, and she did, on a sigh, giving him access to all that sweetness.

In seconds he was drowning, pulling her even closer, spreading his hands down her back to her pert behind. He almost forgot… But at the last moment he remembered and pulled back, taking great satisfaction in seeing how long it took for her to open her eyes. Feeling the rapid rise and fall of her chest next to his.

When she was finally focused on him he said through the clamour of his blood, 'There's nothing fake about *this*, Skye. It'll be a real marriage in every sense of the word, believe me. As real as it gets.'

As real as it gets in his world, thought Skye. *Where no emotions are involved.*

She hated him for making her admit that she wanted him, and yet she was reeling from the kiss. Trembling.

She pushed herself back and out of Lazaro's arms. 'I'm going to go and do that sketch now.'

Lazaro looked infuriatingly cool. 'I'll see you on Saturday, Skye.'

She turned and fled, before she could humiliate herself further.

CHAPTER SEVEN

The day of the wedding

'*MUY BONITA, SEÑORITA.*'

Skye forced a smile for Almudena, who had a suspiciously bright look in her eyes. She'd become a friend to Skye, and it made her feel even more like a fraud.

The stylist and a couple of assistants had left after getting her ready for the wedding. Now a car was there to take her to the town hall, where Lazaro was apparently waiting.

The journey was short. Too short.

Only a few days ago she'd been angry and upset that Lazaro had all but abandoned her, but now she wanted to prolong the moments before she would see him again. She wasn't ready for this gargantuan change. For giving her life up.

But then, she reminded herself, it wasn't just about her. She didn't have that luxury any more. And, anyway, she wasn't her mother. She wanted to put down roots and give her child a solid, stable life.

The car pulled up outside the town hall, where an officious-looking woman was waiting, looking at her watch.

She opened the car door for Skye and helped her out, smiling. 'I'm Sara, Lazaro's assistant. I'll be one of the witnesses.'

Skye got out, wobbly in the high heels. She drew a couple of glances from passing people with her bright red hair, but she was oblivious.

She said to Sara, 'He's waiting?'

The woman looked anxious. 'Yes.'

Skye stood there for a moment in her fancy new clothes, with her make-up and hair done. Behind her was her old safe life. The one she knew. Ahead of her were uncharted waters. Life with a man who wanted her but who didn't really care about her.

At that moment Skye felt something tiny inside her, like a very faint fluttering. She put her hand down over her belly, which seemed to be growing daily. She knew realistically that it couldn't possibly be the baby's movement that she could feel...not yet...but it reminded her, as if she needed reminding, of what was at stake.

She could only go forward.

Lazaro knew Skye had arrived when he felt a subtle shift in energy. The few people in the registrar's office hushed. His skin prickled with awareness. He didn't turn around to watch her walk towards him even though he wanted to.

She came alongside him and her scent reached him. *Her* scent. Light and delicate. Not the overpowering one she'd had on the other day.

The constriction inside him eased. A constriction that had been there since his fraught phone call with his half-brother the day before.

Gabriel Torres had said to Lazaro, 'I underestimated you, Sanchez. No one was under any illusions about your motivation in marrying Leonora Flores, but the fact that you're marrying the alleged mother of your child shows some balls. She couldn't be bought off, then, no?'

Lazaro had been surprised at the depth of rage his brother's words had aroused in him. He'd controlled himself with effort and said, 'Not everyone and everything is for sale, Torres. My plans for the old market space in the centre of

Madrid are infinitely better than yours. I actually care about this city. That's all you need to worry about.'

Gabriel Torres had made a dismissive sound. 'Please don't insult me by pretending you have an altruistic streak. Your interest in this is purely personal and against me, because of this ridiculous claim that we're related. It's just a shame that Leonora had to become one of your casualties.'

Lazaro had counted to ten silently. 'My claim is not spurious, Gabriel. I want nothing from you or your family except acknowledgement. And do you expect me to believe that your own marriage to Leonora isn't strategic? She's a good woman, Gabriel—not someone you should be using as a pawn.'

Gabriel had responded tersely. 'She's where she belongs, that's all that matters.'

Those words reverberated in Lazaro's head now, as he looked at the woman who'd come to stand beside him. *'She's where she belongs, that's all that matters.'* Strange and disconcerting how those words seemed to...fit.

Skye was looking straight ahead, and she was holding a posy of flowers that looked as if they'd come from a garden, tied with string. Her knuckles were white. In fact, she was pale.

Instinctively Lazaro found himself reaching out. He put his hand on Skye's, willing her to look at him. After an infinitesimal moment she did, and a faint pink washed into her cheeks.

Lazaro raised a brow in silent question. After a moment she nodded her head. Her hair was sleek and pulled back into a low ponytail. She was taller in high heels, reaching almost to his shoulder. Make-up covered her freckles. *Again.* And once again Lazaro had the desire to muss her up.

The registrar started talking and Lazaro faced forward again, repeating his words where necessary, hearing Skye's soft, clear voice do the same. Their witnesses were both employees of his.

He acknowledged how different this wedding was from the one he'd had planned with Leonora, which would have been in the cathedral in Madrid under the full glare of the world's media. He realised that there was something about that scenario now that was distinctly unpalatable.

'You are now married. You may kiss your wife, Señor Sanchez.'

Lazaro looked at Skye. His new wedding ring felt heavy on his finger. Solid. She wasn't so pale any more. She looked up at him warily. He put a finger under her chin, tipping it up. He felt resistance and he frowned.

She whispered, 'Do we have to do this now? In front of these people?'

'Yes. We do.'

The irony of the fact that he had just married the one woman who seemed intent on resisting him at every turn was not welcome. Nor was the vivid memory of how it had felt to be embedded deep inside her, the exquisite clasp of her embrace.

Irritation made him pull her into his body, an arm around her waist. Her body was soft against his. He lowered his mouth and touched infinite softness, and he cursed her pull on him even as he couldn't help deepening the kiss.

Skye had really hoped Lazaro wouldn't kiss her in front of these people, because she was afraid she wouldn't be able to control herself around him. But it was too late. He was kissing her and she was drowning.

When he finally drew back his eyes were two burning green gems and she was clinging to him. She let go and would have staggered back in her high heels if he hadn't been holding her. She scowled at him.

He frowned. 'What's wrong?'

She forced her features into the semblance of a smile, aware of their audience. 'Nothing. I'm fine.'

He took her hand and led her to a back room, where they signed the register. Then he led her back out and said, 'There will be photographers from the press waiting when we go outside. Are you ready for this?'

No.

But Skye just nodded. She had no choice but to get used to this.

They walked outside into the bright sunshine and for a moment Skye was blinded. Lazaro put his arm around her waist and pulled her close. She was still holding the small posy of flowers she'd impulsively picked from the garden at the *hacienda*.

When she could see again, she heard their names being called.

'Lazaro! Skye! Over here!'

'Please...*una màs*, one more!'

But Lazaro put up his hand and signalled that they'd got enough pictures.

Then one voice called out, 'Hey, Sanchez, how do you feel about Gabriel Torres marrying your ex-fiancée?'

Lazaro went very still, and then he turned in the direction of where the question had come from and said coolly, 'My wife and I wish them all the very best, of course.'

My wife and I.

As if they were already a unit, speaking as one.

The speed with which Lazaro seemed to be adapting to married life with a woman he would never have married under other circumstances demonstrated to Skye just how ruthless he was—and how determined he was to make things work. To keep up appearances.

He guided her over to where a sleek SUV was parked

and helped her get into the back. He joined her on the other side and the driver moved into the traffic smoothly.

He looked at her. 'Okay?'

Skye was still seeing stars after the blaze of cameras, but she nodded. 'Fine.'

'After the wedding breakfast we'll leave for Venice. I asked the stylist to pack a bag for you.'

Lazaro's cool unflappability, when she felt frayed and on edge after that kiss—after *that ceremony*—made her say sharply, 'That's how it is now, is it? You'll tell me where we're going and what we're doing?'

He answered smoothly. 'I'm a busy man, Skye. My work takes me all over Europe and to America. I'll bring you with me as and when I need to, but once the baby comes obviously I won't expect you to be as mobile as before. To that end,' he continued, 'I've already selected some properties to view in Madrid, with a view to moving somewhere more suitable for you and the baby.'

'*And* you?'

He looked at her as if he was humouring her. 'Yes—and me. But I will keep the penthouse apartment at the hotel for convenience, if I'm in the centre of town or conducting events at the hotel.'

For a second Skye was bombarded with a vision of Lazaro, passionately kissing a tall, sleek, beautiful woman in front of one of the massive windows in his penthouse apartment, while Skye walked back and forth in some suburban house soothing a fractious baby.

The spike of jealousy shocked her with its strength.

'I don't want to be treated like some commodity you can just move around, Lazaro. If you're going to do that I'd prefer to get on with my life in Dublin.'

'Living in a mould-infested basement flat and working as a waitress while doing street portraits for extra money?'

Skye flushed. 'At least I'd be independent. And I know

it's not just about me any more…but I won't go back to a life where I'm at the mercy of the whims of someone else.'

'I'm your husband, Skye, not your mother. This is a partnership.'

Skye stayed silent at that, afraid of what more might spill out of her mouth if she opened it.

The breakfast went quickly, and afterwards Almudena and the stylist helped Skye to change into a going-away outfit. It was in the same style as her wedding dress but in a light blue colour. A matching jacket buttoned just above her bump.

Before she left the room to join Lazaro downstairs she saw the posy of flowers she'd picked from the garden earlier. They looked droopy and a little sad. Skye hated to think it, but she really hoped it wasn't a sign.

When she got downstairs Lazaro was pacing and looking at his watch. He'd changed too, into a light grey suit, his shirt open at the neck. He looked up when she came down the stairs, those green eyes roving over her body. Little flames of heat licked at her nerve-endings.

His hair looked slightly messier than usual, as if he'd been running a hand through it. He was so beautiful he made Skye's heart spasm.

No, she told herself fiercely. Not her heart. He didn't have her heart. Yet. *Never,* she told herself with a kind of fatal desperation.

He reached out to her and she went forward, putting her hand into his. His hand was big and firm, closing around hers. Skye didn't like the way his touch made her feel all at once safe and protected, but also as if she was standing on the edge of a precipice about to fall off.

He speared her with that green gaze. 'Ready?'

Skye wanted to say *no*—to pull free, run back up to the bedroom, take off all the new clothes, the make-up, and go upstairs to that empty room and sketch until she felt grounded again.

But of course she couldn't do that. So she just nodded and said, 'I'm ready.'

Skye had slept for the relatively short flight to Venice. As much because she was genuinely fatigued as because she was finding it hard to compute that she was actually married to Lazaro. She really hadn't wanted to investigate the swirling mass of emotions in her gut. So she'd slept. And had been woken by Lazaro to find herself in the bedroom at the back of the small plane.

She was wide awake now, though, being helped into a boat that would take them into Venice along the Grand Canal. It was afternoon, and the sun was high, but the late summer was taking the edge off the searing heat.

The boat rocked as Lazaro stepped on, and he sat beside her on the bench after exchanging a few words in Italian with the driver. They took off, and Skye relished the breeze moving through her hair, which was already unravelling. There was a refreshing fine mist of spray from the water and impulsively she stood up, so she could see when they entered the Grand Canal.

When they did, she sucked in a breath at the sheer beauty laid before her. The ancient Venetian palaces lining each side of the wide canal. The gondolas. The speedboat taxis.

Lazaro stood beside her. 'Is this your first time in Venice?'

She shook her head. 'I was here when I was about sixteen with my mother. We lived here for six months. It was like something out of a fairy tale for me… I've always wanted to come back.'

'Does this mean you're fluent in Italian too?' There was a strange note in Lazaro's voice.

Skye glanced at him and her heart skipped a beat. The

breeze was ruffling his hair and against this backdrop he could have been a charismatic prince from medieval times. Or more likely a marauding pirate.

Skye struggled to recall what he'd said, and then she answered, 'I know enough to get by.'

For a moment they looked at each other, the grandeur of the Grand Canal going unnoticed. Lazaro reached out and twined a tendril of loose hair around his finger, tugging Skye towards him.

'What other languages do you speak?'

'Passable French, Greek... Arabic. We lived in Cairo for a couple of months when I was twelve.'

He said, 'You're a very...surprising woman.'

At that moment the boat made a *thud* sound and came to a halt. Skye broke out of her trance, a little relieved at the interruption. There had been a look in Lazaro's eyes that had made her insides flutter far too dangerously.

They'd arrived at one of the grand *palazzo* buildings fronting onto the canal. Standing on its own, it dwarfed the buildings on either side, windows gleaming. A balcony ran the length of the building on the first floor. It was breathtaking.

They were helped out of the boat and up the steps into the building. Marble floors and Murano chandeliers decorated the reception area. It was deliciously cool inside.

A man in a suit approached, greeting Lazaro effusively in Italian. Lazaro smoothly replied, also in Italian. Skye wondered how he'd become so fluent.

The man introduced himself to Skye as the manager of the hotel and led them over to an elevator. The inside was as elegant as the reception area, with hundreds of mirrors in its gold-panelled walls. Skye avoided her reflection, not wanting to see how bedraggled she must look.

Then she thought of something, and asked Lazaro suspiciously, 'Do you own this hotel too?'

He leaned back against one of the walls of mirrors, hands in his pockets. Supremely at home in this rarefied atmosphere in spite of his background. 'No.' His mouth twitched. 'But I am in talks to acquire it—which is why we're here. I'm finalising some details before I sign the contracts.'

Skye was about to say *oh* but she clamped her mouth shut, trying not to be intimidated at the sheer level of Lazaro's wealth. She couldn't even begin to imagine what a *palazzo* on the Grand Canal in Venice was worth.

The lift doors opened then, and they stepped out and into the most opulent room Skye had ever been in.

The parquet floor was covered with exquisite oriental rugs. There was *chinoiserie* wallpaper on the walls. More Murano chandeliers and elaborate frescoes on the gilded ceiling. Three huge windows opened out onto the balcony which overlooked the canal.

She went over and stood on it, watching the sunlight bounce off the canal and the waves created by the boats and activity.

'It's so beautiful… I've never seen anything like it.'

Lazaro stood beside her. 'Yes…it's pretty spectacular.'

Skye tore her gaze from the view to look at him. 'Why do you want to buy it?'

He shrugged lightly. 'Because I can. Because it'll enhance my portfolio.'

He turned and went back into the room. It was dotted with sleek furniture in a more modern style than the room, but perversely it fitted. Low glass coffee tables, cream couches. Modern art and artefacts.

He went to a drinks tray and looked back at her. 'Would you like some juice or water?'

She came into the room. 'Sparkling water, please.' She kicked off her shoes and gave a groan of relief, slipping off her coat before sinking down onto one of the couches, tucking her legs underneath her.

Lazaro handed her a glass and she took a sip. He had what looked like a tumbler of whisky in his hand. He sat down at the other end of the couch, resting an arm across it. The movement tightened his shirt across his chest, and instantly Skye wanted to undo his buttons and spread the material apart so she could look at him. And not just look at him.

Her face burning, she took another gulp of water.

Pregnancy hormones.

'You're really not that impressed, are you?'

Skye looked at Lazaro, whose gaze was narrowed on her hot face. 'Impressed by what?'

He waved a hand. 'The fact that I'm about to become the owner of one of Venice's most celebrated and oldest *palazzos.*'

Skye looked at him. 'When I lived here with my mother needless to say we were in one of the less salubrious areas, far away from the canal. I used to dream of travelling down the canal by boat and stepping into one of these buildings as if I owned it... But that was just a fantasy. It doesn't really matter to me either way. It's enough for me to be here and experience it.'

Lazaro leant forward. 'But that's the thing—it's not a fantasy. It's your reality now.'

It hit Skye in that moment how different her life would be.

There was a knock on the door and the hotel manager appeared again to check that everything was all right. A porter was behind him with their bags. Skye saw them being taken into what she presumed was the bedroom.

She stood up as the manager put down a pile of papers on a round table and said, 'The evening editions have just come in with news of your wedding. Many congratulations, Señora Sanchez.'

She murmured her thanks as Lazaro walked him to the

door. The porter left too. Skye was drawn to the papers, even though she dreaded seeing what they had to say about her marrying the man whose engagement she'd ruined so publicly.

On the top were the Italian tabloids. There was a picture of her and Lazaro emerging from the town hall. Skye winced. She looked like a rabbit caught in the headlights, eyes wide and startled, clutching her very homemade bunch of flowers and latched onto Lazaro's arm.

She couldn't have looked less like the sleekly perfect woman he *should* have married.

All she could think about now was that he might not have loved Leonora, but he had felt something for her, and he must have desired her—how could he not have? And if they were here right now they'd be in the bedroom—

Skye cursed out loud.

Lazaro came over. 'What is it?' He saw what she was looking at and swept up the papers and dumped them in a rubbish bin near the door.

Skye didn't want Lazaro to see an atom of what she was feeling, so she went back over to the balcony to look out over the canal. They were married now, and having a baby. She had to deal with it and stop feeling so insecure.

But, as if sensing her turmoil, Lazaro came over. 'Skye?'

Stubbornly, she kept her gaze forward.

'Skye, look at me.'

With extreme reluctance she did, turning to face Lazaro, thinking churlishly in that moment that for a man who was fixated on world domination he seemed to have an uncanny ability to push her when she wanted it least.

'What is it? What's going on in that head of yours?' he asked.

'Nothing… Just…' But she couldn't keep it in. She blurted out, 'Leonora—she was so beautiful and perfect… You must have wanted her… She should be here, not me…'

* * *

Lazaro was struck by the fact that Skye was wrong on so many levels.

'I didn't want her. That's why it was so easy to let her go.'

In that instant Lazaro realised that he would never have been as sanguine about letting Skye go. She was embedded under his skin and he hungered for her on a constant basis.

But it was more than that. Just watching the expressions on her face as they'd arrived in Venice had enthralled him. He would have bet money she'd never seen it before, and when she'd said she had a small part of him had felt something disturbingly like jealousy. Because he hadn't witnessed her very first viewing of this magical city.

Desire made you think crazy things.

Skye was frowning. 'You mean you never…?'

Lazaro was almost enjoying her inarticulacy. 'Are you asking me if I slept with her?'

Skye blushed.

It was still amazing to Lazaro every time she did it. And especially here, against this sophisticated backdrop.

'Don't make fun of me,' Skye said hotly.

Lazaro acted on impulse and ran his knuckles down one hot cheek. Her hair was coming undone and her freckles were starting to pop through her wedding make-up. And just the feel of her hot cheek under his knuckle was enough to tip him over the edge of his control.

'I didn't sleep with Leonora, Skye. I wasn't marrying her because I wanted her. Desire complicates things.'

Now her expression shuttered, and everything in him rejected that way she had sometimes of closing off.

'You mean I've complicated things?' she said.

He put a finger under her chin, tipping it up. She was still trying to control her face. He could see the effort.

'Funnily enough, this is one complication I don't seem to care about any more.'

The closed-off expression faded. He could see uncertainty. Vulnerability.

'You don't?'

He shook his head. 'We have much more important things to do right now.'

'Like what?'

He put his hands on her waist and felt its thickness. Her bump was growing daily now. And her breasts were fuller, pushing against the material of her dress. He'd made love with some of the most beautiful women in the world, but not one of them had ever fired him up like this.

'Like consummating this marriage.'

Lazaro pulled her close. He saw the effect of his arousal on her. The way her cheeks got pink and her eyes widened. Glittering a dark blue. He felt a tremor run through her body, the same kind he was trying to control in his.

He wanted Skye. Only Skye.

He shut out all the voices in his head warning him that this was different from every other time. He told himself it was still within his control even as he covered Skye's mouth with his and knew somewhere very deep and secret that it *was* different, and that control was fast slipping out of his grasp with every kiss. With every touch.

Skye was afraid to admit how much it meant to her to know that Lazaro hadn't slept with his ex-fiancée. He wanted *her*. She could feel it in his kiss.

She heard a faint catcall from somewhere out on the canal and she couldn't help smiling against Lazaro's mouth. But it soon faded as the kiss deepened and became explicit. Lazaro was showing her with his tongue and his hands what he wanted to do to her more intimately.

She twined her arms around his neck and felt herself being lifted off the ground. He brought her into the glorious opulence of the suite and into the bedroom, which Skye barely noticed.

She wondered if every time they slept together would be infused with this sense of urgency. Desperation.

He put her down on her feet by the bed and Skye started opening his shirt buttons, exactly as she'd fantasised doing only a short while before.

His skin was warm. Vital. She moved down, undoing his shirt buttons, exposing his chest, the curling dark blond hair that covered his pectorals.

Then he said thickly, 'You. I want to see you.'

He gently turned her around and undid the zip at the back of her sheath dress. It fell forward and down, and with a tug over her hips it fell to the floor. Now all Skye wore was a pair of panties and a matching bra, and sheer pull-ups with lace tops.

She felt suddenly self-conscious—aware that in spite of the circumstances this was effectively her wedding night, even though it wasn't yet night-time outside. Her belly had grown even in the space of time since she'd seen Lazaro before the wedding. It was forming into a proper bump now.

He turned her around to face him. She looked down and he tipped her face up with a finger under her chin. He looked at her—all of her. Slowly and thoroughly.

'You are beautiful, Skye.'

She ducked her head again, bringing her arms up, afraid that he'd seen her insecurity and was just saying platitudes. She hated this new, needy side of herself that she'd never noticed before.

Then she forced her head back up. This wasn't her. Shy and insecure. She was now married to this man, pregnant with his child, and she wanted him. And he wanted her.

She reached around and undid the clasp of her bra, letting it fall open and to the floor.

Lazaro sucked in a breath.

Her breasts felt heavier, fuller. He cupped them, rubbing his thumbs across her sensitive nipples until she had to bite her lip to stop herself from moaning out loud.

Skye was afraid she'd explode there and then, just from being touched. So she dislodged Lazaro's hands and continued undoing the buttons on his shirt. She spread back the material to take in the magnificence of his perfectly defined muscles.

She moved her hands across his chest wonderingly, feeling the slightly springy hair under her palms, the warmth of his skin. Grazing the hard nubs of his nipples. On impulse she leant forward, explored with her tongue, swirling it around the hard piece of flesh.

Lazaro's hand was in her hair, undoing it and combing his fingers through it, massaging her scalp. He tugged her head back and she looked up at him. She couldn't escape that glittering green gaze. He looked back at her for a long moment, and then he cupped her face and he was kissing her again. Sliding his tongue along hers in a flagrantly sexual and drugging dance.

Skye gripped on to him to stay standing, the blood turning to fire in her veins. Her breasts were pressed against his bare chest and she strained to get closer, creating delicious friction.

He cupped her bottom then, lifting her up against him, and she wound her arms around his neck. If she could have climbed into his skin she would.

Then she was falling backwards, landing on the soft surface of the bed where Lazaro laid her down.

She sucked in a breath, dizzy. And watched as he removed his clothing with far more efficiency than she could have managed. He stood before her naked and utterly unselfconscious. His outer layer stripped away, revealing the perfect male specimen underneath.

And he was majestic. Like every glorious statue she'd

ever seen of the male form in dusty Greek museums or Parisian art galleries.

His erection was thick and heavy, and Skye's lower body clenched in anticipation.

He came to her, and with a precision she didn't want to think about divested her of her panties and pull-ups, throwing them aside. Now she was naked, on the biggest bed in the most opulent bedroom she'd ever been in. Cherubs and angels danced among clouds on the ceiling.

But she couldn't have cared less about the celebrated sixteenth-century artist who had created such stunning work.

Lazaro naked, moving over her with a look of hungry intent in his eyes, was far more impressive.

His gaze stopped on her breasts, and then between her legs. Skye had never felt so needy. He rested over her on his hands and dipped his head, his mouth finding hers with unerring accuracy. She reached for him, needing contact. Needing to feel him on her. *In her.*

His hands were everywhere, moulding the shape of her body as if learning it by touch. Caressing her breasts, cupping one soft full mound and moving his mouth off hers and down so he could surround the taut straining peak with heat and warmth, nipping gently with his teeth.

He knelt between her legs and pulled them apart. He smoothed his hands up her thighs and then around and underneath her buttocks, kneading her flesh. And then he bent down, pressing kisses first along her inner thighs and then higher, to the epicentre where every nerve was quivering, waiting, aching...

Her back arched off the bed when he touched her there with his mouth and tongue. Exploring deep inside where she was laid bare in her desire for him. She didn't care. She was undone... And she came in an intense rush of pleasure, her body spasming for long seconds in the aftermath.

Skye opened her eyes and saw Lazaro above her, reaching out to brush some hair off her face. She was panting… sated and yet hungry for more.

'Okay?'

His question touched on a vulnerable point inside her. She nodded, unable to speak. He came between her legs and she felt the blunt head of his erection against her sensitised skin. He massaged her there for a moment, with his thumb, and she bit her lip at the sensation. He was arousing her again.

'Ready?'

She nodded. Lazaro angled his body and with one smooth thrust seated himself deep inside her. She gasped at the sensation, which was almost too much, and then her body relaxed around his…adapting, yielding.

Lazaro started to move, an inexorable glide in and out, ratcheting up the tension, finding her hand and lacing his fingers with hers over her head. Every sinew in her body pulled taut as they climbed higher and higher, until their tension reached the point of no return and Skye's body went still for an infinitesimal moment before falling down and down into a vortex of pleasure that eclipsed anything she'd felt before.

Lazaro's body stilled. He was so deep inside Skye she felt as if he was touching her heart. A fanciful notion she batted away as soon as it appeared. And then powerful shudders racked his frame as he found his own release. Her body pulsated around him, milking his essence.

Skye wasn't aware of Lazaro extricating himself from her embrace… She had fallen into oblivion.

CHAPTER EIGHT

WHEN SKYE WOKE she could hear the sounds of water nearby—a rhythmic lapping against stone. The sound of a horn from a boat roused her completely. She looked around the room at the fantastical ceiling. The gold inlaid décor. The massive, very rumpled bed.

Heat flooded her body. She turned her head and saw the indentation on the pillow where Lazaro had slept. It was dusk outside, the sky an inky lavender colour.

Had she dreamt it or had Lazaro tucked her into his body after making love to her and spread a hand across her belly?

She heard a noise and looked up. Lazaro stepped into the room, hair damp and curling after a shower, wearing black trousers and a snowy white shirt.

He held up his hands. 'I need help with the cufflinks.'

The event.

Skye sat up, holding the sheet to her chest. 'There's a thing? Tonight?'

'Yes, we have to leave in forty-five minutes.'

Skye felt sick, and grabbed for the nearest covering she could find—a robe that Lazaro must have left out for her. She pulled it on and got out of bed, panic spiking.

'I need to get ready...' She looked at him. 'I have no idea how to get ready.'

Without even looking she knew her hair had reverted to its default unruliness. The make-up so painstakingly applied that morning was well and truly gone.

'I'll call for someone to come up and help.'

She went over and did up his cufflinks, feeling shy all of a sudden, in spite of what had just happened.

'Thank you.'

She looked up. He was clean-shaven, and she wanted to reach up and press her mouth against his jaw. But she didn't.

She stepped back. 'I should take a shower.'

She went into the bathroom and it was as impressive as the rest of the suite. A huge bath. Two sinks. A shower big enough for—

Skye's mind was immediately full of X-rated images. She shut them down and dropped the robe, twisting her hair up and turning on the spray, willing down her growing panic at the thought of her first public function with Lazaro.

As his wife.

When she went back into the bedroom she saw a dress laid out on the bed. She'd tried it on in Spain, for the stylist, and it was intimidatingly beautiful.

It was champagne-coloured and long, and covered her from neck to toe, even her arms. The material was so light and delicate, though, that Skye was afraid to touch it. Not to mention the hundreds of thousands of tiny mother-of-pearl beads and crystals sewn into the fabric that shimmered when she moved.

There was a light knock on the door and a young woman put her head around it. 'Señora Sanchez? Your husband said you might need some help?'

Your husband. She hated how much she liked the sound of that when she'd always considered herself an independent woman.

She forced a smile. 'Yes, thanks so much.'

The woman came in, smiling. She said conspiratorially, 'I'm under strict instructions not to straighten your hair.'

Butterflies erupted in Skye's belly. Dangerous. Just because Lazaro evidently preferred her hair in its natural state, it didn't mean anything. At all.

The girl looked at the dress and said efficiently, 'We'll need flesh-coloured underwear.'

Lazaro was surrounded by a group of important contacts—people he had come here specifically to meet. Usually in this kind of scenario he was focused and single-minded when it came to getting what he wanted out of his peers. But this evening...for the first time...he was distracted.

Lazaro's attention was fixated on where Skye stood a few feet away, in animated conversation with an older woman. When she'd emerged into the salon from the bedroom earlier his mind had blanked. His first thought had been: *She's naked.* But she wasn't naked. The dress was the most provocative thing he'd ever seen. And yet not a sliver of skin could be seen below her neckline.

It was flesh-coloured, and clung to every curve the woman had—including the small swell of her belly. And her breasts. It shimmered when she moved. Her hair was up, loose tendrils framing her face. He didn't know what she'd done with her make-up but she looked more like *her.* He could see her freckles.

When they'd walked in to the party—her hand holding his in a death-grip—he'd seen the way people—*men*—looked at her, and for the second time in his life he'd experienced a feeling that had to be jealousy.

But eventually she'd let go and gravitated towards others. Now she looked as if she couldn't care less where Lazaro was, throwing her head back and laughing at something the woman said, drawing the attention of more men.

Lazaro was about to move over to where she was when someone said, 'Sanchez...tell us, are you really signing the contracts for the Palazzo Rizzoli tomorrow?'

Lazaro dragged his gaze off his wife, resenting the intrusion. Suddenly he went cold when he realised how close he was coming to forgetting why he was even there in the first place. To continue to secure his place in this world where people whispered behind his back and waited for him to show his lack of breeding.

He turned his attention back where it needed to be.

Skye knew the moment Lazaro's intense gaze moved off her. She felt it like a physical thing. She glanced over and saw he was talking with a group of important-looking men and women. All very serious.

She sighed. Her feet were starting to hurt her, and the nice older woman she'd been talking to had had to leave. So now she was on her own.

This function was being held in another beautiful palace on the Grand Canal. Candles and low lighting imbued everything with a golden hue.

The crowd was exactly like the one that had been in Spain the night Skye had gone to find Lazaro. Exclusive and moneyed. Entitled. Skye wondered what it must have been like for Lazaro to grow up knowing that he *should* have been part of this world, but had been cruelly and brutally cast aside due to an accident of birth.

She could understand where Lazaro's drive and ambition stemmed from. But she wondered if it would bring him the satisfaction he craved.

Her hand went to her belly. She couldn't fathom inflicting such cruelty on an innocent child. How a mother could have let her baby go just like that.

Skye became aware of the way people around her were looking at her. She tried not to fidget in her dress, and decided to go to the bathroom to check that everything was in place.

She looked at Lazaro, to let him know, but he was turned away from her, talking to someone. Ridiculously, Skye felt old hurt resurface. There had been too many times in her childhood and young life when her mother had turned her back on her to pursue her own whims, leaving Skye to her own devices.

She reminded herself of what Lazaro had said to her, *'I'm your husband, not your mother.'* She needed to grow a spine if she was going to survive in this world. Lazaro had never pretended to feel anything but desire for her. She simply amused him with her observations and quirks.

Angry that she was letting his inattention get to her, Skye didn't bother interrupting him and went to find the bathroom, sighing with relief when she got there and it was blessedly empty.

She was just checking her back view when a woman came in. Tall, stunningly beautiful, with long glossy dark hair. Wearing a simple strapless dress that instantly made Skye feel overdressed.

The woman smiled at Skye but it didn't reach her eyes. Skye smiled back and washed her hands perfunctorily, not liking the chilly vibe.

The woman was reapplying her lipstick, but before Skye could leave she sent a pointed look to Skye's belly and drawled, 'The oldest trick in the book… Well done, Señora Sanchez, you caught the biggest prize of them all.'

Skye stopped. 'Excuse me?'

The woman turned around. 'You might look as though butter wouldn't melt in your mouth, but you don't trap a man like Lazaro Sanchez so easily. When are you planning on divorcing? A year after the baby? Two? You're set for life anyway, so it probably doesn't matter.'

Skye was speechless.

The woman walked to the door and looked back. 'Enjoy him while you have him. It won't be long before a man like Lazaro is back on the scene. I don't see him playing happy families for long, do you?'

* * *

Lazaro knew when Skye had disappeared from the crowd. He'd felt a prickling on the back of his neck, and when he'd looked around he'd just caught a glimpse of red hair before she'd gone from view.

The conversation he'd been having was boring him, so he'd made his excuses and walked away. And now he stood in the general vicinity of the bathrooms and leant against a golden pillar.

Where was she?

Irritation mounted, along with something else quite alien to Lazaro: concern. What if something was happening with the baby? What if she was alone and in pain?

Lazaro stood up straight, panic rising from his gut. And then he saw her, emerging from the bathroom. He went over, took her arm.

She looked up at him, surprised. Lazaro felt foolish for having panicked. Exposed.

He realised she looked pale and was avoiding his eyes. 'What's wrong? Did something happen?'

She looked at him and he had a sense that she felt guilty. 'No. Everything is fine. Honestly. I didn't tell you where I was going because you were busy.'

'Are you tired? Do you want to go?'

He saw the expression that crossed her face before she could disguise it. *Relief.*

'I'm fine,' she said. 'I don't mind if you still have people to talk to.'

Lazaro's mouth twitched. 'You're a terrible liar—do you know that, Skye?'

She looked sheepish. 'Sorry. My feet are killing me. But I can find a spot to sit down—honestly, don't worry about me.'

This was such an unusual conversation for Lazaro to be having, because generally he was at these things on his own, or the women he brought were clinging to him like limpets—so much so that he'd find himself ending the date early due to claustrophobia.

'No,' he said, surprising himself. 'I'm done too. Let's go.'

He guided Skye out of the thronged room and down into his private boat. The trip back up the canal to the *palazzo* was made in silence. Lazaro found the silence…peaceful. He felt the tight knots inside him loosening.

He sat back and observed Skye, who was looking into the buildings as they went along. 'What are you thinking?'

She glanced at him and then away, looking embarrassed. The moon cast her features in a milky glow, highlighting her pale beauty.

'I always wonder about who lives in these kinds of places. My life was so nomadic I always wished I lived somewhere. I envied families for the everyday rituals they take for granted…'

A tightness formed in Lazaro's chest. 'I used to stand outside the houses of my parents…they lived near each other, in an exclusive part of Madrid. I'd watch them come and go. I'd wonder what it must be like, to know where you were from. To be accepted.'

He could feel Skye looking at him, but he couldn't look at her. At those huge blue eyes.

'What those people did to you was shameful. Inhuman. They don't deserve to know you.'

Her voice was low and he could hear the emotion in it. An unfamiliar sensation eased the tightness in Lazaro's chest. Empathy. Something he'd only ever experienced before with his close friend Ciro. It was disconcerting to experience it with a woman, when his own mother had abandoned him as a baby and his lovers had always seen him as an object of either lust or wealth.

* * *

Skye looked at Lazaro but he was looking ahead. He didn't respond to her words.

Just thinking of how his family had treated him made her so angry. Especially his mother, who had nurtured him for nine months. The thought of having this baby and then giving him or her away made Skye feel sick.

The boat pulled in at the steps leading up to the *palazzo*. Skye couldn't help the lingering sadness she felt to think of Lazaro's words. She couldn't look at him for fear of him noticing. But he seemed locked in his thoughts as they returned to the suite.

When they went into the main salon she took off her shoes with a silent groan of relief. Lazaro took off his jacket and draped it over a chair. He undid his tie, unknotting it so it hung open rakishly.

Skye felt exposed. A little raw.

She said, 'I think I'll go to bed. It's been a long day.' She'd almost forgotten that they'd got married only that morning. It felt like a lifetime ago.

Lazaro was undoing his top button. 'What is it, Skye?'

She looked at him. Damn her too-expressive face. She tried to look as bland as she could. 'What's what? I'm just tired.'

He shook his head and walked over. 'It's more than that. You were animated earlier, and then you disappeared, and since then you've looked…melancholic.'

Skye shrugged. 'Maybe I'm just not good in those situations.'

'Skye…'

She looked at him, and eventually she said, 'Fine. There was a woman in the bathroom…she wasn't very nice.'

Lazaro frowned. Skye went and sat down on a nearby couch, her legs too weary to keep standing under Lazaro's exacting gaze.

'What did she say to you?'

Reluctantly Skye answered. 'She accused me of trapping you and said I was set for life and that you'd be back on the scene soon.'

Five years, if not sooner, according to the pre-nuptial agreement.

Skye felt a pain near her chest.

Lazaro's face turned hard. 'What did she look like?'

Skye described her.

'That sounds like Alessandra Basanti. She's a model.'

Skye felt nauseous. 'Was she a lover of yours?'

Lazaro shook his head. 'No, and I don't think she took my lack of interest well.'

'Oh...'

A wave of relief flooded Skye. A wave of relief she shouldn't be feeling. Because it shouldn't matter to her who Lazaro had been with before. Because she shouldn't care. Because that meant emotions were getting involved.

He came over to the couch and sat down. Close. Too close. But not close enough.

Skye was full of conflicting thoughts. She wanted him, but she was afraid he would see how much.

'That's not all, though, is it?'

Skye looked at Lazaro, hating it that he could read her like this. 'Since when did you become a mind-reader?'

'Since I met someone who shows everything she's feeling as it happens.'

He tucked a wayward piece of hair behind Skye's ear and she had to fight hard not to turn her face into his hand. She was losing it. Flutters were erupting all over her body—not just near her heart or in her belly.

She said, 'I'm not good around negative people. I'm not naïve enough to expect everyone to be nice, but she threw me. She was so...bitchy.'

Lazaro said, 'She is a bitch. And so are many more in this kind of environment, where the stakes are high.'

Skye shook her head. 'The woman I was talking to before I went to the bathroom—she was lovely.'

Lazaro smiled. 'Because you're about forty years younger than her and not a threat.'

Skye scowled. 'So cynical.'

He smirked. 'So true.'

Impulsively, she asked, 'Do *you* think I trapped you?'

He went still. 'I have to admit at first…when I was angry…it was one of my first thoughts. But then I had to acknowledge I was as much to blame for not protecting us. And since getting to know you… No, I don't think you trapped me.'

Skye didn't like how emotional that made her feel. 'Thank you.'

He leaned forward. 'How would you like me to restore your faith in humanity?'

Skye looked at him suspiciously. 'How?'

'A very clever distraction technique I know…'

Skye knew even before Lazaro's mouth touched hers that she was in big trouble. And she knew it for sure when he pressed her back on the couch and took their kiss to a deeper level. She was falling for him. And all the kissing in the world couldn't distract her from that very unwelcome revelation.

She'd broken every one of her own rules the moment she'd locked eyes with Lazaro Sanchez in Dublin. She'd let him in. And now it was only a matter of time before she faced the kind of hurt she'd spent her whole life avoiding.

'*Where* is she?'

Lazaro's head of security answered him. 'She's in Piazza San Marco.'

Lazaro turned away from the table full of people in the boardroom. 'Please tell me she's not sketching someone?'

'Er...no. She's sitting at a table drinking what looks like iced water, and she had some ice cream before that.'

Lazaro terminated the call. He faced the room and said, 'I'm done with discussing the contract, I'm ready to sign.'

Immediately his legal counsel stood up. 'Lazaro, is this wise—?'

Lazaro held up a hand and said dryly, 'Sebastian, we've combed through this contract for weeks now. Let's get this done. I've got somewhere to be.'

Within twenty minutes he was striding out of the *palazzo* and taking the short walk to the Piazza San Marco. He'd just signed the contract for one of Venice's oldest and most notable buildings, cementing his place among a very few exclusive real estate owners in the world. And yet he wasn't basking in a glow of satisfaction. Or feeling any measure of peace. He was...distracted.

And the distraction only dissipated when he entered the square and found her. His wife. Her red hair gleaming in the late-afternoon sunshine. Her pale shoulders bare in a sundress with skinny straps and a buttoned bodice that made him want to undo the buttons so he could free her breasts.

Suddenly Lazaro stopped dead. What the hell was he doing? People flowed around him—the thousands of tourists that thronged Venice every day. He'd just cut a meeting short. A meeting he'd spent months preparing for. He'd spent last night in a haze of sensual pleasure to the point that he'd overslept today and been late for that very meeting. Another anomaly.

He hadn't spent years climbing out of the gutter he'd been left in to let everything unravel now.

He turned around and went back the way he'd come, ignoring the prickling of his conscience.

* * *

Skye tipped her face up to the sun, relishing the warmth. And if she felt a bit lonely, she told herself she was being ridiculous. This wasn't a real honeymoon. It was… Skye sighed. She didn't know what this was. And she didn't like the way that, as the heat between her and Lazaro only seemed to grow, any attempt to define it only seemed to get more elusive.

One minute Lazaro bared a side of him she didn't expect, and that made her heart ache, and the next he was charming her and seducing her so thoroughly that she couldn't speak. And the next minute he was the aloof, stern man she'd met in Madrid, when all hell had broken loose.

This morning he'd been distant and distracted. Late for a meeting. Skye had got the impression that wasn't a usual occurrence for him.

She sighed and put money down to pay for her ice cream, then got up to leave. She waved at the taciturn security guard who was following her and he cracked a small smile. Skye took it as a good sign.

When she got back to the *palazzo* Lazaro was on the phone, pacing up and down. Shirtsleeves rolled up, baring his strong forearms. His hair was messy.

He ended his conversation, which had been in French. 'Did you have a nice morning?'

The question was perfectly innocuous and civil, but Skye detected a tension in the air that she couldn't read. It made her nervy, and when she was nervy she babbled. 'Yes, lovely. I walked all along the canal down to the Piazza San Marco. I found a gelato shop that was my favourite when I was here before. Guido's. It's famous. The pistachio and walnut flavour is to die for…' She trailed off, feeling silly.

Lazaro looked at his watch. 'We're leaving for Madrid in an hour—someone is packing your things for you now.'

'Oh, I didn't realise we were leaving today. You should have told me sooner. I would have come back.'

He waved a hand. 'I knew where you were through Luis.'

The security guard.

Lazaro hadn't actually told her how long they would be in Venice. She'd just assumed. He wasn't remotely interested in visiting some random gelato shop. He was here to work.

'Did you sign your contract?'

He nodded. 'Signed and sealed. I'm now the owner of this *palazzo.*'

'You must be very pleased.' But she noticed that if anything, he looked irritated.

'I am,' he said tightly.

His phone rang again. Skye made a *don't worry* face and went into the bedroom to help the staff pack her things, before changing into something more practical for travel.

She looked at herself in the mirror of the bathroom. Her hair was springing out of its confinement and her nose was red from the sun. More freckles had exploded across her cheeks and shoulders. She sighed. Whatever fascination she held for Lazaro, it wouldn't last long. She turned sideways and saw that her bump was protruding more. And especially not when she started to waddle.

That evening, when they'd finished eating dinner in the Madrid apartment, Skye said, 'So what happens now?'

Lazaro put down his empty wine glass. 'I've got some meetings here for the next couple of days. I'm working on a bid to renovate and rejuvenate one of Madrid's oldest indoor markets. I want to turn it back into a functioning market space—which it hasn't been for nearly fifty years. There'll be flower shops and craft shops, food stalls... A performance space, and an art gallery.'

'That sounds really cool.'

A grim look came over Lazaro's face. 'It would if I wasn't up against—' He stopped.

Skye ventured a guess. 'Up against your half-brother?'

He nodded. 'Gabriel Torres wants to turn it into a multi-functional space too, but more commercial—a restaurant, hotel…car park.'

Skye could sense his tension and said, as lightly as she could, 'I might be biased, but I like your idea better.'

He said, 'I have to go there in the morning, to finalise some details on the bid which is happening in a couple of weeks at a public consultation. Come with me, if you like?'

Warmth flooded Skye, and she couldn't stop a smile forming. 'Oh…okay. I'd like that.'

Lazaro smiled. *'Oh?'*

She made a face. A moment stretched between them, light and delicate. Skye felt breathless when she realised Lazaro was smiling more. Really smiling. In a way that made him look younger. Carefree.

He stood up and her heart beat fast. If he touched her now… She felt as if she had no armour to protect her from falling even harder…

But he said, 'I've got some work to do this evening. You should relax— it's been a long couple of days.'

And nights, Skye thought.

A mixture of relief and disappointment flowed through her, but she affected a breezy tone. 'That's fine. You don't have to worry about me. I can entertain myself. I'm quite tired, actually.'

He nodded. 'See you in the morning, Skye.'

When he'd left Skye sat back and deflated like a balloon. She realised she *was* tired. Achingly so.

She helped the housekeeper to clear the table, in spite of her protests, and then she went to her bedroom. Lazaro hadn't said anything about sharing a room with her, so she wasn't sure what would happen, but she was grateful for some time to process everything.

She decided to take a long, luxurious bath before she went to bed, her hands travelling over the compact swell of her belly under the water. She was tempted to dream of what it might be like—her, Lazaro and the little one—but she was afraid to.

Because she knew the reality would be far different. And she needed to prepare herself for the inevitable.

It was a mistake to bring her, thought Lazaro as his attention wandered again to where Skye was walking around the balcony on the upper level with one of his team, who was pointing things out to her.

She was wearing jeans, and she had a hi-vis jacket on and a hard hat. Yet he wanted her. Even now. Here. He'd wanted her last night too, but he'd forced himself to resist the overwhelming temptation to forget about everything and lose himself in her.

He told himself that he was a fool. What man married to a woman he wanted, who wanted him, denied himself the pleasure? This desire was finite. *It had to be,* Lazaro thought with a sense of desperation.

He gritted his jaw and turned back to the people he was with, trying hard to focus on what they were saying.

'I loved it,' Skye said a couple of hours later when they were in the back of Lazaro's car. 'I love the fact that it's covered, and all the wrought-iron and glass. It looks like something futuristic but also old.'

Lazaro ran a hand through his hair. 'My team seem to be having trouble trying to figure out a logo and branding for it. But you've grasped its essence after one viewing while they've been looking at it for months.'

A burst of pleasure made Skye's heart thump. 'Sometimes it's easier to see something with fresh eyes. May I?' She held out a hand to look at the bid proposal Lazaro was holding.

He handed it to her. 'Be my guest.'

Skye flicked through it, and as she did so she was already seeing possibilities, imagining things.

Lazaro's car stopped at the hotel and he said, 'I'm going into the office for a few hours. We'll be leaving for Paris in the morning.'

Immediately Skye felt anxious. 'Oh, yes. The gala function tomorrow night.'

Lazaro put his hand over hers, a glimmer of humour in his eyes. 'It's one event. Pack the black strapless dress. Leave your hair down.'

It was only when Skye got out of the car that she realised she was still holding Lazaro's bid proposal document, but the car had already pulled away. She took it up to the apartment and found herself settling down with it, and a cup of decaf coffee, sketching out some ideas on a blank piece of paper.

That evening, it was late when Lazaro got back to the apartment. He'd sent a message to Skye earlier, telling her to eat without him. For the first time ever he was experiencing a very novel thing. The desire for something else outside of his relentless ambition and his focus on work.

His wife.

And, disturbingly, it went beyond the physical attraction. He liked spending time with her. Seeing her reaction to things. She always surprised him. And, even more novel, she was a nice person. Something very unusual in his world. A genuinely compassionate, caring person.

Almudena in Andalucía adored her. His concierge at the hotel had just told him to thank her again for bringing him pastries earlier. He'd noticed his usually taciturn Madrid housekeeper smiling. And it wasn't because of him.

For the first time in his life his well-worn cynicism felt like a burden. He noticed it all the time.

He walked into the main salon, pulling at his tie, opening his top button. A few low lights were on. He expected that Skye would be in bed by now, and already felt the frustration in his body.

But then he saw a shape on the couch and went still. He walked over. She was asleep. He saw the bid document on the low table beside her, and some sheets of paper with drawings on them. He picked one up. It looked like a logo. A logo for his project.

He realised instantly that it was brilliant. He looked at Skye. She was still wearing the jeans. Her shirt was askew, showing a hint of curved belly under the elastic top of the maternity jeans. Her hair was in a wild tangle around her head. Her mouth was soft and inviting.

And just then, as if aware of Lazaro's intense perusal, she opened her eyes. Slumberous. She focused on him and smiled a slow, sleepy smile. And before he could stop it Lazaro felt his gut twist with something he really didn't want to investigate. A nameless emotion. Something he'd never felt before.

Never allowed himself to feel before.

Then she obviously realised where she was and scrambled to sit up. 'What time is it?' She saw the piece of paper in Lazaro's hand and her cheeks went pink, hair tumbling over her shoulders. 'Sorry, but the visit to the market earlier sparked some ideas...'

Lazaro sat down beside her. 'It's really good. I have been paying a team of creatives thousands of euros and not one person has come up with something so simple and perfect.'

'Really?'

He put the paper down and looked at her. 'Yes, really.'

She blushed even more profusely and said shyly, 'You can use it if you like.'

He looked at her. 'I like…'

Skye's eyes widened as she obviously realised his explicit meaning. And then she surprised him, by lying down again and slowly undoing the buttons on her shirt, pulling it back to reveal her breasts, nipples pressing against the lace of her bra. She lifted her arms over her head, looking innocent and wanton all at once.

'Unless you're too tired…?' she said.

Lazaro bent forward and snaked a hand under her back, finding the bra-clasp and undoing it with a snap. As he peeled down the skimpy lace triangles covering her breasts he said throatily, 'I've never been less tired in my life…' And then he cupped one voluptuous mound and closed his mouth over the pouting nipple, very effectively closing his mind to annoying questions and revelations.

CHAPTER NINE

THE FOLLOWING EVENING, in a sumptuous suite in an exclusive hotel in Paris, Skye inspected herself in the full-length mirror on the back of the bathroom door. It was her first time getting herself ready for an event, but she couldn't see anything too obviously out of place.

The dress was black silk. Strapless. Its empire line meant the fabric flowed over her belly. Lazaro had said to leave her hair down, and she'd done her best to tame it into some kind of order. She felt very pale and bare with her shoulders and neck exposed.

After making sure she had no lipstick stuck to her teeth, and that her eyeliner wasn't smudged, she went out into the bedroom.

Lazaro looked at her through the mirror, where he was tying his bow-tie. His hands stopped moving. Skye sucked in a breath at the look in his eyes.

He turned around, his gaze dropping and then lifting again. 'You look…stunning.'

Skye blushed. 'Thank you.' She touched her hair self-consciously. 'I couldn't do much with—'

He came over. 'It's perfect.'

Taking her hand, he led her into the living area. 'My friend owns a jewellery shop called De Villiers. He sent over some things for you this evening.'

Skye stopped. '*The* De Villiers? That's more than a jewellery shop…it's an institution.' She'd used to look in the display windows when she was younger, in Paris with her mother, in thrall to all the glittering jewels.

He tugged her over to the flat velvet boxes on the table. He let go of her hand and opened them.

Skye gasped. One contained a sapphire and diamond necklace... Lazaro took it out.

Skye backed away in awe. 'I can't wear that. It must be worth a fortune.'

Lazaro's gaze narrowed on her. 'Skye, I know you're not like most women—'

She sent him a look.

'I mean that in a good way. But will you just try this on? Please?'

Torn between fear and fascination, Skye turned around and lifted her hair up. She felt the cold weight of the jewels land on her skin, sitting just on her collarbone.

'Come to the mirror.'

Skye went over to the mirror and looked at herself. *She looked like one of them now.* The people she'd seen that night in Madrid. All sleek and dripping with jewels.

She glanced up and met Lazaro's eyes in the mirror. Their gazes held. 'It's beautiful...it just doesn't feel like... me.'

He turned her around. 'It *is* you. A new version of you.'

Maybe he was right.

He let go of her shoulders and went back to the table. 'Try these on.' He held up some long earrings.

'There's more?'

He nodded. Skye came over and looked at the selection. She plucked out a smaller pair of earrings than those Lazaro was holding. Sapphire studs. And chose a matching bracelet.

He handed her the clutch bag. 'Ready?'

Skye nodded, even though she wondered if she'd ever feel ready for one of these events. The sobering thought occurred to her that she shouldn't get too used to this attention. Because one day, after she'd divorced Lazaro, he'd be giving it to a much more appropriate wife. The kind of woman who wouldn't need constant reassurance.

Skye stuck close to Lazaro at the gala function. It was a dazzling display of wealth and glamour in one of the city's most impressive buildings near the Arc de Triomphe. It was Paris Fashion Week, and the event was in aid of a very high-profile charity.

She'd never seen so many A-listers in one room. She had to consciously close her mouth when one of her favourite movie stars of all time brushed past her and apologised before moving on.

She looked at Lazaro, but he was holding court, surrounded by a starstruck crowd of his own. Skye was quite happy to sip her water and people-watch...until she felt an unmistakable flutter in her belly—something that was more than a flutter. It was a movement. A definite movement. She went very still, everything falling away as that tiny but seismic movement came again.

The baby. Moving.

A surge of wonder and euphoria rose up through Skye and she only realised she must have gripped Lazaro's hand when he looked down at her.

'Are you okay?'

Skye was about to blurt it out. She wanted to take his hand and put it on her belly. But suddenly she realised everyone was looking at her. It was too fragile and private a moment. And she didn't think Lazaro would appreciate the domesticity of it.

She shook her head. 'Bathroom. I just need to go to the bathroom.'

She needed a moment alone. To process this.

She threaded her way through the crowd, trying not

to trip over her own feet as she did so, and at the last moment spied some open French doors, leading out to a quiet balcony.

She ducked outside. It was blissfully peaceful out here. Candles flickered, giving the flower-bedecked balcony a romantic vibe. They were on the top floor, and Skye could see the Eiffel Tower twinkling on the other side of the Seine. It was like a glittering bauble.

The distinctive skyline of Paris with its tall, elegant buildings stretched out all around her. She could see people moving about in their apartments nearby. Families sitting down to dinner. Babies in high-chairs. Couples snuggling up on sofas. A young girl sitting at her desk, obviously doing her homework.

For a moment she felt absurdly emotional. She didn't need priceless jewels, as nice as they were. Or to mingle with A-listers, as exciting as that was. All she wanted was a simple existence like that. A secure base. *A happy family.* And yet, in spite of the heat between her and Lazaro—

She heard a noise behind her and her circling thoughts came to a stop. She composed herself, and turned to see a woman stepping out onto the balcony, looking as relieved as Skye to be alone. Then she saw Skye and stopped, her mouth opening. Both of them froze as recognition sank in.

'*You...*' Skye heard the word emerge from her mouth, recognising this stunning brunette beauty, in a classically simple and elegant dark blue gown that skimmed her perfect figure. Her hair was up in a simple chignon and she wore jewels as effortlessly as Skye wished she could.

Leonora Flores de la Vega—Leonora *Torres*—said in accentless English, 'Sorry, I didn't realise there was anyone here.' She turned to leave.

Skye acted on impulse and said, '*No.* Please, don't go.'

The tall woman stopped, and Skye saw the tension in her

body. Her guts twisted painfully. Leonora turned around, her beautiful face expressionless. But Skye was sure she saw something in her grey eyes—something human. Kind.

She blurted out words before she lost her nerve. 'I just wanted to say how sorry I am… I never intended on ruining your engagement like that. I just… I'd tried to get in touch with Lazaro but it was impossible. I sneaked into that room and I saw him… I had to let him know.'

For a long moment there was a tense silence, and then Leonora seemed to sag slightly. 'I know,' she said. 'I get that now. You met before he proposed to me.'

'Yes!' Relief flooded Skye. 'I would have hated it if you'd been with him when…'

Leonora came closer. She gave a small smile. 'No, that would not have been nice. But he would not have done that. These men…they have integrity at least.'

'You mean Lazaro and…?'

'Gabriel—my husband.' Then she looked at Skye's belly. 'Congratulations. I wish you all the best in your future with Lazaro.'

Skye put a hand on her belly. 'Thank you…' She bit her lip, and then said impulsively, 'I felt it move just now…a proper movement.'

Leonora seemed to go pale in the dim light.

Skye said, 'I'm sorry—did I say something?'

The other woman seemed to collect herself and she smiled. 'No, not at all. I really do wish you all the best in your future with Lazaro and the baby.'

She was turning away, and Skye reached out to take her hand. 'I'm sorry again…and I wish you all the best too.'

Leonora squeezed her hand. To Skye's surprise the other woman's eyes looked suspiciously shiny.

She said, 'Thank you.' Then she let go and walked back inside, leaving Skye looking after her, feeling sad and relieved in equal measure.

Sad because she sensed that Leonora would be a nice person to get to know, possibly even a friend. And that was never going to happen.

'Sanchez.'

Lazaro tensed. He'd been looking for Skye, and getting more and more irritated because he couldn't find her.

He turned around slowly to face his nemesis. *His brother.*

'Torres.'

Gabriel held a drink and stood in a relaxed pose, but Lazaro could feel the tension crackling between them. Height for height, they matched. And in looks too, even though they were quite different. Gold and dark.

'Ready for the public unveiling of your bid next week, Sanchez?'

'As ready as you are.'

Gabriel lifted his glass. 'May the best bid win. But we both know whose that will be.'

Lazaro had to control his anger—an anger which stemmed from a place so deep and old that for the first time it felt like a burden.

'Maybe this time you'll be surprised, Gabriel, and maybe the best bid will win—the one that has the good of the city at its heart, not just the insatiable Torres need for domination in all things.'

Gabriel took a step closer. 'I do remember you, you know. I remember that day when you confronted my father in the street and claimed to be his son. You have a chip on your shoulder, Sanchez, and it's time to get over it and stop telling yourself you were hard done by.'

The two men were locked in a silent battle of wills for long seconds before they heard a low voice say, 'Hello, Lazaro, it's nice to see you.'

Lazaro blinked and looked to see Leonora standing

beside Gabriel, who immediately slid an arm around her waist, pulling her close. Lazaro saw something in her face. A brittleness. Fragility.

He pushed down his anger. 'Leonora. I'm sorry again for what happened. It was never my intention to do anything to hurt or embarrass you.'

She gave him a small tight smile. 'I know. I just met your wife. Congratulations on the baby.'

'Thank you.'

Lazaro looked at Gabriel and inclined his head. 'Till next time, Torres.'

He walked away, aware of feeling many conflicting things. That strange sense of his anger being a burden, but also the buzz of exhilaration he always got from sparring with his brother. There were very few people who matched up to Lazaro—Gabriel Torres was one of them.

His brother's words circled in his head. *You have a chip on your shoulder... I do remember you...claimed to be his son.*

It was suddenly more important than ever that Lazaro won this bid over his half-brother. It would be the first time anyone had ever bested a Torres, and even if Gabriel wasn't willing to acknowledge they might be related, then he would at least respect Lazaro as an equal.

But as he scanned the crowd now the recent interaction with his brother faded into the background. Where once before Lazaro would have relished the opportunities an event like this could offer him, right now all he wanted—

There she was.

She was standing in the doorway looking hesitant. Clearly overwhelmed by the event and this crowd. But even as he watched he saw her smile at someone who passed her, and saw that person transformed from taciturn to surprised and then smiling back, all in the space of a few seconds.

Lazaro shook his head as he made his way towards her. She was a liability. Far too naïve for this world.

Or was she in fact just what this milieu needed? asked an inner voice. *Someone who was genuine. Sweet.*

She saw him then, and those blue eyes locked on to his. When he got to her he had to curb the ridiculously primal urge to pick her up and carry her out of there. She made him animalistic.

'I'm done here—ready to go?'

She couldn't hide her look of relief. 'Yes, please.'

He took her hand and led her outside to where his car was waiting. They got into the back and Lazaro immediately undid his bow-tie. The car moved sleekly through the Parisian streets.

Lazaro looked at Skye. 'You met Leonora?'

She turned to face him, a guilty look on her face. 'How did you know?'

'She told me. How was it?'

'I apologised to her. She was fine about it. Really fine, considering. She's nice. I liked her.' Skye sounded almost defensive.

'She is nice. Too nice for Gabriel Torres.'

Skye tried not to let Lazaro's obvious regard for the other woman get to her. It was stupid to feel jealous. Nothing had ever happened between them. And yet...

Skye knew that if she hadn't fallen pregnant it would have been Leonora sitting in the back of this car. Not her.

Then he said, 'I showed your idea for the logo to my team today. They really liked it. If we use it I'll make sure you're paid.'

A rush of pleasure made Skye blush. 'That's not necessary, really. I enjoyed doing it.'

'You're very talented, you know.'

Skye shrugged, embarrassed. 'I would have loved to go to art college, but it was never really a possibility.'

The car pulled to a stop outside the hotel and Lazaro came around to help Skye out. For the first time she was starting to feel slightly unwieldy. Aware of her protruding belly.

That reminded her… When they were back in the suite she vacillated for a moment before saying, 'I felt the baby move earlier…'

Lazaro stopped and turned around. She put her hand on the bump. 'It's stopped now. But it's the first time I've really felt it.'

Lazaro felt the strangest urge to go over and kneel down at Skye's feet, spread his hands across her belly. The thought of his baby moving…making its presence known… It was unfathomable and deeply moving. Because he couldn't help but think of his own mother, who would have felt similar sensations.

Would she have had the same look of wonder on her face that Skye had now? Or had she been hidden away out of sight until the baby was born and she could get rid of him? Why had she even put herself through the pregnancy?

As if reading his mind, Skye said, 'I know this must bring up a lot of stuff for you…'

Suddenly Lazaro was aware that he wanted only one thing. To eclipse these disturbing thoughts and revelations in the most effective way he knew how.

He walked over to Skye, taking off his jacket as he did so, throwing it over a chair.

He put his hands on Skye's waist, pulling her towards him. 'Do you know the only thing I'm really interested in discussing right now?'

'Lazaro—'

He cut her off. 'The fact that from the moment I saw you in this dress I wanted to take it off you.'

The clutch bag dropped out of Skye's hands to the floor, unnoticed as Lazaro pulled her even closer—close enough to feel the press of his arousal against her soft curves. One of which held his growing baby.

He was vaguely aware of the distant sound of his cellphone ringing, but that was easy to ignore when his hands were on Skye and all he could see and smell was her.

A sense of futility rose up inside Skye in the face of Lazaro's blatant distraction technique. But also, like him, she felt a desire not to rock the boat unnecessarily. Not while this heat burnt so bright between them. This was the one pure place where Skye felt endless possibilities existed. It was when he wasn't touching her, kissing her, that reality reminded her of its existence. And, right now, if he wanted to avoid that she would too.

Coward, whispered an inner voice.

But it was easy to ignore, because Lazaro was kissing her and nothing else mattered.

The following morning, as dawn broke over Paris, Lazaro lay awake. Skye was draped over his chest, her breasts pressed against him, one leg hitched up over his thigh, close enough to the centre of his body to cause pleasurable discomfort when his body reacted predictably to her proximity.

He could feel her belly pressing against him, the hardness of the small swell. He couldn't feel any movement— not that he would be able to at this stage, when she was only just starting to notice it herself.

It seemed that the more he had of her, the more he wanted her. Their desire, if anything, was increasing. Becoming more urgent. More distracting. Even the thought of her body growing and ripening induced a big enough spike in his arousal levels to make him carefully extricate himself from Skye's embrace, so he could take a cold shower and not expose how badly he wanted her.

Again. Already.

When he came out of the shower, knotting a towel around his waist, he looked broodingly at Skye where she lay on the bed. What was it about her that caught at him so easily? Like a sharp tack under his skin?

She wasn't the most beautiful woman he'd ever been with. Or the most accomplished.

She was...utterly unique. Different from anyone else.

Lazaro shook his head at himself. Since when did he stand mooning over a lover? *Or even, a wife?*

He heard a noise and went out to the main salon. It was his cell-phone, and he remembered hearing it the previous night too, but ignoring it. He picked it up. Numerous missed calls from his assistant and legal team. His skin prickled.

He walked over to one of the windows as he listened to the messages.

Apparently a business associate he'd been trying to have a meeting with for weeks had been at the event last night, and Lazaro only remembered now that he'd agreed to meet him in the hotel bar for a drink before leaving. The man wasn't impressed that Lazaro had failed to show.

His legal team had been looking for him because they needed him to sign off on some important documents before the public bid for the market in Madrid.

Lazaro's gut clenched. He'd spent years undoing people's misconceptions of him. Because of his playboy reputation. Because he was new money and had come out of nowhere. Because he had dubious roots. He knew his success was down to his diligence and his focus. He let people believe he was a louche playboy—but only when it suited him, so he could take them by surprise.

He thought of Skye, and the way he'd left the event last night. That exchange with Gabriel had touched a raw spot. And she'd called to something in him to escape. To rebel.

But he couldn't afford to make those little missteps. Gabriel Torres and many like him were waiting in the wings for any opportunity to take a chunk out of Lazaro's success and fortune. And he was all but handing them that opportunity.

No more. He had to focus, or everything that was important to him and all he'd worked for would be in vain. He couldn't afford to let Skye continue to distract him. He knew what his priorities were.

Skye was sipping herbal tea with her legs tucked underneath her, taking in the spectacular view of the city outside the apartment windows. They'd arrived back in Madrid earlier that day, and Lazaro had gone straight into his study.

When Skye had woken that morning in Paris she'd been alone in the bedroom, her body aching from the previous night's passionate lovemaking. She'd been glad of the time and space to get herself together.

Each time she came together with Lazaro another piece of her soul and her heart cleaved to his. Another vital part of her defences was decimated.

But he'd been cool and solicitous when she'd emerged. Proof that, for him, when they made love it was just a physical release. A by-product of their arrangement.

The baby was growing daily now, forming into the small person who would bind them together for ever. Skye's heart palpitated at the thought of the day when Lazaro would start to lose interest and distance himself. Because it was coming. Of that there was no doubt. No matter how urgent their desire felt right now.

She heard a sound and looked up to see Lazaro striding

into the room. He was wearing dark trousers and a polo shirt and he looked vital and breathtakingly gorgeous. He was holding something in his hands, and when he came closer he handed a bunch of brochures to Skye.

She put down her cup to take them. They all had houses on their covers. 'What's this?'

Lazaro put his hands on his hips. 'I've arranged for an estate agent to come and pick you up tomorrow to look at some houses. Pick out a few you like and then I'll come with you to see them again.'

She looked up at him. 'You trust my judgement?'

'You're an artist, aren't you? You have an eye for aesthetic detail. But also for practicalities. All of these houses have good playgroups and schools nearby.' He looked at his watch. 'I have to go to a function this evening…'

Skye didn't relish the prospect of getting dressed up, but forced a smile, standing up. 'Should I get ready now?'

A look crossed Lazaro's face that she couldn't decipher. Something that looked suspiciously like guilt.

'No, actually, you don't need to come this evening. I'll go alone. I'll talk to you after you've seen the properties tomorrow.'

He turned and left the room. Skye looked at the empty space and did not like the cold breeze that skated up her spine, reminding her of too many times when her mother had left her behind.

She turned around quickly and went to stand at the window, wrapping her arms around herself. She hated it that he could get to her like this. Tap into her deepest insecurities and fears with such ease. Because she'd let him in.

A couple of hours later Lazaro stood in the middle of a vast ballroom, surrounded by the most important and wealthy people in Europe. A man was talking to him, but he was only half taking in what he said.

His tuxedo felt shrink-wrapped to his body. He wanted to undo his bow-tie. He looked around and his heart stopped beating when he glimpsed red hair. A thousand things ran through his mind—chief of which was, *Why the hell has she come?* He'd told her she didn't need to be here. And yet he couldn't deny the sense of something lightening inside him.

It was only when he was within touching distance that he realised it wasn't her. The woman had turned around. She was too tall, for a start. Too angular. No curves. Brown eyes. And her hair was clearly not her natural colour.

Nevertheless she was a strikingly beautiful woman, and Lazaro saw her instant recognition register and how her eyes immediately became covetous.

She moved towards him, seizing on his interest. Lazaro backed away, muttering something about mistaken identity.

A very uncomfortable revelation hit him then. *Not* bringing Skye was actually more distracting than if he had brought her.

'You can see here, Señora Sanchez, that the state-of-the-art security system has cameras all over and around the property.'

Skye smiled politely, while privately thinking that this house felt more like a prison than a home. They were in the security room of the house and it felt disturbingly like the set of a sci-fi movie.

'It's…er…certainly well-protected.'

The officious young man nodded. 'Oh, yes, our clients value security above almost anything else these days.'

They were walking out through the vast entrance hall when the estate agent said, 'We have two more properties in this area. Would you like to see them today?'

Skye knew she should say yes—after all this was important. But she couldn't stomach viewing another massive, architecturally designed glass box, set in a lush private paradise with not another building in sight.

She declined politely and agreed to call him and set up another appointment in a couple of days.

On their way back to Lazaro's apartment they passed by a big green space. Skye leant forward and asked the driver in Spanish what it was. He told her it was El Retiro Park. She asked if they could stop so she could take a look.

It was beautiful—a nineteenth-century park, bordered by tall, elegant buildings. There was a large lake, dotted with boats filled with couples and families, and a stunning glass palace.

Skye sat on a bench and drank it in. She had to face up to reality. She was here on her own because Lazaro didn't care enough about their future together to invest time in looking at houses with her. Because he didn't intend sharing the space. That was why he was keeping his apartment.

He hadn't needed her to go to his function the previous evening. Gradually she would be more and more sidelined, until she was on the periphery of his life with their child.

And yet there was a tiny rebellious flame inside her, hoping against hope that a future could exist for them.

At that moment something blocked the sun and Skye looked to her left. All she could see was a tall, broad shape. A man coming towards her. Wide shoulders. Long legs. A flash of dark blond hair. Slightly too long.

Her heart started to beat fast. *Lazaro.* He'd come. He did care.

The exultant rush of euphoria inside Skye was almost overwhelming. She was halfway out of the seat before she realised that it wasn't Lazaro at all. It was just someone who had a similar build. He wasn't even as tall. Or as handsome.

She sat down again quickly, her heart plummeting like a stone to the bottom of a pond. Her face burned with mortification as she avoided the eye of the man who looked at her questioningly.

If she hadn't been fully aware of it before that little incident, she was now. She was in deep trouble.

In the week leading up to the public bid for the market project Skye hardly saw Lazaro. Her sense of unease was growing even as she told herself she was being ridiculous. This was a big project. And they weren't exactly living in a conventional domestic relationship anyway.

On Wednesday evening she was falling asleep, watching a documentary, when she heard him come home. She turned off the TV and stood up. He came into the living room, tugging at his tie. He looked tired and Skye felt a rush of emotion.

'Hey…'

He looked at her, and she saw that green gaze sweep up and down. She tried not to feel self-conscious in her sweats and the loose oversized shirt. Albeit *designer* sweats and oversized shirt.

'You're still up.'

'It's only nine o'clock.'

She hated it that he could make her feel so shy. Awkward. They'd been intimate. She was carrying his baby. And yet she felt like a blushing teenager.

She said, 'Maria cooked a casserole earlier. There's some left over. I can heat it up?'

She saw Lazaro's mouth tighten, as if she'd said something he didn't want to hear.

'No, thanks. I ate at the office.' He ran a hand through his hair. 'Actually, there's something you should know before you come to see the bid on Friday. We decided not to use your logo in the end.'

'Oh…' Skye was surprised at the level of disappointment she felt—which was crazy, considering she'd almost forgotten about it. 'That's okay. I was only playing around with ideas. It wasn't serious.'

But, actually, being involved in something Lazaro was working on had felt nice. More than nice. His approval had meant more to her than she would ever admit.

She spoke quickly, in case he saw her disappointment. 'I was out with the estate agent again today. I think I've found a house I like.'

Lazaro was pouring himself a whisky at the drinks cabinet. He turned around. 'That's good. Where is it?'

'Beside El Retiro Park. Los Jerónimos.'

Lazaro frowned. 'But that's in the city.'

'Yes... But all those other houses...they felt cold. Isolated.'

'They're in the best areas. Where—' He stopped talking.

Skye said quietly, 'Where Gabriel Torres lives? Where your parents live?'

She'd guessed it must be where they all lived. There were many huge walled estates with grand-looking houses just visible from the road.

Skye shook her head. 'I'm sorry, but I didn't like it out there. There's no centre...no atmosphere. Everyone is locked behind their huge gates and walls with more security than a head of state. It's not natural.'

Lazaro put his drink down. 'I came from the streets, Skye. I won't bring up my child across the road from the park where I used to sleep at night.'

Skye winced inwardly and moved closer, instinctively wanting to soothe Lazaro's rough edges. 'Well, I don't want my child to be brought up in a place where the only people he'll see are domestic staff and drivers—where he's ferried in blacked-out cars from exclusive place to place. I want him to be able to walk out through the door and go to the park. Play with neighbourhood kids. Go to a local school. Have as normal a life as possible.'

* * *

Skye stood in front of Lazaro and all he could see were those huge blue eyes. Full of something that caught at his insides like a fist and squeezed tight.

Like a coward, he'd been hoping she'd be in bed by the time he returned. But she wasn't. Here she was, wearing jogging bottoms and a shirt that was loose enough for him to see the lace of her light blue bra. For him to imagine the full voluptuous curves of her breasts. Her hair was in an untidy pile on the top of her head. Golden red tendrils falling down. She epitomised earthy sensuality.

Por Dios... He wanted her. But what she was saying had touched on so many raw wounds inside him he almost couldn't see straight.

He said, 'You paint a picture of an idyll that doesn't exist, Skye. Not for people like me—like us. It is not that simple.'

'I think it can be. You walk out of here every day and nothing happens to you.'

She didn't get it. 'You and the baby are much softer targets than me.'

'I think you want to live out there because you stood outside those houses, watching those people. Wanting them to notice you. I understand what that must have been like...'

Emotions were rising inside Lazaro—dark, tangled emotions.

Skye was continuing. 'If you think living amongst them will bring you peace then—'

'Enough.'

Something had snapped inside Lazaro. He'd never wanted to touch Skye as much as he did in that moment. Worse. He needed to touch her. To quiet the tumult in his head. Which was exactly why he had to resist.

'I've heard enough pop psychology for one evening, Skye. We will discuss this another time. I have some work to catch up on. You should go to bed—it's late.'

He turned away from her and walked away, with the image of those huge blue eyes, watching him the whole way, branded onto his brain.

Skye watched him leave. She knew, to her shame, that if he had touched her she would have been too weak to resist him. So she had to give thanks for his not exposing her. And for revealing the chasm that existed between them when he wasn't touching her. For reminding her that there was far more keeping them apart than together.

CHAPTER TEN

ON THE DAY of the public bid Lazaro's driver came to pick Skye up from the apartment. She'd chosen a cream silk shirt-dress and matching jacket. Nude court shoes. She'd even gone to a hairdresser to get her hair tamed, not wanting to draw any adverse attention to Lazaro.

When she arrived at the market where the bid was taking place she was met by Sara, who had been there on the day of the wedding. Skye was glad to see a familiar face. She still felt raw after the exchange with Lazaro the other night.

Sara pointed out where Lazaro was standing—looking serious—with a group of other people. Skye recognised Gabriel Torres and scanned the crowd for Leonora, but couldn't see the brunette beauty.

'...your logo.'

Skye realised Sara had been talking to her, but she'd been too busy scanning the space to take in what she'd said. 'I'm sorry, what was that?'

The girl looked around and said, 'Señor Sanchez would kill me for saying this, but we all preferred your logo and your design for the project.'

'Oh, thank you,' Skye said, touched. 'But I understand how these things go. If the agency didn't want to use it then—'

'Oh, but no—that's it. Everyone wanted to use it but Señor Sanchez vetoed it in the end, saying that it wasn't appropriate.'

Skye didn't have much time to take in that revelation, because Lazaro was walking over to where she was standing and his assistant melted away.

He took Skye by the hand and led her over to where there were some seats. He explained that the two presentations for the bid would be shown and then, after the public had had about a month to view the plans, their vote would be added to the councillors votes and the winner would be announced.

Skye tried to put out of her mind what Sara had said, telling herself it wasn't important. But the feeling of hurt wouldn't disappear. *Why* had Lazaro decided not to use her logo?

The two presentations got underway, with both Gabriel Torres and Lazaro producing very slick videos detailing their plans for the space. Gabriel's was focused more on maximising the utility of the space, and Lazaro's centred around it being used primarily as a market, encompassing craft shops, galleries, restaurants and shops, along with a traditional fruit and vegetable market.

As Skye watched his presentation she felt emotional. The man who spoke so lovingly about this space was not a man who wanted to live in a glass box in the stuffy suburbs. She knew it.

Afterwards there was a reception, and Lazaro came over to Skye. She could see the intensity on his face, in his eyes. Going up against his half-brother was taking so much out of him. But he wouldn't want to hear her *pop psychology*.

'It was brilliant,' she said.

He looked at her, seemed about to say something, but just then his attention was caught by something above her head and he went white.

Skye reached for his hand. 'Lazaro, what is it? You're scaring me.'

His lips were bloodless. She'd never seen his eyes look so haunted.

He said, almost to himself, 'It's my mother.'

Skye went cold. She turned around to look where Lazaro's gaze was directed. The woman was tall and elegant. Light brown hair. Imperious. She was looking at Lazaro with an arrested expression on her face.

And suddenly Skye grew hot as a rush of emotion nearly felled her with its force. She felt the flutterings of her baby in her belly—and that galvanised her to move, without thinking, towards the woman.

She vaguely heard someone say, *'Skye...'* behind her, but it was too late. She was standing in front of the woman now, looking up into patrician features. And those distinctive green eyes that Lazaro had inherited.

Shaking with adrenalin and emotion, Skye said, 'How could you?' She put a hand on her belly. 'How could you just abdicate your responsibility and abandon your own baby?'

The woman was icily aloof, but Skye thought she saw a flicker of something like pain in her eyes before it quickly disappeared.

'Because my world is a cruel one, Señora Sanchez,' she said. 'But I am glad my son has you.'

Then she turned and walked away, slipping on big sunglasses as she did so.

Skye was still trembling from the rush of emotion and adrenalin. Her arm was caught in a big hand and Lazaro came and stood in the spot his mother had just occupied. The resemblance was even more acute.

He was angry. Livid. Where he'd been white before, now he was flushed. 'What the hell do you think you're doing?'

It took Skye a second to understand that he was angry with her for confronting his mother. Because, no matter what the woman had done, she was his mother.

Skye couldn't have been told in starker terms where she came in Lazaro's life. Beneath the woman who had abandoned him at birth.

The hurt was immense. She could feel her emotions bubbling over and was terrified about what might spill out.

She pulled free and said, 'I'm going to go back to the apartment.'

She turned and walked quickly outside and got into the first cab she could find. She didn't hear anyone call *Skye*... this time.

Lazaro watched Skye leave, his jaw clenched so hard he had to relax consciously. The bid—everything—was forgotten.

Seeing his mother had been like a punch in the gut. He'd only seen her periodically through the years, but this time she'd been alone and looking at him. As if she'd come for him.

And then, before he'd been able to stop her, Skye had marched over like a tiny virago.

He'd heard her. *'How could you?'*

She'd articulated the words that had resounded in Lazaro's head all his life, and yet as soon as he'd heard Skye say them out loud on some level he'd known that he'd needed her to do that. Because he couldn't. Because the emotions his mother roused in him were too volatile.

But Lazaro wasn't feeling grateful to Skye for her intervention. He was feeling shame, resentment. Discomfort. Raw.

And then from behind him came a voice. 'Still airing your dirty laundry in public, Sanchez?'

Lazaro whirled around to see Gabriel Torres, those dark eyes seeing every inch of exposure Lazaro was feeling. His arm was drawn back and his hand was in a fist, ready to punch his brother before he even knew what he was doing.

Gabriel's eyes flashed. 'Do it, Sanchez. Go on. You've

been dying to ever since that day you followed us to the restaurant.'

Lazaro wasn't sure how he found the strength to resist the overwhelming urge to punch the condescending look off Gabriel's face, but somehow he did.

He told himself it wasn't because of Skye. Because he could imagine her huge blue eyes entreating him. Because he could imagine her soft, delicate scent and her hand touching his arm, pulling it down.

He's not worth it, she would say.

And, damn it, as he lowered his hand and swallowed down his pain he'd never resented her more for coming into his life and ripping open every wound he had. He'd operated alone his whole life. He did not need anyone else. Not then, not now.

The blotches on Skye's face were finally going down. She was a pale redhead, and her crying was not pretty. She felt calmer, though, as she waited for Lazaro to return. Calmer because she knew what she had to do now. For herself and the baby.

She heard a sound and turned around, steeling herself. Lazaro walked in, tie undone and hair messy. She pushed down her concern.

That green gaze zeroed in on her. His face was stark. Lines seemed to be etched there that she hadn't seen before.

He came further into the room. 'You had no right to say anything to my mother.'

Skye said in a low voice, 'I am your wife and the mother of your child. I think that gives me some right.'

His gaze dropped to the wheelie suitcase beside her. 'Where are you going?'

'I'm going back to Dublin. I've booked an early-evening flight. This isn't working, Lazaro. I'm not prepared to live in isolation in the suburbs while you maintain a separate life in the city. You've made it very clear where I come in your priorities and it's not high enough.'

He didn't say anything. He just looked at her.

'I know you were the one who vetoed using my logo for the project. Your assistant told me that everyone else wanted to use it except you. And the only reason I can think of is because you didn't like how I was infringing on your business.'

Your life.

Skye saw a tinge of colour score across his cheeks at that, but she didn't feel better to know she was right.

'I looked up the requirements for divorce in Spain. As long as we've been married for three months we can divorce within two months. I want to have this baby in Dublin. By the time he or she is born, we'll have been married long enough to initiate our divorce.'

She took a breath.

'I've been talking to my mother and she's going to come back to help me when the baby is born. We can discuss going forward from there. I'm giving you your life back, Lazaro. You need a wife who is your equal in this world. I'm not that person. I never will be.'

She clamped her mouth shut, afraid of what else might come out. Things she was too vulnerable to say.

Lazaro had said nothing this whole time. He was expressionless. He walked over to one of the windows and looked out. After a long moment he turned around, arms folded.

'Maybe it is a good idea for you to leave for a while. What you want…what you're asking for…it's not a life I ever envisaged. I don't need a defender, Skye. I never asked for that.'

Skye stifled the hurt and pain blooming in her chest and her heart. 'It's not something you should need to ask for. I've got a taxi coming. I should go.'

'No, my driver will take you. And you need to let me know where you are so I can set you up. You're not going back to that dump of an apartment. Where will you stay tonight?'

The fact that he was letting her go so easily crushed her.

'With a girl I worked with at the restaurant. She's got a spare room. I'll stay with her until I find somewhere.'

'You'll have access to money. You won't need to work.'

Skye said nothing. She had no intention of using Lazaro's money.

She walked to the door, pulling her small case behind her. She turned. She had a sense of déjà vu—back to when she'd been delivered to Lazaro in this very room like a toxic package.

He was as remote now as he had been then. As if nothing had changed in the meantime. As if there wasn't this insatiable tug of desire drawing them together in spite of everything. But clearly not even that was enough. She'd overstepped the line the other night, and today, and he wouldn't forgive her.

Lazaro existed in a fog for a few days. Barely aware of going through the motions. He found himself standing in the vast open space of a glass box on the outskirts of the city one day, with genuinely not much recollection about why he was there, beyond a vague memory of making an appointment to meet the estate agent to look at the houses Skye had viewed.

Her words came back into his head—how she'd accused him of wanting to have a house here just because it was where his parents lived. *'Everyone is locked behind their huge gates and walls with more security than a head of state. It's not natural.'*

She'd told him it wouldn't bring him peace to live here. And he knew with a dull feeling of pain inside him that it wouldn't. Yet he'd been prepared to put Skye and the baby here, as if he could use them to quiet his demons.

A sense of shame burnt through the fog numbing Lazaro's brain. And with the shame came clarity, for the first time since he'd watched Skye walk over to his mother to confront her.

He cut off the estate agent, who was saying something about security. 'There was a house my wife looked at in the centre of the city, near the park. I'd like to see that one.'

A week later

'You can go in.'

Lazaro took a deep breath and walked into Gabriel Torres's office. The man was standing by the window, hands in his pockets.

'To what do I owe this pleasure?'

Lazaro walked over to the desk and put down a padded envelope. He tapped it lightly before looking at Gabriel.

'There is all you need in there to find out if we are related. Which we are. Again, I don't want anything from you, or your family—simply an acknowledgment that I'm of your blood. It's the least I'm due, I think. Also, I've decided to pull out of the bid for the market. I still think my bid was the better one, but it's not my priority any more. And, yes, you're right: a big part of my motivation *was* in going up against you. You're a worthy adversary, Gabriel, but I've lost the appetite for battling with you.'

Lazaro turned to go, and he was almost at the door when he heard Gabriel say, 'What's changed?'

Lazaro turned around. He smiled, and realised he felt lighter than he'd felt in years. In his life. 'I've just realised what's truly important in life...that's all.'

He turned again and walked out, but not even the expression of confusion and shock on Gabriel's face could distract him from what he had to do next.

Skye tried to put everything out of her mind except what was in front of her. A heaving restaurant on a Friday night. Her old boss had given her a few shifts, and she was grateful to be kept busy so that her mind didn't keep circling back to that last conversation with Lazaro. And to the pain near her heart.

Ha! Near her heart? The pain *was* her heart.

She hadn't heard from Lazaro in two weeks, and it couldn't be clearer that he'd already moved on from whatever they'd had.

'Stop scowling, Skye. You look like you're going to take someone's head off.'

Skye rearranged her expression with effort. 'Better?'

The friend who was letting her crash in her spare room said, 'Marginally. Now you just look deranged.'

Skye smiled properly at that. And then she kept that smile on her face as she dived into the fray, using the hectic pace to take her mind off her pain.

She was so intent on distraction that she didn't even notice him at first.

She'd walked over to the table on auto-pilot, pulling her pen from where she'd stuck it in the bun on top of her head. She moved to a new page in her order book and looked up, pen poised—and fell into two green pools.

The shock was so profound that she swayed on her feet, her blood rushing south.

Lazaro grabbed her. 'Skye. Do not faint on me.'

Something in the autocratic tone brought her back to her senses, like smelling salts. She blinked. He was still there. The sheer reality of his physicality was overwhelming.

She scrambled back, almost landing on the table behind her. 'What are you doing here?'

'We need to talk.'

'I'm working. This is not a good time,' she hissed at him.

She turned to walk away, and then she heard him speaking from behind her, in a loud voice.

'This woman is the mother of my child and I'm here to talk to her. But she refuses.'

She turned around in horror to see Lazaro appealing to the people in the restaurant. Everyone was looking at him, rapt. She saw one woman take out her phone to take a picture—or, worse, maybe a video.

Then her boss came up behind her and said, 'Skye? Do you want to take this outside? Please?' He took her order book from her and handed her her bag and coat.

She was outside in the brisk autumn air before she knew how it had happened. Lazaro was looking darkly handsome and effortlessly gorgeous in an overcoat. And smug.

The shock was beginning to fade. All the anger Skye had been feeling towards him boiled over. 'How dare you embarrass me like that in front of everyone?'

He folded his arms and arched a brow. 'You mean the way you embarrassed me in front of all my peers and several members of the press just a couple of months ago?'

That took the wind out of her fury a little. But not totally. 'What are you doing here, Lazaro? You could have phoned me. I gave your assistant my contact details.'

'I could have, yes. But that wouldn't have been as satisfying as this.'

'This? What do you—?'

Her words were stopped because Lazaro had crushed her mouth under his in a deep, drugging kiss, arms wrapped tight around her body. Her bag and her coat fell to the ground.

When he lifted his head Skye's felt heavy. Blood was thundering through her brain, wiping out rational thought. But it trickled back slowly, as oxygen returned to her brain cells. The fact that their desire burned as hotly as ever was a bittersweet revelation.

She pushed herself out of Lazaro's embrace and bent down to get her coat and bag. When she straightened up she saw Lazaro's eyes resting on the swell of her belly, evident under her very boring stretchy black top.

'It's bigger,' Lazaro said.

'Yes,' said Skye, suddenly shy. The enormity of him being here sank in. 'Lazaro...what do you want?'

He lifted his gaze. 'I'm in the same hotel as last time. Come with me? Please? I have some things to say to you.'

That sounded ominous—in spite of the kiss, which Skye put down to a moment of madness. But they did need to talk. 'Okay.'

He helped her to put on her coat and then took her bag. She decided not to fight the battle to get it back. A part of her was enjoying seeing such an Alpha male carrying a small patent cross-body bag over his shoulder.

They walked the short distance to the hotel in silence. And when they entered the lobby Skye felt a sense of déjà vu wash over her again. She remembered how excited she'd been. How in awe of Lazaro. How life-changing that night had been. Literally.

The feeling of déjà vu got worse when they stopped outside the same suite. And then went in. Not that Skye remembered much about it from the last time. Her head had been too full of Lazaro and what was to come.

Now it was different. Even though she couldn't deny the awareness humming under her skin.

Lazaro took off his coat, revealing a long-sleeved sweater and dark trousers. He looked totally urbane, but when he turned to face her she could see the strength of his chest under the thin material and her mouth dried.

'Do you want tea, coffee?'

Skye shook her head. He came over to her.

'Let me take your coat.'

Ridiculously, she felt like saying no, but she let him take it, wondering if it was her imagination that his fingers lingered on her neck.

Tension wound tight inside her. 'What do you want to talk about?'

Lazaro stuck his hands in his pockets. 'I want you to come back to Madrid with me. I don't want you living in another city. I want you to have the baby in Spain. And I'm prepared to compromise on the house. I looked at that one you liked near the park…it's beautiful. The kind of place I would never have considered. It needs some work, but it should be ready by the time the baby is here.'

Skye absorbed this, and then realisation sank in. 'You've bought it already?'

He nodded.

'But…what about the park across the road…? Won't it be difficult for you?'

He made a face. 'If anything, I fantasised about living in one of those palatial houses by the park more than I ever did about living in the suburbs. I'd just forgotten…'

'I didn't think you were going to live with us.'

'I don't think I'd truly considered doing that either. But I want something different now. I want to give this a go properly. A life together.'

Skye's legs felt suspiciously wobbly. She moved over to a chair and sat down. 'What's changed?'

Lazaro started to pace, taking his hands out of his pockets, running one through his hair, messing it up.

He stopped and faced her. 'Everything. Me. I went to see Gabriel Torres. I left him a sample of my DNA and told him he could do a test if he was interested in finding out if we're related. But even if he doesn't, and even if I never know for sure, it doesn't really matter. Just like the bid for the market doesn't matter either. I told him I was pulling out.'

'But I loved your bid,' Skye said in dismay.

Lazaro shook his head. 'Gabriel was right. It was more about my feud with him than anything else. And you were right too. The only reason I didn't use your logo was because I had to push you back somehow...'

He looked at her.

'I was too harsh on you about my mother. It was just so shocking to me...to see you go after her like that. I've only ever seen her a few times in my life. We've never spoken. My feelings about her are...complicated. I'm so angry at her, and yet whenever I see her I see some vulnerability. I feel a need to protect her for some bizarre reason. Which makes me feel more angry. No one has ever stood up for me before, Skye. I've been on my own for ever. I didn't know how to respond... I felt exposed.'

Skye felt the tiny flame of hope she'd quenched upon leaving Spain bursting back to life. She told him what his mother had said—about hers being a cruel world and that she was happy he had Skye.

Her face was hot. 'I think she assumed there was more to our relationship. But, more importantly, I think she was saying that perhaps things weren't so black and white— that maybe she had a reason for giving you up. Maybe she didn't have a choice.'

Lazaro's face tightened. 'Perhaps. But I'm not here to talk about her now.' He pulled a chair over to sit opposite Skye. 'She was right about one thing, though...'

'What...?'

'I never expected to meet someone like you, Skye. You're a free spirit. You're not the kind of woman I thought I needed in my life. And yet... I don't want anyone else in my life.'

Skye looked at him, trying to read his expression, his eyes. He'd bought the house. He was clearly prepared to compromise—to give their life together a go. But she had to protect herself.

'You might be willing to compromise, but I don't know if I am.'

Lazaro frowned. 'What does that mean?'

Skye stood up. She couldn't think straight so close to him. She walked over to the window, which looked out over Dublin's leafy St Stephen's Green. A far smaller version of that park in Madrid, but equally charming.

She battled to keep the emotion she was feeling out of her voice. 'I spent my life with someone who didn't love me enough to put me first. My mother dragged me from pillar to post in her endless quest for peace, or whatever it was she was looking for.'

She turned around to face Lazaro, who had stood up. The shadows in the room made him look taller, darker.

'I don't want to come second again. I want to be someone's first choice. I want more than compromise. I deserve more. And maybe some day I'll find it. But that's not what you're offering, Lazaro. I know we have this amazing chemistry, but that won't last…will it?'

She hated the hopeful note in her voice and hurried on.

'And when it's gone I think whatever we have won't be strong enough to sustain a relationship. I thought that the most important things to me were setting down roots, stability and security. And they are. But I want more than that. I want a life that's rooted. Not just an existence. I want a *family.*'

Lazaro moved over to where Skye stood.

She put out her hands. 'Please…don't touch me. I can't think when you do, and you make me forget everything—'

He took her hands in his and laced his fingers with hers. She looked up at him, her eyes roving over his face. Over the perfect symmetry that she knew could distract people from the much deeper and more complex man.

'I forgot to tell you the most important thing,' he said.
'What's that?'

He tugged her towards him. She came reluctantly.

He smiled. 'That I love you, Skye Blossom O'Hara Sanchez. I love you so much it scares the life out of me. I realised how much I loved you when I saw you take on my mother, but I was in too much shock to take it in. And too threatened and terrified. I had my whole life planned out before I laid eyes on you, and as soon as I did it all went out through the window. I only realised how lonely I was when you came into my life, and yet the more I came to depend on you, the further I pushed you away. It felt like a weakness...wanting you, needing you.'

Skye was afraid to believe everything Lazaro was saying. If he was just saying this to get her to come back...

'How can you be so sure...? How do you know it's not just physical...or the thought of the baby...?'

'Did you not hear what I said? Falling for you has been the most terrifying and threatening thing I've ever experienced. We're not so dissimilar, you and I. I haven't trusted anyone in...ever. I've never let anyone get close. Until you.'

'I'm scared too, Lazaro,' Skye whispered. 'So scared. I love you so much. But I always vowed never to let anyone close enough to hurt me. And you really hurt me...'

Lazaro lifted his hands to her face, cupping her jaw, his thumbs wiping at tears she hadn't even been aware she was shedding. *Great.* Now she'd be all blotchy.

'I'm so sorry. I was an idiot. Please come home with me...let me show you how much I love you.'

Skye searched Lazaro's face and his eyes, not fully believing what she saw. Too afraid.

Then Lazaro took his hands away and said, 'Wait. I have something.'

He pulled something out of his pocket and she looked

down to see her wedding ring and engagement ring in the palm of his hand. She'd left them behind at the last moment.

He got down on one knee and took her hand. 'I never asked you to marry me. I told you we would marry and you had no real choice. But now you do. And I want you to choose. Skye Blossom O'Hara, will you please consent to be my wife, the mother of my child and hopefully our future children?'

She wanted to—so badly. But what he was asking her to do was to forget the lessons of a lifetime and put herself in someone else's hands again.

As if he could see her turmoil, he said, 'I saw that sketch you did of me…and it scared the life out of me. No one has ever seen me before—really seen me. Except you. And I think it's the same for you. No one has really seen you either. But I see you, Skye. I love you, and I know you love me too. You just have to trust me, my love. I won't let you fall.'

Skye looked down into the eyes of the man she loved and she believed him. 'Yes… I'll be your wife, Lazaro Sanchez.'

And she fell right into his arms and into his heart.

They landed in a tangle of limbs on the floor, and at some point resurfaced for long enough to make it into the bedroom, where they relived that first night all over again—except this time one night would last for ever.

EPILOGUE

Eight months later, Andalucía.

'HEY, WAKE UP, SLEEPYHEAD.'

Skye smiled into the kiss Lazaro pressed to her mouth. She reached for him, but he caught her hands.

'Not this time, you insatiable woman. I have something to show you.'

He helped her out of the hammock strung between two trees in the back garden of the *hacienda*. It was early summer and the air was redolent with the perfume of a hundred different flowers.

Skye stood up, her sundress falling around her legs. Her breasts were heavy with milk and she smiled at their four-month-old son Max, who was sleeping peacefully against his father's chest in a harness. Lazaro had taken him for a walk after his last feed.

'How is he?' She touched his plump cheek and he stirred softly before settling again.

She didn't blame him. Her favourite thing to do was to fall asleep on Lazaro's chest and feel his heartbeat under her cheek. But that was usually after—

She blushed and said hurriedly, 'What do you want to show me?'

He smiled at her and she blushed harder—because he knew exactly what she'd been thinking.

He took her hand and led her into the *hacienda* and up

the stairs, all the way to the stairs that led up to the top room where she'd sketched her first portraits.

She looked at Lazaro, her excitement growing. 'It's ready?'

He nodded and opened the door that had been closed to her for months on Lazaro's instructions. He led her up the stairs and into the space, and emotion filled her heart so much it was all she could do to take it in.

It had been transformed into a dream artist's studio. The windows had been made bigger. There were several easels. Brushes...paints. Paper. Every kind of pencil. Literally everything she might need.

The walls were white, reflecting endless light. There were new floorboards. Rugs. Plants. Candles.

'Do you like it?' Lazaro sounded worried.

She nodded, tears filling her eyes. 'I love it.'

He squeezed her hand. 'It's yours. Your space. To become the artist you are.'

Skye nodded, too overcome to look at him just yet. When she could, she turned and looked up. 'After Max, this is the best gift you could give me...you have no idea how huge this is...'

He wiped her tears away. 'If it's anything as huge as how grateful you make me feel every day then I have some idea.'

Skye smiled as her heart overflowed. She reached up and pressed a kiss to Lazaro's mouth, saying, 'I love you.'

When she pulled back she could see the emotion in his eyes too. She smiled and put her arms around him and their son, feeling the love all around them, binding them together and sinking roots deep into the ground. For ever.

* * * * *

MILLS & BOON

Coming next month

PROOF OF THEIR ONE-NIGHT PASSION
Louise Fuller

The coffee shop was still busy enough that they had to queue for their drinks, but they managed to find a table.

'Thank you.' He gestured towards his *espresso*.

His wallet had been in his hand, but she had sidestepped neatly in front of him, her soft brown eyes defying him to argue with her. Now, though, those same brown eyes were busily avoiding his, and for the first time since she'd called out his name he wondered why she had tracked him down.

He drank his coffee, relishing the heat and the way the caffeine started to block the tension in his back.

'So, I'm all yours,' he said quietly.

She stiffened. 'Hardly.'

He sighed. 'Is that what this is about? Me giving you the wrong name.'

Her eyes narrowed. 'No, of course not. I'm not—' She stopped, frowning. 'Actually, I wasn't just passing, and I'm not here for myself.' She took a breath. 'I'm here for Sóley.'

Her face softened into a smile and he felt a sudden urge to reach out and caress the curve of her lip, to trigger such a smile for himself.

'It's a pretty name.'

She nodded, her smile freezing.

It *was* a pretty name—one he'd always liked. One you didn't hear much outside of Iceland. Only what had it got to do with him?

Watching her fingers tremble against her cup, he felt his ribs tighten. 'Who's Sóley?'

She was quiet for less than a minute, only it felt much longer—long enough for his brain to click through all the possible answers to the impossible one. The one he already knew.

He watched her posture change from defensive to resolute.

'She's your daughter. Our daughter.'

He stared at her in silence, but a cacophony of questions was ricocheting inside his head.

Not the how or the when or the where, but the *why*. Why had he not been more careful? Why had he allowed the heat of their encounter to blot out his normally ice-cold logic?

But the answers to those questions would have to wait.

'Okay...'

Shifting in her seat, she frowned. '"Okay"?' she repeated. 'Do you understand what I just said?'

'Yes.' He nodded. 'You're saying I got you pregnant.'

'You don't seem surprised,' she said slowly.

He shrugged. 'These things happen.'

To his siblings and half-siblings, even to his mother. But not to him. Never to him.

Until now.

'And you believe me?' She seemed confused, disappointed?

Tilting his head, he held her gaze. 'Honest answer?'

He was going to ask her what she would gain by lying. But before he could open his mouth her lip curled.

'On past performance I'm not sure I can expect that. I mean, you lied about your name. And the hotel you were staying at. And you lied about wanting to spend the day with me.'

'I didn't plan on lying to you,' he said quietly.

Her mouth thinned. 'No, I'm sure it comes very naturally to you.'

'You're twisting my words.'

She shook her head. 'You mean like saying Steinn instead of Stone?'

Pressing his spine into the wall behind him, he felt a tick of anger begin to pulse beneath his skin.

'Okay, I was wrong to lie to you—but if you care about the truth so much then why have you waited so long to tell me that I have a daughter? I mean, she must be what...?' He did a quick mental calculation. 'Ten, eleven months?'

Continue reading
PROOF OF THEIR ONE-NIGHT PASSION
Louise Fuller

Available next month
www.millsandboon.co.uk

Copyright ©2019 Louise Fuller